"*Free Chocolate* is quirky, fun, and loaded with sci-fi chocolaty goodness! This book is a calorie-free treat."
  Beth Cato, *author of* Breath of Earth

"Exhilarating fun in a galaxy muy loca for Earth's most sublime delicacy! Bodacious lives up to her name, and not even certain death can slow her down. *Free Chocolate* proves that romance, intrigue, space opera, mortal peril, and culinary ambition can be served with a sweet side dish of humor."
  Sue Burke, *author of* Semiosis

"You had me at laser monkey robots."
  Arianne "Tex" Thompson, *author of the* Children of the Drought *trilogy*

"Soap opera drama mixed with sci-fi high stakes, *Free Chocolate* is a muy thrilling ride!"
  Laura Maisano, *author of* Cosplayed *and* Schism

"Earth has a monopoly on chocolate. The aliens will do anything to get a cacao sample, and the planetary government will do anything to stop them. What a premise!"
  Daniel M Benson, *author of* Groom of the Tyrannosaur Queen

"¡Muy deliciosa! Amber Royer's *Free Chocolate* is nonstop fun on every page! From strangely delicious sounding cosmic treats to Spanglish-speaking intergalactic diplomats to the relentlessly breathtaking feartastic adventure, this is a unique read and a total page-turner! Not only does Royer introduce the first university-student Mexican sci-fi heroine, with a host of wildly eclectic friends, but she builds a believable universe around them that is a true delight to visit."
  Eden Unger Bowdich, *author of the* Young Inventors Guild Series

AMBER ROYER

Pure Chocolate

**ANGRY
ROBOT**

ANGRY ROBOT
An imprint of Watkins Media Ltd

Unit 11, Shepperton House
89 Shepperton Road
London N1 3DF
UK

angryrobotbooks.com
twitter.com/angryrobotbooks
A sign of good taste

An Angry Robot paperback original 2019

Cover by Heri Irawan
Set in Meridien and Infinity by Argh! Nottingham

Distributed in the United States by Penguin Random House, Inc., New York.

ISBN 978 0 85766 753 3
Ebook ISBN 978 0 85766 754 0

Printed in the United States of America

9 8 7 6 5 4 3 2 1

To my husband and alpha reader, Jake,
who went above and beyond on this one.

PROLOGUE
Eight Years Ago – Kaimoan City, the planet Evevron

Awn clutched her son to her chest as she skidded to a halt. Damn. She'd been so close, could see the spaceport behind the wall of warriors clad in black body armor. Her husband had said to meet him at the ship. Maybe he'd made it. Please, let him have made it.

Hult stepped forward, gesturing for Awn to hand over the child. The vertical slits of his pupils had almost disappeared in the intense sun. "Is the boy infected?"

Awn bared her teeth, the grit of Evevron's amethyst sand blowing into her mouth. She spat on the cracked dirt. She would love to sink her sharp enamel into Hult's smug face. He thought this would stop them. But Awn's connection to the source wasn't the same as the others. Capturing her did nothing to stop the spread.

"Well? Is he?"

"No." Awn was glad of it. She'd hoped her son would become one with the others, but they hadn't had time. But now that she'd been captured – at least he wouldn't be executed alongside her.

Hult wasn't a monster. He thought of Awn as a criminal, but he wouldn't hurt a non-infected child.

They marched her to the lab, down in the cavern, past the

waterfall. She felt the connection inside her reaching out, trying to find her husband, trying to find the rest of the people she loved. All she got back was terror and anger and dread.

In the lab, they'd arranged five cryostasis pods in a ring. Everyone knew that cryostasis didn't work. Awn's heart sank. No one had ever been able to overcome the issues with cell revival. The researchers who'd brought Awn into this whole mess – unwillingly, mind you – just used them to store experiments long term.

The new set of researchers wanted to preserve her, study her. Try to find a way to cure the galaxy of what was insider her. As though it were an evil to be eradicated. Not a beautiful way to connect all creatures in the galaxy, the one true way to peace.

The young medic approaching her with an analgesic gun looked as terrified as Awn felt.

"I'm sorry," he said, glancing at the soldiers behind her. "They're not giving me a choice. I promise, it won't hurt. And I'll stay with you the whole time."

A dull rhythmic thudding came from four of the capsules, in perfect unison. With horror, she realized that the sense of anguish that had been protruding into her mind came from inside these pods. Her husband was in one of them, being pumped full of the fluid that would replace his blood to minimize the damage of freezing. The slow process would take hours. And it was happening while he was awake.

But this had gone far beyond just the five of them, the first on Evevron to be infected. Some of the infected had gotten offplanet. Their five bodies' deaths meant nothing, since what they had become could no longer be contained.

CHAPTER ONE

"Where's Kayla?" Mertex asks, his polite smile showing a wide mouth full of razor-sharp shark-like teeth. The bald lemon-yellow alien is wearing a brightly-colored collared shirt and long shorts combo, casual beachwear that contrasts with the crisp black uniform he'd had on the last time we met. Mertex is small for a Zantite. He's still big enough to have once picked me up, carried me under his arm, and forced me to my knees so his superior officer could try to eat me. It was not his best day, nor mine, pero, we've moved past that, no?

In fact, we're having dinner together, eating just-caught seafood at a restaurant overlooking one of his home island's many beaches. Sí. I lived up to my promise and made it to Zant. Bo Benitez on her glitzarazzi tour of the Major Fourteen. The whole galaxy is watching.

"Kayla and Kaliel are coming in a couple of weeks. After Kayla's graduation."

Everyone at the table looks at me with sympathy. Kayla was my roommate at culinary school. We were supposed to be graduating together – if I hadn't spent the last few months on Earth trying to sort my legal problems.

My stylist, my publicist, and my assistant chef are all still staring, like I might shatter from the disappointment.

I shrug. "Que? I'm just happy to still be alive. I could easily have gotten shaved, no?"

Shaved, as in public execution by guillotine.

I have no illusions. Nada. Nunca. If HGB hadn't needed me to come here to Zant, my head would no longer be connected to my body.

Pero, the fate of Earth hangs in the balance. This alien race is in the process of filing paperwork with the Galactic Court to legally invade my planet. Earth needed to send a diplomat. They needed a persuasive powerhouse.

They got me. A washed-up never-quite-was holostar turned culinary academy dropout and her entourage.

So why exactly are *we* here? It's because of chocolate.

Chocolate is the only unique commodity Earth has left that other species in the galaxy want. HGB, the company on Earth that controls cacao, will sell the aliens all the chocolate bricks and cocoa powder they produce. Just not the unfermented beans.

I'd stolen a pod worth of beans and given them to the Nilka and the Krom, in an attempt to forestall war. I'd been naïve, thinking it would be that simple, no?

A number of planets that didn't get cacao still want to force open Earth's borders at railgun point. Pero, they can't say it's to rip away our commodities. They have to claim it's because we're acting aggressively towards the rest of the galaxy. Which, given our closed borders and outward-pointing planetary defenses, is kinda true.

I had been guilty of treason against Earth for selling chocolate to the aliens. But the Zantites' King, Garfex, had liked me, had actually danced with me aboard a Zantite warship – long story – and challenged me to prove my objections to him invading my world. Minda's on our side in this. She's also one of King Garfex's favorites. He's capricious, and changes the law to suit himself. He's already changed his mind once, when it was Minda doing the asking.

If we can sway Zant to back out, by proving we're not

dangerous monsters, then the rest of the coalition loses half their warships and mucho momentum. We're here to convince Zant that Earth deserves a spot in the galaxy. And we're going to do it with a cooking show.

Pero, no pressure, right?

I can't complain, though. I'd put myself in this position the minute I left school and committed treason by freeing chocolate. And I'd capped it by volunteering to tour with Minda Frou, Zandywood's most popular star.

When I'd been in cooking school, I'd had amigos, a goal, una vida.

All that is gone, and for what? I may have shared chocolate with a few other planets, pero those cacao beans have barely sprouted into seedlings, and HGB intends to keep the supply of unfermented beans as limited as possible. I'm sure they're already planning to sabotage the off-Earth plantations. That way, chocolate stays expensive – and with such a galactic commodity they still have a reason to be the most powerful corporation on Earth.

Mi hermoso Brill catches his hazy reflection in the wall's polished black rock surface. Most of the buildings on Letekka – the only Island-continent I've seen so far of Zant – are made of the same stone, inside and out. Brill runs his hand across the damaged skin on his cheek and nose, where it's rough and tinted orange.

Brill's from Krom, a planet that's still not on the best of terms with Earth, despite being one of the ones to wind up with a nascent cacao grove.

So many of the tiny vessels carrying his iron-rich blood had burst when Mertex had thrown him into a blast freezer, inside a muy grande chocolate mold, not so long ago. Again, not Mertex's best day. Pero, it had been Brill's, when he'd stopped thinking about himself first and become un verdadero héroe. Him stepping in front of Mertex had saved my life.

Mertex notices, and his yellow skin blushes green.

"It's not done healing." It's hard to tell exactly who Brill is talking to. Is he acknowledging the history between him and Mertex? He looks over at me, "Don't worry, Babe. It probably won't even scar."

It probably will, pero I keep that thought to myself. Let him hold on to his hope and his vanity, and who knows? Maybe that healing balm he keeps slathering on every time he thinks I'm not looking will do the trick.

Even if it doesn't, I still think we make un bien encarado couple. He's tall, well-built and strawberry-blond, with a chiseled jaw and those distinctive Krom chromashifting irises. I'm slim and dark-haired, with a wide smile and a slightly hooked nose that highlight my Mexican ancestry. I'm also just tall enough to fit perfectly in his arms.

Mertex bites at his lip and looks from me to Brill. Then he changes the subject, gracias a Dios. He asks Brill, "Are you sure you don't want to try the lenmakf?"

"Nah, Su. I'm good with the soup." Brill's OK with eating some kinds of fish when he's in a group where others are eating it, pero today he's gone strict vegetarian. It's a Krom thing, especially on un nuevo planeta. It makes sense, given their fragile cardio systems, combined with their do-no-harm explorer nature. While there are limits to the foods I will try, I am more open to exploring local proteins. Still, it's never been an issue between us.

A Zantite at another table waves at Mertex. Murry smiles even bigger, and my stylist Valeria lets out a muffled, unhappy noise. Which tugs at mi corazón. I can remember being that terrified of a Zantite grin. Zantites are capable of unhinging their jaw to fit something larger than they should be able to into their mouths – and once that something was me.

I flash back to being in the mouth of a Zantite, a single breath away from having my spine severed with razor-sharp teeth. I put my fork down to hide the trembling in my hands as the remembered fear battles with the permanent side-effects of my unwanted drug addiction – forced on me by that same Zantite.

Mi publicist Tawny's staring out the window, her ice blue eyes intent. Down on the sand, the leaves of some of the plants and the curving edge of the ocean are lit with a phosphorescent glow. This place is muy bonito. I follow her gaze to a dark cliff, level with the restaurant, where shadowy shapes, their hands and faces outlined with fuchsia, are leaping one at a time into the water, then running back up a path to get in line again.

"I used to do that," Tawny says. She has pixie-cut brown hair and warm-toned brown skin. She's mixed race, part of it Hawaiian. "When I was a kid, we used to do back-flips off Black Rock all day long, then at sunset, a guy would dress up like an old-time Polynesian warrior, and they'd tell all the tourists that it was going to be dangerous when he leapt from the rock into the sea. We'd never do it at night, though. That *was* dangerous."

Mertex looks confused, and I'm sure I'm about to have to explain human cultural history, pero he says, "Weren't you with your pod? Would they not have cast light-buoys on the water to keep you safe?"

"So those *are* children," Brill says. He's been quiet tonight. I can't tell if something's bothering him, or if he's just trying to appraise the situation. "Learning pods only last until you guys are what, sixteen?"

"Roughly that, though years are longer here than on Krom."

No lo sé what that means in terms of years on Earth.

What would it have been like for Mertex to have been a child here? I study the kids out on the rock, and suddenly, the line of moving hands becomes a circle, and in the middle, there are two pairs of hand-outlines, grappling with each other, waving wildly. Then one of the hands disappears.

Oi! Shock knifes cold through my stomach. "En serio? Did one of the kids bite that one's hand off?"

Brill stands up from his chair so fast that he knocks it over backwards. "We have to get down there!"

"No," Mertex says. "You'd get hurt trying to break up brakks."

"But those are kids," Brill protests.

Mertex pulls aside the neck of the tunic to expose his right shoulder, where a thick scar runs over the outside, outlining a shiny patch where a graft was once required to keep the arm. "And I was a shy kid, Brill. But don't worry. No one will die out there tonight. Their lives are all bound to each other, and if one of them comes up missing, it would be... bad... for the rest. Executions here are swift, and our justice is without mercy."

I look down at my plate, not hungry anymore. I sneak a look over at Mertex. He'd said his life is bound to mine and Brill's, that he is our protector on this planet. It's suddenly a chilling thought.

Brill slowly sits back down.

Tawny looks over at him. "I never realized you were so protective of children, Mr Cray. Do you have any of your own?"

"Of course not! Ga!" Brill looks from Tawny over to me, and I can't read his face. It's always seemed that even asking Brill if he wants niños would be pushing our relationship too far. Most Krom see humans as an inferior species, and a Krom/human crisscross is bound to be an outsider everywhere.

Heat floods my face and suddenly I need to get out of this room, surrounded as I am by a hundred giants who would be so quick to dispense justicia against niños, but even more by one man, whom I love more than anything, but still don't completely trust with my heart, or my future.

"Let's go down to the beach." I'm on my feet, headed for the door before anyone has a chance to respond.

I don't want to get too far ahead, so I sit down on a bench by the doors. After a minute, this Zantite guy sits down next to me, keeping his hands in his pockets. I guess he figures it's non-threatening. He's wearing the beachwear, pero his pants are long.

"You're Bo Benitez, aren't you?" He's speaking Universal, but with an accent that sounds a bit like he's gargling rocks.

I don't deny it. "It is an honor to make an initial impression of you…"

"Rex. I apologize thoroughly. Where are my manners?" He falls into the proscribed language. "And I also, Bo, bearer of the Invincible Heart."

I make solid eye contact. "I also cook and do things I actually have control over, mi amigo."

I'll never understand the Zantite fascination with me for having taken the rage drug that they give to suicide soldiers – taken it and survived. Which is yet another reason I am here, instead of a more traditional diplomat. Even if, back home, hardly anyone knows about my addiction. It's been kept out of the Earth feeds, and the Zantites have shown enough respect to do the same. But that doesn't stop their rumor mill.

"Shame about you and the IH. I understand Earthlings never get over it, that the need to feel that power again just keeps getting stronger and stronger, no matter how long it's been. How bad is it for you?"

I shrug. "It's manageable."

Which is a lie. Him just talking about it has me sweating, has my hands itching to reach for something that isn't there. I never wanted IH in the first place, had been forcibly injected with it aboard a Zantite warship. It's not fair – but then addiction never is.

"I suppose it must be manageable, if you have no choice." He leans back, causing the bench to creak under both of us.

The Invincible Heart is a controlled substance – one that even the Krom, with their mission of "discovering" commodities to trade throughout the galaxy, consider too much of a menace to touch.

I hold up a hand, letting Rex see the tremors. "Coffee helps control some of the symptoms, pero I haven't found a place to get any since we landed."

"There's an excellent coffee shop just a few streets that way." He points inland, then leans towards me, the scale of him intimidating, the hints of teeth revealed when he smiles down at me feartastic. "But how much would it be worth to you to have another dose of what you really need?"

I blink. "You have military grade rage drugs on you right now?"

He shrugs. All Zantites are bald, and the moonlight glints off his head. "I can get it. I'm a doctor's assistant aboard the *Infinite Destruction*, and I've had to hand it out to the guys going on those missions before. Twice. Hard to do, you know." Because IH is lethal to Zantites after the effects wear off, no exceptions. Having to administer the drug is exceedingly rare – unless the ship's captain is loco. Pero, the fact that they will do it at all makes the thought of them invading Earth even more terrifying. The guy looks down at me. "At least it wouldn't kill you."

"Shows what you know." I hop down off the bench. "That stuff keeps building up in the Earthling liver. Takes longer, and more doses, but it kills us just as dead."

I head away from the guy, down the path toward the beach, sure mis amigos will follow. And in the meantime, it's nice to be alone.

As in Tawny-free.

HGB doesn't trust me. They've bugged my dorm, my phone, my jail cell – and now my person. Not that I can blame them. After all, I did commit theft/treason when I stole a cacao pod out of one of their facilities. Pero, they'd had me bugged well before that, just for consorting with a Krom.

They'd have chosen someone else for this diplomatic mission, if they'd had any choice. Pero, I had volunteered aboard a Zantite warship, where I had just risked my life to find out that the Zantites were looking at colonizing a planet at the edge of Earth's solar system – and that they were holding a conference to discuss whether or not it made sense to invade mi planet. Minda chose me. King Garfex approved her choice.

It would have been awkward for HGB to say I'd been executed and they were sending someone else. Tawny's here officially as my publicist. She's really my babysitter.

I ditch my jacket – along with Tawny's camera, which she doesn't know I spotted – in a nearby trash bin.

I'm wearing a sleeveless blouse underneath, and I'm enjoying the feel of the cool night air against my skin as I walk down the path towards the sand – right up until an oversized hand grabs my arm.

At first I think the Zantite I'd been talking to on the bench followed me, pero he hasn't moved, and this guy had been standing so still I'd mistaken him for a tree in the dark. He pulls me off the path, into the shadows cast by the real trees. There's still enough moonlight to get a look at him. It's the tall Zantite with the concave area on the right side of his skull that I'd met at the spaceport, the one who had come in the same welcoming party with Mertex. Murry and Dent Head had seemed to be on the verge of a fight.

When he leans down close to me, this guy's breath smells like fish and rum – pero mostly rum. That can't be bueno. Mi corazón's hammering.

Brill comes out the restaurant door, looking around to see if I waited for him.

If I shout, this Zantite might panic. He hasn't done anything overtly violent, hasn't even said anything yet. I've had a sublingual installed in my head since I was a teenager. The device is wired to both my brain and my vocal cords. More than just a phone, it helps me process and remember languages. Pero, the handiest feature is that I can use it without needing to speak. I open my channel and make a sublingual call to Brill's handheld.

He answers immediately, his voice warm and concerned inside my head. *You OK, Babe? You seem upset.*

Halfway down the path to the beach, I bubblechatter at him. *I'm in trouble, but I'd rather not cause a galactic incident.*

So no guns, Brill says, starting to wander towards me. The pitch of his voice doesn't even change.

"Say," the dripsy Zantite slurs in passable Universal, "is it true that you shot that brat Crosskiss with his own vapgun?"

"I did." I try to slide my arm out of the guy's fist, but he's not quite alchafuzzed enough.

"That makes you a hero. Good thing I don't have to kill you to give Mertex the fright of his life."

When we'd landed, Mertex had met us at the spaceport, pulled me aside and said he'd vowed to Minda to keep me and Brill safe, which somehow links our lives to his. So whatever's about to happen to me should leave the poor muchacho terrified.

Dent Head brings my hand up, closer to his mouth.

I squeak. He might not realize humans bleed a lot more than Zantites when we get bitten. And I'm rather attached to that arm. "Wait! There's still enough IH in my system to make you sick." I speak slowly, in Zantite, in case he's drunker than I thought – and to give Brill, who's hearing all of this over my sublingual, time to do something. "You know – Noble Race – suicide drug – Crosskiss tried to use me as a murder weapon."

The Zantite laughs. He raises my arm higher, till he can get a good look at my wrist, which he touches with a device that was concealed in his other hand. There's no pain, pero the world goes dark and the last thing I hear as my consciousness falls away is Brill, both over the sublingual and in the darkness, saying, "Babe?"

CHAPTER TWO

I dream I'm trapped in a bottle, floating in green liquid. Minda, even more giant than in real life, has an eye up to the glass, squinting in at me. She starts chanting, "Mentiroso, mentiroso, mentiroso." I know this is a dream, because there's no way Minda knows the Spanish word for *liar*.

And part of me knows where this dream's coming from: my friends and I had found cases of green liquid in the lab inside HGB's cacao plantation inside the rainforest in Brazil. We analyzed it. Serum Green is an additive they've been putting in HGB chocolate for decades to make it literally addictive. Frank Sawyer, who works for HGB, had followed us back into the rainforest. Porque Frank y I have a history, he made us promise at gunpoint to keep it a secret.

Instead of just shooting us to ensure our silence.

Dream-Minda holds up a giant brick of HGB Dark and uses it to smash the glass. I go careening away on a waterslide of green. Minda plucks me up and holds me out to a horde of screaming Zantites, who are all mad about being addicted. I try to tell them the serum's mostly harmless. One of the Zantites licks my face, tasting me, deciding if I should live or die.

I rise towards consciousness. Something really is licking my face.

My heart pounding with fear, the dream mixed up with surfacing memories of having been abducted, I open my eyes to full daylight. This squatty looking creature with a long, dark tongue and four hand-like feet is licking me from the next branch over.

Because I'm in a tree.

And because it's high tide, the trunk of that tree is in the water.

Incongruously, my abductor has thoughtfully wrapped a blanket around my torso and legs. Who knows what happened to my shoes.

I think about that blanket, and about all the practical jokes the crewmen had played on each other in the short time I'd been aboard that Zantite warship. This feels more like a prank than an intentional attempt to hurt me.

If I had been another Zantite, maybe it would have been just that, pero Dios mio, I've been out here all night. Anything could have happened. And there could be Galactic repercussions.

Another of the creatures is hanging upside down from a branch above me, clinging on by three of its feet. The fourth foot-hand grips my left shoe, the creature chewing on it with all the zeal of a teething puppy.

"You don't happen to know how deep the agua is down there, do you, muchachos?"

The creature that had been licking my face sticks the tongue up its own nose and pulls out a booger which it waves at me before sucking it into its mouth.

The other one offers me the shoe, as though I might want to share in its breakfast.

"Gracias, pero no."

I call Brill over my sublingual.

Babe? He sounds groggy, and a little hoarse. *Is that you? Avell, tell me you're OK.*

The desperate way he says the Krom word for please strikes something inside me.

"I'm fine, pero I'm in a tree, somewhere at the edge of the coastline."

Can you see any landmarks?

I turn over carefully and start to make my way to the trunk. I spot the black cliff the kids were jumping from last night and… suddenly I'm not in the tree anymore.

I suck in a shocked breath just before I hit the water. I open my eyes, sure I'm about to crash into a rocky bottom, pero it's deeper than I thought and teeming with life. Dozens of the same striped fish I was eating last night scatter at my impact, then hesitantly return to feeding on something growing on the trunk. A flattish creature slides away, glittering like a sea-pirate's treasure trove as it burrows into the golden sand.

The agua is muy claro, even as it gets deeper past a drop off. There's a crashed ship down there, in the process of becoming a reef. I can tell from the distinctive shapes of the writing that its markings are in Evevron. Pero, I don't know how to read it.

I'm going to check out this shipwreck. Por favor, come get me. I'm not far from the cliff we saw last night. And bring Valeria. I'm going to need serious help with hair and wardrobe.

Shipwreck? Brill bubblechatters. *I thought you were in a tree.*

I swim towards the wreck. The hull's gashed, the windows fissured. It must have been a horrific crash. Imagine having come so far, from Evevron to Zant, only to wind up at the ocean's bottom. Are there skeletons inside? Cargo that should be recovered?

If I bring something back, maybe that will give Tawny something positive that she can spin for the media. I surface for a good deep breath before diving to within inches of the glass, peering inside. There's a silver-tone inoculation gun rusting away on the pilot's chair. On the floor, there's a locked box that looks like someone had tried to hack it open.

What could that be?

Inside the ship, something moves. I jump as a blue blob with tentacles sucks itself onto the spiderwebbed glass, obscuring my view inside. It has a ring of teeth – each one bigger than my hand – that all arc in the same direction.

Maybe I don't want to explore in there quite on my own.

I swim to shore.

A crack of thunder sounds close to me, and it starts to trickle and then pour down with rain. More dog-monkeys are sheltering under an overhang of rock. Running barefoot through the sand, I join them. Once I've entered the shelter, I turn, staring miserably out at the rapidly clouding sky. I let out a squeak as lightning hits the sand farther up the beach.

When the van finally arrives, Valeria gestures me to the back seat, where she's been waiting, warm and dry. We brought the van packed with supplies, pero now that it's empty it feels huge.

As Tawny drives us back, Valeria tries to get a brush through my tangled hair. She's the same stylist I had back in Brazil, for the brief time when I was working there for HGB. She's in her forties and has long, dark hair, a dramatic counterpoint to her sensible cardigan and striped tee.

I can't quite make out what Brill and Tawny are saying to each other in the front, not over the radio, which is spilling out a Zandywood song medley. The announcer introduces a song by Verex Kowlk. The live recording opens with a bunch of screaming fans.

Cringing at the noise, Valeria says, "These Zantites are terrifying. We should just give them what they want."

Brill turns the radio down. "I suggested that we bring some cacao seedlings with us as a good faith gesture. I nearly got arrested just for asking."

Earth can't give anyone else chocolate. The fact that two planets are already growing chocolate seedlings is problematic enough – because of Serum Green.

HGB didn't modify the cacao genetically. They're adding

Serum Green during processing. Which means that whatever the aliens harvest is not going to be the chocolate they're expecting. Which means they're going to find out we've been manipulating them to buy our product. Oye! Think how angry both the Nilka and the Zantites are going to be. Forget invasion, hola annihilation.

Pero, if we can keep the borders closed, no one will be able to prove what we're growing is not the same as what we're selling. But even HGB has to know that's not a viable strategy long term – not with the Krom having a cacao plantation.

The Krom make it their mission to spread commodities throughout the galaxy, the equivalent of open-source software hackers. If this invasion coalition could wait long enough, the Krom would give them cacao seeds. They just have to let the Krom plantation's trees mature, or give Krom researchers time to find a way to overcome the resistance to cloning that HGB bred into the beans.

Pero, because of Serum Green, the coalition members are choco-addicted. They may not even know why they're so obsessed with getting chocolate for themselves. And that's partly HGB's fault.

"I understand you've been arrested before, mijo," Valeria says to Brill, yanking my hair unnecessarily hard. She blames Brill for getting me involved with the whole stealing chocolate thing in the first place. She is not wrong. But she doesn't understand the complicated reasons behind what he did.

Brill shrugs. "Wal. A couple of times. Kind of comes with the territory." Brill's a trader, mostly in luxury foodstuffs, especially fine wines. A gray market trader. Pero he has his boundaries.

Valeria whispers to me, "Nacido ladrón, criado mentiroso, en el krom del corazón."

It's a proverb about the Krom, relating to the fact that the word Krom in their language means center: *Born a thief, raised a liar, at the center of the heart.*

"That's not true." I bite my lip to keep myself from saying anything stronger. I've had this fight before – most people on my home world consider all Krom pirates and galactathieves – and I've never managed to change anyone's mind.

The Krom/Earth First Contact was Earth's first First Contact, and it did not go well. Krom look enough like Earthlings – hot, built Earthlings – that they figured they could pop in some opaque contacts to hide the chromashifting eyes and walk among us. A Discovery Vessel landed in Iowa, and a couple dozen of them got jobs and pawned stuff and started buying samples of plants and animals with Earth currency. Only, we caught on in the middle of their commodities cataloguing, and they left in a hurry – without getting a sample cacao tree.

Chocolate became the center of Earth's economy, and our basis for trade with the galaxy. We fought a global war over it, restructured our entire world over it, wound up with HGB, a megacorp built out of the world's chocolate companies, having too much power because it held a monopoly on this one resource.

The megacorp has only been in charge of chocolate for about forty years. But in that time, they've re-shaped the way the world thinks about candy, getting rid of much of the fun and whimsy, subtly discouraging humans from eating it – while at the same time, trying to find ways to grow more, to be sold as high-cost offplanet exports.

Most humans still blame the Krom for everything that happened during and after the First Contact War. They forget about how much of that we did to ourselves, forget about the riots that swept the globe *after* the aliens left, when people were accusing their neighbors of being not of Earth.

I don't know how Brill puts up with the insults and the slurs without becoming bitter, pero when I ask him about it, he just says he's used to it.

"El ciego no distingue colores," Brill tells her. Literally, *a blind man should not judge of colors*. More bluntly, *you have no idea what you're talking about*.

I'm not about to tell Valeria that Brill learned that – like most of the Spanish he's picked up – watching telenovelas. Especially not now, with her cheeks going red.

CHAPTER THREE

Back on set, Valeria is doing touchups to the work she started in the van. She's made me look like I spent the night on a featherbed instead of in a tree. I could get used to having a stylist, no?

"Here." Tawny opens a drink can. She pulls a package of teal straws out of her bag and drops one through the hole, because she doesn't want me to touch the rim. "It's an electrolyte drink to help you recover."

"Gracias." I take a sip. It's pleasantly citrusy.

I look over at Mertex, who is hovering like a mother hen. I ask him if he knows anything about the reef-ship I saw. I'm hoping he's going to say, *What reef ship?* and then I can tell everyone about my discovery.

He shrugs. "It crashed here eight or ten years ago. The people on board were Evevronian criminals, and their government wanted them back. They were eventually captured and taken home, but nobody wanted to pay to move the ship, and us kids were already making dive trips out to it, so they just left it."

"People survived that crash?" I ask. Dios mio! "Then why hasn't anything been salvaged out of it?"

Mertex shudders. "It's a phkhekk fiekksk."

Plague ship? Bad luck?

Before I can ask, the same uniformed soldiers who had met us at the spaceport troop in... including the muchacho who knocked me out. I sit up straighter, leaning back so fast I bonk Valeria in the nose.

"Ow!"

"Lo siento!"

She waves me away as I try to look at the injury.

One of the Zantites leans forward in an awkward bow. He has a squarer, more defined jaw, and his eyes are oversized for his face. "I'm Dghax, head of the local police. I apologize thoroughly that I failed to introduce myself yesterday. It didn't seem necessary for an honor guard."

So they're police officers, not soldiers, though the uniforms are quite similar.

Somehow that makes what Dent Head did to me seem even more irresponsible. I make eye contact with him, and he looks away, a bit of green coming into his cheeks. He wasn't so fuzzfaced that he doesn't remember.

I look back at Dghax. "I wish to belatedly say I was pleased to make an initial impression of you."

"Me too."

It's an informal response. What does that say about the policeman? Or my situation?

Mertex, who had been speaking softly to one of the uniform guys, steps over to me, rests a gigantesco hand on my shoulder. "Since your disappearance was reported to the police..." Mertex glances at Tawny, unable to completely hide his distaste, "they are here to collect a statement."

I've seen enough Zandywood holos to know that you don't report things to the police unless you're hoping to get someone executed. Does Tawny not know that? Or does she just not care?

They're considering whether what Dent Head did was an abduction. He can't exactly claim it wasn't.

I lean in towards Murry and ask, "What's the penalty for kidnapping here?"

"If the victim was put in physical danger – as Tawny is insisting happened – it could be death. Or maybe just assignment to a warship." Which is a life sentence.

Tawny's not likely to let it go, or laugh it off as a prank.

I've said so much to Tawny about how horrible it is to lie. Pero, this time, if I tell the truth, my abductor might not leave this room. Who'd have to kill him? On the warship, that honor had gone to the highest-ranking officer. Dghax seems to be in charge here, so it will probably be him.

Dent Head swallows visibly and goes a bit greener. His hands ball into fists at his sides. And yet, he's not trying to escape this. There's a hint of hero to him after all.

Dghax holds out a voice recorder. "Did you see the face of or speak with your abductor?"

I look up at Mertex, who is encouraging me to speak the truth, even though he can't know that it will implicate his rival or enemy or whatever Dent Head is to him. I look over at Dent Head, who has flattened his rubbery lips with resolve. He takes a step forward, about to confess.

My heart lurches, as I picture his neck meeting Dghax's teeth. I don't want to see Dent Head die for one drunken mistake.

"No!" I say, mostly to him. Pero, I smile at Dghax and repeat more calmly. "No y no. I remember being on the path, then I remember being in the tree."

"Are you certain? That seems to contradict the statement given by Mr Cray last night."

I shrug. "Earthlings go into shock very easily. We tend to block out things we'd rather forget."

"Sí," Valeria says. Her eyes are round and she's backed up against the mirror. Pero, she seems to be doing better than last time she was surrounded by Zantites in uniforms. She gestures at Mertex. "They say I fainted yesterday at the spaceport. But I don't really remember."

Dghax puts his recording device away. "If you do remember

anything, please let us know."

He and his men troop out. Dent Head gives me one last amazfused look, and this time Mertex catches it and arches one questioning non-eyebrow at me.

"Later." I'm still freaked because I just had Dent Head's life in my hands. It's a feo, feo feeling. Not a power I'd ever want. I'd been where he was – slated for execution over something blown out of all proportion.

"That's right." Tawny moves closer, missing or ignoring the subtext between me and Mertex as she examines my makeup. "We've kept our sponsor waiting long enough."

I was hoping for a minute to talk to Brill, who is sitting in one of the other beauticians' chairs, trying to stifle a yawn. His eyes are gold with love, pero they're more slypered than I've ever seen them. He was up all night, looking for me, and that makes me feel all soft and warm in my chest. Tawny follows my gaze.

She starts to say something, thinks better of it, then tilts her cabeza and smiles at Brill. There's something predatory in her eyes as she looks at him. I manage not to make a noise as I suck in a startled breath. I recognize that look, from about a million telenovelas, when the obligatory *other woman* enters the scene.

It's hard to believe, though. Could Tawny really have designs on my boyfriend?

"Don't keep my girl busy too long," Brill tells her.

Tawny's expression changes, pero I can't read it.

Brill walks over to me. I put a hand on his chest, sliding it between his leather jacket and his tee, feeling estúpido for being so demonstrably possessive as his Krom heart beats like a hummingbird against my palm. Pero, Tawny needs to be clear that Brill's off limits.

Tawny holds my hand, squeezing a little too tight the whole way down the hall to Minda's dressing room.

"I need you on your best behavior, Bo." Tawny gives me a plastinique smile. "Earth can't afford you pulling any more stunts."

She means HGB can't afford another scandal. Their monopoly on chocolate is partially dependent on the good graces of the Global Court of Earth – and part on public opinion and the trust of the people. They've already lost enough of that, over the years, to make a lot of people question whether HGB really is the best solution for Earth's future. Everyone thought that the debacle a few months ago with one of HGB's pilots was going to be enough to tip Earth into another global war.

Pero, what does Tawny think I'm going to do? She doesn't even know that I know about Serum Green – Frank promised that much, when I agreed to keep it secret. And if I make Earth look bad – well, then what was the point of coming here?

"Have I been anything but cooperative?" I ask.

Tawny puts a hand on the door. "Bodacious–"

From the other side, something explodes, then someone coughs repeatedly. Tawny and I look at each other. Then we barge in.

Minda's standing next to a portable oven, waving smoke away. She's wearing an apron with a print of pink fruit, over a tight black outfit. Cake batter is streaming down her giant yellow face.

"One of you get me a towel." She holds out a huge slender-fingered hand without even looking to see who we are and whether we've agreed.

There's a basket with a dozen small white towels rolled up inside a glass-fronted cabinet. I pull one out and give it to Minda. She dabs at her face. "How can cake be liquid inside, when outside it's charcoal?"

"What did you put in that?" I ask.

"Bo! You're here to save me." She turns around and breaks into a wide smile, showing the heavily serrated edges on her teeth. Tawny doesn't flinch, even when Minda moves towards us to wrap me in a hug.

Minda pats my hair. "I am hopeless in the kitchen and we're streaming out our first episode live tomorrow. I'm counting on you to make me look good."

Que? I want to end this whole adventure as a culinary arts teacher, pero I was not prepared for a Minda-level student. "Minda, por favor!"

"You can do this," Minda says. "I don't care what the polls say."

Tawny's posture stiffens. "I have counseled Bo not to look at the polls. Reminders that people find her... problematic will only make her nervous."

Problematic. That's an understatement. People are still saying they think I deserve the shave for selling out Earth for a couple of chocolate beans.

"You're always going to have detractors," Minda says. "If you go around doing the things that other people are afraid to do, you will be slandered. If you try to change from the person people thought you were into something better, people will make up lies so that they still get to feel superior. This isn't a maybe for those of us in the public eye. It is what will happen."

"Not to you." I study her gigantic face, literally larger than life. "You have a grande fan base, and nobody dares buzzbash you, even in my planet's media. You have the power to change things, because people listen to you. Which is why it is estúpido that I'm here. This should be you and mi mamá."

"You think I've never been lied about? Or that I've always been popular? The only way that you get to grow up to become me is by refusing to care." Minda gestures with the towel. "You're here because everyone loves an underdog. And because you're the one who made your life forfeit to do the impossible already. Do you imagine your mother would have done the same in your place?"

Probably not. "Mamá would have done something smarter."
Tawny snorts a laugh. "Tell me about it."

Mi mamá is Mamá Lavonda, one of Earth's most popular
celebrity chefs at a time when foodies are bigger than rock stars.
She's also a cookbook author, and occasionally teaches classes.
Mamá's entire career was financed by HGB, who sponsors her
feeds. She provides positive publicity for them on Earth, and
encourages people from other planets to give Earth-produced
exports a try.

Basically, she gets the ratings HGB is looking for, and they let
her do whatever she wants. Which doesn't mean that she's not
incredibly talented, as a chef and at making captivating footage.

I call Mamá for help. Things are still not easy between us.
She has never apologized for not supporting me when the
media shredded my holostar career. Still, if I make her feel
needed here, that will make her happy. And despite my past
hurt, I want her to be happy.

After I've explained my Minda problem, she says, *Set up the
kitchen and holocall back. Then we will do a rehearsal, like it is a
scripted show.*

We pair up the holofields so that it looks like Mamá's
kitchen is the other half of our set kitchen, obscuring the
audience bleachers. Only Mamá's not at home. The space looks
suspiciously like a ship's galley.

I hear a masculine voice in the background. Frank Sawyer.
Blegh.

Mamá rarely goes offplanet, and when she does, it's for a
FeedCast big enough that I'd have heard about it. Is she going
somewhere now? With the same Frank who forced me at
gunpoint to keep another one of HGB's secrets?

Frank's the HGB agent who tried to stop me from taking
cacao offplanet. He's shot at me before, killed a man right in
front of me for trying to protect me.

Pero, he is also the one who leaked the holo that helped me

escape having mi cabeza detached from my shoulders.

Frank's *still* Mamá's boyfriend. Anyone else would have thrown Frank out the minute she found out he was the HGB assassin who killed mi Papá, el amor de Mamá's vida, *the love of her life*. Or that Frank fell in love with her afterwards because HGB tasked him with watching our family.

Pero, not mi mamá. No y no. She is, after all, Mamá Lavonda. Whatever Mamá wants, Mamá gets. Currently, that includes Frank.

After the run-through, I go looking for Brill. He's not waiting for me on set, so I call him. There's hysterical laughter in the background. "Babe! We're on my ship. Jimena made the worst snacks. Avell, come help!"

I feel a little left out, pero, what did I expect him to do, sit around all night? Mertex, who is waiting sleepily just outside, sees me looking flustered.

"Want a ride over there?"

"Please." I follow him to his vehicle, a blocky silver hatchback with six tires. He looks more relaxed behind the wheel than he ever was on board the warship, where he came across as nervous and petulant. This place suits him.

"Ever think you'd be friends with the biggest star in Zandywood?" Mertex asks.

I stifle a laugh. "Weren't you the one who once told me that term is both inaccurate and insulting to the Noble Race?" Meaning the Zantites.

He leans his arm on the window frame. "Minda says Zandywood. She keeps telling me to lighten up."

When we get to the *Fois Gras*, Brill has turned the bridge of his ship into a theater, using the oversized nav and representational viewing screens and attendant holofields. The screens can become clear, providing windows across the bow. It's an incredibly flexible design, and part of the upgrade HGB gave Brill's ship in exchange for bringing us here. They also sprang for deluxe chairs at Brill's table to replace the old ring bench since Tawny's back can't handle "primitive" seating.

Valeria and Jimena are sitting on the sofa, and some of Brill's friends are playing Varan at the table. There's a thin-lipped guy I've never seen before trying to talk to Jimena, pero he's not getting very far. They're all watching a Spanish language cheesecast with Krom subtitles.

Brill gives me a hug. "I was telling Valeria about how I got un poco addicted to telenovelas trying to learn Spanish, and it turns out we both like this show, and some of my friends were in the area, and hest, instant party."

I look at Valeria, who notices me looking and seems a bit embarrassed. I'm filled with wonder. Brill's won her over, at least a little.

The guy Jimena's been talking to heads for the bathroom, and Jimena asks Brill, "Who *is* that guy?"

"Commodities broker," Brill says. He means *fence*.

"Qué lástima. I was hoping he was somebody famous." Jimena straightens her gauzy floral blouse and crosses legs clad in lime green leggings. She doesn't seem to own anything in neutral colors. "I thought you would party with a higher class of people."

"I should be getting back," Mertex says. Pero, the way he's been shadowing me, that probably means he's planning to wait in his car.

"Ga, su. Stay." Brill gestures to the table. "These sus could use one more, since I'm done playing. Ever tried Varan?"

Mertex shakes his cabeza, pero he starts watching the game.

"Careful, Murry," I say. "Varan against three Krom? You'll lose fast."

"Ven?" one of Brill's friends says. *So what?* "Krom don't gamble, so what's he out but time?"

"If you're sure it's OK?" Mertex looks ridiculously oversized perched on a vacant chair. Pero, nobody laughs as they start explaining the rules. I don't think he ever got invited to this kind of thing back aboard the *Layla's Pride*. He looks so happy right now he might pop.

Together Brill and I head towards the galley, where they've broken out the booze. There's a tray of something wrapped inside biscuit dough on the counter. I start to reach for it, pero Brill says, "I wouldn't, Babe."

"Que?" I pick one up and break it in half and smell it. Puaf! No lo sé what Jimena was thinking, pero you don't mix bleu cheese and plef. Whatever the last kitchen she worked in was, it must have been muy experimental.

I yawn. It's late. Pero, I've earned a Tawny-free good time. "Don't worry, mi Vida. I can fix this."

CHAPTER FOUR

The live recording isn't going well.

Jimena looks all of twenty years old, with large innocent dark eyes, though the restaurant experience on her resume implies she's closer to thirty. I'm only twenty-four. Which is probably why she's been blowing me off and doing things however she wants. She won't even take her headphones off.

She bumps into one of the Zantite production assistants and drops the entire bowl of pitted cherries – produce Brill had carried from Earth.

My fuzzy brain sees it in slow motion, unable to adapt. I'd been up half the night, tag-teaming with Mamá to get Minda ready to do this and the other half partying. With Jimena. Which makes it my fault, if she's too slypered to work. Ay-ay-ay.

There's a wet squish, and Minda says an unfamiliar Zantite word that I'm guessing is a swear. I look over and see cherry juice staining the side of one of her pale silk slippers.

I feel the same way. Cherries take forever to pit, and I can't just substitute something else. Minda has already advertised that we're kicking off the tour with mi mamá's choctastic Black Forest Cake.

Brill calls my sublingual. He was in the audience, pero his seat's empty. *Don't worry, Babe. There's more to that shipment. Be right back.*

I turn to Jimena, who finally has the headphones off.

"Lo siento, boss." She doesn't look sorry, though.

I don't have time to take that personally. "Happens to the best of us." I grab two blocks of HGB dark and toss one to Jimena.

She catches it, holding it out away from her like it's radioactive. "What do you want me to do with this?"

"Melt it." I try my best not to, pero I roll my eyes. She's supposed to have had more experience in the kitchen than me. I'm starting to wonder.

"Fast," Minda adds, in Universal. "Or I'll have them take you back to the spaceport." She nods towards that same group of policemen, here today as crowd control.

Jimena blanches and the block starts trembling in her hands. "No, por favor. We *have to* make it to the capital."

Which is the show's last tour stop.

I don't get it. What's with the implied *or else*? It's not like Minda said, *Or we'll show them how to cook you as an entrée.*

Minda whispers, "Is there something wrong with that chocolate?"

I blush. Like all HGB products, that chocolate is laced with an addictive substance.

I wish I could tell Minda that. But if I did, I'd find myself back home and being prepped for execution before Minda could even lodge a protest.

"No, chica. The chocolate's standard." Which isn't actually a lie.

I talk to the camera in slow, careful Zantite about how tempered chocolate has a snap to it, shaving off a piece and then breaking it to prove it. Just in time, Jimena brings the pot of melted chocolate over and lowers it towards the table.

Minda says a close approximation of, "Muchas gracias."

Startled, Jimena jostles the pot as it touches the table, and chocolate sloshes onto her arm, and splatters up onto her face.

Gasping, she says something in dismay, but all I hear clearly is, "semilla de la muerte." *Seed of death.*

"Que?"

"Nada." She retreats, wiping furiously at her eye with a towel. What is wrong with that chica? Why would she sign up for this gig if she's that nervous on camera?

I forget about my prep chef's problems when Brill shows up Krom-fast, hauling another crate of cherries in his arms. He puts them down in the prep area.

Brill opens the crate. Jimena takes out a bowl, fills it with cherries, then starts attacking one with a knife.

I hand Minda my spoon. "She's going to cut herself."

I gesture Tawny over. "What did you do with that pack of drinking straws?"

She digs in her bag and pulls out the package.

I snag the straws, then walk over to Jimena. I take the knife away from her and hand her a straw. "Watch."

I push the straw into the cherry, and the pit falls out onto the prep table. I drop the cherry into the bowl. There's one. All I need is about two thousand more. I sigh.

I reach back into the bowl, and a male human hand reaches in from across the table. Our fingers touch as he scoops out a handful of cherries. I look up into beautiful, smile-crinkled gray-green eyes, lighter than his cool-toned black skin.

"Kaliel?" My heart starts thudding overtime, even though I had promised myself that the next time I saw him, I wouldn't let it do that.

He takes a straw from the pack. "Looks like we got here just in time to help."

"I thought you guys weren't coming until next month. What about Kayla's graduation?" Kayla. As in my former roommate and mejor amiga. His girlfriend.

He pits a few cherries, dropping them into the bowl, staining his hands. He smiles and leans closer to me – whispering distance.

"Don't tell her I told you, but Kayla's going to graduate here. With you. Minda's getting special permission from your school."

His face is so close to mine, I back away.

I'd kissed Kaliel, just twice, but that's enough to remember what his lips felt like on mine, his hands running confidently along my arms, my fingers against his stiff super-short hair.

But I'm back with Brill now, and Kaliel is with Kayla. And… this is going to be a long tour.

It's incredíble that Kaliel and Kayla wound up together at all, since they'd only met because he was on trial for blowing up the SeniorLeisure galactourist vessel that had Kayla's grandparents on board.

Brill had helped me and my friends prove that Kaliel had been set up to take that shot. The gritclip we'd found as evidence showed another vessel for a few frames, an inky black ship outlined against a lighter background. The com array on the cruise liner had been disabled, and the mystery ship had made Kaliel think he was being pursued and fired upon.

In an area where space pirates often disable ships to take cargo – after spacing the crew – Kaliel's fear was reasonable. Especially because he'd been working for HGB, carrying a load of chocolate that was worth more than the equivalent weight of gold bricks would have been, back before First Contact.

The liner wouldn't respond when he'd tried to clarify who he was – an official HGB pilot, and no threat to them – so he'd scuttlepunched it.

HGB had had no choice but to allow Kaliel to go to trial for the manslaughter of everyone on board. If he'd been found guilty, the media and the public would have demanded his head in a basket. Pero his innocence barely made the news. And the existence of the black ship was never made public.

For Kaliel, skipping the shave was enough. He didn't care who had set him up.

I wish I could move on so easily. At the same time Kaliel had been counting down days to his trial, HGB had threatened mi familia in an attempt to get me to give them back their precious unfermented cacao beans. Frank had come close to murdering mi mamá, on the grounds that he always follows orders – even if they are personally distasteful.

HGB isn't just the company that controls chocolate production and distribution. They're the face Earth shows to the galaxy, and they have a huge amount of influence over Earth's Global Court. Even though I can prove Frank killed my father eight years ago, I've got to play nice, because with the threat of invasion, a power vacuum right now – or the descent of my world into another internal war over who gets to control chocolate – would be disastrous.

"Here, hun." Kayla comes up behind Kaliel and hands him a white apron. The juice leaves clear handprints near the hem as he takes it. It looks like blood

Kayla pulls masses of her curly brown hair away from her milk-pale cheeks and stuffs the locks up under her favorite green knit hat. She's wearing a bright pink tunic top and jeans, with an apron that matches Kaliel's. "Just point me at the prep sink." Her wide-set, intelligent dark eyes glitter with happiness. She can't wait to be on camera.

Minda comes over and peers into the bowl. "Bring the cameras. This looks like fun." She looks out into the audience. "Who wants to be on the feeds?"

Half the audience raises their hands, and Minda calls people down to help, until we run out of straws.

Brill's studying me and his smile looks tense. He knows I kissed Kaliel. I'd apologized for the betrayal, but it had nearly broken us up for good. Later, Brill had said he was over being jealous, and I'd said I was over Kaliel, pero this is the first time we've seen the pilot since he got reinstated with HGB, and Brill and I were obviously lying to each other.

Minda spears cherries all the way up her straw and pushes eight of them into the bowl at once. "We should keep this as a regular feature. You show us a fun food prep hack, and audience members get to try it."

I nod. "Sí, sounds perfect."

I look over for Brill, pero he doesn't like cameras. I'm not surprised that he has melted away. Pero, I hope that's all it is.

With so many hands, it doesn't take long for us to get the cherries re-prepped, and Jimena gets them cooking down behind us at the quaint gas range. Minda assembles the cake batter and I pop it into the top oven – then I pull the completed, baked, cooled cake out of the bottom oven. We start discussing frosting. I might just make it through this.

By the time we're handing out cake slices to the audience, I have forgotten the cameras. Right up until Jimena sinks to the floor, holding her arms across her stomach.

I rush over to her – and so does a camera drone. I try to bat it away. This is, after all, live. "Jimena!"

"No me siento bien." *I don't feel so well.*

Hot, sticky guilt fills my gut. I've been criticizing her while she's ill.

Unless – panic replaces the guilt – it's food poisoning. I look around. I don't see a cake plate, pero that doesn't mean she didn't have one. Or that she hasn't been sampling the ingredients. Nobody else is showing any signs of getting sick. If I can get her out of here quietly, maybe this will all be OK.

Jimena throws up. Loudly. The pleasant chit-chat that had filled the room goes silent.

Someone says in Zantite, "The Earthlings have brought disease to our planet."

I bristle at the insult, pero it could have been worse. At least they're not claiming to have been poisoned.

"Wait," someone says. "What if she's accidentally poisoned

herself? These aliens are angry about our expansion into their solar system. Who knows what she might have added to our food."

And... now it's worse. I can't make out what any one Zantite is saying in the chatterclash that follows. Mertex is making his way over to me – presumably to keep me safe if this breaks out into a mob. So is Dent Head. Dent Head gets there first, pushing me behind him, close to the oven, which somebody turned on to bake Minda's cake.

"Wait a minute!" Minda shouts, her voice commanding in the large space. "Shouldn't we consider what the Earthlings will think if one of their delegates has contracted one of *our* diseases?"

The dead silence is broken by a lone female voice, from the very back of the audience. "I'm a doctor." The Zantite makes her way down the stairs, pulling up a holo that looks like an anatomy course. She looks around Dent Head at me. "I've never studied humans, but will you consent for me to examine your friend?"

Bang! We both jump. Cake batter's dripping down the inside of the oven door.

En serio? I'd watched Minda mix that batter myself. How did she mess it up?

I glance over at Minda, who is peering with dismay at the oven.

"Bo," Mertex prompts. "She asked you a question."

I nod. "Sí. I've been treated by a Zantite doctor before myself." Besides, it's not like we brought a human doctor with us. Which, in retrospect, seems like bad planning on HGB's part.

"You have to say you have no complaints," Mertex says. "You're waiving liability in case the treatment doesn't go well."

"I have no complaints." Is Jimena's condition that serious? Or do they ask that from everybody?

"There's a cot in one of the dressing rooms." Mertex picks up Jimena, who is conscious but in no condition to walk. Dent Head gestures for me to go with them.

As soon as we're out in the hall, Mertex asks me, "Seriously, what is the deal between you and Fizzax?"

I glance back at the doctor, who is only two steps behind us. "It's complicated." We've reached the dressing room by the time I think to ask, "What is the deal between *you* and Dent Head?" Fizzax. His name's Fizzax.

Mertex places Jimena in the oversized cot, then moves aside so we can let the doctor work. "Fizzax considers me a coward." A green blush grows on Mertex's cheeks. "He's not wrong."

The doctor places a blinking band around my wrist. "I need a baseline comparison of vital statistics. Try not to move too much."

"I'm not a good baseline," I protest, pero nobody's listening. "Murry, you're not—"

"Please sit down, Miss Benitez," the doctor says. She turns to Mertex. "Refusing a duel is not the mark of a coward. It is a sign that you respect the preciousness of life."

"Thanks, Sonda," Mertex says. "But that's not how most people see it."

This must be a muy muy small island if these two not only know each other, but Sonda knows Mertex's business. She turns back to Jimena.

I ask Mertex, "What did Fizzax want to fight you over?"

He shrugs. "He claims I dishonored his sister. He was mistaken. Why should I die for something I didn't even do?"

I put this together with the story he'd told me on board the *Layla's Pride*. "So to get out of it, you volunteered to crew a warship."

"Something like that."

"After he gave his entire life savings to his cousin so she could start a squidriding and boat tour business."

Mertex nods. "It was worth it. She's the only one who wrote me the whole time I was stuck on the *Layla's Pride*."

Sonda turns back to us. "There's no sign of any of this area's more common poisons, but if I'm reading the standards for Earthlings right, your friend has a high fever and rapid heart rate. I don't know what's wrong with her. It doesn't seem life threatening. Still, I'd like to keep her under observation until tomorrow, just in case I've missed something." She points at me. "You, on the other hand, have measurable organ damage and a cocktail of toxin residue in your bloodstream. What exactly happened to you?"

"She got bit by a Myska," Mertex says, that horror-happy gleam back in his eyes.

Sonda's round eyes go even wider. "How are you even alive?"

"The guy gave me an antivenin." I shrug. "We're friends now."

"And she took the Invincible Heart," Murry adds.

Sonda's mouth gapes open.

Mamá calls my handheld. I hold it up, grateful for the diversion, pero a little worried. She never does that unless she has gran news and wants to see my face. Por favor. Tell me she's not eloping with Frank.

I step into the hall. "Hola, Mamá."

She's a bubble away from the kind of domed-in megamall you find on spaceports across the galaxy. People crowd the street behind her. Most of them have long, thin necks and heads shaped like peaches, with narrow beaks in the central dent.

Frank walks across the frame, heading towards the building. I stiffen. He has Botas, the corgi he rescued, on a leash. The dog starts sniffing, and Frank smiles down at it as it takes its time to find a spot to do its business. Mamá follows my gaze.

"What will it take for you to forgive him, mija?" Mamá looks like an older version of me, with the same wide mouth and slightly hooked nose. Which means we have almost identical frowns.

"I don't hate Frank, Mamá." It's been a long time since Mamá and I have been this honest with each other. "Frank was doing his duty, pero, that duty was killing mi papá. I can live with the logic of that. Pero, he can't step into the family he tore apart and find a place to belong."

"There is a big difference between not hating and forgiving. You are going to wear the past like a bag of rocks until you figure that out." She wags a finger at me. "Carry it long enough and you will break your back."

I blink at her, glance over at Frank, who is now bagging dog poop. "After he admitted we were just part of his assignment, how can you trust anything he says?"

Mamá smiles. "How did you forgive Brill for using you to get closer to what he wanted from Earth?"

She has a point. Brill did lie about meeting me by chance, when in reality he had sought me out because he thought I could help him claim chocolate as a Krom "discovery." I'd broken up with him when I'd found out – and it had taken a lot for us to patch things up.

How had I forgiven Brill? "He proved to me he wasn't using me anymore, that he could be the hero I needed. Pero, Frank's still working for HGB, still putting our familia in danger."

"You should try getting to know Frank. Maybe you will see he is more than what you think he is, too."

I sigh. "Just promise me you're not going to elope with him. Wherever you two are headed."

"Oye!" Mamá looks offended. "Elope? If I get married again, it's going to be the media event of the season."

I let her go and check on Jimena one last time before leaving her with the doctor. Sonda wants to transfer Jimena to the hospital to keep an eye on her for a couple of days. When Jimena's better, I am going to have to ask her what she meant by *seeds of death*, and who the *we* are she's so intent on getting to the capital with. Because it didn't sound like she meant me and Minda.

CHAPTER FIVE

The show *had* been a success, by force of will on Minda's part, and she intends to celebrate at her favorite dance club.

We of an Earthling scale – minus Jimena – all pile into the van to head across town for the afterparty. Tawny is still fuming over the groundless accusations the Zantite audience had made, and everybody else is trying to avoid drawing her attention. Brill seems so withdrawn compared to last night, when we'd been with his friends. Maybe it's because Kaliel y Kayla are here. Maybe it's just Tawny.

Once we get inside the club, the music is hard-edged and undulating, but with oddly operatic trills to the sopranos' voices, transforming the rough Zantite words into flowing honey. Brill holds my hand as we wind through the crowd toward an open area on the dance floor that seems reserved for couples who are taking turns dancing for the cameras. I doubt Brill wants to be on camera – even though he's learned to dance.

We pass Mertex, just as he offers a green fizzing drink to Minda. I stop to watch and Brill lets go of my hand.

Minda's changed into a knee-length silver dress and stacked her wrists with bangle bracelets. She looks like a go-go dancer from the early days of Earth's flat video – or like how that era's science fiction films thought aliens would dress.

Minda giggles as she takes the drink, dipping her cabeza, the better to look up at Murry. When Mertex, the most awkward

Zantite on a ship of misfits, had first confessed he was in love with a movie star he'd never met, it had been an impossible daydream. We'd been discussing how, if you have to die, you'd prefer to go, and he'd said in Minda Frou's arms, with her singing him to sleep.

Pero, now that he's working for Minda, it looks like he's grown on her. He might wind up in her arms after all, and not even have to die to do it.

"I love that color on you," she tells him, running a hand along the collar of his dark blue shirt. "It brings out the green undertones of your skin."

His face goes teal. "Thank you," he splutters, maybe understanding for the first time that the girl of his dreams is into him.

Minda notices me. "You should have seen how proud Tawny is of you, Bo. She told me you really made HGB look good today. I got the impression before that you didn't like her company. So why are you working for them?"

"That's the deal I made to keep my life. Better the devil you know, and all that, no?"

Minda scrunches her flattish nose. "The absolutes of good and bad are rarely as clear as they seem."

I want to tell her that HGB's been manipulating people since they began. That they're not above killing people to keep their secrets. Sometimes people from their own planet. Pero, maybe she won't be shocked. Maybe every planet does that. Maybe every planet has their own Pure275 and their own Serum Green.

I sigh. "It will be years before we know for sure whether chocolate can even be grown successfully on other planets, and HGB's going to be doing everything they can to make sure that doesn't change anything. If your planet doesn't destroy mine when they invade."

Minda's rubbery lips pucker with distaste. She doesn't seem to believe her people capable of such barbarity. Yet I can so vividly see Earth exploding into a bajillion pieces, trying to repel the invaders.

A familiar tenor voice chimes in with the sopranos. It's the Zantite singer from the radio. Desperate to change the subject, I ask, "Is that Verex Kowlk?"

Mertex nods. "They just wrapped on his first feature-length holo, so he's on a publicity tour, like you."

Verex looks just out of the learning pod, pero he's hot by Zantite standards. His skin's so yellow, it's almost orange, and he's muscled like a whip. Verex leaves the stage and heads for a nearby table.

An Earthling comes out of the kitchen, carrying a plate with an elaborate dessert on it. He's Aidan Ace, the teen prodigy/independent HoloCaster the polls say is set to replace Mamá as Earth's most popular celebrity chef. He's maybe even younger than Verex. His spiked-up hair's blond, his eyebrows so light they almost don't exist, in contrast to his deep brown eyes, which are full of mirth and trouble. He puts the dessert on the star's table, and Verex asks him to sit down.

"What's *he* doing here?" I ask Mertex.

Surely Aidan's not planning to replace *me*. He's not exactly the kind of person to show Earth's mature enough to belong in the galaxy. Y, if I get made irrelevant or sent home, it could put me back in line for the shave. I'd prefer all my cameracentric time to not involve being strapped to a board and tipped onto a guillotine for ratingstastic blood-splattering entertainment.

"He came to chronicle people's reaction to your show. I got him a job here to keep him out from underfoot." Minda rolls her eyes. "He wanted a job ON the show."

Dios mio! The impertinence.

"There you are." Tawny's suddenly at my back, pushing me forward onto the dance floor. "I've requested a special song for you and the hero who showed up just in time today."

"Where is he?" I'm looking for Brill, who brought me the

replacement cherries, pero she's pushing me towards Kaliel, who is standing at the edge of the dance floor, minding his own business, holding a beer. He looks startled at me coming toward him and glances at the stage as a samba starts playing. One of the singers is doing her best at pronouncing the unfamiliar Spanish.

I stifle my own panic. Tawny knows how badly Brill reacted last time to that bumpclip of me and Kaliel dancing. Either she's mad at me for what happened with Jimena – which was not my fault – or she's still trying to drive a wedge between me and Brill, even though she's so not his type.

Tawny takes Kaliel's beer and sips from it, making a face at the taste. No straw or anything. She puts it down on a table behind her. "Everyone's waiting to see this episode's stars dance together."

The reserved dance floor's gone empty, because nobody else here knows how to samba – except Brill, who knows the basics, pero there's no way he'd do it in front of these cameras. I can't even find him in this crowd of giants.

"I don't think this is a good idea," Kaliel says, pero Tawny places my hand in his, and pushes us onto the dance floor.

Kaliel's other hand comes around my waist as we move to the music. He draws me close to him, and my heartbeat skyrockets. This is a very bad idea.

I try to focus on something other than the scent of his cologne and the strength of his arms as he pushes me into a spin. The music is fast, and he's showing off a little with quick changes, pushing us apart, bringing us back together, pulling me into a turn where my feet come completely off the floor. I'm flying in mi cabeza too, unable to deny the ease with which I fit together with Kaliel, even though Brill must be watching. The feeling is confusing and slippery, laced with guilt even though Kaliel and I are just dancing.

Tawny's slapped a bug on Kaliel. The tiny circle glitters on the sleeve of his tee-shirt as he moves us across the floor. He pulls me to him, lifting me off the ground again, and as the song's last notes die away, he's holding me up by my waist, our faces inches apart. His eyes don't have to be capable of chromashift for me to be able to recognize the attraction reflecting back out at me. He puts me down.

We both hesitate in that moment of stillness, and it's all I can do to make myself pull away.

Kaliel turns, peering down at the floor. Then without saying anything, he walks away. And my heart squeezes.

I know. It doesn't have any right to. Pero, I can't just leave it like this.

I follow him into the crowd, even as a song more fitting to Zantite dance steps starts. Kaliel's headed for where several Zantites are playing with an electric game that looks like a giant pinball machine got crossed with holo-darts.

I grab his arm, turn him back towards me, not even caring about the bug. His eyes go wide with surprise. "Bo, I–"

I cut him off. "Gracias por today. You showed up just in time to save me. Again."

Kaliel had helped me escape when Frank was closing in back in Brazil after I'd been caught stealing cacao from the plantation. I'd asked Kaliel to leave the planet with me, offered him things my heart had no business promising. He looks at my lips, and I bet he's remembering that night in the rainforest. Remembering the intensity of his lips on mine, just like I am.

He returns his focus back to my eyes. "You mean with the cherries? It wasn't that big a deal."

"It was to me." My hand's still on his arm. I pull it away. "Mira, we need to talk."

A waiter carrying a tray of tiny choco-boozy shots walks by, leaning down to offer us some. Kaliel shakes his head. "Thanks anyway. I don't like chocolate."

"Que?" I let out a startled laugh. "See, this is why we were never meant to be together." I mean it as a joke, pero I realize it's a mistake, even as the words are leaving my mouth.

His lips tighten into a serious line. "I'm not going to deny I'm still attracted to you. We just proved that back on the dance floor. But that can't mean anything. I love Kayla, and I wouldn't hurt her for the world. Loyalty's important to me."

He's that kind of guy. Which is what makes me want to keep him as an amigo. And he's put into words exactly how I feel about Brill. "Entiendo. I understand, and—"

"Do you?" Brill's come up behind me. I turn towards him. His eyes are rosy orange – embarrassed and frustrated. He holds up his phone. "This has me questioning your definition of loyalty."

Pain knifes through me. The paparazzi must have been mixing flashback malcasts in with the post-show feeds. What weak moment of my past could they have captured that he wouldn't have already seen? "You promised you wouldn't let the pops color how you think of me. A lot of it is outright buzzbashing."

I glance towards Kaliel, like he can vouchspeak the truth – which he can't, I didn't even know him then – and that's a mistake, too.

Brill's eyes drop towards angry maroon. "I'm talking about your little dance exhibition." He plucks the bug from the fabric of Kaliel's shirt and drops it to the floor, where he crushes it under his boot. He pops up a holo on his phone. "Tawny sent me this."

The gritcast is mostly of me, from the point of view of Kaliel's tee-shirt sleeve. Mostly, all it caught is the outline of my hair, or my profile spinning away. Pero, there's audio, of me and Kaliel talking in Spanish. Eh? We hadn't said a word.

Holo-him says, muffled and indistinct, "Meet me tonight. They'll never have to know."

And I – me, my actual voice – replies, "Do you really think we can hide our love?"

Holo-Kaliel says, still muffled, "We've been doing well so far. He hasn't found the e-mails–"

"No, of course not." Me again. This conversation is starting to sound familiar, pero I can't quite place it. "I'll leave him as soon as we've gotten what we want."

Brill turns off the holo.

"I didn't say any of that!" I squeak.

"She didn't, I swear." Kaliel takes a step backwards as Brill looms menacingly towards him. "Maybe I should go."

Brill's hands ball into fists at his side. "Ga. Su, I'll go."

I watch his brown leather jacket disappear into the crowd. I thought that after all we've been through together, how hard we'd fought for each other, Brill and I had something real. So how can it still be this fragile?

Kaliel says, "That actually was your voice. What e-mails were you talking about?"

"Ni idea." Pero, then it hits. I gasp. Tawny is even more devious than I gave her credit for. "Actually, I do. That was from the one scene I did in *Bullets for Luiz*. We were on the next soundstage, and one of their regulars called in sick. They holoed the whole thing so you couldn't see my face."

"So Brill wouldn't have seen that?"

I shake mi cabeza. "Nunca. It was uncredited."

"I still bet you were better than the actress who normally played that part." He winks at me. Kaliel and I are going to be OK. No lo sé about me and Brill. The electronic game lights up and starts blinking and a blizzard of paper tickets shoots out of it. I ignore the winners' dancing and booze-sloshing.

"Brill's a kek," I sigh. "I told him it wasn't what it looked like, and he didn't even listen. What am I supposed to do with that?"

"Cut him a break." Kaliel puts a hand on my shoulder. Then he quickly removes it. "We guys have a hard time not believing our own eyes. Let me go talk to him."

I try not to think about the warmth of that contact. "Are you sure that's a good idea?"

Kaliel shrugs. "It's not like he's armed or anything."

"He might be."

Kaliel's eyes go wide. "I'll be careful, then."

I make my way over to the bar, climb up on one of the tall stools. I need one of the fizzy green drinks Minda was having. Or maybe two or three.

But before I can even order, a deep voice asks, "Is this seat taken?"

I look up. Dent Head – Fizzax – is standing there, one hand on the stool next to mine.

"It is now."

He sits down, orders twek, and gestures for me to get what I want. I describe Minda's drink to the bartender.

Fizzax takes out a recording device, pero he cradles it in both hands, not turning it on. "Officially, I'm here to ask about your assistant's illness."

"Pero, that's not what you really want to talk about."

The bartender passes me the drink. I sip liquid fire and barely manage to swallow it. My throat burns and I'm coughing. This stuff is like pineapple-flavored turpentine.

Fizzax grins. "That's the begekk. You'll get used to it." But the grin fades just as quickly. He turns his hands over, trapping the recorder against the bar. "Why'd you cover for me? You had every right to watch me die yesterday."

"For what? My wounded pride?" I put a hand on one of his giant ones. If he feels the IH shaking in mine, he doesn't react. I look up at him. "By all rights, I should have been executed for stealing cacao on Earth. That made me appreciate what a gift mercy can be."

I don't believe that, not really. What HGB showed me wasn't mercy, just calculation. It's just something to say to make him feel better.

Fizzax's eyes turn soft and thoughtful. "I am a man of honor, and lies do not sit easily with me. I should turn myself in and accept the consequences."

I take another sip of turpentine. It goes down easier this time. "I'm not mad. Tawny doesn't really care. And I'll be sickened if I have to watch your execution."

"But why aren't you mad?"

"Honestly? It's the blanket." I smile, remembering it wrapped around me. "A guy who cares whether I'd get cold doesn't deserve to die."

He looks dumbfounded. "Then what do you want? To make things right?"

"An apology would be nice." I swirl the drink, watching the fizz climb as a cloud of steam. "And I'd love for you to drop this thing with Mertex."

He starts to protest, pero bites back his words into a growl. "I will consider it." Then he dips his cabeza. "I apologize thoroughly."

"And I forgive you thoroughly."

It's not part of the proscribed language, but it does get a laugh from Fizzax. He turns on the recorder. "Do you know of anyone who would wish to injure your assistant Jimena Duarte or who has a grudge against any member of your cast or crew?"

I consider his question. "Some people both here and back home find this a laughable attempt at diplomacy, pero I doubt those people take us seriously enough to try to poison anyone."

"Then you do believe she was poisoned?"

I shrug. "Ni idea."

Kaliel walks back over towards us and drops a hand on my shoulder, more casual this time, like he's testing the just-be-friends thing. "Brill's outside and he wants to apologize to you. I gotta go."

"Go where?"

"I need to find my girl." Kaliel turns and scowls into the crowd. "Tawny sent Kayla that malcast too. So Kay told Brill she's packing her things and going home." He huffs out a breath. "Do you ever get the idea that Tawny might be trying to break all of us up, because from a media-spin standpoint, you and I make a better couple?"

Krom aren't popular on Earth, having raided the planet for commodity samples during First Contact and all. And having Kaliel turn out to, not only have been set up for the crime he was nearly shaved over, but to have formed a romantic alliance with the hero who brought that information to light...

It's possible. And if Tawny does want Brill for herself, that's a bonus. She's the one that ought to be compared to a spider, media-spinning a gossamer web we're all stuck in. "That heartless little–"

Fizzax laughs. "You know he's gone, right?" He gestures toward the door. "We can talk later."

I get up from my stool. I open the sublingual channel and call Kayla. It tries repeatedly to connect, pero there's no answer. I hope Kaliel's found her and they're talking.

Outside, it's dark. I can see Brill's pale pink irises reflecting in the lights from the club's sign before I spot the rest of him.

"Sorry, Babe." He sighs. "I'm a kek." Which is Krom for either *idiot* or *jerk*.

"As long as we agree on that point, no?" I step closer, not touching him, though I really want to bury my face in his leather jacket. It's heartshattering when you're mad at the person who should be comforting you. Though, honestly, I'm more upset at Tawny for manipulating all of us. Especially Kayla, who didn't do anything to anybody. "Promise me you're not going to listen to Tawny anymore."

"Promise, Babe."

"She's not your type, is she?"

"What?" He cringes, visible even in the dark. "You don't think I'm looking for an excuse to break up to be with her? Because that's kalltet–" *stupid* "–and just gross."

"I need to know that what we have isn't going to disappear over nothing. I've put too much of myself into this for that." I fight to speak around a lump in my throat. "You have a point about Kaliel, I know that. Pero, it's still not fair for you to throw accusations at me in public."

"I'm sorry." He holds a hand out towards me. "I wouldn't have come to Zant for anybody else. I wanted to protect you. But I keep hurting you. I know you're not looking for a make-up present." He winces – he'd learned the hard way that techniques that work with Krom girls don't always equate for Earthlings. "So what do I do here?"

Tears bite at the back of my eyes. I make a noise deep in my throat and rush forward and bury my face in his jacket. "Just trust me. And keep me safe."

CHAPTER SIX

The next morning, I'm dressed for the day in a cotton top and shorts. My head's pounding and my mouth feels like I've been chewing cotton, like my shirt. I suspect it has something to do with the pineapple turpentine.

It's also that Kayla still isn't answering her phone. We've been uña y carne – *fingernail and flesh, inseparable friends* – for heading on three years. And now she's not talking to me.

I've seen Kayla give people the silent treatment before. It's just never been me.

There's a knock on my door. I'm afraid it's Tawny – I don't have anything on my agenda, so she's bound to have scheduled an interview or twelve – pero when I open the door, Brill and Kaliel are both standing there, in swim trunks and water shoes, towels slung over their shoulders. Mertex is with them, wearing his tunic getup, also carrying a Zantite-sized towel.

I blink then pull my hair back away from my pounding forehead. "One of you had better have brought coffee, no?"

"Hanstral, Babe." Brill holds out two empty hands. *Sorry.* "I can go find you some decaf."

A growl's building at the back of my throat, the edginess of my need for another dose of IH spilling over into irritation. Brill knows decaf does nothing to slake the itchiness inside my blood. I know he's worried I'll overtax my system, pero, en serio?

"Pass." I glance down. Then I can't look away from those two sets of washboard abs. Brill's got a faded surgical scar running down one side of his, from an operation when he was a niño. Kaliel has a scar too, slashed diagonally across his chest. Ni idea where that came from. He's also got a tattoo on his shoulder of Icarus crossing the sun. Probably a pilot thing. And... I need to stop staring.

Brill already noticed.

"We're going squidriding," Kaliel announces. "Wanna come?"

Squidriding is a Zantite extreme watersport made famous by the *Princess Squidrider* tooncast. It doesn't look like anything a real live person would want to do. "No. Y no. And I can't believe you even asked that without bringing coffee."

"It's not as dangerous as they make it look in the cartoon." Mertex straightens the folded edge of his towel. "We have safety buoys, and emergency air tanks, and sonar trackers in the harnesses. Half the crew's going, so nobody'll get left alone. And these squids are old – like one tentacle in the grave."

"Geesh. Take all the fun out of it, why don't you?" Kaliel says.

Mertex shrugs. "There should still be enough challenge for an Earthling. Few species have the air capacity or natural swimming ability of the Noble Race." Mertex gestures at Brill. "Although for deep diving, your guys have surprising maneuverability in the water."

Both Brill and Kaliel look like they aren't quite sure whether they've just been insulted. And that's the kind of day I don't really want to deal with. I turn towards the sliding glass door, leading out onto my balcony, which looks out over the ocean. "You go, muchachos. I'll watch from right here."

Brill steps over to me. "Love ya, Babe."

He gives me a quick beso on the cheek, and for a second, I want to hold onto him.

"Wait!" I say, then feel estúpido. If Mertex is going, how lethalriffic can it be? "Take some pain au chocolate. The hotel sent way too much porque they're afraid of making Tawny unhappy."

Tawny. Both Brill and Kaliel get very similar sour expressions. Yet, Brill takes a croissant. Mertex does too.

Kaliel shakes his cabeza. I forgot, he doesn't like chocolate. He fans through the brochures on the desktop. He stops at an ad for *Authentic Earth Convenience Bread* and shows me the pic. "I already ate. This place has some cool options for pizza toppings, so I had leftovers from last night."

Pizza is one of the few Earth things that has become a fad throughout the galaxy. Mamá, who is usually content to stay in Brazil, even left Earth a couple of years ago to lead a tour of the top ten places in the galaxy to have adapted it.

"We need to go," Mertex reminds them.

Mertex steps out into the hall, followed by Brill.

I ask Kaliel, "Are you OK? After last night?"

"Yeah. I'm feeling pretty good." He plucks the branch of flowers from the vase on the desk and sniffs it. "I got some good news."

He takes the flowers with him as he follows the others out into the hallway, looking happier than I've ever seen him. Well, that was cryptic.

After they've gone, I take another croissant, and a glass of the juice that arrived with it, and move to the balcony, where there's a cushioned lounge chair. It's a beautiful day, with just a few puffy clouds in the sky. The waves crash rhythmically onto the beach below. I slip off my sandals, enjoying the feel of the breeze against my legs and bare feet. No matter where I am, the ocean always feels like home.

I try calling Kayla's phone again. This time someone answers. It's not Kayla.

"Argvekka Spaceport Lost and Found Department." It's a Zantite voice.

Uh... I'd feel stupid just hanging up after calling so many times. *I'm looking for my friend. If you find her, could you have her call me back?*

"Look, lady, I only picked it up because it won't stop ringing and we're not allowed to shut them off in case the police call."

I apologize thoroughly. I hesitate. *Can you at least tell me where this phone was found?*

"In the waiting area outside hanger nine. Now will you please stop calling?"

I call the spaceport's automated number, manage to get prior flight times. Last night, a shuttle left from that hanger, heading for Skadish, which is at least in the same direction as Earth. Logically, Kayla left the planet and was still so upset that she forgot her phone.

And yet, I can't let it go. I start calling our mutual friends, classmates from cooking school, even Chestla – who is on her home planet, Evevron, the same as that wrecked ship was from – pero nobody's heard from Kayla. Finally, I try her brother, Stephen.

He doesn't pick up, which isn't surprising. He's one of my exes, and it's always been awkward. After the fourth consecutive call, he gives in.

What? He sounds angry. At that point, anyone would.

I hesitate. *I was just wondering if you heard from Kayla yesterday.*

I did, actually. She's going back to Earth for a while because she needs her life to be less complicated.

Well, that's that then. Her travel plans confirmed, I should be able to stop worrying.

Pero... she'll miss graduation. Surely, as soon as she's not so angry, she'll realize that and turn back, right?

After a pause, Stephen asks, *Did you two have a fight?*

Something like that. Mira, tell her that I'm sorry and that it isn't what she thinks. And that I'm going to be heartbroken if she doesn't show back up here in time for graduation.

Shapes move on the water now, too far away to make out clearly, pero it must be Brill and Kaliel and the crew, tethered to animals that aren't like Earth squids at all.

Why don't you just tell her yourself? Stephen asks.

Because she left her phone at the spaceport. Or because she's not talking to me. Take your pick.

The shapes are moving fast, across the horizon, arcing around the point of land that will take them out into rougher seas.

I'll talk to her when she gets to Mom and Dad's, but that's going to be a while. Stephen hesitates. *You're a good friend for checking in. Sorry I didn't answer.*

Stephen's a good guy. Sometimes I have a hard time remembering why things didn't work out between us. I hang up and close my eyes, just lazing in the sun.

Who knows how long later, someone shouts. There's a commotion on the sand down below my balcony. I don't understand all the words, but something's gone wrong. I dash to the railing.

Two guys are carrying Mertex, who looks only half-conscious, towards the hotel, as the rest of the crew who went squidriding race across the sand, heading for the cliff.

"What happened?" I shout down at the guy holding Mertex's feet.

"One of the offworlders disappeared in the middle of the excursion, and this guy nearly killed himself trying to find him." The Zantite gestures with his chin at the retreating figures. "They're headed up top to try to get a better view."

I suck in a breath as my chest goes cold. The only two offworlders out there were Brill and Kaliel, and now there's only one human-sized form moving among the Zantites, keeping pace with the others. Which Brill might do, even though he could move faster, if he didn't know the path. And

Kaliel would be pushing himself to keep up.

Even from this distance, it should be obvious which one it is, given their vastly different skin tones and hairstyles, pero he's wearing a protective suit. When distance perspective takes away the fact that Krom are naturally bigger, the two guys I'm attracted to have remarkably similar physiques.

And I may never see one of them again.

My heart squeezes, and shock narrows my vision. Por favor, let it be Brill in that suit.

I know that's feo, that if something did happen out there, Brill, who has Krom book lungs and blood that contains natural antifreeze, would have the better chance of surviving in the frío airless ocean. Pero, he's mi vida. And Kaliel's not.

I stumble back through my room, force my uncooperative jelly-legs to stabilize as I race out into the hallway and down the stairs. I spot Mertex in the lobby, sitting up in a chair, holding a wadded-up shirt to his forehead. It's soaking through with azure blood. He's more alert now.

"Who?" It's all I can manage. Please don't let it be Brill.

Mertex closes his eyes. "We got separated between the troughs in the waves, and by the time I circled back, he was just gone."

My heart is hammering in my chest. "He who?"

"Kaliel."

"Gracias a Dios." I'm still upset and worried, pero the raw panic is gone. Brill is safe. And I'm relieved that Mertex doesn't know a word of Spanish, so doesn't realize what I just said.

"He was wearing a flotation vest, but those currents are strong. He could be anywhere." Mertex sits up straighter, drops the wadded-up shirt onto the plush carpet. There's still an open greenish-blue gash on his forehead, pero the bleeding's stopped. "I'm going to join the search party."

"Me too." I offer Mertex both my shaking hands to help him up, and he takes them in one of his. He's not putting all his weight behind it, pero it still nearly pulls me over when he stands.

"The helicopter should be on its way. It'll take us down between the teeth."

That sounds ominous. "Right."

Mertex gestures down at my feet. "You're going to want heavy duty shoes. And long pants."

I turn towards the staircase. "Don't leave without me, por favor." One hand on the railing, I look back. This is a different side of Mertex, one capable of taking charge in an emergency. I gesture at his wounded forehead. "I guess you proved you're not a coward."

Mertex blushes green. "I fell off when my squid flipped through the wave to get back to where Kaliel went down. After I was under, I stayed down too long thinking Kaliel's dive suit would be easy to spot, and when I came up in a panic, I hit the oxygen generator at the back of the buoy rig."

I laugh. "Pero, you stayed under. That's the important thing."

A voice from the doorway says, "If you say so." Fizzax is standing there, his recording device in his hand. "Vaveskkent, Mertex. Another missing offworlder report? It's like you miss seeing me or something."

I race up the stairs before I can get drawn into the conversation.

By the time I change and get back downstairs, Mertex and Fizzax are waiting by the helicopter. Brill is with them. He's changed out of the protective suit, is wearing his standard jeans, tee and leather jacket combo. His hair is still wet.

Fizzax asks Brill, "...and when the swell subsided?"

Brill shrugs. His irises are deep gray. "He was gone. He'd been tugging on the tubes, like he wanted to access the oxygen supply. But they're mounted into the rigging, uan it's not like he was going to use it to dive. Revwal?"

He's asking for agreement, pero Fizzax ignores it – or doesn't know the word.

"Mr Cray," Fizzax says. "You had a fight with Johansson last night. And out on the water, no one remembers seeing you for at least five minutes before he disappeared."

"Just what are you implying?" Brill asks, though it's obvious.

Fizzax doesn't expect us to find Kaliel. And since squidriding is supposed to be relatively safe, it looks like Kaliel's disappearance might have been foul play, even murder. Because Brill stormed out of the bar last night, and no one saw him and Kaliel resolve their differences, Brill's just become Fizzax's prime suspect. Dios mio!

If we don't find Kaliel, I could lose them both.

My heart is thudding in paniterroration. A noise escapes my throat. "Mnrhpn."

Fizzax looks at me, his expression embarrassed, appropriate given our discussion last night. Mercy won't be involved if these guys decide Brill killed someone.

"Come on, Fizzax," Mertex says, gesturing towards the helicopter. "We're in the middle of a search and rescue mission. If we find the guy soon enough, you can just ask him what happened."

CHAPTER SEVEN

We all pile into the helicopter, alongside a group of young Zantites wearing fluorescent orange vests. The seats are big enough that Brill and I share one, buckling into the same belt, so they can get one more searcher aboard. I don't recognize any of the faces.

A couple of Tawny's camera drones fly in like mosquitoes. They bob against the ceiling. I try to ignore them.

I whisper to Brill, "Where's the rest of the people who went out there with you?"

"Leapt right off the cliff to search in closer to the point." He gestures out the window. "They were all freaked out. Apparently, accidents like this just don't happen."

"Are you sure it was an accident?"

I'm wondering about the rest of the crew, pero an odd look crosses Brill's face. It's a lot like the way he'd looked this morning when he caught me staring at Kaliel's bare chest. I try to read the color of Brill's shifting eyes, pero it's like brick-tinted sand, some complex blend of emotion I can't tease apart. He obviously thinks I was asking if he knew more than he was telling. And I hope that color isn't a shade of guilt.

I know Brill's killed a handful of people in self-defense. Dealing with space pirates and gray traders is dangerous work. He'd never commit murder, though.

And yet, I find myself staring at his jacket, where he keeps the heavy, lethal weight of his gun. Jealousy is a powerful motive, and I know Brill already wasn't happy seeing me around Kaliel again. Could I have pushed him too far?

Brill's eyes darken. "You don't really think I offed Dork Face?"

"Did you?"

"No!"

"I believe you." I put a hand on his. He doesn't move it, pero he keeps looking at me strangely.

Mertex points down at the landscape as we turn, flying over the channel leading between the southern island and the northern two. From up here, it really does look like an open jaw edged with sharp teeth. "The currents around the point tend to whip things through here. They're going to drop us off at intervals, then the chopper is going back out to look over the ocean."

"Sounds like you've done this before, su," Brill says.

"Not in a long time. But everyone has to serve on the rescue squad in their last year as a learning pod."

I take a closer look at the rescue squad in question. One girl raises an arm towards her face, as if to adjust the goggles perched on her forehead. She's missing the hand, and obviously not used to it yet. I gasp. These are the kids who were fighting on the beach. I try not to stare. No lo sé how rude that is in Zantite culture.

The chopper comes down low over the water. The channel is wider than it looked from higher up. I can see the shore on this side, pero not that of the southern island.

The one-handed girl and the Zantite sitting next to her move to the open doorway and leap out of the helicopter, into the agua.

A minute later, a speaker crackles at the front of the chopper. "Safe and ready to proceed."

The chopper moves on, dropping two more pairs of rescuers.

I am not dressed for diving. I can already feel myself walking in squishy shoes, chafing from wet jeans.

"Don't look so nervous," Mertex says. "We're the shore crew."

The helicopter hovers over one of the "teeth" and the guy sitting nearest the doorway throws out a nylon-looking ladder. He turns back to us, "Your turn."

We climb down the ladder and the helicopter moves on, leaving us in a wild, beautiful place, part-beach, part-riverbank, with stumpy lavender-barked trees and tangled yellow vines trailing down into the water, all decorated with driftwood and shells and tumbled bits of glass.

"Stay close, you guys. It would be embarrassing to lose part of our rescue party." Mertex scans the area like Kaliel might appear if he looks hard enough. "If you see any mounds of dirt, or any giant green eggs, leave them alone."

"What are they?" Brill asks.

Mertex shudders. "Yawds are vegetarians, and they're shy, so as long as you don't disturb their nests, they won't stomp on you."

"Good to know." Brill takes a few steps down the shoreline, then hesitates, waiting to make sure we're following him.

We walk for a couple of hours. I'm thirsty. I should have brought along some of Tawny's bottled agua. Mertex didn't bring any water either. Apparently Zantites can go longer without rehydrating.

"Babe." Brill hands me a bottle of agua he had tucked in his jacket. I drink it greedily, while he sips at one of his own. An animal jumps in the channel, making a splash about ten feet out. Brill grabs my arm. I freeze, afraid I'm about to be Zandy-gater food.

Brill brings his face close to my ear, like he's brushing my cheek with un beso. "Someone's following us."

In the stillness behind us, a twig snaps. We stand still,

listening as Mertex keeps getting farther away in the other direction. I catch a flash of orange caught on a fallen tree that's half in and half out of the water. Pero, nothing else looks out of place and no other noise comes – for minutes. And Murry doesn't come back looking for us.

"Maybe it was an animal," I suggest softly.

"Maybe," Brill says. Pero, he doesn't look convinced.

"I'm going to check out that orange thing." I take off my shoes, roll up my jeans and wade out into the water. Even though I haven't gone deep, the current is strong. I grab onto the tree to keep from falling in.

An orange life jacket, crudely hacked down to Earthling size, is caught in a mass of dirt and sticks. It has to be Kaliel's. I work my way over to it, and shout, "Maybe he took it off!"

Kaliel could be somewhere out in the woods, hurt or lost. Maybe that was him earlier, cracking that twig.

"Maybe," Brill calls back from the bank.

The agua gets deeper fast. The bottom half of my jeans get soaked as I grab the life jacket and yank. The mass of sticks crumbles, releasing it. I turn back towards the bank, holding the life jacket up.

Brill gives me a thumbs up.

Then he gasps.

Behind me, three pale green eggs, each the size of a laundry basket, are rolling from within the half-rotted foliage towards the water. Brill is a blur as he races past me, trying to catch the eggs before they fall. He gets his hands on the bottom one before it even gets wet, but the next one bumps hard against it, and there's a sickening crack.

I manage to push the two whole eggs back into the nest. Brill lets the ruined one fall into the water, where the current drags it down-channel.

He looks in distaste at the goo covering his hands, then washes them in the water. Brill eats eggs – sometimes. It depends on what kind. "Shtesh! There was exactly one thing Mertex told us not to do."

"I know. Where is…" I let my words trail off. I don't care anymore where Mertex went.

Down below the nest proper, half-submerged in the agua, there's a terrolting pile of bones, about the right size for a Zantite child – or a human. I can't see the skull clearly enough to make out the jaw. "Dios mio! I thought Mertex said these things were vegetarians. There's a person's skeleton here."

"It could have killed someone that invaded the nest. People here have to be tempted to harvest such big eggs." Brill moves up next to me. "Erkh." His eyes shift gray, then a purple so dark it's almost black. "That can't be Kaliel. Unless there's a type of fish in this channel that can pick bones to polished in a couple of hours flat."

As if to prove him wrong, a thumb-sized seahorse with a human-ish face swims out from under the bones, gnawing on one of the ribs with needle teeth while blinking warily at us with bright blue eyes – almost the same shade Brill's eyes get when he's really happy.

I think I'm going to be sick.

I put both hands over my mouth and breathe slowly through my nose, trying to keep myself from throwing up. After a few breaths, I decide I'm going to be OK.

I've seen those creatures before, for sale at spaceport fish markets, and even dead, they weirded me out.

"Wal. We need to get a DNA sample." Brill reaches through the branches toward a double-bone that looks like part of an arm, which has separated from the rest of the skeleton. The branches shift as Brill leans against them. "Shtesh! My hand's caught."

One of the thinner offshoots has slipped between his wrist and his proximity bracelet, a silver band that works as an anti-theft device for his ship. It's a solid piece, on tight enough that someone would have to cut it if they wanted to take it off him.

I move to help him, pero the hairs at the back of my neck start to rise, like someone's watching me.

There's a melodic song, like an oboe or a low-pitched bird, coming from shore. I turn. At the base of the fallen tree, still on dry sand, there's an overgrown sea otter. It's maybe five feet tall at the shoulder.

It's like something out of an antique science fiction flick where they couldn't afford to build aliens, so instead they just superimposed an out of scale image of a gila monster or a lobster or whatever to look like it was menacing the poor, screaming Earthlings.

Incongruously, I want to laugh.

Then it moves.

"Brill!" I shout, pero the animal is already leaping fifteen feet across the dead tree, grabbing onto the wood and slapping at me with a thick whip of a tail as the tree breaks into pieces. The bit I'm standing on rolls. Ay! No!

I take the blow full in the stomach and splash into the water, hardly able to breathe. Brill's arm was still caught. He rolls under.

"Mi vida!"

I fight panic. He's not likely to run out of air. I'm the one in more immediate danger.

The two eggs float out of the mess, and the otter monster looks from them to me and back again.

I try to get up out of the water, pero my movements are slowed by the sand.

This time when it leaps, the yawd hits my back with its front feet. My stomach can't keep up as I fall. My scream turns into a strangling gurgle as my face hits the water, gets ground into the sand.

The yawd holds me under with its body weight. I already didn't have much air and my lungs protest this refusal to breathe. Oy! I am going to drown two feet from shore.

My heart's pounding. My vision sparks. My hands clutch at the sand, and I accidentally grab onto a sharp shell. With a slice of pain, my blood's in the agua.

The otter monster pulls back, and when my ears break the surface, I can hear it singing reproachfully at me for bleeding too much while it is trying to kill me.

I scramble towards the bank. The yawd lunges again.

I turn around and hit the beast square in the nose with the shell's sharp side. It screeches as it moves backwards, taking the shell with it, the massive tail thwacking at the ruined nest, which comes apart, sending debris and bones – and Brill – shooting down the channel. The yawd grabs the shell with one paw-hand and pulls it out of its own nose.

I try for the bank, but I can't keep my feet under me. The current catches me, dragging me into the middle of the torrential flow. I'm flailing, even though that's the worst thing to do. I force myself to stop, to let the current drag me until I manage to catch onto a floating piece of the tree and get mi cabeza above water.

"Bo!" Mertex's voice is coming from above the channel bank. He's hanging upside down from a rope trap, and I put together a plausible scenario: a local hunter's living out here, trying to trap yawds. His kid finds the nest and decides to steal one of the eggs. And is never seen again. Which means that Kaliel isn't dead. Necessarily.

One of the drifting eggs has fetched up against another one of the "teeth," and the yawd turns towards it.

Pero, I'm still being whisked along by the unforgiving current.

"Babe!" Brill's managed to get up on the bank. He's holding the end of one of the yellow vines, and the rest of it fans out across the water's surface. I have to let go of the log piece to grab it, and I bob under. Panic bubbles through my chest.

My fingers tangle in the vine, and my shoulders protest the

tug as Brill pulls me free from the current. Pero I get my feet under me, find stable sand, take some of the pressure off the vine. It still breaks with me chest-deep in the agua, pero I'm on the sheltered side now and I'm able to make my way to the bank.

"Thank the Codex!" Brill pulls me out and crushes me against him. My back hurts so bad I whimper. He lets go. "You hurt?"

"I don't think anything's broken." I run a hand along his uninjured cheek. "You?"

"I lost the bone, and I feel guilty about destroying a family of yawds."

I sigh. "We have to get past mamá yawd to rescue Mertex. And then we have to find my boots, because they're my only pair, and no one here sells my size."

"Not a problem, Babe." Before I can protest, he's scooped me up and we're racing through the scrub trees.

I would complain that I don't need carrying, pero there's not really a path here, and I'm barefoot, and a lot of poky-looking plants are blurring by. He sets me down near Mertex and races off to get my boots.

I move over to the rope securing Murry up there. "I can't undo this knot."

"Here!" Mertex tosses down a Zantite-sized pocket knife. "Hurry, please. That bird's been circling for a while now."

I open the knife and start cutting through the rope. "How'd you even wind up there?"

A huge bird squawks and wheels in the sky. Mertex makes a hiss-splatting noise at it, and it changes course.

"I thought I saw a piece of yellow fabric, like Kaliel's suit. Turns out it was a hkkvaka wrapper, open in the middle of a trap." Murry's face is getting a bit green from all the blood rushing to it, and the cut on his forehead has started seeping again. "Yawds like sweets. People who camp in this area are advised against bringing them."

"Good to know." I've almost cut through the rope. "I don't know how to put slack in this, so get ready to fall."

"Anything's better than being up here."

The rope snaps, and there's a thud, then Mertex says, "Oww!" Once he's righted himself, he blinks at me. "Why do you look so cold?"

I guess I am shivering a little. "Because humans don't handle dunking in frío rivers very well. We have less insulation than you, and unlike Brill, there's no natural antifreeze in my system."

Mertex blushes. He has firsthand knowledge of how handy Krom antifreeze can be. "I never have apologized for what happened to his face."

"You were trying to kill him, mijo. In a blast freezer, inside a vat of chocolate."

"But he was fine. Except his face." Now that's Zantite logic for you.

Brill reappears, carrying my boots. "I thought I made it clear I was over it when I helped you get off that warship. But thank you. Apology accepted."

"I'm glad I failed," Mertex says. "Because otherwise, I wouldn't have gotten to know how cool you are. But I still can't believe I didn't get executed for it."

"Which is why I don't hold it against you, su." Brill holds the boots out to me, clearly done talking about it. "Reshdo, Babe." *Here.* "Or should I help you put them on? Like Cinderella?"

A month ago, Brill didn't know who Cinderella was. As I take the boots, I tell him, "You've been watching too much holofeed."

I examine the boots to make sure nothing has crawled into them. Gracias a Dios, my socks are still in there – and nothing else.

Mertex picks up his radio, which is lying near the brightly

printed candy wrapper. "It was still so cool, watching the warmth come back into your face. I've never seen anything like it."

"It wasn't so litoll for me," Brill says. "And I'd prefer not to think about dying, especially when I was just holding a bone that might belong to a friend of mine, so can we talk about something else?"

Eh? Did Brill just call Kaliel an amigo? Am I still misjudging how he sees things?

CHAPTER EIGHT

I roll my shoulders. "I can't believe I got stomped on by a yawd."

Mertex laughs. "You do know that was a juvenile, right? Probably a sibling left to watch the eggs." He points to a bare spot of mud closer to the bank, where there's a footprint, easily two feet across. "Now that's the size of an adult."

I shudder. I would never have survived that.

"When you were up there, did you see a boat anywhere?" Brill asks.

"Yeah. By the hekkjet the guy who set this trap's staying in. Why?"

"Because if I'm the prime suspect in a Zantite murder investigation, I'm not leaving here until we find out if that really was Kaliel."

By the time we steal the boat and drag it down to the water, the sun has gone behind a mass of clouds, casting bits of the landscape into shadow, and many of the plants are glowing with pink or yellow traces of phosphorescence. It's one of the most breathtaking things I've ever seen, pero it isn't making an impact. Not much can past, *I was holding a bone that might have belonged to a friend of mine.*

Brill must have been more disturbed by what had happened to him inside that blast freezer than he'd let on. That's why he's been putting off dealing with the damage to his face. If it can just heal on its own, then maybe it wasn't as bad as it seemed. Maybe he hadn't come a few heartbeats away from dying.

Brill's got his phone out, tracking our location, though he's holding it gingerly, like his hands hurt from gripping that vine. He glances repeatedly at our surroundings to verify what he's looking at in the holo. "A little way past the teeth, there's a narrow spot where the channel bends and a whirlpool area that sucks things inland. Some debris must have wound up on the far side."

I follow his directions, cutting back the engine, which makes it quieter. Birdsong's coming from the bank, and I turn to look for an otter monster. This time it *is* a bird, which flies lazily overhead – and then takes a poop, which splatters down on the bow of the boat. Which about sums up my experience so far on Zant.

At one point, we pass part of the diving squad. The one-handed girl waves at us.

Mertex waves back and points further up-channel.

She gives him an approximation of the Zantite military salute with her remaining hand –three fingers up and wiggling at the forehead, thumb and pinkie flat across the palm.

By the time we've lost sight of them, a fish glides by next to the boat, as big and club-faced as a log. Mertex doesn't seem worried.

Before long, we come to the bottleneck where the current gets even stronger.

"You want to anchor the boat on this side of the bend," Mertex tells us.

When I cut the engine, he hauls a spade-shaped piece of iron out of the back and drops it overboard. The boat jerks as we reach the end of the chain. We hop into the agua instead of beaching the craft and then wade to shore.

The plan is to hike around the bend and the whirlpool, pero there's still not a decent path. I manage to hold my boots out of the water to keep them dry, but the rest of my clothes get soaked again.

As we make our way around, I spot something white dropped on the ground. The plants are trampled around it, like there had been a scuffle, or a large animal had moved through the area. I hesitate to reach for it, because it's in a bed of thick yellow sawk-vines.

I point. "Oye, Murry, what is that?"

Mertex crushes the vines away from it with his boot, then picks it up. "It's a police-issue data recorder."

He punches play. Fizzax's voice comes out of it. "And you are certain that Mr Cray had blood on the towel he tossed into the laundry chute at the hotel?"

"Fairly certain," a muffled voice says. "But I only caught a glimpse. He pulled something wrapped in the towel out of his suit."

Brill puts his injured hands over Mertex's and shuts the recorder off. "That's enough."

My heart's thudding. Fizzax thinks he has evidence that Brill's a killer, had that recording on him when he got with us on the helicopter.

Pero, what happened here? He wouldn't have abandoned that data recorder on purpose.

"Do you muchachos think Fizzax ran into the real killer?"

Brill looks at me, like he's still not sure I believe he's innocent.

Pero, I'd seen the way he looked at that bone. He was horrified at the thought it might be Kaliel. I look steadily back at him. "Lo siento, mi vida. I shouldn't have doubted you."

There's relief in his face as his eyes shift from gray towards blue.

Mertex says softly, "We had better find proof that that wasn't Kaliel's body. Especially if Fizzax... I have no idea what happened here, but he would have been in radio contact with the group. I told them we thought we found something."

We all start walking faster. I keep staring at the device in Mertex's hand. "What does it mean if something happened to Fizzax?"

Brill's eyes go solid black. "I'm likely to get blamed for that, too. Zantites don't have to have a body to prove a crime. They just have to wait seventy-seven hours and hold a funeral, so the missing person can be officially declared dead."

"They can only execute you once," Mertex says. When we both turn to stare at him, he shrugs. "Old Zantite military saying. In other words, it can't get any worse, so you might as well do what you want. Like the Earth equivalent, in for a penny, in for a pound."

"That's not comforting," Brill says.

We can see the whirlpool now, and the pond-like area on our side of it. There's a flicker of motion in the yellow reeds growing near the bank.

"Don't worry," Mertex says. "Those are just dakka fish."

There's a ton of debris and as we get closer, I can make out some of the rotted branches from that dead tree. Brill changes something on his phone, and wades into the water. The hologram is showing the density of submerged objects. Brill heads towards a promising spot, while Mertex and I stand on the bank.

Mertex turns around, looking into the woods. "Did you hear that?"

"No. Nada."

Pero then there's a soft *whoosh*. Brill cries out and clutches at his neck. He drops his phone, and it sinks into the murky agua as I run towards him.

"Ga, Babe, don't! Get out of here!"

I freeze, not sure where to go. If there's a sniper, there's nothing I can do. But whatever hit Brill's neck, he's still able to speak, hasn't fallen over.

"Come out of the water, Mr Cray." It's Fizzax, from

somewhere in the trees. "Get Bo to help you. It would be pointless to dart her, don't you think?"

"Don't touch me!" Brill holds out both hands. They're trembling. "He doesn't realize humans are a lot more responsive to conductivity than Zantites are. Or Krom. In this water..."

Tawny's camera drones circle in close – then fall into the murk.

"You know darting a Krom's considered cruel." Mertex makes a face at Fizzax. Then he looks at me, and there's a concession in his features. "Though it is rather ingenious. Because how do you catch a Krom, when they're faster than any bullet they can see coming? You mess with their ukewellet, so that they're too dizzy to move."

Mertex wades around me and picks up Brill, carrying him to the bank. I hurry to follow.

Brill pulls the dart from his neck, despite the obvious pain to his hand. It falls from his fingers, and he puts the palms of both hands to his temples. He's paler than I've ever seen him, and his eyes are a dull orange. "Shtesh! It's embedded in my skin. The dart's just a carrier."

Fizzax emerges from the trees, a zip-tie in his hands.

Brill sees it and backs away. Zantites don't believe in prisons, or in detaining suspects. Fizzax shouldn't be arresting Brill unless he's ready for interrogation and judgement. "Avell! Please! Kaliel hasn't been missing long enough to be declared dead." Fizzax keeps advancing. Brill says, "I have so many complaints."

"We have evidence. Headquarters radioed. They took a look at the squidriding equipment. Kaliel's blood was all over the harness. You killed someone over jealousy of a girl. That's cowardice. You don't get any complaints." Fizzax grabs him, throws him to the ground, zip-ties mi vida's hands in front of him.

"Mertex, do something!" I shout.

Mertex tries to reason with Fizzax. "If you arrest him, that's as good as executing him here. The death hasn't been declared. Vaveskkent, we don't even know for sure yet there *has* been a death."

Fizzax isn't listening. He's unhinging his jaw. He grabs Brill's shoulder with his other hand and pulls him up towards his mouth.

My heart goes cold. "No!" I rush forward.

"I demand to speak to a Galactic Inspector." Brill still sounds somewhat calm.

Fizzax's mouth opens, and Brill's cabeza and shoulders disappear, eclipsed by the Zantite's gaping maw. Mertex lets out a high-pitched squeal loud enough that I cover my ears.

"You can't eat him!" Mertex has an arm on Fizzax's shoulder, trying to pull the dented head back. Mertex makes a hiss-splatting sound as he hits Fizzax hard on the side of the cabeza. "We have a treaty with his people. It could start the war with the Evevrons all over again. They're allies of the Krom, you know?"

I stare into Fizzax's eyes, pero this isn't even fazing him. Something's deeply wrong. Fizzax's a rule-follower. Shouldn't he honor Brill's request to speak to a Galactacop? What happened to the guy I'd shared a drink with at the club, the one so uncomfortable with injustice?

Maybe he'd been hit on the head during whatever happened back in that patch of sawk vine. Pero, knowing that is not going to save mi vida.

Murry hits Fizzax again, and when Fizzax rears back, Brill comes into view. He's in one piece, looking incredibly grossed out. Fizzax drops Brill's shoulder, pero he's still dangling mi vida upside down.

It takes my heart a second to slow down enough to not feel it's going to explode.

Fizzax gets his jaw back into place. "I have an accusation

from a witness who saw him with a bloody towel. I have a public fight with the victim. He's the only one who could have been in the water long enough to fight Kaliel and get Earthling blood on the harness." Fizzax looks over at Mertex. "I need to get this case tied up quickly. People are talking. It's disruptive."

"But it's not our law!" Mertex protests.

"Put. Me. Down."

Fizzax looks down at Brill. Even hanging upside down, with blisters all over his zip-tied hands and that chip in his neck, Brill's managed to get his gun out of his jacket.

Fizzax grabs for the gun, lifting Brill as high as he can with one hand, while scooping down with the other. Brill fires. The bullet goes through Fizzax's arm. Fizzax drops Brill, who then barely manages to stand. Fizzax makes a hiss-splatting noise as he punches Brill in the chest. Mi vida falls backwards into the agua.

"Brill!" I try to run to him, pero Mertex catches me.

"Electrocution, remember?"

The surface settles. I have to remind myself Brill doesn't need to breathe, not for hours.

It takes minutes before Brill slowly breaks the surface. He wobbles to his feet.

Fizzax spits light blue blood from his split cheek. He moves towards Brill again.

"No!" My chest sparkles with icy shards of panic.

I can't let this happen. I race into the water, getting between Fizzax and Brill. Fizzax towers over me, teeth bared in earnest. I'm about to pee my pants, but with them already being wet, no one will ever know.

Because I'm going to save Brill's life and lose my own.

I lie to Fizzax. "I did it! I confess. I killed Kaliel."

Fizzax was poised to push me out of the way with his giant hand. Now he just stares at me, and the malice in his bared teeth becomes open-mouthed confusion. "But you couldn't possibly. Eye-witnesses have you on the balcony at the hotel the entire time."

I shrug. "I don't care. I did it. If you need a life for a life, I'm offering mine." I'm trembling as the IH tries to gather and give me the strength to get through this. Choosing execution this time doesn't make it any easier to face.

"But why?" Fizzax's wide eyes are childlike, like he honestly doesn't understand.

"Because I love him. And I'm the only reason he's even on this planet. And if I hadn't kissed Kaliel all that time ago, you wouldn't even think he has a motive. I promised to make my actions on this planet count." Not bad for last words.

Too bad people never get to live long enough to enjoy having gotten them right.

"Babe, no," Brill protests. "I couldn't live knowing you did that."

Ignoring him, Fizzax advances on me. I try not to flinch away, but I can't help it.

I force myself to close my eyes so I won't run. "I told you before, I'm contaminated with the Invincible Heart." I don't know why I care if he gets sick. But I do. It feels surreal, but I add, "It's safer for you if you shoot me instead."

He laughs, and his breath blows over me. "Tell me about the kind of love you would die for."

"Que?" I open my eyes.

His jaw is still hinged. Fizzax cocks his head. "I'm not going to execute you. It would not be justice. I just… I need to understand. You showed me mercy, and you don't even know me. What did this Krom do to earn the kind of love you have for him?"

"H-he," I stammer. How do you put the whys of love into words?

Before I can even try, the one-handed Zantite girl turns the bend and lets out an ear-piercing squeal. She tries to stifle it, blinks, looking from Brill in the water to Fizzax still leaning over me, a bullet wound in his arm. She picks up the data recorder, where Mertex left it on the bank.

There's no hiding what happened here, even if Fizzax was willing to let us try. The girl has the "evidence." Brill is still going to be put forward for murder.

Fizzax straightens up. "There hasn't yet been a recorded death. I will try my best with all my might to keep there from being one, Bo the Merciful, Bearer of the Invincible Heart."

My mouth drops open in surprise. "Que?"

Mertex has been in sporadic communication with the other search teams. As we approach, they're all standing there, waiting for the helicopter.

Brill's holding a tissue to the side of his neck, where Mertex used fishing pliers we found in the boat to get the chip out. Fizzax is traveling with us, pero not talking to us.

The sky starts turning rose, then purple, then the helicopter shows up, a crisp streak of black in the finger-painted sky. An overwhelming bolt of despair hits me in the gut. We didn't find Kaliel. If he's still in the water, he doesn't have a flotation device. If he's on land, he didn't leave a trail leading anywhere.

My back aches, and I'm slypered. I should cry, pero I'm too worn out. Probably mañana, when I get a basket of those estúpido chocolate croissants, I'll cry then.

CHAPTER NINE

Tawny shows up the next morning before the croissants do. Before the sun. Once I let her in, she turns on all the lights, swishes open the curtain to the balcony.

She gestures me over to the glass. "Let me see your face."

Like that orange glow peeking over the horizon's going to help her see.

I try to stifle a yawn, which winds up pretty much in her face, though I haven't had time to brush my teeth. She doesn't even seem to care as she uses the fingertips of both hands to tilt my chin so she can get a better look. "This looks like you took sandpaper to it. I'll have Valeria get with the spa staff to put together a healing facial."

"What about for Brill? Could she do something like that for him?"

"On HGB's dime? No. If he's too cheap to see a cosmetic reconstructionist, that's his problem."

"It's not that he's cheap," I protest. "He's still hoping it will heal on its own."

Tawny rolls her eyes. "Typical Krom. They have *all* the time in the worlds, so they sit back and wait for problems to resolve themselves."

The way she says it, emphasizing *all* the time, expresses such longing. Maybe that's why she's attracted to Brill. Given the emphasis she puts on youth and beauty, it would make an odd kind of sense, no?

"As long as I also get to soak in those therapeutic mineral baths, I'm in." My back aches. And the shoulder with the old gunshot wound hasn't hurt like this in ages.

"What were you thinking, going out into an alien wilderness like that?" She snaps her fingers. "Let me see your hands. If they're anything like Brill's–"

"I was thinking mi amigo had gone missing, and I'm a human being with feelings." I hold out my hands.

She flips them over to examine the palms. "Those yellow vines you guys touched yesterday are an irritant." Tiny red dots spot the middle of my hands, where I'd gripped the vine the hardest. Tawny uses a pair of tweezers to pop one, and it starts itching like crazy. "This doesn't look too bad. I'll add the doctor to your list, though, just in case." Then she makes eye contact with me, and for once her smile isn't plastic. "You think I don't have feelings? That I've never lost someone I care about? That I don't understand what you're going through right now?"

"You never…" I have no idea how to finish that sentence.

"I keep my personal life and my work life separate, and you're part of my work life, so no, I never did." She runs an alcohol wipe over the tweezers. "I have a job to do, and if I screw it up, then it puts everything I've worked for *and* everyone I care about in jeopardy. You may not like some of the decisions I make, but I will not apologize for them."

"Then just make them. Stop trying to manipulate me and–"

There's a knock on the door. It's a Zantite bellboy delivering my basket of chocolate croissants. All I can see is Kaliel's face, hear him saying he doesn't like chocolate. And I was right, the tears do want to come, pero with Tawny here, I don't dare let them.

"Because of you, one of my last memories of Kaliel is of all of us having this gran fight. That, at least, you should apologize for." I pick a croissant out of the basket, pero I'm not hungry. "You could have told me what you wanted instead of lying to people. And trying to pass off holonique."

"Because you totally would have listened if I told you there's no place for a Krom in your life while you're the center of Earth's last-ditch diplomacy? Nobody's forgotten they stripped us of everything at First Contact, and as long as you're with him your motives here are going to be questioned. His people aren't our allies, and they also aren't particularly friendly with the Zantites, so there's no strategic advantage to the pairing." Her light blue eyes are hard like ice, and I think I preferred the plastic smile to the grim frown.

"That's just so calculating." I bite into the croissant and chew slowly, making her wait for the rest of what I want to say. "And the Krom are the Evevron's allies, so maybe also short-sighted."

She rolls her eyes. This is obviously not news. "Brill is going to be executed for murdering Kaliel. I'm sorry my attempt at separating you drove him to it. Losing Kaliel's appeal for the cameras is a blow. But that's a Krom killing a human in cold blood. You have to distance yourself from this."

"Brill's innocent. I won't abandon him just when he needs me most. I've been through the spotlight-wringer before, no? Had the stardiggers tear my life apart twice – twice – already over what things looked like, and what people guessed my motivations were. I've found someone who loves me, who for all his flaws, is a hero at heart. And I'm not giving that up."

Tawny takes a croissant and sets the basket down on the desk. "Zantites don't believe in prisons, but Brill has already been warned that if he tries to leave Zant, it's an admission of guilt, and he can be executed by any police official present. They're claiming that after you found that lifejacket, Brill destroyed the evidence. But they have to wait until Kaliel is declared legally dead to do anything else."

"He saved my life yesterday." I'm close to shouting now, and the shakes are getting bad enough that she's bound to notice. I take a deep breath.

Tawny peels up a layer of dough on her pastry. "He's still a murderer."

"Brill did not murder Kaliel."

"Are you sure? Krom have a complicated system of honor and rank. And you don't exactly fit the description of a loyal girlfriend. That audio may have been holonique, but the attraction in your eyes was real."

My face is hot and the shakes are getting worse. "Brill has never lied to me. Omitted things, sí, allowed me to make a few flawed assumptions, OK. But he's never outright lied." That's not strictly true. He has lied a couple of times, to make himself look better. Pero, not over anything like this.

"You asked him *outright* if he killed Kaliel?" She stares at me until I nod. "Then maybe you should be asking yourself if you're really so sure he didn't, if you felt the need to ask."

"And maybe you should ask yourself if you're really keeping your work and personal life separate." She doesn't dignify my cheap shot with a *what do you mean*, so I continue, "I've seen the way you look at Brill, and there's definitely something there you want. We both know Brill's capable of ending a life and I don't think that'd be a deal-breaker for you. But you don't know him if you think he'd do it unprovoked, to someone who considered him an amigo."

Even as I'm speaking, I realize how stupid and hurtful my moment of doubt must have been to Brill yesterday. Because it's true. He wouldn't. And I think Tawny sees that in my face, because suddenly the plastic smile is back in place.

"Whatever ulterior motives you think I have, Bo, I'm the one who's going to get you through this. Kaliel's funeral is tomorrow afternoon, and hopefully by then, the salvage team will have come up with a body so that we're not sending home a coffin with nothing but his boots and his pilot's license in it.

I want you to think carefully about who you show up to that funeral with."

Kayla's not going to be there, not if it's mañana. She's in transit, pero too far away by now to get back in time – if we could even get a message to her somehow.

"There's no chance left of finding him alive?"

Tawny's smile cracks. "The search team called it. Believe me, this isn't something we wanted to announce prematurely. The negative spinoff is going to be horrific."

"Then can I have my privacy? I have a few calls to make."

The first person I call is Gideon Tyson. He's the reptilian Galactic Inspector who shot me when I tried to run with that cacao pod – and then later, he bit me as I escaped after he'd captured me. Sí, he's venomous, and sí, he'd been justified. I was guilty, and he'd been charged with bringing me back to face charges of treason. In the end, though, he'd helped save me. We're friends now.

Tyson is all about interplanetary law. If anyone can find me a way out of this, it'll be him.

It rings a long time before Tyson picks up. *Sparkly bounce party, Bo! It's good to hear from you.*

I explain that this isn't just a social call, and after I detail the situation, I ask, *How can I save mi vida?*

Tyson hesitates. *Have you considered getting him a dose of te Invincible Heart?*

I gasp. *Brill told me if a Krom took that, his heart would explode.*

He's saying there's no hope, which caves me in, like he's punched me in the chest. It's the last thing I expected from him.

Tyson sighs, though through his reptilian mouth, it sounds more like a hiss. *But it's so instant it's painless.* Unlike being chompcrushed into tiny pieces. *And it would leave a body to send home to te family. Krom are big on tat.*

A body. I can't help picturing Brill lying cold and peaceful, like he's asleep. Icy terror dances through me. Mijo! I'm not giving up.

Te treaty Brill's people have with te Zantites mean he's treated as a citizen under tere laws. I'll try to get tere in time to help. If I can. In the meantime, work wit Mertex to try to find proof. He has as big a stake in tis as Brill.

Que? I know Mertex feels guilty about Brill's face, but why would he care so much? It's not like he failed in his duty to keep us safe on his planet.

If he's taken a formal vow tat bound your lives to his, if he can't protect Brill even from tis, ten he'll also be executed for his failure.

Well, jrekt, as Brill would say. It literally means *the sound a bat makes when dropped down the well*, pero it's used more like *oh, crud*.

Exactly, Tyson bubblechatters.

Sorry. I hadn't meant to think that at you.

I was already tinking it.

And then I try to find someone who can tell Kayla her boyfriend's funeral is tomorrow.

For some people, it wouldn't be odd not to have used the shuttle's public phones, pero for a girl like Kayla, in the middle of relationship drama – it's odd that she didn't give a return contact code by calling *somebody*. Maybe she realized after the flight left that she was overreacting, and got embarrassed. Pero then, shouldn't she have called Kaliel? Maybe she did. Maybe that's why he was in such a good mood yesterday morning. Maybe she told him she loved him before he died.

And that's when I lose it. Fat tears drip down my face, turning my eyes red and my nose snotty.

Brill sends a note that he and Mertex are in the hotel restaurant, and they've ordered me a coffee. Sometimes mi vida really is sweet. And that makes me cry harder.

• • •

"Babe!" Brill stands up when I come in. His face and the front of his hair are glowing with translucent pink paint.

I raise an eyebrow at his appearance, pero I just say, "Mi vida."

He hugs me, and there's a strong herbal smell coming off him. "We were just talking about how odd that thing was with Fizzax yesterday." He's holding his hands awkwardly out of the hug, and when he pulls back, I see he's wearing thin yellow gloves – of a shade that approximates a Zantite skin tone. They appear to be the source of the smell.

I ask Mertex, "Has he ever acted extraño before?"

Mertex shakes his massive head. "No. He's one of the most level-headed people I know. And there at the end – he sounded like a child asking about love. Like he was somebody else inside. That was scarier than when he tried to eat Brill."

"Speak for yourself," Brill says. His irises are black just thinking about having been in Fizzax's mouth. "I need a charter, to get back down to the channel."

Mertex adds, "He thinks he can find those bones, prove they're not Kaliel."

Brill nods. "I figured I'd better be proactive. Revwal?"

"Pero you don't know for sure that skeleton wasn't him. Whoever did kill him could have dumped him in the nest to disguise what really happened." It's horrortastic: my friend, a guy I'd kissed, might have been stripped of his flesh by carrion eaters on purpose. I force myself to continue, "What if whatever you find makes it worse?"

"I didn't do it, so whatever it is can't prove anything against me." He reaches into his pocket and a mini camera drone flies out. Even through the gloves, he winces at the contact. "I borrowed this from Tawny. She was being incredibly sweet to me this morning. But maybe it's just because she knows that she can FeedCast the holo if I fall into the channel again."

Mertex asks, "How are you going to verify that they're the

same bones, if they're not even in the same place?"

"I can't. But how many dead sus are in that river?"

Mertex's mouth drops open. I'm guessing maybe a lot. Mertex clears his throat. "Kaliel didn't just fall off the squid. He was bleeding before he hit the water. Who – other than Brill – might have wanted to hurt Kaliel? And why?"

"I'll ask around here." Pero, my face feels gritty and tight, and I have had zero coffee this morning. I'm not equipped to deal with this level of logic puzzle right now. "Pero, like, what's up with the pink paint?"

He frowns at Mertex. "I went back to my ship and tried to make you coffee. It seems someone's trying to start a practical joke war."

Mertex drums his fingers against the chair arm. "You're not mad, though, right?"

Brill's eyes tint an amused violet. "Just don't expect me to retaliate."

"I have something at the hotel that you can use to get that stuff off. Let me see your hands." I get a flash of déjà vu. Tawny had asked me the same thing.

"Ga, it's nothing." He leaves his hands at his sides. I give him a look that means I'm not buying it. "Haza." He takes off the gloves. His hands are covered with orange blisters, from his fingertips to past where his wrists disappear into his jacket.

Mertex lets out a low whistle. "That's the worst sawk-vine reaction I've ever seen."

For a species of explorers, Krom certainly are prone to allergic reactions.

"Put the gloves back on," I tell him.

CHAPTER TEN

We are running out of time. Brill wasn't able to find anything in the river and is on his way back. And I've talked to half the people on this island. I'm back at the hotel, talking to the janitor, before I meet Valeria for my facial. The guy keeps wandering off on tangents, wasting precious moments.

"But did you see anybody hanging out near the laundry chute?" I have to get this conversation back on track. Fizzax's recording talks about blood on a towel Brill supposedly threw out the laundry chute.

"Now, I wasn't here for part of the day, but while I was cleaning the office areas, I saw a couple of the old guys who come in for breakfast every morning getting their coffee from the vending machine. Since they're regulars, the restaurant doesn't mind them bringing it in. Have you tried the restaurant yet? They make amazing skhalb."

"Anyone else?" I prompt.

"An offworlder girl asked me for some extra towels, and that couple from Room 203 made out in the hallway from the time I started cleaning the bathrooms until I finished vacuuming the conference room." He shrugs. "If you want to talk to the old guys, they went out with the salvage operation."

He gestures in the general direction of where I'd seen that wrecked ship becoming one with the reef.

My eyes widen. "I thought that was off bounds."

"Not everybody believes there is such a thing as a phkhekk fiekksk. And if it was, nothing could have survived this long underwater." The janitor shrugs. "Besides, they got an offworlder commission, and the money's good."

I need to talk to those Zantites, find out if they saw anything that could help clear Brill. If they're here every day, they probably have a better bead on the area than anyone else.

I make my way down to the beach. I only spot Mertex trailing me once.

There's a truck idling on packed sand that makes a road heading away from the shore. Three Zantites are carrying blocky items from a small boat and piling them into a truck. One guy has the locked box I'd seen.

I try to get their attention, pero they deposit the items in the truck, get in the front and drive away before I can get close enough that ignoring me becomes obviously rude.

The boat driver makes eye contact with me, then revs the engine and heads for deeper water. I don't know if it's because I'm an offworlder, or because they know I'm bound to be asking about Brill and they don't want to get involved.

With a sigh, I head for the spa. Minda's already there, waiting to talk to me. It has to be about Mertex's vow, no?

Valeria makes her wait. My stylist takes a good look at my face and tuts over all the scratches. "You've been out in the sun, too, but it's all on one side. I hope your skin is smooth enough for foundation by the time we film again."

She spreads a layer of cooling goop on my face and wipes her hands on a towel.

"A side effect of the Invincible Heart is that my skin's the smoothest it's been since I was a niña. If not for the weird color of my nails, it'd be great." I hold out my hands, where the polish has chipped off, revealing the shade the natural nail has grown in, between pea and puce.

"Egad!" Valeria grabs my hands to get a closer look, at the same time smearing cream all over my fingers. She drops them when Tawny stalks in, Mertex in tow. Murry's face is bright green.

"What. Did. You. Do?"

I may have made a statement to a Zantite reporter that I believe Brill is innocent. "I told the truth."

"Which could lead to your show being cancelled. Is that what you want?"

"What I want is to keep Brill breathing." I stare at the green showing through the cracked polish on my nails. It's not growing out any lighter. There's no getting out of any of this. "Pero, if I can't, I'd at least like to find a way to unbind Mertex's life from mi vida's."

"That was supposed to be an honorary title and assignment. This wasn't supposed to be dangerous. We're making a cooking show, for Garfex's sake!" Minda's been about to pop, waiting to say that.

Tyson and I have been discussing this at length. "If Brill dies, you're supposed to execute him. Mertex's life belongs to you."

"And what would I do with it?" She pokes me in the shoulder. "Tradition and peoples' expectations be damned, I will not destroy someone I'm in love with. After all, mercy is a gift."

"You're what now?" Mertex sounds flabbergasted.

I stare at Minda. A bit of the goop Valeria stuck on my face falls into my lap. I ignore it.

Had Minda overheard me at the bar? Does she know what I did – or rather didn't do – for Fizzax's sake?

She stares straight back. It's definitely a reference. "You heard me."

Mercy for mercy, I've started something here. Too bad it's not enough to help Brill. Or Mertex. Or anyone.

"I'd like to talk to the Galactic Inspector you've been consulting with," Tawny says. "See if there's anything I can spin."

"Sí." I take Valeria's towel and try to wipe the goop off my hands.

Brill walks in, stooped and defeated, his eyes iron gray.

My hands are still sticky. "Can you forward Tyson's contact to Tawny?"

"Reshdo." He gingerly holds out a hand for my phone.

I raise an eyebrow. "Did you get a new one?"

"Ga. Didn't seem that important."

Brill must really believe he's going to die. His phone is key for both his business and his social life. It's the only possession – besides his ship – he cares much about.

I fight a hitch in my throat.

"Bo, he is absolutely glorious. I am thoroughly sorry for your loss." Minda gives me a sad smile, and steps over to put a hand on my arm. There's nothing different about Brill. Praising him must be part of Zantite comfort. She turns to Brill, "Kiss her well, that she may wear your valor on her lips forever."

They use that line a lot in Zandywood holos, and it's cheesetastic, pero it still leaves moisture glittering in Brill's eyes.

CHAPTER ELEVEN

The next day – Brill's last day – we watch the sunrise from my balcony, and then head down to a little coffee shop. Once I've got my coffee, Brill laces his arm through mine, and guides us to a table.

"I have to give you something." His eyes are stormclouds.

My chest suddenly feels tight. "Por qué do I get the feeling I'm not going to want it?"

He winces. "You probably won't, at first. It's a Krom tradition for someone who's dying to give his friends a... I guess the closest English is a parting gift. There's a galactic antiques shop on the southern island, and one of the imports they specialize in is Krom. I stopped there yesterday."

"Oh." I take another sip of coffee. There's ice burning in my chest that isn't soothed at all by the coffee's heat. "On Earth, a parting gift is what they give a contestant on a gameshow who's lost and is about to get booted off." I try my best to smile.

"That's not too far wrong." He takes a silk pouch out of his jacket. "The box for these is on my ship. There's seven pendants in a full set of paladzian, because in the Codex, six hearts are the most that you can hold in your hand. It means six friends and loved ones are the most you can really be close to. You are the only one on this planet I want to give one to."

"Tyson's coming," I insist. "You can't give up hope. Por favor."

"Oh. Su. That's the thread of hope I'm holding onto." Brill closes his eyes. "The pendants are supposed to be worn close to the heart during the stress of grieving because the ore conducts energy that helps stabilize the heartbeat. Wearing mine will help me get through today. And yours will help you cope after I'm gone. Even if you're not Krom."

"This means a lot to you." I pull the pouch towards me. The piece inside is bonita, disk-shaped and engraved with a woodland scene, the crystal forming the sun. It suits his taste perfectly.

"They ought to have been specially commissioned, paid for with ore I earned trading, but I'm too young to have had them made. The guy at the store felt sorry for me, and gave them to me. He told me to use the money to do whatever that one thing is that I've always wanted to do before I die."

I let him take the pendant from the pouch and fasten it around my neck. His hands must still hurt, pero he manages it. Then he puts on one himself.

Brill's hands ball into painful fists. "I am so sorry, Babe."

"Lo siento por qué?"

"I'm the one who got you involved with all of HGB's secrecy garbage. The black ship. The poisoned chocolate. I planned to be there in case it all blew back in your face when the publicity tour is over. And I can't be." His eyes are mahogany.

"Mi vida." I can't manage anything else past the sudden lump in my throat. Finally I get my breathing under control. "Kaliel was cleared. That's all in the past, no?"

Brill looks at me like I'm un poco estúpido. "Frank said that you stay alive as long as you stay in line. Look good for the cameras. Tout HGB as Earth's last hope. But what happens when they don't need you anymore? Are you going to join the corporation your dad died fighting against? Because if you don't, they're going to decide at some point you're a liability, and Frank's going to make your death look like an accident."

"Frank wouldn't really give up Mamá." *Pero,* we both know he would, if he thought the alternative was losing his planet.

"Listen to me. You need to make Chestla stop looking into that black ship we found in the bumpclip of Kaliel blowing up the SeniorLeisure tour, and you need to forget about Serum Green. If you need to run, my ship's in the hangar, and the title is in the same compartment where I store my gun. I've signed it, so all you need to do is add your signature, and it will be made over to you. There's money in there, too. Find Gavin and tell him that I made a parvbada," *death promise,* "declaring you his trevhonell." *Responsibility something.* "Don't worry. It's not sexual. But he'll live up to it, even though you're an Earthling and he's a bit prejudiced. You–"

I put a finger on his lips. "I'll be fine." The tears in his eyes match the ones escaping my own. "Somehow."

I close my eyes, losing myself in the raw ache, and moments later, Brill's arms are around me.

He's given up. I need to remind him why he wants to live. I cross my arms over my chest, the crystal embedded in the pendant poking coldly into my skin. "Que? What is it, then?"

"What is what, Babe?"

"The one thing you want to do before you die?"

His brows crease together. "You're going to think it's kalltet."

"This whole situation's stupid. Try me."

He holds out his hands. "Nobody's ever been able to collect a commodity from Zant before, and this sawk stuff could be weaponized against Krom, so it'd be good to have an antidote. I want to get samples into a live box and mail them home. It would be my legacy."

"Then let's do it." I put the van in gear and reverse onto the road.

"You would participate in a Krom discovery?"

That gives me pause. The Krom "discovered" Earth. Our peoples hate each other over it. He's asking where my loyalties lie. And that's complicated.

"I basically already did, when I helped your amigo Jeska get credit for selling cacao." I keep my eyes on the road. "I'm still conflicted about what you guys do. I can see your point, that commodities need to be open-sourced, pero I grew up with the results of when you crashbang it." I can't help but remember the CastClip of the vlogger that found out Earth – and all its major commodities – had been *discovered* and traded across the galaxy. The shock on her face when the guy had told her, *Girlie, your planet's been mugged!* The road curves and I take a deep breath with it. "Pero, te amo." I say I love him again, this time in Krom. "Tesuaquenell. I want to understand you."

"Harvesting plants is going to take time. Tawny's going to kill us if we're late getting back. Or if she finds out you were part of a discovery."

"No, she's not. Nunca. Because they can only execute us once, remember?"

I just thought my bruised back hurt before. By the time I've spent a couple of hours trying to dig out vines with intact roots, and making out a little with the Krom who makes me feel whole, and hiking back to the van, I'm so stiff that I can barely drive.

When we stop by the postal center, Brill already has the package prepped. Pero, he takes out an envelope and goes to talk to the Zantite at the window. He puts a thin stack of cash in the envelope, writes something on it and hands it over. When he comes back to where I'm waiting, I ask, "Did you have to bribe him to send it, mi vida?"

Brill's eyes tint violet. "Ga. When Krom take a commodity, we pay for it, or at least try. Since the sawks aren't available commercially, I'm honoring that shopkeeper's intent by donating the amount he didn't charge me to the local wetland fund."

"The logic of commodities," I tell him.

"Everyone has them." Then he asks, "So what's HGB's new product?"

"Que?" It sounds like he's saying HGB, which had been allowed the monopoly on cacao because it had promised to leave everything else alone, wants to branch out. Impossible, no?

He takes my phone and pulls up a CastClip, where the CEO of HGB is being interviewed. He talks about how Earth's biodiversity is vast, how we can find something else the galaxy will buy from us even if we can't hold onto chocolate. He says there's something promising – that just needs a more stable delivery system. And that we have all the time in the worlds to develop it, because it would cost the aliens too much in money and lives to actually invade Earth. Therefore, it will never happen.

Persuasive, no? Especially with his shoulders-back, set-jaw herocast posture. Pero, for all his words, he hasn't really said anything. He's hinging our future on the idea that the invasion is not a cost-effective proposition. Even though the coalition is moving forward with plans to file with the Galactic Court.

Besides, what is this product? How does it justify giving HGB a new monopoly?

I bet Tawny already knows, is planning the spin. Asking her is pointless, though.

I wince. Brill puts a hand on mine. I feel horrible that he's the one comforting me.

We do get back before the funeral starts, with just enough time to change into somber clothes. In my room, Brill gives me one final kiss. Our last beso. I try to sear myself onto his lips, a memory of our love to give him courage.

I put everything that I am into this one moment, this one kiss. And when he breaks it, it's like a bubble popping, cascading from the warm pool of love into icy agua.

CHAPTER TWELVE

They're having the funeral at Minda's studio, which seems kind of tacky.

When we arrive on set, Tawny's fluttering around setting up the funeral music, making sure they're getting everything on camera. They even let Jimena out of the hospital to attend.

Tyson still hasn't gotten here. That caves in my heart.

Mertex *is* here. He's not a coward. Even if he is wearing two of those mothball necklaces Zantite soldiers sometimes put on to forestall summary execution: when disappointed superiors are expected to execute you with their teeth, making yourself unpalatable is a legitimate survival strategy.

At Zantite funerals where the body is intact, everyone touches the coffin, which is at the entrance to the room, as they enter. Some people are patting it, or knocking on it. I just slide my hand along the smooth wood. Kaliel's not even in there, so it's not creepy.

I drop my hand to my side and walk into the room we've been using to FeedCast the show. The kitchen set has been curtained off, until after, when all the food we made last night will be served. They've set up a stage with a simple podium.

If only Kaliel was in that estúpido box. If only we knew what happened. Pero, it's too late. The pendant hanging heavy around my neck is proof of that.

"Look, Babe." Brill points at a vase, where pieces of sawk-vine are intermixed with tiny white flowers and undulating spiny things that look more like rainbow-colored caterpillars than plant life. "It's a funeral flower. I need to add that to my notes now, while there's time."

"Sí." Time's a funny thing. Ours is gone, pero it doesn't feel like anything's about to end. Which is probably just another side effect of the IH.

There aren't many empty seats – this funeral with no body is something of a public spectacle – pero we find two near the end of a row, towards the back.

As we sit, the Zantite to my left leans over. He's young, maybe not even as old as the learning pod that had served as Kaliel's rescue crew. He says in halting English, "You're from Earth, right?"

I nod.

"Cool!" He holds up one of his flexible hands and spreads his fingers apart in a Star Trek-inspired salute. "Live–"

"Please. No." I hold up both of my own hands, cutting him off. I can't hear that right now, not in English, not when Brill's about to die.

He looks kind of hurt. "I didn't mean–"

"No. Lo siento. I'm sorry. It's just me, feeling too homesick." I manage a smile. "You do realize Vulcan isn't a real planet, right?"

He pops me the salute again. "You never know, maybe we just haven't found it yet."

This kid – his optimism and appreciation for my planet's stories – is exactly why I'm here. It could all be so different. I wonder if he will still feel the same after watching a Krom die.

The funeral starts, soft flute music playing as everyone stands. I can no longer see over the Zantites in front of me. Brill's on his tippy-toes, pero I doubt he sees anything either.

I hear Minda's voice. "Gatherings as large as this may not be our tradition for honoring the dead, but we know, if nothing else, how to be good neighbors in the galaxy. We choose privacy. This man's people choose community."

Everyone sits back down.

My handheld buzzes. I fumble it out of my pocket and get it switched to silent. It's an all caps text from Fizzax – in English. *WHAT IS BRILL HOLDING?*

I look down. Brill has slipped a syringe out of his pocket. It is unmistakably the Invincible Heart. The murky liquid, flecked with swirling gold, holds everything I need to scratch the itch in my blood, plus a few hours of vitality and lack of anxiety to cope with the horror of what's about to happen to someone I dearly love. I want that syringe, to the core of my bones.

Pero, for Brill it is instant death.

With shaking hands, I text back, *IH*.

Almost instantly, Fizzax sends, *WHATEVER YOU DO, DON'T LET HIM TAKE IT. THERE IS SUPPOSED TO BE A LAST-MINUTE RESCUE.*

I look around for Fizzax, pero I can't spot him in this room. I don't know what he's planning. The only thing that would save Brill is for Kaliel to walk in here and announce he's not dead after all. That's exactly what would happen on a telenovela – the over-the-top drama drawn out until the last second, then crashbanged by a too-easy solution. I would love for that to happen right now. Pero, we are not on a set. OK, we are on a set. Just not casting in a genre known for cheesetastic storytelling.

So I text back. *????????*

And then I wait. I get no reply, even as the service draws to a close.

I know Minda's not going to execute Mertex. Could she be the one with the last-minute plan? If so, Mertex doesn't know about it.

The Zantite policemen are starting to assemble at the door, and silent tears have begun rolling down Mertex's teal cheeks.

Some people are leaving, though more are waiting to witness the executions.

I don't want to deny Brill his easy out. Pero, if there's even a chance Fizzax knew what he was talking about... I need to grab the IH before Brill injects it. Pero, he's quicker than me. Krom-quick. I slide my hand towards his, hoping I can catch him unawares.

Brill looks at me, his eyes going wide and umber as he realizes what I'm trying to do. He whispers, "It's hard to say goodbye, Babe."

Then he gets up and dashes a few rows away, saying, "Excuse me," to a guy whose foot he stepped on getting out of our section. Typical Krom. Polite to the end.

He bows his head for a moment and cradles the syringe in his palm. The policemen, obviously realizing what he's planning, are making their way towards him. He turns to face them. I get there first.

Brill is trembling, holding the IH, pero he can't make himself uncap it. While he's distracted, I knock it out of his hand.

It goes skittering under the next row of chairs, landing between the feet of a female Zantite who's wearing an exceptionally short skirt.

He looks at me, reproachful sadness the color of whiskey in his eyes. "Babe."

All he knows is that I've taken away his chance to die without pain.

"Lo siento. I can't give up." I move to block any chance of him slipping under the chair. Whatever Fizzax had planned hasn't happened. May not happen, at this point. Pero, I can buy Fizzax a few more minutes. I turn to the policemen. "I have something to say. About Kaliel."

"What about me?" The voice comes from behind the casket.

We all turn to stare. Kaliel steps forward, staring curiously back.

"Mi Dios! Kaliel!" For a moment, I think maybe I am living in a telenovela, of the worst caliber of cheesetastic storytelling. Pero, I don't care.

"What's going on here?" Kaliel asks.

"Excuse me!" The lady in the short skirt holds up the syringe. "Someone lost this."

Dghax takes the syringe and hands it to Brill. "I trust this will be properly disposed of. I'd hate to have to examine it and identify the contents. Especially since you've escaped execution once today."

Brill looks at it, then at Kaliel, and the strength goes out of his legs. He sits down, right there at the policeman's feet.

CHAPTER THIRTEEN

"Where have you been?" I demand, staring right into Kaliel's beautiful eyes and not feeling even a hint of a zing.

Kaliel shrugs. "Trying to get back here. After I lost my lifejacket, I floated until I washed up on the southern island. I hiked inland, found a village, and the guy who handles their package delivery service was kind enough to fly me back here."

"This happened after you were attacked?" Dghax looks skeptical.

"Attacked?" Kaliel laughs. "It was an accident."

"But we found your blood all over the rigging and a puncture in the oxygen tubing," Dghax says.

Kaliel smiles, but it looks Tawny-level fake. "I had some of those food sticks they use as treats for the squids, and when I was lowering it into the water, one of those curly-horned dolphin things leapt right up onto the rigging to get it. A horn went through the tubing and put a big scratch in my neck. I was so startled, I fell in, and my life jacket got tangled in the horns of another one, and it dragged me around the point before the straps broke."

Dghax looks over at Jimena. "What about the Krom's bloody towel and the murder weapon?"

I squeak, "She's the witness?"

She was supposed to be in the hospital. What had she been doing at the hotel? Had she just wandered out of her room, delirious with fever?

Brill whispers, "I swear I saw this on *En la Falta de Flores*."

In Want of Flowers is one of the biggest cheesecasts to come out of Mexico in the last five years.

"Ga," I whisper back. "That character had amnesia."

"Evidence of what?" Kaliel's staring at the photograph of himself propped on top of the coffin. "Who's in there?"

"Your pilot's license and your boots." My voice sounds strange, halfway between a laugh and a wail. I'm relieved and freaked out and confused, and for once, stronger than the need for the Invincible Heart. "You know what? We should celebrate Kaliel's return with those cookies we made for after the funeral." I dash through the curtain to the kitchen and come back with one of the silver trays, offering them to various Zantites as I make my way back.

Fizzax pulls me off to the side. He bites nervously at his spongy lip with his razor-sharp upper teeth. "I just want to ask. Are you sure Brill didn't see what actually happened to Kaliel?"

"Sí. He would have told me. Que?" It shouldn't matter, now that Kaliel's been cleared of murder.

Pero, Fizzax lets out a sigh, like I've just told him he's safe. Extraño, no? He stammers, "No, no reason. Just an impression I had from the first time I talked to him."

I blink, confused. "So what happened to your last-minute rescue? Or did you somehow know Kaliel was coming?"

I mean that last part as a joke, pero half of Fizzax's cabeza blushes green. Did he know?

"Oh, look. Cookies." He shovels in a mouthful, basically changing the subject. He chompcrushes once then swallows, and a look of dismay fills his huge whale eyes. "Did those have chocolate in them?"

"Sí." I take a cookie for myself and break it open. I hope he's not allergic to chocolate! "They're inside-out chocolate-covered cherries, with cherry-infused cookie dough. Oye! Where are you going?"

"I have another case to deal with," he says, without looking back.

Extraño. Pero, I'm not going to try to stop him.

Mertex sidles over to me, a plate of food in his hand. He points with a shrimp-like geskk at Kaliel, who's chatting with Minda. "That story he told us doesn't make any sense. He wouldn't have wound up on the southern side, which is why we didn't even look there. That's not the way the currents work."

I'm just glad that Kaliel's alive, and that no matter how jumbled his memories are, he didn't claim anyone tried to hurt him.

My hand goes to the pendant. I look down, realizing I've grabbed it, then I look over at Brill, and suddenly, I've had enough. Of this place, of this day, of this whole loco situation.

I turn and walk out of the room. Mertex is following me – he's not very subtle – pero he doesn't try to stop me, just trails me all the way back to the hotel.

I pull on the tall, heavy front door. I'm starting to get used to the scale of everything around here. Once the door closes behind me, he doesn't keep following.

My sublingual rings. It's Chestla. *Hey! I have news about Kaliel.*

She's a bit late on this one. *I know he's back.*

He was gone? Chestla sounds confused.

What are you talking about?

I think I know why he got set up to blow up the SeniorLeisure vessel. He's a Sunrunner. It's like an extreme sport. HGB nearly fired him for slingshotting too close around stars to save on fuel. So the guys who set him up probably picked him because HGB already thought he was a hot-head.

Brill just now told me to stop digging into this. Pero – that was when he thought I was going to be on my own. No?

I sigh. He can't expect me to give up on finding out the truth about HGB. But I can't expect him to be able to protect me from Frank – or whatever other assassin HGB might send.

I can't right now, chica. I need to think of a safer way to find the truth. *Brill told me to tell you to stop looking into it.*

Chestla's disappointed noise bubblechatters through my brain. *I thought he was more supportive than that.*

She has no idea.

When the knock on my door comes, it's Brill. I can just see Mertex's back retreating down the hallway. At least he trusts mi vida to protect me.

Brill wraps me in a crushing hug. We stand that way for a long time.

Then I move over to the dresser and pull out a casual top, since Brill's alive to take me to dinner later.

Brill turns, looking at himself in the mirror, then sneaking a look at me in the reflection. "Don't wear the pendant."

"OK." I take it off, start to hand it back to him, pero he balls his gloved hands into fists, which must hurt.

"Ga. I'm not asking you to give it back. But if you wear it, it's like you're asking for us to be separated. You can wear it if I'm dying, or give it back if I break your heart. Because once you've worn it, it goes back in the box when you're over me, vivo o muerto."

Brill's taking our relationship a lot more seriously than I realized. "Where's yours?"

"Back in the box. Which I shouldn't have for another century, unless I was an invalid." His jaw is tense, and he's trembling. "I wasn't supposed to survive this day, and now everything feels wrong."

"Pero, you did survive. And I for one am happy about that." I wrap my arms around him, pressing my cheek against his jacket.

He rests his chin on the top of my head. "It's just – I was holding that syringe and I couldn't go through with it." He drops his arm lower on my back, against one of the worst bruises, pero I don't flinch. "I thought – this is kalltet – but I thought that if I loved you enough, that when you grow old, and your life ends, that I'd want mine to end too. That it would be even. And fair. But I can't promise you that."

"I wouldn't want that." I turn mi cabeza, so that my forehead's against his chest, feeling his hummingbird heartbeat. The pendant's chain still dangles from my fingers. "You couldn't give yourself that injection because you never give up hope, no? Even when it was hopeless."

I feel him laugh. I look up at him, and he tilts his face down towards me, pero before our lips touch, there's a knock on the door.

"Who is it?" I call. Please don't let it be Tawny.

"Is tis a bad time?"

"Tyson!" I hug Brill harder for a second, then I let him go and hurry to open the door.

The Galactacop's standing there, wedge-shaped reptilian head ducked forward, spine compressed down so that he's only about six and a half feet tall. He's another leather jacket, jeans and boots guy. He sweeps me into a hug that practically crushes me, then he lets me go. "I am so sorry. I don't blame you if you don't forgive me for letting you down. It's only dumb luck Brill's even still alive."

"La, not dumb," Brill says. He snagged the pendant from me, and I didn't even notice. He's sliding it into a dresser drawer.

My relationship with Tyson – who's a Myska, one of the galaxy's most lethal beings even without his toxic bite – is one of the oddest friendships I've ever had. Before I'd succumbed to the Invincible Heart, just looking at the guy's fer-de-lance face had rendered me unable to move.

Now, I give him a hug. "We're all headed down to the club to celebrate Kaliel's return. You have to come with us. Por favor."

"But I'm not needed here," Tyson protests.

I shrug. "You have to at least stay in town long enough to see me graduate, no?"

"Graduate?" Tyson catches his reflection in the mirror, brushes something I can't see off his gray and green facial scales.

Brill says, "Bo's going to get credit for doing the show, and they're teleconferencing in some of her teachers."

"También," I add, "Minda's got some mystery guest star that she says is going to make the audience go loco."

Tyson's reptilian tongue flicks between his lips. He has no front teeth. Hence, his inability to say th. "How could I miss tat?"

He still doesn't come to the club.

Kaliel's there though, dancing with a stick-like orange-skinned offworlder. Her tall boots and short skirt make her look even more like a go-go dancer than Minda had.

I turn to Brill. "I promise I won't dance with him."

"Go ahead, if it's to this." Brill's eyes are violet with amusement. This dance has more of the uncoordinated throwing about of limbs of the Chicken Dance than the scintillating romance of the samba or the tango.

"If that's what you want." He probably didn't actually mean for me to do it, pero I walk over to Kaliel, who turns away from stick girl. She huffs, then turns and steals another dance partner, and I try to copy Kaliel's movements. There's no real pattern to what he's doing.

"Have you heard from Kayla?" I shout over the din of the music.

"Why? She broke up with me, remember?"

"Pero you seemed to be happy the other morning, before you went squidriding. I thought she might have called."

"My mom sent me a message. I had asked her permission to get my grandmother's ring out of the safe deposit box when we got back to Earth, and she'd said it was cool. I assumed at that point that Kayla just needed to calm down, so I was still excited. But she's not going to get over it, and I have to deal."

I'm flailing my arms in the seemingly accepted manner, pero I hit a passing Zantite in the chest. "Lo siento. Sorry!"

The guy just keeps dancing.

"This dance is stupid." Kaliel stops flailing. He grabs my arm. "There is one thing."

I follow him away from the dancing, to a quiet little corner. He must have realized something about what happened to him, something that can help solve the mystery of why everyone's been acting so extraño.

I go to sit in one of the chairs, pero before I can he grabs me and kisses me. It's nothing like before, when his lips had been gentle and sweet, yet on fire with need. Even closed-lipped, Kaliel's current beso is invasive, and when I squeak a startled protest, he sticks his tongue in my mouth. And that's a lot less coordinated – and far more slobbery – than last time, too.

I push him away.

He wipes at the corner of his mouth. "I'm sorry. He… I really wanted to do that."

"He?"

"You're so beautiful, and I think about you so often."

"Stop it. I'm with Brill." Where's the zing I used to feel for Kaliel? Where's the temptation?

He doesn't walk, talk or act like the same person. En serio. It's like Kaliel came back from the dead as his own evil twin. And if that's not a true soap opera moment, I don't know what is.

Brill's walking over towards us, and he looks deep-maroon mad. I move to intercept him.

"Don't say anything, por favor." I link my arm through his. "We barely survived the last fight you two had."

It takes him a moment to calm down. Even when he does, concern still lights his eyes honey-hued. "You don't look OK."

I shrug. "Would you think I'm loco if I said I'm afraid my life was turning into a telenovela?"

"Not if it means we get our happily ever after."

It's cheesy, and perfect. And the closest he's ever come to a proposal.

CHAPTER FOURTEEN

Eleven days later, we're back at the spaceport to pick up Mamá. She's going to make a cameo on the last episode we're holoing here in Letekka before moving on to Hoftbek. I'm still not supposed to know Mamá's really here to see me graduate. I wish they'd told me sooner, so I could have stopped worrying about her running off to marry Frank.

It's just me and Brill in the van, and so far, there's no sign of the shuttle. Brill still has that syringe in his pocket. I'd felt the outline of it yesterday when I'd hugged him, wanted so badly to take it from him, couldn't bring myself to remind him he's supposed to destroy it. Don't know why he hasn't already. Maybe it's like his face, a reminder of how close he's come to death.

Brill takes out his shiny new phone. He's still wearing healing gloves. Ni idea what the skin looks like under there, pero he seems to be moving less gingerly. "I got the information back on Jimena. Tawny needs to vet her employees better. Jimena's there in the databases for HR, but when my friend went in person, nobody at the restaurants she's supposed to have worked for has ever heard of her."

I hesitate. "What should we do?"

Brill shrugs. "You could ask her why she lied to get the gig, and go from there. Unless you think she's dangerous."

I'd asked Jimena what she'd meant that day, when she'd

117

looked into that pot of chocolate and talked about the seed of death. She claims to have been delirious with fever. Only, I could tell she'd remembered exactly what I was talking about. And the way her face had lost color and her hands had trembled – it terrifies her.

I look up at the sky, at the puffy clouds not so different from Earth's. "Somebody had to hacktack a number of HR databases to put her data there. That took money, or skill or both, no? Pero, why? It doesn't seem safe to ask."

"Then just keep an eye on her."

"Sí, I have been. She looked sick for almost a week, and she's been complaining of headaches. She seems fine now. Aunque, she's still refusing to work with chocolate." Which is going to be a problem. And she won't explain why. "None of this matters until we get to the capital. Garfex's wife is supposed to be a special guest on the show, and if she has fun, she might get her husband to call for a vote to reconsider the invasion."

"You didn't tell me that." He leans towards me. "That's awesome."

"I just found out last night. It was Minda's plan from the first, pero she wanted to have a few successful episodes before she talked to Layla." I rest mi cabeza on his shoulder, inhaling the smell of leather and guy.

"Babe, you truly are Bodacious." He shifts his shoulders so that I'm facing him, and he kisses me. I close my eyes and enjoy the feel of his chest pressing against me, his fingers tangling in my hair.

I can do that, right? Just enjoy the warmth without wondering too much about where our relationship is headed. Pero, I have to admit, we're past the just-having-fun stage, and I want something more. But his family hates me, and he has a life span three times longer than mine. He'd be giving up so much if he committed to me. So I don't even know how to ask what he wants, without scaring him away.

For a moment, the hummingbird rhythm of his heartbeat double-matches the slower drumming of my own, like I'm the treble to his bass, like he's calming my heart. And it feels like this could really work, no matter how different we are.

That rhythm changes slightly. It only takes me a few seconds to wonder if I imagined the synchronization. Wishful thinking brought on by the heat of his lips.

There's a knock on the window, and Brill pulls back, startled.

Frank's frowning in at us. Brill rolls down the window. That beso must have lasted longer than I thought. I didn't even see Frank's shuttle enter atmo, let alone land.

Frank thrusts an envelope through the open window. "I'm not supposed to be worried, huh? The future of Earth is at stake, and you let your guard down to play tonsil hockey?"

"Sorry, sir," Brill mumbles. "It won't happen again."

"Damn right it won't." Frank opens the sliding door and slips into the seat behind Brill. Frank is an assassin, and the way he's looking at mi vida gives me chills.

Brill's irises have gone dark gray, which means he's feeling the weight of that stare too. I don't blame him for being afraid. After all, he still has a scar from when Frank shot him in the arm. Frank had been trying for the center of his forehead. Brill swallows visibly. "What do you mean, Mr Sawyer?"

Because it sounded like Frank just threatened to shoot him for kissing me instead of guarding me.

Frank plucks one of Tawny's bugs off Brill's jacket and throws it out the window. He checks for more. Which is odd. I mean, he *works* for HGB. "I mean I'm going to see that you get some decent training. Tawny already reported that you let Bo go missing, and she implied that it was over some fight you two had. She recommended I–" Frank stops mid-sentence and glances over at me. My chest squeezes in.

I'd thought Tawny had been flirting with Brill.

Had she really recommended he be killed?

Brill makes a soft, startled noise.

"Relax, Brill, you get to keep breathing. For now." Frank leans back in his seat. "My orders are just to take her recommendation into consideration as I evaluate the current situation."

"Thank you, Mr Sawyer. I enjoy breathing. Very much."

Frank thumps Brill on the back of the cabeza. "You're not likely to keep doing it long term. I've dealt with a number of self-taught space pirates. And they're all sloppy."

Brill's shoulders hunch up. Mi vida, usually calm under any kind of threat, looks like a niño. "I'm not a pirate." He forces his shoulders down, forces his eyes back to a carefree blue. "But I do welcome any training you'd care to offer."

Frank growls a noise of assent.

"Por favor, Frank. Stop intimidating him. We've kept your secret."

Frank looks levelly at me. "It's not my secret. It's Earth's secret, and by extension your secret, too. I've told you before. I'm a weapon in service to HGB. I always follow orders."

"I know, viejo." Frank truly believes HGB is acting to secure Earth's place in the galaxy.

"Your father..." Frank trails off.

"Que?" I snap to attention, heat burning in my chest.

Frank looks vulnerable for a moment. Ni idea why. "Your father died over a vial of what you call Serum Green." Frank does not say *I killed him over...* "He had that, and a sample of some yellow liquid from the lab, and HGB needed to keep those samples safe. Please don't make me kill you over the same thing. I like you. And your mother would never forgive me."

I let out a tiny squeak. Did Frank just express some sort of regret over murdering Papá? I'm trembling, and this time it's not the IH.

Brill looks in the rearview at Frank. "Bo's still important, alive. We're making progress here. Did Tawny tell you that

Queen Layla has agreed to be a special guest on the show, once we get to the capital?"

Frank looks startled. I guess Tawny's intelligence isn't as complete as he thought. After a long moment, Frank says, "She did say that Jimena... isn't working out."

Frío fear knifes through my heart. Tawny wants Frank to assassinate everybody. "Frank, don't you dare. I did not spend two weeks of my life tutoring that girl in the kitchen just to have to start over with someone else."

"Calm down. I'm going to talk to her first." Frank buckles his seatbelt. "You need to take this seriously, Bo. A lot of people are angry about you selling cacao. It's a betrayal of everything Earth has stood for, for decades. Jimena could have been sent to kill you."

I splutter out a laugh, pero I reach for the canned coffee in the van's cupholder. The shakes have gotten bad the last couple of days, which is why, in the kitchen, I've kept handing Jimena the knives. I can't suppress a shudder. "She's had plenty of opportunity, if that's what she wanted to do, viejo."

"You've been alone with her? After she was acting erratically?" Frank's face tints pink. "You're the most valuable asset Earth has right now. You can't take chances like that."

"A couple of months ago, all you wanted was proof of my death," I shoot back. "And you just threatened me with death again, if I step out of line. So stop acting like I mean something to you."

Brill puts his seatbelt on, and the quiet click sounds loud in the compartment. He opens the envelope Frank gave him and pastes the sticker that's inside on the windshield. "Let's go get your mom."

The sticker gets us back through security, to the tarmac. Brill's ship's been moved into a hangar, pero the HGB shuttle Mamá took is still in the open.

Mamá is standing by a pile of luggage, fanning herself. She's wearing a white caftan and oversized sunglasses, and she looks ready to hit the beach. She turns back to the open shuttle door, says something to someone still inside.

My brother Mario appears in the doorway and I choke on my coffee, spluttering milky drops onto my shirt. "What's he doing here?"

Mi hermano's a historian and a homebody, so he never goes offplanet – not even to resort places like Praxis. The idea of him coming to Zant is loco.

"Your whole family wanted to be here for your show," Frank says. "I thought you'd be touched."

"My whole family," I repeat, as Mario hands down both of my little sisters and all three of my nieces to mi mamá, before helping his wife out of the shuttle. After I take a few calming breaths, I turn around and glare at Frank. "If you think someone's trying to kill me, what are the niñas doing here?"

Frank shrugs. "The risk to them seems minimal, especially compared with the chance for Feed-time showing adorable, tiny Earthlings. Make the coalition see who they're threatening to invade as real people."

My mouth is open, and a noise is coming out, pero it's not words.

Brill has no such trouble. "So it was Ms Kamaka's idea. I thought you cared about Bo's family. How would Mrs Benitez feel if she heard you say that?"

Frank shrugs. "Lavonda and I discussed it. She agrees."

"Did you tell Mario?" I ask.

"That didn't seem prudent."

I bring both hands to my face, pressing in on my cheeks like that's all that's keeping them from exploding. "If it's so safe, viejo, where's your granddaughter?"

He has custody. She should be with him, no?

"She spends a couple of weeks with her other grandparents every year. She was already there. I asked them to keep her if it takes longer than expected to get back."

Which sounds suspiciously convenient, no?

The door behind me slides open, and Mario pokes his cabeza in. "Surprise!"

The girls talk nonstop the whole way to the set, telling me about their trip, about the simple problems in their lives. My nieces are two, three and six years old, one of my sisters a tween, the other barely a teen. Still young enough to see me as a hero, and to be fearless about being on an alien planet.

Pero when we pile out of the van and they get their first view of Minda, they all fall back, hiding behind Mario and Frank. Botas the corgi seems to like Minda, though, putting his front paws on her leg, begging to be petted.

"Who wants a set tour?" Minda scratches the dog between the ears. "Or would you rather play with the puppet stage upstairs?"

At that, Angelina and the girls abandon us, leaving Minda, Mertex, Mamá, Mario, Frank, Brill and me.

Minda holds out a basket of cookies. "I baked these all by myself. Bo's been teaching me how to do the one thing I thought I'd never be good at."

"Bo's always been a patient teacher," Mamá says. "I think it's growing up with two little sisters."

"And let's not forget her big brother." Mario steps closer to Mamá, pero he's looking at Minda. "Bo didn't always used to be good in the kitchen. After our papá died, we were broke. Mamá had a block of HGB dark in the pantry, and Bo thought she'd cheer everyone up by making chocoflan, but she didn't know you're supposed to melt chocolate in a double boiler. She scorched that chocolate to carbon, trying to figure out how to fix it. We had to throw away the pot."

Mario's story always drops a little ice into my heart, and right now, with Kayla missing and, I'm starting to have to admit it, possibly injured or dead – it feels like he's punched me.

It was a tough time for all of us. Papá died in a fire – thanks to Frank, though I didn't know it then – and the acrid smell of choco-carbon had lingered in the kitchen for days. The sound of the spoon when I'd tried to rake the char out of the pot got mixed up in my brain with the sound of shovels raining dirt onto the coffin containing Papá's charred body.

And Frank, hearing about the poverty he'd caused us, doesn't even have the good grace to blush.

Frank tugs Mertex aside while Mario is still talking to Minda. "This place is a logistical nightmare. What have you done to secure it?"

Mertex points to the block of seats with the tooth-mark symbols. "The local police force plans on sending six officers for the show. They'll ensure that no one brings in any weapons."

Frank snorts. "Because that's useful." He's looking at Mertex's mouth with all its natural knives.

Brill, Frank and Mertex form a small knot, absorbed in the conversation of how best to keep everyone safe.

The tour continues without them, into the area where we've been storing foodstuffs and other supplies. There's an elevated lip around the edge of the room, and shelves lining everything. The floor's center slopes down to a central drain. I had nearly died in a room like this, once meant for duels and interrogations. That drain's there to make it easy to clean the blood that's been spilled. I've been spending as little time as possible in there. Hence the usefulness of a prep chef.

I feel better once we get outside.

Minda says, "This studio produced *I Don't Want to Keep Her* and *Don't Lose My Heart*, two of Zant's earliest holographic immersive story experiences. The resolution wasn't great, but for the first time, the audience could look out through the character's eyes. It was too disturbing, though, when the characters were in danger, and quickly fell out of favor." Minda runs a hand across the black stone. "My first acting job was here, as a kid. Back then, every space was used for multiple sets, and designed with that in mind. Our storage room used to double as a starship deck, and an interrogation room – and when frozen over, an ice rink."

Somehow, knowing that that floor had been a prop, that no actual blood had been spilled on it, doesn't make me feel better.

"I moved back here and bought the place to start my own studio just a few years ago."

Mamá puts a hand on Minda's arm. "Being in the right place at the right time can change your life forever, no?"

My phone rings as the others head back into the main area. It's Stephen. I pause where I am and answer it. He's on the bridge of his mining ship and looks like he hasn't slept in days.

I say softly, "You still haven't heard from her."

We're counting down to the episode I've figured must be grad time. Would mi amiga really miss that – on camera – just because she's mad at me?

He frowns. "She's not dead, Bo!"

I take a step back, though I'm holding the phone, so of course, he goes with me. "I didn't say she was."

"We're twins. I would know." He rubs his hand against the side of his nose, leaving a dark streak. He's been tinkering with the engine. Stephen sighs. "I left Larksis 2 the day after the last possible day Kayla should have made it to Earth."

"You're coming to Zant?" I'm not excited at the thought of seeing him again.

"I'm more than halfway there. I'm going to try retracing her steps, maybe catch something the police missed. I know Kayla better than anybody."

"Be careful. Things around here have gotten un poco extraño." I hurry to catch up with the others. "Let us know when you get here so we can meet your ship."

When I hang up, Mertex is heading in my direction, and

Mario's in the middle of the quad, looking left out, though people keep walking past him. It's actually a busier space than I'd expected, almost like Minda built a park for everyone in the middle of her buildings.

It worries me that now Brill and Frank are alone somewhere together. Pero, he promised Brill he'd keep breathing.

I try to relax. "You're from here, right?" I ask Mertex.

"So?"

"So. This is a small island, Murry. Minda just said she moved *back* here a couple of years ago. If she lived here before she got famous, surely you met her somewhere."

Mertex blinks. "I'd have remembered that."

I glance at Minda, who's still chatting away with Mamá on the courtyard's far side. Her eyes go soft with affection as she looks over here. She certainly seems to have remembered him.

Two Zantites come up to Mario.

One says, "You're Mario Benitez, right?"

"Yeah." Mario sounds hesitant.

"I knew it!" The muchacho opens his bag and pulls out a print copy of Mario's book, *The History of Cacao*. "We're fans. Please, sign our books!"

Mario frowns at me. I'm the one who always got asked for autographs, so I'd expect a note of triumph in his expression, and that smugness he specializes in. Pero he looks more accusatory. Or maybe scared. Still, he forces a smile. "Who do I make this out to?"

Mario's book has crossed out of the history niche market onto the bestseller shelves. I've read it. He's a careful researcher and a natural storyteller. It hurts that he's not proud to sign his work.

Pero, there's nothing I can say that won't make him mad.

I spot Fizzax sitting at a picnic table over towards the edge of the manicured grounds, drinking something out of a blue cup. He nods at the other side of the table. I make my way over and sit down. He looks pale and there are greenish circles under his eyes.

"Are you OK?" I ask.

"I'm doing a little better today." He takes another sip out of the cup, which is filled with a viscous clear liquid that smells medicinal. "I got so sick right after Kaliel came back – threw my guts up for the next two days."

"That's horrible." Pero not my fault. Everyone else ate those cookies, too, and nobody else puked. It is, however, close to what Jimena came down with. "You been having headaches?"

"And a fever. But that went away when I stopped puking. I think I'll be back to myself in a day or two." He nods, then brings his fingers to the bridge of his nose. Apparently, he still has the headache.

Three people on this island have been acting strangely. Both Fizzax and Jimena had gotten sick after being exposed to chocolate. Kaliel doesn't like chocolate, so hasn't had any. Could there be some kind of connection?

"I feel like parts of last week were a bad dream."

"You and me both, mijo." Especially that day where I'd offered to let this guy eat me.

He snorts. "I'm serious. I've been a cop for over a decade, but I made accusations on the barest circumstantial evidence. Yet, it all seemed to make perfect sense at the time. I'm not usually that impulsive."

I give him a skeptical look. I had, after all, found myself in that tree.

He blushes, and it's the most color his face has had all day. "At least when I'm sober. But I haven't had a drink since the one we shared at the club. All I can think is that I've been coming down with this illness for a while."

Brill walks over to us. "Everything OK over here?" He looks at me. "Frank just gave me a crash course in self-defense. In case you don't feel safe."

"She's fine." Fizzax scratches at his wrist, with a fully functional hand attached to the arm Brill had blown a hole through. The bullet wound seems fully healed. The sawk rash not so much. He cuts a look over at Mertex. "Don't tell Flat Face over there, but I realized he's not a coward after all, the minute he grabbed me and made me spit you out."

"I never thought he was," Brill says.

Which is interesting, considering the way Mertex had acted towards Brill aboard the *Layla's Pride*.

Fizzax reaches into his pocket and pulls out a wrapped box. "I know you are a collector of oddities, and that your people are big on apology gifts. I want you to have these goggles." Fizzax's not the only one who's been acting strangely. Could they all have a judgement-altering virus? That sounds like a badly written cheese-fi episode, pero strange things do happen out in space.

No lo sé how that would fit in with the chocolate connection I'd been trying to figure out.

I need to talk to both Jimena and Kaliel and see if there's anything Frank needs to know before he gets carried away "evaluating" the situation.

CHAPTER FIFTEEN

The next morning, I'm up early for filming. Pero, there isn't enough coffee in the worlds to have prepared me for what Minda's telling me. And I forget about my plan to talk to Jimena and Kaliel.

Zantites make these jelly sweets, with sort-of seahorses in the middle, a crunchy savory-sweet treat that looks like a niño's ball. I've never eaten one – mainly because of the human-ish face and needle teeth. And because those seahorses are bottom-feeders.

After all, we'd found one chewing on the bones that we thought might have been Kaliel.

I swallow against a suddenly dry throat. "You want me to make what?"

"Prakk."

"No, por favor." I've done whatever Minda wanted thus far, and I agreed to do this surprise episode – which is obviously my graduation exam. We're backstage and I can already hear the audience out there, murmuring. There's no time to change Minda's plan without embarrassing her. And no point, if they've already steamed the sea creatures, with their bright blue eyes. Unless she's planning that as the audience participation part. Dios mio, please not that. "It doesn't even contain chocolate."

I sound desperate, even to myself.

"Relax." Minda takes me by both shoulders. "You know I'm

not cruel. I talked with... well, with your school – and they're OK if we replace the grepiskks with chocolate containing crisped grain and seaweed. I just need you to use edible nanites to create some kind of spectacular effect."

"Something worthy of a graduation exam?"

Minda laughs. "Something like that. I got the idea for this project from Earth's chocolate turtles."

My eyes go wide. Chocolate turtles were a pre-HGB candy made of pecans and caramel. The pecans were arranged to give the impression of feet and a head inside a round caramel patty covered with chocolate. Even after all the independent chocolate producers crashbombed, the flavor combination was still popular, so even without the shape, the chocolate, caramel and pecan goodies are still called turtles. "You've done your history research."

Minda shrugs. "I'm not as ditzy as everyone thinks."

I shake mi cabeza so hard my chunky white earrings brush arcs on my neck. "Nobody thinks that, nunca."

Minda dabs at her lipstick. "You should see some of the questions I get from my fan club." She points to a group at the top left of the stands, wearing blue shirts with individual letters plastered on them, that collectively spell, *We HEART Minda*.

In English.

Which means they're trying to interact with the people watching this on Earth. Which feels like progress.

They've spelled out the word *heart*.

"The core members all came out for the special episode."

Which means everybody's here – except Kayla. She wouldn't miss this, not if she had any choice.

Minda and I discussed it.

Kaliel's been keeping to himself, saying he's tired after his ordeal. Pero, when pressed, he's admitted he's still heard nada about his hermosa.

Even though Kayla's parents are refusing to report her

officially missing, we're going to make an appeal at the end of this show for mi amiga to contact us. Her parents are OK with that, as long as we only use her first name and don't FeedCast her picture. Kayla hadn't even told them she was going to be on the show, and they seemed more upset about that than anything.

Why aren't they doing everything in their power to find their daughter?

They don't seem to believe she's in danger. Maybe, secretly, she's reached out to them – though they keep saying nada, nunca.

I follow Minda out onto the set.

Minda smiles at the audience, and it's magnified on holos that pop up right in front of the stands. My family's all there, right in the front row, and when mi littlest hermana Sophia sees that razor-toothed grin, she screams and dives into Isabella's arms. Isabella's all of fourteen years old and she looks terrified herself. She's always been the shyest of my siblings.

Frank thought this was going to be una buena idea? I look for him to give him an I-told-you-so smirk, pero he's not here. My heart jumps.

I can't remember having seen Jimena today.

Frank had insisted he wanted to "talk" to her, even after I asked him to back off.

Could he be interrogating her right now? Or burying her?

A dog barks, and I look over to find Botas sitting in the seat next to Mamá. I thought Frank and that corgi were inseparable. Botas opens his mouth, lolls out a happy tongue.

My stomach clenches as ice tickles my spine.

"Oye." I try to say it quietly, pero Minda gives me a questioning glance. I gesture with my chin for her to address the cameras.

"Who's ready to learn how to make chocolate grepiskks?" Minda's looking straight at her fan club, who are cheering the loudest. "Today's skill tip is how to keep crispy inclusions crisp, while pouring chocolate into a mold."

Minda really has thought this through, pero I can't concentrate. I use my sublingual to call Jimena. She answers on the first ring, as though expecting my call. At the sound of her voice, a ball of worry inside me collapses.

Hola, Bo. Lo siento I'm late. I've been having coffee with this fascinating older gentleman–

The worry's back, kneeling on my chest. I force a breath. *Is his name Frank?*

To someone on the connection's other end, she says, *Bo knows you.*

I force my hands to uncurl themselves from fists. He said he wanted to talk to her. Maybe that's all this is. *Can you put him on the phone, por favor?*

I guess. Jimena sounds confused.

When he comes on the line, I ask, *Well? Does she get to live?*

Frank laughs, like this isn't serious at all. *So far, the results are inconclusive.*

I'm not doing this with you again, viejo. You start threatening people, and I'll be on the next ship off this rock.

This has nothing to do with your mother. I'm not the kind to cheat. In other words, he's not trying to leverage anybody to get me to do what he wants.

In the background, I hear Jimena squeak, *You're seeing someone?*

"Bo?" Minda says, and I get the idea it's not the first time.

I gotta go. Don't do anything rash. I wonder if Frank gets as strong of a sense of déjà vu as I just did. *Por favor.*

I mean it, though. I'm willing to leverage myself – leverage Earth – to keep from winding up in the middle of HGB's web again.

Minda's fan club has made their way down from the stands. There's only so much room at the prep table, and one of the guys nips at one of the girls, pushing her out of the way as she cradles her bleeding elbow.

Minda turns back to the audience. "And while they're working, they'll be serenaded by our special guest, Verex Kowlk."

The crowd goes loco.

Tyson's in the back row, looking broody and lethal and unimpressed.

Verex comes out, a squatty, barrel-like instrument in his hand. He plays a few electronic chords, and the fan club girl forgets about her bloody elbow, which Brill is trying to patch up for her. She swoons in mi vida's arms, dragging him to the floor with her weight.

Brill's eyes are violet. He's not hurt.

I launch into teacher-mode and get these fan clubbers working on their project. Verex starts singing, and half my volunteers stop working to watch. I sigh. This is going to be a long show.

I motivate them the best I can, then I step over to the workstation where I must program the nanites. The culinary curriculum I'd been a part of on Larksis 9 brings together an eclectic set of skills necessary for coping in an inter-planetary kitchen. In addition to working with unfamiliar food, we'd studied linguistics, diplomacy, first aid – and coding, which is my weakest area. Fortunately, I can use the bits and swatches of code I've pulled together for different assignments – my entire school archive has been downloaded onto this laptop – as long as I string them together to create something new. The image of prakk as a child's ball has given me an idea for a carousel, where the balls bounce up and down and change colors to the tune of one of Minda's songs.

A slow breath moves my hair. Brill is standing behind me, watching. He is so curious by nature, so intently enamored with being alive and every possibility that brings.

"You forgot to close your brackets." Brill is a whizz with code.

"Gracias."

"De nada, Babe."

It suddenly embarrasses me, him watching my clumsy work. Especially after he corrects me a couple more times. Which saves me hours of debugging – which I don't have – but still makes me feel estúpido. Another camera drone's following something occuring on the other side of the kitchen. "What's Minda doing, mi vida?"

"She said the audience needs something to watch while you're staring at a computer screen."

The fan club's done, the molds with the mock sea creatures are all chilling, and Verex is sitting in the audience next to my sisters – who seem to have gotten over their fear of him. Isabella's even playing a game with him that involves touching hands and making shapes with their fingers. And yes, Tawny's making sure the cameras are capturing that, from several different angles.

"Pero what is Minda actually doing?"

Kaliel's in the prep kitchen, chopping up some of that sticky glowing fruit, and it's not for anything I'm working on.

Brill points out another failed bracket close on my screen. "She's determined to make a proper cake. Didn't you hear her tell the audience that this is her graduation exam too?"

"No, mi vida. Unlike some people, coding takes every bit of my concentration."

He puts a hand on my shoulder, brings his face even closer to my hair. "But you're doing an amazing job. I never would have thought of bringing some of these elements together."

"Pero I keep making mistakes."

"La, everybody makes coding mistakes. Fixing them's just rote patience. It's the creativity behind it that's hard."

Heat floods my face. I turn back to the screen and try to

work faster. It still feels like forever before I can simcheck it, and another eternity before I can eject the tubes of prepared biodegradable nanites.

Jimena should be preparing the jelly that will hold the whole thing together, pero Valeria got pressed into doing it. The pots are all lined up, and there are quick tape-strip labels in neat hand-lettered Spanish detailing the flavors in each one. If she wasn't already so skilled as a stylist, I'd offer her Jimena's job.

Minda pops her cake in the oven, and together, me, Minda and Valeria get everything molded and prepped. Then Minda declares an intermission while everything sets – and the FeedCast rolls Verex Kowlk's first – and so far, only – film. About half the audience sits raptly watching the holoproduction. Everyone else starts milling around, heading for the bathrooms, or going outside to find some actual food.

CHAPTER SIXTEEN

Kaliel comes up to me. "I'm sorry I was such a jerk. Can we talk outside for a minute? It's about Kayla."

"Did Stephen report her missing? I know her parents are against it, pero–"

"I'll tell you when we have a bit more privacy." He casts a sour glance at Tawny, who is looking over my work.

I understand how he feels. As I follow him out the door, I catch a peripheral glance of Brill, trailing along behind us, trying to look casual about it. I blink as we come out into the bright sunlight. Mamá and Minda already have a table set up across the lawn, prepared to sign autographs. Botas is running in a circle nearby, chasing something that, if I squint real hard, looks like a butterfly.

"They're outside?" Kaliel sounds surprised.

Minda sees me and comes over. She looks sourly at Kaliel. Somebody probably told her about what he'd done at the club. She takes my arm, obviously anxious to separate me from him. "Bo, you should come sit with us. You're as much of a star here as me or your mother."

I'm blushing. "Sí. Just let me grab a Sharpie." I turn to go back in.

"Wait." Kaliel moves, barring the glass door.

There's a bang from inside. Minda blushes green. "My cake! I was so sure I'd got it right that time."

Pero, then there's a series of three shatterclashing bangs, and Brill comes flying through the door, gloved hands shielding his face from the shattering glass. He bowls into Kaliel, knocking him flat. I fall backwards against Minda, and she holds me steady as the impact of the blast rocks me.

"That hurt," Brill says, rolling away from Kaliel. There's a cut above his eye, on the same side as the half-healed freezer-marked cheek, pero otherwise, he looks OK. He's said before that thick leather jackets aren't just decorative.

He unzips his, pulls the syringe halfway out and, while trying to shield it from onlookers, examines it for cracks. I can't believe it didn't break. I can't look away from that dark, inviting swirl, even when he says plaintively, "No more putting it off. I need to get this to someone who can dispose of it properly before I wind up stabbing myself with it."

He remains sitting on the ground while Minda and I rush back into the building. Some Zantites are emitting those high-pitched wails. My baby sister screams – glass-shatteringly loud, feartastically close, distinct even over the Zantite noises of pain and distress. Pero, I don't spot her.

"Oh, no." Minda races to where my family had been sitting. A bloody blue and yellow mess wearing the same clothes as Verex Kowlk is lying awkwardly in front of the seats. Minda rolls him backwards, off Sophia and Isabella. He'd leapt in front of them to protect them from the explosion. His head lolls and his eyes are open in surprise, his rubbery lips a line of final determination.

The cops are moving through the crowd, trying to keep everyone from panicking. The shakes are the worst I've ever had them as the IH tries to cluster in my blood to give me what I need to get through this – tries and fails.

The counter where Minda was working has been jangleblasted to rubble, pero the table with my borrowed laptop is still in one piece.

Minda moves to the center of the room, wiping azure goo off her hands onto her pants. "We need everyone to move outside in a slow and orderly fashion. The officers will be escorting you, a section at a time. Until then, please stay seated."

Amazingly, everyone listens to her. Isabella and Sophia are safe. Mamá's outside. But what happened to Mario and his family?

Tyson makes his way towards me, despite the acid scowls he's getting from the Zantites who were just directed to stay put. He holds out my bag, which looks unscathed.

"Have you seen Mario?" I ask.

Tyson shakes his cabeza, and at first I think he's answering my question. "I can't hear you!"

Maybe his reptilian vibration-ears are more sensitive than I thought.

Extra policemen have come, and are looking for more bombs, examining the places where the others were set off.

I get outside as soon as I can and start asking everyone if they've seen a family of Earthlings. It's not hard to pick up their trail, which leads to the food court of a nearby shopping area. They would have thought they had a good hour and a half, while the holo played. I ask to be let through the barrier the police have set up, and after I give him my autograph, the cop lets me through.

When I find Mario, all three of his niñas are eating dough balls soaked in nkeh syrup, and a small group of Zantites are holding print copies of *The History of Cacao*. They're laughing, and Angelina's at least smiling. Mario still looks unhappy. Y todavía, from his expression, I can tell he hasn't heard about the bombing.

One of the Zantites sees me coming. "Bo! Will you sign it too? Right by your picture?"

I'm the main subject of the last chapter of Mario's book, and the Zantite flips it open to the relevant page.

I don't want to steal Mario's thunder, pero he gestures at the book. "Por favor, Pequeña."

He uses the shift in attention to escape. I sign the books quickly – those are some of the most lop-sided stars I've ever drawn – and then I follow him to where he's standing in line for something resembling a beer.

"You don't like having fans?" I ask.

"That's none of your business, mi hermana." He steps away as the line moves up. "What are you doing here anyway?"

"Trying to make sure you and the girls were safe. Somebody bombed the set."

His face goes slack with shock. "Mamá?"

"She's fine."

"But Sophie and Isabella. I left them with that actor guy because they wanted to watch his movie."

"The niñas are OK. The actor's not." Mi hermano looks like he's going to crumble, so I put a hand on his arm. I can't remember the last time I did that. "You couldn't have known it wasn't safe."

Because Frank didn't bother to warn him. It's got to be extraño to be the only non-gun-toting guy in the group, the one left out of the plans.

"Why would someone do this?" Mario asks.

I shrug. "Best guess? Some Zantite has a vested interest in this invasion happening. Minda's too determined to bring peace, and they want Verex Kowlk's ruined face paired with Earth all over the feeds." Pain spikes through my chest again as I remember Verex scrunching up his nose, mimicking my youngest sister. "Though I'm not exactly popular back home either. So I could have been the target."

"You haven't been popular for a long time." Mario looks down at the intricately patterned floor. "I should know. I got a lot of flak for things you did, en tiempos pasados." *Back in the day.*

"Is that why you won't ever let me forget it?"

Mario looks surprised. "Lo siento. I don't mean anything by it."

"Whatever." I leave him to scramble over to his family, collect them together, and be thankful that they're safe. I look back, and he's watching me walk away.

I can't get rid of what's burning in my blood – and I can't use it either. When I get back, Brill's being examined by the selfsame doc's assistant who offered to get me IH my first night here. He's left his jacket slung over a chair near the door of the improvised exam room, with his shirt folded on the seat.

"Babe?" Brill can't turn around, because Rex has his arm up over his head, testing the joint for range of motion.

"Sí. You OK?" I'm going to regret this. It's weak. Pero I quietly zip open his pocket and take out the syringe. I slip it into my own jeans.

"Cuts and bruises. This su doesn't believe me when I say nothing's broken. Except my phone. I hadn't even gotten all the contacts in it yet."

"Phones can be replaced, mi vida." I slip out the door.

There's a nice breeze, blowing away the smell of burning, and I make my way over to the same picnic table where I had sat with Fizzax, not so long ago. Someone has set up a row of white tents off to the side of the tables, for people to get out of the sun. They're facing the other way, so despite the soft voices coming from inside some of them, this spot feels private, as I look away from the set, towards the tangled undergrowth between here and the beach.

I take out the syringe, trying – and crashbanging – to remember the horror I felt the first time, when this stuff was forced on me. Four or five hits of IH and my liver fails. It's not a question. Pero I should be able to survive this one, and maybe when it burns away, there'll be enough left over to make me feel strong.

Unlike Fizzax, I don't have a fever, or a new kind of headache, so I'm probably not suffering from the virus, or whatever it is, that's crashing people's judgement. This is all me, looking into darkness and waiting for the darkness to flinch.

I uncap the syringe, press lightly on the plunger to make sure there isn't any air in it. I've never given myself an injection, but I've seen enough medical holo to know I need to do that much. It's harder to figure out how to find a vein.

I hear footsteps behind me and Brill sits down next to me. He doesn't look surprised. Pero his eyes are so gray, they're almost black.

"You here to stop me from doing this?" Without me even meaning to, my grip on the syringe tightens.

"Not by force, Babe." He looks at the tents, the light fabric tinted by the very beginning of the sunset. "I just wanted to remind you of a few things. Like how strong you are, and how it might literally break my heart if you die."

I sigh. I don't cap the syringe. "I never wanted this, mi vida. Despite what the sleazarazzi said, I never took drugs. I had a bit too much alcohol when I was with Fabian." Fabian, despite being a huge star now, had been the biggest mistake of my wannabe days. "I was brainblurred when he got both of his DWIs. Pero that's as far as it went."

Brill leans against me. "I'm sorry this happened to you, but you don't have to give in to it. I've never had an addiction, so I can't sit here and say it's easy. But I do know you always have a choice in life."

The fabric of one of the tents bends, then tips to the side. There's a startled, "Hey!" from the next tent over as the whole thing collapses, leaving Mario standing there, looking caught out. He shifts his face from little-kid-with-hand-in-cookie-jar to stern-older-brother-about-to-teach-a-lesson.

"Bo, what is that?"

"Nothing." I cap the syringe and throw it on the ground

behind the bench. Which is equally childish. I can feel my
cheeks going crimson, and I can't decide if it's because of what
IH is – or because Mario is seeing me in my weakest moment.

"That didn't look like nothing." He sits down across from me
and Brill. "I have no right to ask, after what I said to you today.
Pero – you really never took drugs?"

I fight not to roll my eyes. "Ay, I was impulsive, not stupid."

Mario looks down at the table. "I'm sorry I listened to
Ana buzzbashing you. I should have realized – since you
stole Fabian."

"Who's Ana?" Brill asks.

"A FeedCaster who claimed I was hitting on her guy – even
though he had broken up with her well before we got together.
Eventually I realized Fabian was just using me to make her
jealous, pero by then things had gotten a little out of hand. She
always hated me."

"That's an understatement," Mario says. "She had an
anonymous malcast called WhoHatesBoBenitez, with voice
changers and everything."

"I knew that was her!" I had just never been able to confirm
it. And here, I could have asked Mario and saved myself years
of pain.

Mario looks down at the table. "Look, why don't we go for
drinks later?"

Que? We've never done that. Pero, he's serious. This could
change everything between us.

"Sí," I say. "I'd like that."

Brill holds out his arm. "You OK if we go back now? Rex
wants to examine you next, even though I told him you were
outside when the bombs went off."

I take his arm. "I can't wait."

We're halfway to the improvised med center when I realize
I left the syringe on the ground. "Be right back."

I head back to the table just in time to see Mertex sliding

the syringe into his pocket. He puts his hand to his side. He's injured, and his torso's been wrapped with yellow gauze. He spots me. "You shouldn't leave things lying around."

He doesn't move to give it back to me, though. He's probably still worried about our lives-bound-together thing, afraid of what I might do under the influence.

"Sorry about that."

He shrugs. "You know the time you took it is the only other time I've seen it up close. It looks like a child's toy, full of glitter and swirls, but there's hero-stuff in there. And death."

He's still sounds fascinated with IH, pero there's no chance he's going to take it. Which makes it easier to walk away, despite my body's insistence that I *need* that glitter and swirls. Girls and glitter go together after all.

I force myself to say, "So you'll give that to Doctor Sonda for me, right?"

CHAPTER SEVENTEEN

It's getting dark. The people stuck milling around are clamoring to go home. And the cops are everywhere.

Tyson looks uncomfortable, because the Zantite cops are deferring to him. He glances at me, a hint of accusation in those golden whiteless eyes. If I hadn't asked him to stay to see my graduation, he'd be nowhere near here.

Frank's standing next to him, wearing a dark gray pea coat to protect against the chill in the evening air. It feels like it may rain soon.

Police Chief Dghax holds out a ragged piece of metal, which Tyson takes carefully by the edge. There's a partial handprint on it – an Earthling-sized palm and two fingers, formed of softly glowing sticky sap. "The team who did the security check before the show is certain there was nothing attached to this as of early this morning. But you can see the adhesive where one of the bombs was taped."

Tyson looks over at me again. This time he tilts his cabeza, questioning, and at the intensity of his peligroso gaze, I feel my bladder tense up.

Only a few people here have hands that small. One in particular leaps to mind: Kaliel. He was cutting up glow-fruit earlier on the show.

En serio though, Kaliel may have had a few lapses in judgement lately, pero he wouldn't attack people.

And yet, he had barred the door, like he had known something was about to happen.

Tyson tilts his cabeza even farther and stares at me, trying to figure out what I've just figured out.

Dghax says, "I recommend we get a list of names and contact information and let these people go home. It's obvious who our suspect is." He looks over at me.

My heart jolts. Me? My hands ball into fists as the shakes get worse. "Por qué? One of those bombs nearly blew up my sisters!"

Dghax shrugs. "I've heard humans don't care much for their children. Leave them in dumpsters sometimes if they think they're ugly, or out on mountainsides if they come out the wrong sex." He leans down, hands on his knees, until he's my height. "You've been at the center of three criminal incidents, and you've only been here a couple of weeks. That's not normal."

"It has to have been Kaliel," Frank says. "Otherwise, why'd he run?"

I turn to Frank, give him a pleading look to shut up. I can't deny that Kaliel had flitdashed, right after we came back from that picnic table. Brill tried to stop him from leaving and gotten socked in the jaw for his trouble. I turn back to Dghax. "Un momento, por favor."

Once Frank and I are far enough away, I ask, "Couldn't it have been Jimena? She's the one who was acting extraño when we filmed the first show, like she wanted it to crashbomb."

"That's not possible."

"Por qué? Because she's such a mousy girl?"

"Because she couldn't have been here." He turns his head to look me straight in the eye, and as he shifts, I see a splatter of blood on his jaw, right beneath his ear. Like he'd missed it when he wiped the rest away. "Not all day."

My chest feels all sparkly, and goosebumps run the length

of my limbs. He'd killed Jimena. Not only that, he'd spent an entire day with her before he'd decided she was dangerous and ended her life. How can mi mamá love someone so cold?

"Right after you talked to me on the phone, Frank, really?" I gesture at the blood. "Good thing you're so good with knives. Because you just volunteered to be my new prep chef."

Not that I expect there to be another show after this.

"Guns, actually," Frank quips. "She had one too."

I hold up a hand to stop him sharing the grithorror details of his gunning down my prep chef. "I really, really don't want to know."

"Tell me about the chef from Earth. Aidan what's-his-face."

My face goes hot, and my chest goes cold. "No y no. You leave him alone. He's just a kid, and he hasn't been anywhere near Minda's set."

"He knew Verex. They were seen together at the club." Frank straightens his coat collar. "Kids can be dangerous."

"Not like how you're dangerous."

"I still ought to look into him. What if he's been working with Jimena to–"

"Por favor, Frank. Don't. Mamá keeps saying I should forgive you, and then you keep doing things like this."

"I was protecting you." He rubs at his jaw with the back of his hand.

"Unless I get blamed for Jimena's disappearance, too." I sigh. "I'm surprised they haven't said I did something to Kayla." Wait. Could Frank have killed Kayla too? I stare at him for a second. Pero no, the timing doesn't line up.

Frank gives me a reproachful look. "Your friend's shuttle landed safely at Skadish, but nobody remembers seeing her get off, and she didn't book a flight from there back to Earth, or to anywhere else."

"You looked into that? Because I was worried?"

"I keep telling you, I'm not a monster." Ironic, given the way he's rubbing the bloodstain from his face onto a handkerchief. "But if Kayla went off the grid, and then Kaliel took off running, maybe Kayla was laying the groundwork for his escape."

"Kayla wouldn't be a part of something like that."

Frank puts a hand on my arm. I force myself not to jump. He's never touched me before, certainly not in a way meant to bring comfort. "She's your friend, Bodacious. Trust your gut here. What do you think is going on?"

"No sé." *I don't know.*

"Do you think Kaliel killed her? If there's something wrong with him mentally–"

"No. Por favor. No." I pull my arm away. "None of this makes any sense, nunca. Kaliel has always been a good guy."

Word comes over the radio that they found something else, and Frank goes inside to check it out. I try calling Kaliel again. If he would just answer, just explain why he ran, maybe I could stop this here, before it gets loco.

After a few minutes, Frank says something to Tyson and they both say something to Dghax. Dghax starts shouting into his phone, sending out orders to lock down the spaceports and halt the ferry service, putting half the police force on an island-wide Earthling-hunt. For Kaliel. Because whatever they found inside ties him to the bombing.

It's a small island, and as far as I know, Kaliel has no experience hiding out from anyone. This will end soon, likely with his muerte, and that breaks my heart.

Kaliel's the guy who wouldn't flitdash to save his own life back on Earth, even knowing he faced the shave, because running would make him look guilty.

So why would he run now? It doesn't add up.

Unless whatever came back from the river isn't Kaliel at all.

Could he be a doppelganger, the science fiction version of an evil twin, after all?

Pero, that's loco, no?

Mertex would have told me if there were shape-shifting monsters in the woods.

So I'm left with the idea of a virus, which sounds loco too, or a brain injury from his accident, to explain why Kaliel's acting in opposition to his own moral code.

Minda walks towards us, her face lit in an ethereal glow from the frosting of the cake she's holding in her hands. "Mertex rescued the layers for me from the bombing site. Even though he was injured." She smiles, and there's a bit of frosting glowing on one of her front teeth. "It didn't blow up this time."

There is something to be said for small victories on a day like today. I tell her, "That looks beautiful. It makes you look beautiful, too."

"Bo, my ego's fine. You don't have to say that." But then she blinks. "You can see Zantites as beautiful?"

"Some Zantites, sí. Then again. I only think *some* Earthlings are beautiful too, no?" It never occurred to me to wonder what Minda sees when she looks at me.

Minda hands her cake to Frank, and peers at me, though surely she can hardly see me in the dark. "One aesthetically pleasing thing about you is your hair. It balances the smallness of your face, adds shadows of motion when you move. It doesn't have heat-coloration like the rest of you, but that's what makes it fascinating."

"Heat coloration?" I ask.

She explains that Zantite vision combines something resembling the way I see, plus detail based on ambient temperature.

"I never knew that." I wonder what Mertex looks like to her. It might explain why I think he looks like a dork, but she's so smitten.

And when Murry had said it was amazing watching the warmth coming back into mi vida's face – that small miracle must have looked more beautiful than I could ever have imagined.

I look over at the cake, which must be even more spectacular through Minda's eyes. "Small victories, right?"

"What?"

I don't explain, just walk over to the cluster of cops and announce, "I think Kaliel has a virus. Or something."

I look back at Frank. Jimena might have had the virus – or whatever it is – too. Could she still be alive if I'd explained my loco theory when I'd had Frank on the phone? Heat blooms in my face, and I realize that to a Zantite, that's as much of an emotional giveaway as the shifts in Krom eyes.

"Is he contagious?" Police Chief Dghax asks, stepping away from me as though I'm the one who's sick.

"I don't know. Just... there was something off about the way he kissed me. Like he was a completely different person." I can't mention Jimena here, or Fizzax, so it sounds un poco estúpido. I lie, adding their symptoms to Kaliel. "He's had fever, nausea and headaches. Try to bring him back alive, por favor, so that we can find out what's really going on."

Dghax asks, "Have you had any of those symptoms?"

"No, gracias a Dios."

Tyson sucks at his mouth, skeptical, yet he keeps silent.

Doc's assistant Rex – not so much. "That's preposterous. There aren't any viruses on Zant that cause those symptoms. And if something like that came from Earth – well, you guys would know about it."

My cheeks flame even hotter. Dios mio. At least Brill has some control over what his eyes are doing. "It's the only thing that makes sense."

"Offplanet viruses do happen," Dghax says. "Not everyone who lands planetside comes through decontamination. You remember that Evevron ship that crashed here about a decade ago? Their people said they were sick."

Rex sniff-snorts. "They only said that so we wouldn't eat them. Space spores only happen in Earth movies."

He's talking about *Invasion of the Body Snatchers*. Which is kind of what this situation feels like.

That ship I'd seen in the water really was a plague vessel. And people have been swimming out to it for years. Something about it starts to click in mi cabeza, pero before it can, Mertex comes hobbling up, holding onto his side. "My cousin called to check on me after she heard about the bombing. Kaliel had just rented one of her boats."

"Even if he makes it across to the southern island, the spaceports are closed." Dghax pulls out his phone. "We just need to widen the search area."

CHAPTER EIGHTEEN

"Come on, Bo, we're leaving." Mario's hand lands on my shoulder. Mi hermano glares at the Zantites, then at Frank. Then he drags me away from them.

"What are you doing?" I whisper.

"I came here – brought mi familia here – because I wanted to support my little hermana finally getting her life together. And then I find out people are trying to blow you up. And you are getting yourself in deeper. It's time to go home, and let all these aliens sort things out for themselves."

"All these aliens? Kaliel is just as human as we are, no?" I pull away from him. "Earth's position in the galaxy is still precarious. Back home, HGB's stockpiling weapons to stave off an invasion they won't win. Earth survives only if we convince *all these aliens* that we deserve a place in the galaxy. And Kaliel – *if* he did it – just killed one of their most popular heroes."

"How are you going to change that?" He looks like he wants to grab me again, pero doesn't dare. "You're a chef, Bo, at best, and a screwup. You think you belong with those guys?" He gestures at the knot of cops, and Frank and Brill, all with their leather jackets and thick pea coats and uniforms and guns and scowls.

"I've kept myself breathing this long." I cross my arms over my chest. Mario still has the power to make me feel like I'm eight years old.

"Some niño told me what that drug you're addicted to does. And that no human who's ever taken it has managed to last as long as you have without dosing themselves again and again until they die. Do you know they're pooling bets on how long it takes you to give in and kill yourself?"

I did not know that. Pero, I'm not about to tell Mario how much that hurts. "I've outlasted the expectations. I'm stronger than you think. And you might know that if you hadn't shut me out." I'm breathing hard, and the shakes and the need are catching up with me, pero I will not let mi hermano see me cry.

"*I* shut *you* out?" Mario, ever the historian, shifts into his teacher voice when he says, "Bad things happen, Bo. You can't change it. Things never end well for anyone who has something somebody else wants. Look at the Opium Wars. Look at Montezuma."

"Maybe this time it will be different, no? After all, we're not the only ones that have chocolate now."

"The Zantites still don't have it."

"If the Krom First Contact had gone right, they would."

Mario gasps. "Are you defending them?"

There's a soft noise behind me, a shoe shifting on gravel. I turn. Brill's standing there. Mario, who spent weeks hanging out with Brill, bonding over bad science fiction flicks and soccer, at least has the good grace to blush and look away.

"There's been a development. Tyson wants to speak with you." Brill turns to Mario. "You're right. Things do often end badly. We Krom know that better than most. Have you ever asked yourself what might have motivated Povika and his children to write the Codex? Why we bother expending so much effort for what amounts to such little monetary gain?"

"Why?" Mario says it, pero I'm suddenly asking myself the same thing.

Brill shakes his cabeza. "Read the Codex. And then we'll talk."

While I've read parts of the Codex, I never could get through the whole thing.

Brill's silent as he walks me back over to the knot of cops. Tyson's gotten taller, uncoiling his spine enough that there's a gap of several inches between the bottom edge of his leather jacket and the top of his jeans, and his snakelike head is down almost against his chest. I'm frozen at his frío anger, despite the IH residue.

"We underestimated Kaliel, dark want supernova." Tyson blinks his translucent eyelids, then focuses on me with such predatory intensity that I nearly wet myself. "He killed tree guards and two crew members and stole a government transport to get offplanet."

"There must be some mistake. Kaliel wouldn't–"

Tyson moves towards me, like he's flowing agua and stardust, and his gold slit-pupil eyes are only inches from my face. I can feel the air blowing past his fangs when he says, "Tell me where he's going."

At first I can't get my mouth to move, but then I blurt, "Ni idea."

"Murder, Bo. Five bodies, not counting te four from te bombing." He studies my face, looking for signs I'm lying. It's all I can do not to look at Frank if we're counting up murders, because I'm not sure what Tyson would make of what had happened to Jimena.

Finally, Tyson turns away.

I manage to speak. "Tyson, please." He looks back. My stomach turns icy. I almost can't continue. "Something extraño has been going on ever since I got to this planet. At least consider the possibility that Kaliel's a victim of it."

Tyson tilts his cabeza, scrunches up his mouth, then says, "Your judgement's compromised here. How many more people will he have to kill for you to realize that?"

Frank says, "Kaliel was involved before, in an incident

where people got killed. You got him exonerated on the basis that another ship was there, and his testimony that he was framed. I've seen the holo. But no one knows what ship that was, or who it belonged to. Given this–" He waves his hand at the still smoking building, "–is it possible that everyone misinterpreted that evidence, and he was actually working *with* that ship?"

Maybe I'm wrong. Maybe I'm a horrible judge of people, and Kaliel scuttlepunched that SeniorLeisure transport on purpose, as the beginning of a loco killing spree.

"No. No y no!" I can't be *that* mistaken. "Why would he hurt Kayla? Or any of them? What's his motive?"

A helicopter passes overhead, and I assume it's the police. The chopper swings back around, landing in the open quad.

A lithe figure bounds out of it, green eyes glittering in the darkness, long hair swishing. She turns and waves at the pilot before it takes off again.

"Chestla!"

Chestla turns towards me and grins. She looks a little like an ocelot, with those vertical-slit pupils and reflective green irises above a predator's smile. Pero, she's humanoid, tall, has smooth beige skin on her freckled cheeks, and long honey-colored hair. I reach out and hug her. As I let her go, her mouth gapes open in shock, revealing fang-length incisors.

"You," she starts, in Universal Standard. Then she closes her mouth.

"I what?"

Chestla continues in Universal, which she's never been comfortable with. She, like most non-humans, doesn't want a sublingual, so the improved language skills are all the more impressive. "You've never hugged me before. Aren't you afraid of me?"

What I've termed the Chestla Effect, that natural response of most sane creatures in the presence of an alpha predator, just isn't hitting me. "I guess not."

"You shouldn't have come here." Brill sounds nervous. "Whatever it is, you could have holocalled without... you know." He gestures towards the cops, who are giving Chestla sour looks.

"Did you break some law here, chica?" I ask.

"Nah." Chestla wrinkles her nose. "The war between these people and mine was long and ugly and ended not so long ago. But I have a favor to ask you. And it's the kind of thing you ask in person."

"Me first." Because I have an idea, a gleefully loco idea born of desperation. With Chestla's tracking skills and Brill's fast ship, I might have a chance to out-Tyson Tyson. "Would you be willing to help me track somebody?"

Tyson asks, "What are you doing, Bo?" at the same time Chestla says, "Yeah, sure. Who?"

I answer Tyson. "I'm making you a proposition, muchacho. The Kaliel I know wouldn't have run, and certainly wouldn't have killed people to do it. I believe he's sick. Or that there is some kind of mistake, and whoever we're chasing isn't him." I keep my doppelganger theory to myself – for now. "If we find Kaliel before you do, then you make sure he gets checked out by a doctor, and you try your loophole magic to find a legal way to help him. *Before* he comes back to Zant."

Tyson's mouth scrunches in, and it looks like he's about to explode with frustration or anger. His cabeza moves towards me, and I flinch back. He's already bit me once, no? But then he bursts out laughing. "Tat's never going to happen."

"Pero if it does?"

"Fine. Party happy cupcake frosting." Tyson opens his mouth, flicks out his tongue. I'm no expert in his language transliteration, pero that sounded patronizing. "But don't expect me to wait around for Brill's ship." He holds out his phone. "I'll even share te file, to make it fair."

My handheld dings. I accept the share offer, and data fills the screen, including the trajectory of the stolen ship on takeoff. When I look up, Tyson's walking away, and Fizzax is trotting after him. The two stop and Fizzax says something that makes Tyson laugh.

I ask Brill, "What's wrong with your ship?"

Mi vida gives me a sullen look. "You could have at least asked."

I hesitate. "Are you saying you don't want to try to find Kaliel?"

I can't blame him, not after the way Kaliel's been acting lately.

"Ga. I'm saying you asked Chestla, and I don't like to feel taken for granted, especially when it's my ship."

"So will you help me find Kaliel, mi vida? Por favor?"

"That's all I needed." He takes my hand and squeezes it. "We are going to be starting a few hours behind, though. The *Fois Gras* got damaged by vandals at the spaceport right after the bombing hit the feeds. Go get packed."

"After she makes a statement," Tawny says. She's got one of her camera drones trained on me, gently lighting the area where I'm standing. It may have even caught me issuing that challenge to Tyson. "I need a few words disavowing any knowledge of Kaliel's actions."

I force my hands flat and take a deep breath. "You want a statement? Being human is about loyalty and honor, and not bailing on your friends. I'm not giving up on Kaliel until he tells me why all of this happened."

I turn away and run smack into Mario.

"Nice speech." He ruffles my hair, like when we were kids. As I smack his hand away, he says, "I guess you have time for that drink after all."

"Un momento." I turn to Chestla. "What was that favor you wanted to ask?"

"I'll understand if you say no." She won't look at me. "You probably should say no."

"Say no, Bo," Mario says.

I ignore him. "You have to tell me what you want, first."

"The Council of Elders found out why I went to Earth, and given the popularity of your exploits, they're willing to re-evaluate my potential as a Guardian – as long as you come in person to provide a reference."

"Claro está!" *Of course.* Becoming a Guardian Companion to a royal princess on her home planet was her life-long dream – a dream made impossible when she'd failed, and nearly died, on the obstacle course portion of the aptitude test. "I'll be happy to tell them how you saved my life."

Chestla says, "There's a bit more to it than just giving a testimonial. You are the reference. And you would be putting yourself at risk."

"Por favor say no," Mario repeats.

Chestla had never hesitated to put herself at risk for me. "As soon as we find Kaliel, I'll go with you."

Claro está, I have no idea how we're going to do that.

As we walk away, Mario says, "You have any idea how you're going to do that?"

I give him a sour look. Behind him, Tawny is waving at me.

I grimace. "I guess I'm not quite done here. Meet you there?"

Tawny shuts off the drone, and it settles to the ground. "Can I give you one more piece of advice?"

I look at the drone, frío and silent, and a chill goes through me that is more than just the evening breeze. Why'd she shut it off? "Que?"

"I just talked to a few people back home. Don't leave this planet on anything other than an HGB ship, not until you've fulfilled your obligations. It's not... prudent."

"Is HGB making that an order?"

Tawny pats my hand. "No. And I can see you're not going to listen. But there will be implications just the same. For you, and for the people harboring you."

CHAPTER NINETEEN

The mechanics may have replaced the syphoned fuel and repaired the smashed parts, pero nobody had time to paint over the graffiti covering the left side of the *Fois Gras*. All that clean white metal must have been irresistible as a canvas.

I speak a lot more Zant than I read, so I have no idea what most of it says. It can't be bueno.

Brill blinks at it. "Now that's not even physically possible."

"Mi vida–" I put a hand on his arm.

"It's just words. They're angry." He points at a line of Krom writing along the arcing front fin. "Whoever kept writing Zombie spelled it wrong."

I've not heard that particular slur before, pero it obviously comes from the Krom ability to go extended amounts of time without breathing. They can look dead.

"I'm sorry I landed here. I was only thinking that because I can take care of myself, it wouldn't be a problem." Chestla stretches her hands, the claw-like nails catching on the fabric of her jeans. They're still perfectly polished with glittering purple. "I didn't think they'd take it out on you."

"Ga, su," Brill says. "This is about us and Kaliel."

"They think you had something to do with the bombing?" Chestla asks.

"More that Bo did, and I brought her here. It's good that we have a reason to get off this rock. There's already talk of trying

159

her in Kaliel's place. Apparently, Verex was ita ita popular."

"Can they even do that?" I squeak.

"Legally, ga. But if they appeal to Garfex, he can do whatever he wants."

Chestla stares at the graffiti. "Then let's get out of here before that happens."

Brill gets us in the air and out of atmo, and I'm watching Zant recede into a blue marble when my sublingual rings. I brace myself for a scolding from Mario, or even Mamá trying to talk me out of going.

But it's Frank. *What the heck, Bo?*

"Que?" I say it out loud and in mi cabeza.

"Who are you talking to?" Brill asks.

"Frank."

Brill holds up a tiny square. "I may have locked him in a bathroom back at the hotel. After I stole his phone battery."

"You told me he didn't want to go with us."

Frank heard my half of that exchange. *Put Brill on the phone now.*

I can't. It's a sublingual.

"I didn't want him on my ship." Brill's eyes slip towards gray. "I'd like to be able to sleep in my own home without worrying if Mr *I'm a Weapon* is going to get orders to try to kill me. Again."

Which is a valid concern.

This isn't a good time, viejo. I hang up the call, just as Frank's telling me he'll catch up with us if we give him a location. I turn to Brill. "You know he really is going to try to kill you when he sees you again."

"Not if we're successful."

My handheld rings seconds later. Frank must have figured out that Brill never got a chance to replace his phone the second time.

"It's for you." I toss it to Brill. They're going to be talking for a while.

I study the nav. We're following Kaliel's trajectory, pero it's not like he's going to just keep going straight until we catch up with him.

In fact, Brill makes a face at something Frank's said, then changes course so dramatically that the internal stabilization can't keep up. It throws me off balance, and I grab on to the wall. There's a clatter from inside Brill's cabin. He looks up, and suddenly his gun is in his hand. He drops my phone onto the dash.

The cabin door opens, and Tawny's standing there, looking disheveled. She pulls Jimena's old headphones off. "Tell me we're not already in space."

What was she doing in there? Planting cameras on the ceiling so she can watch Brill sleep?

"Did you not notice us taking off?" Chestla asks.

"I've been a bit preoccupied listening to the news." She blinks at us. "Which apparently you haven't heard."

She pulls out her phone and pops up a hologram. It's one of the regular HGB FeedCasters, a twenty-something black guy with frosted hair. "...having given him a second chance. FeedCasts coming from Zant have labeled Johansson, 'The Rogue Earthling.' The families of his presumed victims are demanding swift justice, and have collectively offered a seven billion Bingt reward."

Brill groans, his eyes darkening to black. "It's going to be a zoo out here."

The feed shows still images of each of the deceased, back when they were still happy and smiling. The last photo, claro está, is the beloved Zantite holostar, and it lingers in the air for a long while.

Then the FeedCaster's back. "Earth has disavowed all knowledge of and responsibility for Johansson. If you have any information–"

Brill's eyes turn a strange brick red. "Babe, that means the bounty hunters won't hesitate to kill him."

I'm still reeling. When everything had gone wrong with the SeniorLeisure ship, HGB had lobbied hard to get people to see it as accidental and forgivable. They have less information now, and they're not even going to try to spin-wash Kaliel this time.

I look at Tawny. "Is this the ramifications you were talking about, mija? Or one of your suggestions?"

Tawny looks offended. "This was *not* my idea."

My sublingual rings. It's Tyson. *Do you want to call it off? Tere's going to be a bloodbat. You do not want to see tat.*

Will you help him?

Bo–

Then I still have to try.

I hang up, pero the sublingual rings again immediately. *Tyson, I told you–*

Mija. How can I help?

Moisture shimmers in my vision. *Mamá! Lo siento I–*

Don't worry, Bee. Just let me know when you're in danger from now on. Sometimes influence can help you.

She's referring to how I didn't tell her I was supposed to have been executed aboard the Zantite warship, how I haven't exactly been forthcoming about my experience on Zant. I've wondered, though. How can she be as blasé as she is about HGB – and still have been concerned enough about my safety at their hands to have sent Chestla to protect me? Pero now's not the time to ask about that. *Can you get them to un-disavow Kaliel?*

Don't ask for the moon and Interface Station. Mamá sounds shocked.

Tawny's still got the holo playing, and now there's a foot-high version of my head and torso saying, "Being human is about loyalty and honor, and not bailing on your amigos. I'm not giving up on Kaliel until he tells me why all of this happened."

Then there's a close-in shot of Minda. "Mercy is a gift." She stares intently at the audience, the splice work invisible. "You heard me."

Then bouncing back to me, at the bar, shrugging into my fizzy turpentine. "By all rights, I should have been executed for what I did by stealing cacao on Earth. That made me appreciate what a gift mercy can be."

Then Verex, alive and playing shadow puppets with my little sister, smiling up at the camera. "Mercy is a gift? Yeah, I can believe that."

Dios mio!

I manage to suck in a breath past the shock.

Let me think on it, Mamá, and get back to you. I hang up.

Then I stare at Tawny. "You released that?"

She shuts off the holo. "I had meant for it to be a metaphor about the invasion. And then I had to waste it on Kaliel."

"It wasn't wasted," Chestla says. "People will still see the metaphor."

Tawny smiles for real. "Thanks."

We all realize that that could be good or bad. Because they will see the metaphor, we've just tied the outcome of our whole attempt to stop the invasion of Earth to selling the Zantites on the concept of mercy for one insignificant Earthling.

"Please return me to Zant." Tawny scrunches up her nose. "It's safer than where you're headed."

"Can't." Brill looks like he'd like nothing more than to boot Tawny off his ship. "No spitpod. We're already a couple of hours behind, so there's no way we're turning around and taking all the time and fuel to land."

"Fine." Tawny pockets her phone. "I'll be in my room, trying to sort this mess. I can find a ride back when we reach a suitable planet."

Brill calls after her, "Stay out of my cabin!"

I call Mamá back, using my handheld. I want her to see that

I'm OK. She's sitting on a sofa with Botas half in her lap, half on the seat beside her. There's another hand petting the corgi. Probably Frank's.

I try to ignore that. "I figured out what you can do, Mamá. Talk Minda out of canceling, por favor. Take my place on the tour and show everyone that humans are capable of keeping their word, and that Minda still trusts us."

Is it sad that Tawny's the one who has given me hope? Though her ad amounts to little more than emotional manipulation.

"I could do that." Mamá bats her eyelashes dramatically. "El espectáculo debe continuar." *The show must go on.*

"Absolutely not," Frank says from outside the capture field. "That's going to be a logistics nightmare, and there could be another attempt on Minda's life. I was willing to go with you and Brill," there's a hint of bitter growl in his voice, "because your mother was going home."

"The show must go on, Frank." Mamá sits up straighter. Dios ayude a Frank if he thinks he can change her mind. "Mario can take all the girls home with him in the morning. I'll tell him when he gets here."

The corgi starts whining, picking up the tension between his people.

"Let me talk to Bo for a minute." Frank takes the phone from Mamá and walks over to a balcony that overlooks the phosphorescent bay. "I'm curious. Did Tawny coach you to say that stuff about mercy for her holo, or do you really believe it? Do you feel HGB and the court gave you a gift?"

I start to say that of course I do, pero, looking at his skeptical face, I hesitate. From one way you look at it, I had been shown mercy by the Global Court. By another, I had played the game and earned my escape from the shave.

Claro está, he's implying that by accepting their mercy, I've made my peace with HGB. And I haven't.

I swallow. "I said that on my own. It suited the context. It doesn't matter what I believe."

"I think it does." Frank smiles. "Look, if your mother is staying, I'm staying. I'm going to protect her – at all costs."

"Now that's a switch, viejo." Last time, he'd leveraged my mother against me, threatening to kill her if I didn't turn myself over to the Galactacops.

Frank laughs. "It's better this way, don't you think?" Inside the room, all the girls start giggling. Frank smiles past the camera, and it chills my heart. I can't help it. This is my family he's trying to become part of. His eyes look happy when he says, "Tell Brill I forgive him." He must see something hard in my face, because his smile dims a few watts. "Mercy and forgiveness are related, Bo."

We're not talking about Brill anymore.

"Let me talk to Mamá." My voice cracks.

Frank looks at me like he didn't expect that. Pero, without comment, he gestures Mamá onto the balcony and goes back inside. I hear him make a lame joke and the girls laugh.

"Cómo?" I ask Mamá. "How am I supposed to take your advice?"

Her eyes soften. She looks back into the room that I can't see, where Frank is still joking with the girls. Mi hermano Mario laughs. Somehow, even he has accepted Frank, though he only knows that Frank works for HGB and threatened Mamá. Not that Frank killed Papá.

Mamá says, "You have the biggest heart of anyone I know, mija. Always have."

"Mamá, you couldn't even forgive *me* when you thought I stole your fiancé. What Frank did is so much bigger than that. So how?"

Mamá sighs. "It is not that I did not forgive you. Whatever was happening in your life that got you to that point–" She means the wild parties, the DWIs, the frustangerated FeedCasts, all of which embarrass me now, "–and then whatever really did happen with Hugo – I felt like I had driven you there. You had pulled away from me. I had failed, as a parent, and as an amiga – and my own fiancé had made me feel so old. And I did not know how to face any of that. So I responded to your anger with my own. Lo siento."

I stare at her in shock. "Mamá."

She's done opening up, shifts the topic back to Frank. "Look at it this way, mija. The two men I have loved were on opposite sides of the war." She's talking about the First Contact War, implying that it never really ended, because not everyone accepted the outcome. Even now, there's a fragile balance between HGB's power and anger at their abuse of it that could easily rip Earth apart again. "When I was young, everyone's friendships y familias fractured over something as estúpido as chocolate. Pero, once it was over, the ones left alive had to figure out how to fit back into each other's lives. I do not know what the right side is here, but I do know that whatever Frank has done, he honestly believes it was necessary to keep Earth safe. And I honestly believe that you have done the same."

I try to imagine Mamá as a child during the war. She's a few years younger than Frank, so it wouldn't have been her amigos fighting, pero, I know mi abuelita played some part in it. It obviously affected Mamá more than she has ever let on.

"I will think on that, Mamá."

The minute I hang up, Chestla hands me a broom.

I'm still trying to sort my emotions. I manage to crack a smile I don't feel as I look at the spotless floor. "I know the down time in space can get boring, chica, pero Brill's a neat freak. We don't need to clean."

Chestla rolls her eyes. "Since you refuse to carry a weapon, I need to teach you to defend yourself with whatever's at hand. Take that and try to hit me with it."

Like in the cheeseball training montage scenes from every action movie I've ever seen. "Two sessions on board this ship is not going to turn me into a Jedi." We'd watched *Star Wars* together once, and she'd mentioned then how improbable that kind of instant progress is. Pero, I do have this frustangeration with nowhere to go. I adjust the broom so that I'm holding it more like a light sabre – or, even better, a piñata bat. "Wait. Where are Tawny's camera drones?"

I imagine the electronics bursting out of one of those like tiny bits of candy. Satisfying, no?

"Don't paint me as your Obi-Wan." Chestla steps towards me. "I'm supposed to protect you, not turn you into me. I just need you to be able to help me do my job, because on Evevron, my skills may not be enough."

"We were just on Zant," I protest. "How much worse can it be?"

Chestla takes the broom away, pivots behind me and strikes the back of my knees. I fall on my butt and she throws the broom at me. I roll away, and it clatters to the floor.

Brill's out of his chair, across the room, helping me up. "If I help out, can I get a note for Frank saying you trained me?"

His eyes are violet with the humor of it, pero Chestla smiles predatorily. "Even better. Try to hit Brill."

He gives me a look like, *You wouldn't, would you*?

I look at Chestla. "He's Krom. Eso es imposible."

"Is it?" She picks up the broom.

"Hest!" *Hey!* "I was joking. Frank would never give me credit anyway." He retreats so fast the motion is a blur. "I'm not going to hit a girl."

Chestla says, "You sounded serious enough to me."

Five minutes later, Brill's on his back, one of Chestla's boots on his chest. She points at him, pero she's looking at me. "It's all about patterns, figuring out where the target is going to be."

"Can I get up now?" Brill asks.

"I'm never going to be able to do that," I protest.

"Then how would you use the principle for defense? How

could Brill have avoided me catching him?"

"Seriously," Brill says. "This is embarrassing."

"Then get up."

"*Haza.*" *Fine.* Brill elbows Chestla in the back of the knee, so lightning fast she doesn't even brace for it. He uses her lack of balance to push her away from him, then rolls to his feet.

She stumbles, pero doesn't fall.

In Brill's place, I'd have still been on the ground. I really should have said no to going to Evevron.

Brill's studying the broom. "Patterns, huh." Then he asks, "Can I borrow your phone for a minute, Babe?"

He makes a voice call, while Chestla gives me the broom again. I never manage to hit anything except a box of cargo, and the stink of fermented fish fills the cabin. Chestla coughs.

Brill squints as he holds up my handheld. He looks wistfully at Chestla, who is taking the ultra-expensive box towards the trash chute. "Geckh. That stuff is illegal on a lot of planets for a reason. It's going to be in the air filters forever. But good news, Gavin has a lead on the ship Kaliel stole."

Gavin is Brill's closest friend. He's not the most reputable kind of guy, pero mi vida has good reason to trust him. "That's muy bueno."

"You'd think so. The place he wants us to meet him is a ship graveyard."

My heart clenches. Something bad must have happened for Kaliel's ship to end up there. "Kaliel's muerto, no?"

"No." Brill hesitates. "At least if he is, the body isn't there. We'll be there soon, and we'll figure out more."

I'm tense, and there's nothing I can do here but wait. Pero, I can't just sit, especially not so close to the fish-smell. I retreat into the galley. Brill's got some high quality Krom wine chilling in the fridge, and some vegetarian protein blocks. I can at least make something Gavin might be willing to eat – something portable, since it's too fish-smelly to stay inside the ship. He's much more of a strict vegetarian than Brill, more into Krom culture and traditions. And he was horrified the first time Brill expected him to eat food prepared by an Earthling.

I am never going to be his favorite person, pero Gavin seems more willing to tolerate me since that time I helped Brill save his life.

When we get to the wrecking yard, I wrap the abandt – the Krom version of a riceball or sandwich – individually, while Brill's balancing the atmo and opening the doors. Tawny's sending her camera drones with us, pero she's refusing to leave the ship.

I have never been on an asteroid as bare as this one. Half of the derelicts were simply crashed onto it.

In the middle of all the ruin and spare parts, there's a pristine black cruiser. Gavin is leaning back against it, squinting at us. He has lightly hooded eyes and a thinner frame than Brill, so while he could still pass for human, the impression I get is of a Hadvaxian stick frog.

"Took you long enough." He says it sarcastically, pero his grin and the way his eyes are shifting to a light lavender mean he's trying to be cómico.

"Here, mijo. This should make up for it." I toss him one of the abandt.

He catches it easily and unwraps a corner. "Everything in this come out of Brill's stores? Nothing off Zant?"

I'm not even offended anymore. At least this time he didn't ask if I'm sure it's vegetarian.

Pero his logic fails me here. Brill's a gray trader who buys things from all over the galaxy. Who knows where the stuff in his stores comes from? I shrug. "I didn't bring anything on board."

Gavin takes a bite, and his eyes shade towards blissful blue. I take the subtle compliment.

Brill runs his hand along the sleek hull. Zantites build beautiful ships, and this one has edging that looks like real gold. "Have you cracked into this thing yet?"

"Wal, su. He stripped it. Check out the engine." Gavin finishes the abandt and turns. He bangs his fist against the edge of a hatch, and a long section of the ship's side falls open. I know nada about ship engines, pero I can still tell that this mass of rust and disconnected cables doesn't belong inside.

Brill groans. "He's got a fast engine inside something that looks like a wreck. Great."

"It is great," Chestla says. She moves forward, leaning into the hatch, pulling on the rusted parts. Do Evevrons need tetanus shots? Ni idea. "If he had just tossed this engine instead of trying to hide it, we wouldn't be able to tell what he's driving now." She pulls out her phone to snap a picture. Within about a minute, she's got a holographic representation of the ship the engine belonged to popped up and spinning above her hand. Claro está, it is rendered with the optimism of a blue-book entry.

"Right." Brill looks at Chestla appreciatively. "Now just imagine that it's old and beat up."

"I'll check for sightings," Gavin says, at the same time Chestla – who speaks more rapidly – says, "I can crack through to look for customs hits showing records of entry."

I sigh. What am I supposed to do? I'm the one who wanted to go looking for Kaliel, pero I might as well have stayed on Brill's ship and dried the dishes.

There's a loud hiss overhead, and when I look up, a saucer's arcing down out of the sky.

"Perfect," Brill says. "Tyson's here."

Which means that in just a minute, every Galactacop on this side of the galaxy is going to have our same lead. Only, Chestla leans back into the engine hatch and rips something out of it. The piece is big in her hands. She points out a logo for a brand name I can't read, followed by Sraksian-style numbers. "This will help us keep ahead."

"Tyson? Didn't that guy bite you once?" Gavin asks.

I nod. "We're friends now."

"We have to go *now*," Chestla says, gesturing towards Brill's ship with her chin.

"Wal," Brill and Gavin say at the same time.

Oye! Am I really the only one feeling weird about taking the part with the engine numbers, so Tyson can't make the same logic leap Chestla did? It's tampering with evidence. Claro está, we've made a bet with the cops. I guess that changes the rules, no?

Gavin points towards his ship. It's almost the same design as Brill's. "Send me a spoof of your signature, then when we both take off, he'll have a hard time figuring out who to follow."

"Thanks, su." Brill gives his friend a close-fisted salute. "True heart and safe journey until we meet again."

Gavin returns the gesture, pero with a troubled frown. "Don't act like we're not going to talk, su. I'll have information for you before you even have time to miss me."

Brill shrugs. "Just wanted you to know how much I appreciate the help."

"This is getting heavy," Chestla says.

"Hanstral." *Sorry.* Brill dashes around her to unlock the door. Chestla bounds inside and dumps the metal piece in the middle of the floor.

I rush to follow. We're inside – and only mildly choking on fish-fumes – by the time Tyson's saucer touches dirt planetside. He comes running towards us just as Brill punches the thrusters, and we're taking off straight up, while he's standing there, shaking a fist at us.

"Why's he mad, mi vida?"

"He knows we took something. If he's not going to honor the spirit of the bet, he could arrest us for stealing evidence."

Tyson has to choose between our ship and Gavin's, and for once he must have chosen wrong, because nothing is showing up on our sensors. A little while later, my handheld rings again, from where Brill left it up on the console panel. I assume it's Tyson. I move to get it, pero Brill beats me there.

"It's probably for me, Babe. I gave some of my contacts this number."

I turn back to Chestla, pero her phone dings off an alert, too. She looks up at me, excitement glinting in her slit-pupiled eyes. "Kaliel just pawned a couple of pieces off his trashed ship."

"You know this how?" I lean in, looking at the display, which is showing a flat list of numbers and letters. The numbers are the only things I can read.

"If it's a legit shop, Babe, the numbers have to be registered. Part of the Galactacop initiatives to stop space piracy." Brill's still on my phone, trying to follow both conversations. He gives up and hangs up. "Since Kaliel's ship's not stolen, it's not going to ping as a bad sale."

Chestla says, "I put a flag in the Galactacop database, so it would ping anything involving his name. But he didn't take cash. Which means he used the credit to buy something else."

"What was it?" I ask.

Chestla says, "They don't have to report that part."

My phone rings again. This time it is Tyson. "Tell Brill tat his friend Gavin is about to be charged wit impeding a police investigation."

My heart sinks. Gavin won't resist – part of the whole Krom take responsibility for their actions thing – so he's not in any danger. Pero, he's really good at getting information. It would be hard to do this without him.

I ask Tyson, "You have the whole police force as an information network, no? Do you think it's fair to take one of my few pieces off the board?"

He sucks his mouth inside itself, thinking. No lo sé

how he does that without hitting his folded-in fangs, pero Myska are immune to their own venom, which is bueno when you imagine a lounge of Myska kids having the usual playground fights.

Tyson sigh-hisses. "I guess I could let him go wit a warning. Te rest of his rap sheet is relatively harmless."

"Oh?" I would love to know what is in Gavin's file.

Tyson laughs. "Uh uh. Ask him yourself, if you want to know."

CHAPTER TWENTY

I take a good look at my phone. There's screens' worth of new apps and info. It's such a personal kind of merge – my data with Brill's. He's giving me access to a lot.

I could be reading more into this than he means.

At any rate, now I have Gavin's contact info. I go to text him a thank-you for helping us out. Only, there's something new in the drafts folder. I open it up.

Johansson headed for Yend. Get there first and we both keep Bo safe. Maybe split the reward? It's addressed to Tyson.

"Mi vida?" My voice comes out tight. "You can explain this, no?"

He glances at the phone and winces. "I thought I deleted that."

Chestla leans in and glances at the screen. "Nice strategy. Throw the race to get rid of your romantic rival and profit in the process. You have no guarantee that Tyson's going to kill the guy, though."

"You approve of that?" I splutter.

"I didn't send it," Brill says.

"Things like that happen in court intrigue all the time. Guardian Companions live by a more honest code, but it's not like we don't enjoy watching the game." Chestla shrugs. She must be confident in my recommendation for being a Guardian, if she's already referring to herself as one. "You give your guy reason to be jealous, he's going to act on it."

Brill's eyes go an embarrassed pink. "I didn't send it, because Bo is right. Dork Face doesn't have any reason for attacking a bunch of Zantites – that we know of. If there is a reason, I'd like to hear it."

"Fair enough," Chestla says.

"It turned out to be a bad lead anyway. That's all I'd need – Tyson thinking I'd tricked him." Brill lets his eyes go gray, emphasizing the seriousness of his words. "Do you have any idea what he might do to me?"

"Not much, mi vida." I delete the draft, then point at him with the phone. "Tyson's the most honor-bound Galactacop I know."

Brill snorts a laugh. "He puts up a good front. But I've known that kek longer than you have."

My heart squeezes in sympathy for the look on his face. "He hurt you?"

Brill shakes his cabeza. "Ga. Not me exactly."

Pero, he doesn't offer anything else, and I'm not going to push. The silence gets uncomfortable, so I go over to the sofa and finish my text to Gavin.

Gavin does not reply.

I check in on Mamá. She and Minda are preparing to shoot another show. They don't have a set prepared yet, so they are in Minda's apartment, holocasting from her sofa. They're screening one of Minda's Zandywood spectaculars, and talking together about what made it great – from both a Zantite and Earthling point of view. The polls show the Zantites are loving it.

Maybe this isn't hopeless after all.

There's nothing to do on this starship but wait. I don't know where else to look for Kayla in the present, so I start looking in her past. Her public archive isn't a FeedCast, exactly. More a collection of home-holos and oral history interviews meant for her friends. It isn't fully public, either. She's afraid her tech-paranoid parents will find it.

Maybe somewhere she mentioned un amigo I don't know, or a place she might have gone to feel safe.

She gave me the link a long time ago, pero I never took the time to look at most of it.

The most popular clip in her list is titled *Playing Anastasia*. I pop it up. The opening is a pan over yards and yards of pink chiffon laid out on a table, covered with a couple of packs of sew-on sparkle jewels. Teenaged Kayla is giving a voice-over.

"Today we're making a Romanov-style dress. When I first heard about this project, I wanted to cover Cinderella, but my gran convinced me there never was a real, historical Cinderella, and that since the point here is to explore history, picking apart a folktale is missing the point. My middle name is Anastasia, and I've always loved to read, so I went through this whole period obsessing over the Romanovs. Anastasia was the princess everyone loved – even the guards holding her family prisoner. After the royal family was executed, rumors grew that she had escaped. These rumors caught the popular imagination and were explored in both novels and films, which many people still prefer over grittier history, even after it was proven that the body left behind actually was Anastasia's. In the words of my gran..."

The holo shifts to a gray-haired woman with sun-tanned, almost leathery skin. Pale stripes on her arms mark where the sleeves of her current shirt are shorter than whatever she wore when she got the tan. "Why do they have to go ruining a perfectly good story with DNA evidence? In my mind, Nastya survived. Why? Because being able to believe, that gave people hope. And right now, hope's what we all need."

"Me too, abuelita," I tell the holo, even as she disappears.

Chestla puts a hand on my shoulder, and I pause the holo. She hands me a mug of coffee brewed so thick it's practically mud. I need the caffeine and the comforting warmth so badly right now, I tell her, "Gracias. This is perfect."

She sits at the table, opposite me. "What are you going to do if Kayla is with Kaliel when we find him?"

I take a long slug of caffeinated mud, and not even the room's fish smell can dull my enjoyment of it. "That depends on whether she's helping him, or she's a prisoner. And whether there's a reason for all this."

Chestla stretches her hands out flat against the table's surface. "Do you remember the time Kayla rescued that dupu with the broken wing, back at school?"

I grin. "She kept that thing in our bathtub for two days, until the vet's office opened. The first night, she sat with it for hours, just petting it."

Chestla grins back. "I wonder why she chose cooking school instead of veterinary school. She always struck me as more of a healer."

Eh? Aside from that one time, I can't think of Kayla being anything other than feisty or opinionated. "She told me she decided on Allocogon because she could double-major in intragalactic linguistics. She got into languages early, pero she didn't want to specialize in something that was only useful if she stayed on at a university." What she'd actually said was she didn't want to give her mother the satisfaction. She's always resented her mamá taking so many different fellowships, which may be one reason she was so much closer to her abuelita. "Pero, she was always best in class when it came to decorating cupcakes or making garnishes. It will be easy for her finding a job where she gets to be creative like that."

Assuming she's OK, wherever she is. Because it's hard to mix up pink frosting if you're muerta. Chestla reads the change in my face, because she says fiercely, "She's going to get the chance to make all the cupcakes she wants."

I nod, take another long sip of coffee. "I'm more worried about what we do if we don't find her with Kaliel."

"You know what we don't do?" Chestla smacks both her fists on the table. "We don't give up."

Tawny's voice comes through from the door to her room. "Can you do that again, but look up a little more at the end?"

Chestla bares her teeth at the ceiling. I cannot wait until we can find Tawny a ride home.

CHAPTER TWENTY-ONE

A few hours later, Chestla says, "Kaliel's ship number just pinged in a landing request on Aspeld. That's close."

"I'll call Gavin," Brill says. "He knows everybody. Or somebody who knows everybody. See if he can bribe someone to stall the landing request."

I only half-hear him. Aspeld sounds familiar. I'm trying to place it. Didn't Mamá do a cooking special there once?

I take out my phone to look it up.

One new app is a newswire service that keeps sending notifications on stories Brill's following. It pops up a headline *Attack on New Cacao Plantation*.

The FeedCaster is a frowning Krom in a black sweater. He speaks without intonation, lacking the usual popjoy for his subject. "This morning, a trade vessel was granted opportunity to land at Catha, site of the Nilka's new colony, set up for the singular purpose of growing cacao. There was one soul on board not listed on the manifest, one angry, displaced Earthling. This is what security feeds captured when the Earthling then snuck from the ship to the cacao plantation."

The holo gritcasts a woman dressed in black approaching the edge of a walled area. She's carrying a pair of garden shears. She makes it over the wall, pero the holofield splits, showing she's set off a silent alarm, which sends half a dozen armed guards running through the building, popping open the door to get outside. Nilka are deceptively fragile-looking, built like humanoid butterflies with both a proboscis and a mouth. They're actually one of the most feartastic species in the galaxy. And they can fly.

Their gossamer wings, silver and yellow and white, float them like kites towards the woman, who is kneeling in the dirt, closing her clippers around the base of one of the cacao saplings, which is maybe a foot and a half tall. The sapling topples into the dirt just as a Nilka drops out of the sky, bowling her backwards. There's an interrogation. It only takes a few minutes, and afterwards, that same Nilka picks up the garden clippers. His body blocks the camera, pero when he steps away, the woman is muerta, the clippers sticking out of her chest.

The Kromarazzi reappears. "The woman claimed to have been working alone, but early reports suggest the Nilka suspect Earth Corporation HGB to have had a hand in this sabotage, in an attempt to regain their monopoly on chocolate. Without proof though, the Nilka will likely refrain from retaliation."

The other new cacao plantation is on Krom. Thinking about what could happen between my people and Brill's if HGB sent someone to Krom to try to destroy those cacao plants makes mi cabeza ache. Claro está, the Krom always manage to return invaders unharmed. It's kind of their thing.

Then the numbers three – two – one poofbang into the holofield, and the whole thing vanishes, including the link to get back to it.

What kind of news service is this? I doubt this story will appear on the regular newscasts.

Chestla comes close and I get an echo of the prey response. She says, "I hate that service. You never get to watch the good stuff twice."

"I usually don't watch this kind of stuff once, chica," I tell her.

"That's right." She drops her voice to a whisper, her teeth

coming close to my ear to avoid Tawny's eavesdropping, pero she still sounds a bit miffed. "You told me you weren't looking into Kaliel being setup anymore. He didn't care who tried to have him killed to cover up whatever was going on with that Senior cruiser. So you wanted to just let it go. Only now he's important again, so maybe that information's not completely irrelevant."

I whisper back, "I thought we decided the attack was against HGB. That someone must have been trying to break public opinion about the megacorp's right to control chocolate, if they can't control their own pilots."

"Let me show you something somewhere a little quieter." Chestla casts a meaningful look at Tawny's door, then pulls me into her cabin and takes out a device to scan for bugs. She plucks a nearly invisible camera off the wall and squashes it. Then she pulls up a holo. "I've almost cracked who hired the mercenaries who killed Kayla's grandparents."

My eyes go wide. Was this about Kayla? Had we been completely wrong about it being an attack on HGB? That makes absolutely no sense. Kayla's a nobody. And so were her grandparents. And yet, she had disappeared. Could Kayla have been in some kind of trouble that we didn't know about?

I can't help remember what Frank said, about the possibility that Kaliel might have been working with these guys. I consider fitting him into this holo, a subsidiary part of the bad-guy crew. Pero, I can't. That's just not the Kaliel I had gotten to know.

Besides, he'd come close to getting shaved for his part in the SeniorLeisure incident. He wouldn't have taken a suicide mission. He's not the type of person to just throw his life away.

Which makes what he's doing now just that much harder to understand.

Brill had told me to get Chestla to stop looking into this. I should stop her right here. Pero, I can't look away from the holo of the interior of a crowded bar. "Which one of these guys tricked Kaliel into taking that shot?"

Chestla points at the gritcast. "This guy. Here he's walking into a bar on Plektar and accepting a check from someone whose face never appears on camera, four days before the SeniorLeisure incident." Plektar's the planet where Earth first applied for membership in the Galactic Court, and the bartender's a twelve-tentacled native, with beer mugs in four of her "hands."

One customer is paying for his drink with a bar of HGB dark, which still trades at a more valuable rate than Earth cash. Yet another reason not to mention it's been infused with Serum Green.

Pero, that customer's not the feedclip's focus. It's a guy with a face that looks rough and rocky, patched black and gray. Like he's half-made of countertop material. He's wearing a buttery matt-gray leather jacket and black pants with tailored lace-up dress shoes. Chestla says, "The ship is called the *Onyx Shadow*, and that guy there with the granite skin condition is Grundt." The camera image shifts, panning towards the door. "The girl in the green – that's Junk. I'm pretty sure that's not her real name. The tough guy in black is Flip."

My chest goes frío. This information is dangerous. Those people are dangerous.

What if Tawny still has a way to overhear us? Knowing too much is a great way to get on HGB's most wanted dead list.

I force myself to breathe. Would HGB even care that Chestla's unraveling who hired a bunch of thugs to frame one of their pilots? Their reputation was hurt by everything that happened, and it dropped their public opinion in the media polls to the point where the revolutionaries who oppose their concentrated power are more openly calling for war. Surely, HGB is trying to figure out who framed Kaliel too.

Pero, they don't like people digging into their business. Mi papá died for doing just that. And now Brill wants me to stop, so that I'll be safe.

Pero, I'm pretty sure I'm already past that point. HGB knows I've uncovered some of their secrets. Like he said, I'm only alive because I'm useful to them on this tour. I need to find a way to change the status quo – before we get to the capital.

I might uncover something useful enough to keep me alive. If not, they can only execute you once, no?

After making damn sure there's not another bug on my clothes, I tell Chestla, "Frank has admitted he killed Papá and took back vials of Serum Green, and what I'm calling Serum Yellow. Pero, we still know nada about the tainted chocolate that Papá was looking for."

"Serum Yellow?"

"Ni idea. Frank didn't know what it was either. Pero that chocolate has to be the same as what we found in the warehouse. All those tons of it, all laced with Pure275. Why would anyone put such a selective herbicide in food? A human would have to eat a lot of it, over a period of time, to die from poisoning. Pero, if it got into the batch by mistake, why not just destroy it?"

"It was all marked like it was supposed to be destroyed." Chestla shrugs. "Maybe it wasn't meant to target humans. Maybe it was meant for some other species who's more susceptible. And whoever was going to use it chickened out, because it's the kind of thing that can get you sanctioned by the Galactic Court."

"You mean there's a planet with people who are genetically similar to cacao trees?"

Chestla scrunches up her nose. "Not like that. Not necessarily. But was there anyone who was a threat to Earth before this invasion fleet showed up?"

"Not that I know of, chica. Pero, who'd tell me?"

She gestures towards my phone. "Frank, maybe? He showed up in HGB's tax payrolls in 2093. That was thirty-two years ago. He's got to be what, early fifties? He's been with them for more than half his life."

"Which is why he's not going to tell me anything. Pero, we do know that several boxes of the tainted chocolate got shipped to the SeniorLeisure vessel *CaptureVista* – the same ship Kaliel later got tricked into blowing up."

I believe that the herbicide and Serum Green were created by two different groups of people, even though we'd found them both in the same lab. One contained a poison, while the other had been carefully engineered to be non-toxic. One had been a completed product (the boxes of tainted chocolate marked for destruction, like they might have been an accident or a mistake), the other an additive (the vials of serum and their box completely unlabeled).

Which means they both can't have been created by HGB. Right?

My phone dings, with a headline from the regular news channel: *"Undocumented Earthling Lands on Krom. Misunderstanding Leads to Cultural Exchange."*

Did the Krom news network alert them to what had happened with the Nilka, so they could diffuse the situation? Or is the way they handle things in general just that much different?

Before I can discuss that with Brill, my sublingual rings. It's Mamá.

"Mija! Can Brill get us an interview with the Krom who just hit the newsfeeds?"

I blink. "Mamá! It's not like all Krom know each other."

"Pero Brill is famous now." She says it like that means people should give him anything he wants. "He has fans. If you cannot get the cultural exchange Krom, tal vez Brill will holo onto the show? We need to push this forward while we can. Minda is fighting so hard to bring peace."

I doubt Brill will go for that. He's not going to be happy that Tawny's been FeedCasting enough holo of him for him to even *be* famous.

"Cultural Exchange Krom, Mamá. What's the su's name?"

CHAPTER TWENTY-TWO

Brill says, "Gavin's contact could only delay the landing for so long, Kaliel's already on the ground."

Chestla asks, "What's the plan? Sit by his ship and wait until he comes back?"

"Pretty much." Brill is checking his gun. I give him a pleading look. His eyes turn an anxious gray, pero, he nods and puts it away in the locked compartment molded into his command chair.

I mean, en serio? What is the point here if he's just going to shoot Kaliel?

We have to save the loco pilot and figure out why he's been acting so erratically. We need the Zantites to understand his actions, because right now Kaliel's a stand-in in their minds for all of Earth. He has to live long enough to confess, or apologize, or explain the mistake. And preferably keep breathing after that.

Otherwise, we might as well have just let Tyson take him back to Zant.

"What about Kayla?" I ask softly. "Is she here?"

Brill looks at me, his eyes turning a sympathetic pale topaz. "Ven let's go over there and see if we can find evidence of her having been on board."

"Gracias, mi vida." I hurry him outside, pero I find myself walking slowly across the spaceport, even more so when the battered version of the ship Chestla had showed us comes into view. I've been fighting for evidence of what had happened to Kayla – and now I'm terrified of what I'm about to find.

Some spaceports are high-tech wonders. This is just a paved area surrounded by fences. It's a riot of smells – food and refuse, and whatever animals they're raising on the other side of the fences. There's no way Tawny was getting out here, either.

Chestla looks pale. I ask her, "Are you OK?"

She brings a hand up to her face, covering her nose. "It's overwhelming my sense of smell. I can't think straight."

Brill pulls out a lock-killer device. Mi vida's eyes are stormclouds as he looks back at me. "Promise you'll stay back if we are going in here unarmed."

"Be careful," I say softly.

He drops the lock-killer on the door and disappears inside. After a few minutes he calls back at us, "Diay. Come on in."

Chestla and I move inside the ship. Brill knocks on a door at the back of the space. There is a solid metal clang. "This leads to the cargo hold we saw on the schematics. It's too thick to break and these physical locks will take a while. But unless she's been staying in there, I don't see anything that says Kayla's been here."

There's a single cabin, with the door open. The bunk is made. From what I can tell, there's not much evidence that *anyone* has been staying here.

"You don't see two black travel mugs, or two black trash cans, or two black stereo speakers, do you? Somebody found a receipt that he bought two black somethings. It's all over the bounty hunter forums." Chestla moves into the galley, which looks completely nonfunctional. The range has caved in. If it even turns on, it's an explosion waiting to happen.

He could be eating rations or granola bars. There are a few wrappers in the trash, pero I don't see a big stash of anything.

I remember a conversation Kaliel and I had right after we first met about the best restaurants in Rio. Kaliel's a foodie. I bet he doesn't like rations. He's probably stopping so frequently because he can't cook here and needs food.

That doesn't help us figure out what else he's doing, though.

Chestla's phone rings. She answers it immediately. Eugene blinks back at her. He's hiding under a desk, his hand two inches from the wheels of his rolling office chair.

Eugene is the researcher Chestla was trapped in the rainforest with, while HGB was hunting her. He also helped us analyze both Serum Green and the chocolate laced with Pure275. He's pretty hot from his work in the rainforest, pero he is Earth's biggest nerd. And he is not supposed to be continuing his work in that lab. HGB forgot about him. Nobody wants to remind them.

Eugene whispers, "Somebody just broke in. What do I do?"

Chestla whispers back, "You stay out of sight. Don't call HGB. Don't call the police. Don't be a hero." Eugene nods. He looks terrified. Chestla asks, "What are they doing now?"

Eugene pulls at the collar of his shirt. "They're stealing the poisoned chocolate. Case after case."

Brill says, "HGB is probably moving it. They've done that before."

Chestla nods, and some of the tension goes out of her frame.

Brill leans out the ship's doorway. "Kaliel's coming back."

She whispers to Eugene, "It's their rainforest and their building. They have the right to shoot you, so stay hidden, and I'll call you back when I get a chance."

"Are you in the middle of something?" Eugene asks.

"Kind of. Yeah. You better stay safe." Chestla hangs up.

The three of us leave the ship.

Chestla says, "I'm going to see if I can find out what's going on. Eugene's a sweetheart, but he is not capable of taking care of himself."

She takes her phone and heads for an area with slightly fresher air.

I spot Kaliel on the far edge of the open-air spaceport. He's moving this way, carrying an oversized shopping bag in each hand. He's looking at the ships he's passing, hasn't noticed us yet.

"Mi vida," I whisper, putting a hand on Brill's arm. "What do we do?"

Brill gestures around the side of the ship, and the two of us start edging out of sight. We're watching Kaliel more than where we are going. He's getting close.

And, I realize, so is Tyson. And about a dozen bounty hunters, all ranged strategically to keep sight of Kaliel's front door.

As I squeeze up against the ship's side, a hand comes around my mouth and something frío presses into my neck. I let out a soft, involuntary squeak. Whoever grabbed me had been hiding in a divot formed by one of the ship's thrusters.

"Jack," Brill says. As in the space pirate who tried to kill us aboard the Zantite warship not long ago.

Brill freezes as two of Jack's henchpirates roll out from under the ship, training their weapons on him. Mi vida could flitdash. A Krom can outrun any bullet he sees coming, no?

Pero, we both know that if he did that, then Jack would shoot me.

My heart's hammering as time turns to goo while my brain processes that horror-heavy thought and I try not to picture myself crumpling at the pirate's feet.

Brill raises his hands in surrender. "Avell, don't hurt her."

The hairs on the back of my neck rise in a familiar prey response. I glance up. Out of the corner of my eye, I see Chestla moving silently across Kaliel's ship's roof.

Jack clears his throat. Though I can't see his face, I can still remember what it looks like. Deeply tanned, with short dark hair and deceptively friendly warm brown eyes. "Drop all your weapons."

Brill shrugs. "I'm unarmed, su. Kaliel's a friend, and we didn't want him to get the wrong idea."

"You expect me to believe that?" Jack moves around me, keeping the gun at my neck. He takes a good look at Brill's jacket, which is all scratched up from the explosion. It's the same one Jeska stole off Jack back aboard the *Layla's Pride*. He eyes mi vida. "And you haven't even been taking good care of it."

Brill straightens the cuffs, pulling the leather down over the proximity bracelet that tethers him to his ship. Then he zips it all the way up to his neck. "Does that mean you care enough not to put a hole in it? Because I'd appreciate the consideration."

"I'll have to think on that one." Jack admonishes his henchpirates, "Grab the Krom and make sure he can't run."

"What is it, Jack?" Brill's eyes are still that no-care-in-the-world blue, which means he's hiding being terrified. A henchpirate takes him by each arm. "You must want something more than just Kaliel's bounty, uan neither Bo or I would still be breathing."

Now that he knows Brill can't just grabsnatch me, Jack relaxes the gun away from my neck. It's still pointed in my general direction. Chestla's right above him, looking ready to tackle him as soon as she's got an opening.

Jack says, "I want you to lure in Gavin. That little snot took something from me, and I want it back."

Kaliel looks towards the entrance to his ship. We're not exactly hiding. When he spots us, he drops the shopping bags, and there's the crystalline sound of shattering glass. Then he pulls a long cylinder, like an oversized flashlight, out of his jacket, and crouches, smashing it against the ground.

Brill flinches before anyone else can react, pero his captors keep him from ducking. Chestla leaps, pero she's not aiming for Jack. She lands on me, knocking me flat on my back as a blinding flash of light passes by in a ring, about four feet high. Everyone it touches collapses.

Brill has gone down with both of his captors on top of him.

"No!" I try to move toward him.

"He's not dead," Chestla says as she gets up and turns towards Kaliel, who was kneeling under ring-level.

Kaliel makes eye contact with me, then he flitdashes for his ship, getting there just before Chestla does. She makes a grab for him, and he kicks her off balance. This time she does fall. He slams the door in her face. All she can do is back away as his engines go live and he takes off.

I pull Brill out from under the henchpirates. He's not breathing, pero, that's not uncommon in an unconscious Krom. His hummingbird heartbeat is normal.

Jack fell on his vapgun, and the corrosive blue liquid is all over his new jacket. We should probably get the jacket off him. He is not going to be happy.

Chestla walks over to me, dusting off her pants. "Can you fly Brill's ship?"

I nod. Brill has given me a few lessons. "Well enough to get off an open-air spaceport. Not well enough to chase anybody."

"Good. Go get his ship, while I get these pirates turned in to the proper authorities.

CHAPTER TWENTY-THREE

Once he's conscious, Brill takes over flying the *Fois Gras*. Chestla and I take turns telling him what happened.

Tawny, who's come out of her room for once, says, "You should just let him watch the holo. It's not like anyone else can see it."

Because, of course, it's showing more Earthlings behaving badly.

Tawny crosses to the galley, grabs a bottle of wine and takes it back to her room.

When he sees the clip of Chestla leaping off that roof, Brill's eyes go blue-green. He whispers, "I should keep sparring with her, only I still feel like a kek trying to hit a girl."

Chestla says, "I'm taking that as permission."

Once we get to the part where Kaliel escapes, Brill lets out a noise of frustration. "Jack's a kek. If he'd waited until we'd captured Kaliel, we wouldn't still be doing this."

"Mi vida," I say softly. "If he'd done that, then we never would have gotten away."

Pero, Brill's right. We're volver a empezar desde cero. *Starting over from scratch.* And we have to wait for Kaliel to show up again. If he ditches that ship now that he knows we've seen it, it's going to be even more complicated to find him.

"What was in the bags?" Brill asks Chestla.

She shrugs. "Couldn't tell. It was all smashed up. Whatever

it had been involved glass and copper."

"Glass and copper and two black somethings," Brill muses. "Ven. What does that add up to?"

My handheld rings. It's Tyson. Brill and I look at each other. After leaving him unconscious, neither one of us are particularly fizzbounced to answer it.

The Myska and I may be friends, pero on some levels I'm still terrified of him. I've always feared snakes, even before he bit me. He had delivered a mostly dry bite, intentionally holding back the full intensity of his venom. I had still nearly died, running from him before I'd gotten the antivenin.

And now, he's bound to be angry.

"Fine, mi vida. It is my phone."

Tyson's smiling in the image. "Tank you for te gift, Bo. I'm not sure I should accept it, but I appreciate te gesture."

I smile back, though I'm confused. "Que?"

Chestla moves into the capture field with me. She puts a hand on my wrist. "I put your name on the paperwork when I turned in Jack Wolfe and his crew, crediting Tyson for assisting in the capture. Do you know how much the bounty on those four was worth? You guys get to split it fifty-fifty, in case you need to buy anything to catch up with Kaliel." She looks over at Brill. "Keeps it fair. I got the idea from your text draft."

Tyson smiles, his lips stretching wide. "Just so it's clear, you're not buying my loyalty. I support te law. In fact, I should hang up. I have a criminal to catch."

Brill asks, "What would you spend it on, Babe? If your part of the bounty was going to poof away if you didn't?"

He means for it to be a fun question. Pero, I look down at my nails. The polish has chipped, leaving parts of the puce green visible. *Recovered health. Peace for my world.* "The things I want you can't just buy."

His eyes shift through half a dozen colors, settling on a light green. Flirtation. Then before he speaks, a shift to gold. "You can't buy what I want either."

Giddy little bubbles float through me. He's hot. He's smart. And he loves me. "Que? What do you want?"

He looks so serious. My heart starts flutter-beating and my hands turn to ice. Is he going to propose?

Pero, the gold clouds a little. "If anything were possible? I want us to grow old together."

"Mi vida." He's cut me to the heart, and my chest is caving in around the empty space. An average Krom lifespan tops three hundred years. Three times mine. He's asking for the one thing I can't give.

"I'm serious. Wal, it might be fun to blow all that cash on a speedboat or a balloon trip through the alps, but I've heard rumors of anti-aging treatments that actually work." I'm not sure he understands the exchange rate to Earth currency. With what we've been given we could do both of those things, twenty times over. "And rumors the grain called the Fountain of Youth might still exist. With the kind of money you just got – we could go looking for it."

"And if we did all that and it didn't work, wasn't real? What then?"

"Then at least I would have tried." The gold in his eyes has enough upset brown bleeding in to turn them mahogany.

He's so focused on our relationship being fair – first wanting to end his own life early to pair with mine, now wanting to find a way for my life span to match his – will he be able to deal with something that ultimately won't be fair?

If I had been Krom, he would have proposed just now, no?

The fact that I'm not is not something either of us can change.

So I say, "Let's take whatever is left after we get back to Zant and go looking for this Fountain of Youth… or if you change your mind, we can blow it on some loco fun while we're both still young."

Brill laughs, and some of the brown does fade out of his eyes.

Frank must be watching for hits on my name, because he calls too. I start to hand it off to Brill, pero he pulls back his hands. "Ga. That one's not for me."

I answer the holocall. "Hola, viejo."

Frank looks behind me, sees Brill and Chestla watching and gives each of them a small nod. "Where's Tawny?"

"She's in her cabin. You want to talk to her?"

"Good God, no. I just want to know what the heck is going on out there. Are you and Tyson working together now?"

"Not exactly," I shrug. "It just sort of happened."

"I'm sure it's more complicated than that." Frank waits for me to add detail, pero when I don't, he clears his throat and says, "Your mom asked me to thank you for getting her that interview."

"De nada." I hadn't been able to get her the Krom involved in the cultural exchange, pero Brill had found a Krom family who had been rescued by Earthlings when life support on their ship had gotten fried. It had been a touching interview. As far as diplomacy goes, it probably has had more of an effect than anything I said on Minda's cooking show.

Now that the set's back together, they're still doing cooking segments, pero they've changed the format to allow for more variety.

"I spoke to Stephen, and to some Zantites who were there the night Kayla disappeared. The timing's all wrong. Kayla must have called Stephen when she left the club, not from the spaceport. I'm beginning to doubt she ever left this planet."

As his words sink in my heart sinks too. "You think she's dead?"

"Not necessarily. Leaving her phone at the spaceport and booking her a ticket is not the act of a mugger or random criminal. Is she worth anything to anyone?"

"There hasn't been a ransom demand, Mr Sawyer," Brill says.

I nod. "Her papá's a doctor, pero her mamá's a poet. They don't have the kind of dinero that would make something like that worth it."

Frank shakes his cabeza. "I don't mean money. I mean skills, information, anything worth taking her and keeping her alive."

My brow crinkles. "Like if they need a chef or a linguist? Same double-major like me. She's also good at sewing, and she reads a ton."

"Linguist, huh?" Frank rubs his chin. "I'll keep looking into it."

"Why are you doing this?" I can't help but ask. "Isn't it a little outside of your job description?"

"Ninety-seven percent of what I do is research and talking to people. I recover and protect things – and at times people. This is exactly my job description." He sighs. "I'm doing it for you because I always seem to be taking things away from you. And for once, maybe I can give you something back. Lavonda wants us to talk, but I don't want to come to you without an olive branch."

I look over at Brill, who nods. I tell Frank, "Why don't we talk now."

I head into the galley.

Frank says, "Lavonda says you want to get to know me. What do you want to know?"

I snort a laugh. "*She* wants me to get to know you. I don't think you'd like my questions."

"Try me."

My stomach fills with anxiety, even as I steel my resolve. There's one question I've been wanting to ask for a long time. "OK, viejo. What were mi papá's last words?"

Frank's cheeks and nose blush red. "He asked me not to hurt his family. He said, 'Mi familia knows nada about chocolate except how to eat it.' I'm sorry I couldn't even give him that much." He pauses. "I'm sorry I hurt you. But this whole mess – it's bigger than us."

There are tears in my eyes. I wipe them away. No lo sé what I expected Papá to have said, don't know why I'm so floored by it. "And you're still sure it was the right thing?"

Frank nods. There's no hesitation. "I'm not saying HGB is perfect. But there are things that have happened – things in Earth's past that very few people ever got to know about – that have proved to me that without strategic control of chocolate to give us allies and leverage, we're all going to wind up getting hurt."

"What kind of things?" I ask.

"The very fact you have to ask that question means I've been doing my job."

There's a loud thump from the main living area.

"What was that?" Frank asks.

I poke my head around the galley wall. Brill's on the floor again, and this time Chestla's got the broom poking at his back.

"Nada, viejo."

"I talked to that Aidan kid," Frank says.

My heart lurches. "Ay Dios mio."

I try not to picture the chef prodigy lifeless, though surely Frank's telling me he put a bullet in him.

"Good kid," Frank says. "Smart. A bit of a troublemaker, but bright enough not to cross any lines that would make his co-workers at the club want to eat him. You were right that he has nothing to do with Jimena. He could have quite a future."

Aidan Ace met Frank and is still alive. I let out a breath that is half-sigh, and Frank snorts a laugh.

"You really do think the worst of me, don't you? Sometimes a chat is just a chat. Most of the time, actually."

After I hang up, I sort through Brill's fridge, trying to find comfort by bringing order to my surroundings. Everything's been picked through, and the fresh stuff isn't going to last much longer. I start pulling out vegetables to make a soup. I still can't decide if anything Frank just said changes the way I feel about Mamá and him. Could I sit next to him at a family dinner? Dance with him at una fiesta? All the while knowing he once tried to shoot me?

CHAPTER TWENTY-FOUR

The ship's life support shifts on to recycle the air, and the smell of fermented fish gets pushed back out of the vents. It's fading, pero still enough to make my eyes water.

"Guys," Chestla says from over by the nav station. "You're not going to believe this."

"What?" Brill asks at the same moment I ask, "Que?"

She points at something on the nav array. "I am about ninety-six percent certain that is the engine signature for Kaliel's ship."

Brill's attention snaps to the nav. "He's not alone. Who are those other ships chasing him?"

Chestla says, "One of them is registered to a Tessa Gegg, one to Vinknet Vinkshou, and the third one has had the registration stripped."

Brill whips us around in a one-eighty, and the stabilizers fail entirely. I stumble sideways and smack into one of the bolted down chairs that had replaced the old ring bench at the dining table.

"Babe, call Tyson back. We're going to need his help if we're going to stop these keks from getting Kaliel before either one of us has the chance to win this bet."

It takes a couple of tries to get Tyson to answer, and when I finally do, I hope it's not too late for him to help us help Kaliel. Before I can even say anything, Tyson says, "One of te things Kaliel pawned was a makeup case with Kayla's ident wallet tucked into te lining." He holds out a placating hand. "Just because he is selling off her stuff doesn't necessarily mean he killed her back on Zant." Although we both know that's exactly what it sounds like. "If tere is a chance he left Kayla somewhere alive, we have to try to get tat information before Kaliel is killed."

Tyson's still ready to turn Kaliel over for immediate execution. Which, if he killed Kayla, may well be what he deserves.

Pero, he doesn't know for sure that Kaliel had anything to do with Kayla's disappearance. I still feel like there is something going on that we don't understand.

Why can't Tyson see how important this is?

Heat burns at the back of my eyes. "Kaliel's ship is still near Aspeld. We're following him now, only there's three bounty hunters ahead of us."

"Babe," Brill calls, "tell him Chestla and I are working on a plan."

"You tell him, mi vida." I bring the phone over to where Tyson can see Brill.

Brill addresses Tyson, "Can you catch up with us before one of those keks manages to disable Kaliel's ship and spaces him?"

"Why wouldn't they just blow it up?" I ask Chestla. Horrible as that is, it seems like a lot less trouble.

She looks down at her hands. "They need the remains intact enough to be identified if they want to claim the bounty. The Galactacops won't pay up over just a smear of DNA. I'm guessing those Zantites won't either."

That leaves me feeling hollow. *Remains.* Such a feo word.

"How do you know that, chica?"

"I tried out for the Galactacops after I left home, before I settled on Larksis. I failed their exam too. Just the psych part, though." She rolls her slit-pupil eyes, which is custurbing – cute yet disturbing. "Apparently, I am too friendly and forgiving and not suited to long solo jaunts in space."

I manage not to laugh. "When I first met Tyson, he had a partner. Lately, he's been running solo. How does that work?"

Chestla looks shocked. "Galactacops aren't required to have partners, but their office doesn't break partnerships up lightly. If he's between partners, chances are his previous one died or did something to get kicked off the force. Unless maybe the guy was old enough to retire?"

I hadn't given that guy a second thought.

He's probably muerto. Tyson hadn't seemed to let that affect him at all. I can't decide if that's cold or just sad.

I've missed some of what Brill said to Tyson, pero Tyson hisses out a sigh. "You are aware tat tat means Kaliel will get away."

Brill nods. "That is a very high probability, wal. But it means he stays alive, so when we eventually do catch him, you can find out what he knows about Kayla, and Bo can–" He looks over at me. "Honestly, I'm not sure what Bo's hoping to do here, su. Solve the puzzle of why this happened, I guess."

"Brokeheart icestorm tunderstrikes." I'm not sure, pero I think Tyson might have just cursed. "I'm on my way."

As soon as he hangs up, my handheld rings again.

I check the caller. "It's Mario."

I start to answer, pero Brill snags the phone as a voice call. "Hest! Did you see the game on Saturday?" They talk soccer for a few minutes, first the actual game they'd both seen – and then I'm getting the idea that Kaliel's the ball, and Tyson's the defender and we're trying to keep Kaliel out of the bounty hunters' goal by bouncing him out of bounds.

There's a long pause where I can half-hear Mario talking excitedly about something.

Brill says, "Ga, su. Don't worry about it." Then his eyes turn a startled lime shade. "I don't think anybody'd be offended. But a lot of the archives were lost, uan I don't know where you'd even start." Brill gives me a questioning look as he hangs up.

"Your brother wants to study Krom history for his next book."

"I guess what you said really got to him, mi vida."

Chestla says, "They're closing in. I hope Tyson gets here soon, or Kaliel's going to be breathing stardust."

Tawny comes out of her room. She sits down on the sofa. Chestla gives her a questioning look. Tawny shrugs. "Some things you just want to see for yourself."

I'm trying to follow what's happening on the nav. "Mi vida, we're moving away from the action, no?"

"Wal, Babe. We're going to come in under them." He looks up at us. "Everybody strap in. The sofa converts to crash seats."

Chestla doesn't move, so neither do I.

Tyson's saucer is a faint shadow on the screen now, still behind pero catching up. Maybe the type of engine he uses gives off a different signature.

"Come on, come on," Brill's muttering to himself, or to Tyson, who can't possibly hear. "Naramoosh. Catch up before we get too close."

"Why don't we want to get too close?" I ask, pero no one is answering me. They're all staring at the nav. Don't we want to catch up?

The *Fois Gras'* com system dings. Brill allows the call through from Vinknet Vinkshou.

Vinknet's bass voice surrounds us. "Who are you and what do you think you're doing?"

"Just a friend asking you to stop pursuit of that vessel. We need to talk to that su." Brill's voice is calm.

"And if we don't?"

"Then we're going to put him out of your reach."

There's silence for a long time. "Are you serious? You'd rather blow him up, so that nobody gets the bounty?"

"That's not my plan, ga." Brill adjusts our course, so that now we are tracking along with the other ships, just lower than them.

"Then I'm going to take the odds that you can't stop us. If you fire on one of us, the other two will destroy your vessel before you fire again."

"Hold on, su. I don't plan on firing at all." Brill jettisons something from the *Fois Gras*, a smaller dot heading upwards into the empty space.

"What did you just do?" Vinknet asks. "Was that a mine?"

"Ga. Just our spare fuel cell." Brill looks up at us. "En serio. You sus strap in."

Chestla and I head for the sofa. Tawny punches a button, and foam seat partitions spring out from the wall. Brill changes our course, so that we're angling away from where he sent the fuel cell.

Vinknet figures out what's about to happen pretty much the same time I do. "Why, you little–"

Given the giant holofields, I can still see what's going on with the nav. Tyson's coming in fast, over the top of the other ships, and they've been so focused on Brill, they didn't notice his fainter signature.

Tyson fires on the fuel cell.

We've got a little bit of distance, pero when the shock wave hits, it pushes us from the group, flipping us around like we're a toy top that just got dropped. The stabilizers give up. The seatbelts bite at my chest. Someone is screaming. It's me.

Pero, Brill gets us back under control.

Kaliel gets shot forward, the bounty hunters backwards. They're trying to get turned around, moving towards Kaliel again, pero that takes time. Time equals distance, and Kaliel's speed is giving him more of it.

The bounty hunters give up and turn towards us.

Brill zooms in on an actual image of our pursuers. We've wound upside down in relation to the other ships. Brill doesn't bother flipping us over. After all, there's no right-side up in space.

"We have more fuel than you do right now," Vinknet says. "We're going to make you wish you hadn't done that."

I let out a squeak. They're going to scuttlepunch us.

"I would advise against tat," Tyson's voice cuts in. "As a Galactic Inspector, I understand you have first rights to any bounty you touch, but retribution against someone who keeps you from making contact is against te law, and can get your license stripped."

Suddenly, his saucer becomes more visible on the screen.

"You have got to be kidding me," Vinknet grumbles.

"Afraid not, su." Brill wipes a hand across his face. His irises are black with fear, pero his voice sounds almost playful. "Check the saucer's engine registration."

There's a long, tense moment.

"Fine. Let's make this a long game." Vinknet and his companions head back the way they came.

"Ven, Tyson, are you going to give us that tow?" Brill sounds skeptical. Tyson would be at an advantage if our fuel is too spent to get us to a tradepost or a planet. We'd be able to coast, pero that method can make a two-hour trip take days.

"Sending out a grappler now. Once I get you to te shop, tough, I'm not waiting for you."

Brill looks surprised as the *Fois Gras* rocks when the grappler hits home. "Fair enough."

Tawny goes back in her cabin, perfectspinning the feed of what just happened. Brill and Chestla start debriefing each other on the precision of the fuel cell placement and Kaliel's current trajectory, congratulating each other that nobody got hurt.

We can't keep doing this. Kaliel's gone and we're not going to catch up to him before he really does get wooshwashed.

True to his word, Tyson drops us at the nearest tradepost. It won't take long for them to change out the fuel cell, just an hour or two for the mechanics to get to our turn in line.

Chestla and Brill both want to go get a quick drink to take the edge off the adrenaline. And Brill wants to get a new phone.

I really don't feel like going out. "Why don't you go, muchachos?"

"Are you sure, Babe?"

I hope he doesn't think I'd be jealous of him spending an hour drinking with Chestla. Mi vida is nothing if not loyal.

I assure them I won't leave the ship, won't turn off my phone, and won't open the door for anyone. And Tawny's in the next room – apparently too busy to remember she wanted to find a ride home.

Left alone in the bridge, I think about what Chestla said about patterns. We need to find the pattern here, get ahead of all this instead of just reacting. What do we know? Kaliel's picked up two black somethings, some copper and glass and, according to Chestla's forums, a spool of fiber optic cable.

I know Kaliel's a foodie. And Earth-centric food seems to be the only common denominator between all the places we've wound up.

I pull up the feed archive for Mamá's *Pizza Lover's Guide to the Galaxy* tour. When I have the data overlaid, I just blink at it. Kaliel's been at half of these spots, though not in geographical order. Pero, after a while, it makes sense.

When Brill and Chestla come back, I bring my phone over to them and make the datagraph as big as possible. "This is going to sound loco, pero I think Kaliel's hitting every famous pizza joint between Zant and Earth. At least the ones on mi mamá's list, in order of rating."

I expect them to laugh, pero Brill lets out a low whistle, as his eyes turn gold. He's proud of me.

Chestla nods, examining my work. "One of the best ways to avoid being tracked is to move erratically, but even subconsciously, it's hard to avoid leaving a pattern. So you choose a pattern that makes sense only to you." Chestla points at the data. "And this is a pattern only you would have been likely to spot."

"Then we know where he's going next. Number six. Semolina's, the place with what I would have voted the best pizza in the galaxy."

Chestla gives me a questioning look.

I shrug. "Mamá and I disagree about a lot of things."

CHAPTER TWENTY-FIVE

I'm sitting on Brill's sofa, with a cup of coffee, checking out the news – both public and with the disappearing facts app. Now that I've got my phone back all to myself, I'm not sure if Brill expects me to delete the contacts he's saved, or his apps. Unless he asks, I'm not going to. I might need to talk to Gavin or someone someday. Not that Gavin ever replied to my text – pero he might if it was important, no?

We've been on Watuza for almost an hour. I've already reviewed the bumpclip of Mamá interviewing the chef and customers at Semolina's a couple of dozen times. It's almost like she's walking me through this.

Tawny sits next to me. "Are you sure you want to confront Kaliel in a restaurant? One Earthling murdering another in a setting this public – after everything else that has happened – I'm not sure if we can control the fallout."

"You think Kaliel would kill me for sitting down and talking to him?"

She pulls a tube of moisturizer out of her pocket and rubs it on her hands. It smells floral, with a hint of cherry. "If you are distracting him, and Brill darts him from a distance, there is a significant period between him getting hit and passing out. And that's when bad things could happen." She offers me the tube.

I take it and rub cream on my own hands. It feels cooling.

"You think I don't know that? Pero, honestly, it's like ten seconds."

"Are you ready, Babe?" Brill's loading darts into the little silver gun. He gives Tawny a skeptical look.

She answers for me. "As ready as she'll ever be."

Kaliel's not at the restaurant when we arrive. Brill spends a hundred local money units verifying that he hasn't already been there and gone before we take a table in the bar with an unobstructed view of the door. Chestla moves to cover the rear exit.

We both sit on the same side of the table, hiding behind the table-mounted holo – which is showing a news and sports Galactacast – waiting for Kaliel to show.

Waiting for a long time.

What if I was wrong? What if this isn't the pattern he's been following at all?

The two celebarazzi Galactacasters, Blizzard and Feddoink, start talking about the repercussions of the bombing. Blizzard is a Myska like Tyson, Feddoink a tentacled blob with a huge head. They sit side by side at a desk that seems to grow out of the center of our table, speaking crisp Universal.

Blizzard says, "Eart's position in te galaxy is still precarious. While te borders have opened a crack, it won't win tem enough allies to halt invasion."

"I know," Feddoink replies. "A prolonged war would shut off the chocolate supply to the entire galaxy – and risk damaging the source. My wife is addicted to the stuff – and she's pregnant. What am I supposed to do about her midnight cravings? Men of my species have been killed over less."

"You're braver tan me, Feddoink." Blizzard laughs, fangs visible, secondary eyelids closing over his whiteless brown irises in reflex. He's mostly gray-green, like Tyson, pero there are a few black scales lining the edges of his blade-like face. "But not all of te factions involved are ready to commit te resources needed for an instant crushing defeat of tis planet."

My planet. Earth.

The feed shifts to a Zantite holding up a hand-lettered sign reading MIAG, in Earth Roman script. Ni idea what that means. He's speaking Zant, pero the feed's putting subtitles in Universal underneath his face. "So they're preparing to defend themselves? That's fair. It's not like they're building a doomsday device or anything…"

Brill grabs my arm. "He's here."

The hostess leads Kaliel to a table.

He takes a chair facing away from us. Good. I stand up and walk toward Kaliel's table.

Brill argued against this plan, pero it's our best shot. Shaking with nerves, I force my rubbery legs to keep moving. I'm almost to the table when Kaliel notices me.

I gesture towards the chair opposite him. "Can I sit down? Por favor."

Kaliel's on his feet, scanning the room, putting me between him and the center. "How did you find me?"

"That's not important." I step closer, moving to the side, so Brill will have a clear shot to dart him.

Kaliel moves in front of me again, just as a dart hits the wall where he was standing a moment ago. He gives me a dirty look before he turns and runs.

Ay, no! My heart breaks a little more. I chase him. "Por favor, wait. We want to help you."

Brill flashes past me, moving Krom-fast to intercept Kaliel. Mi vida tackles Kaliel, who pushes Brill hard enough back against a table, which collapses on top of Brill.

Kaliel scrambles to his feet, pero by that time I've caught up to him. I get a hand on his arm.

Kaliel leans over a table where a bunch of kids have just gotten a fresh pizza. He grabs the pizza and throws it at me. I fend off the tray, pero my hair and face get covered in pepperoni and cheese. Egh. By the time I can see again, Brill's blocking the exit, and Kaliel is changing trajectory back towards me. There are two darts in his jacket – one dead center for his heart and one in the sleeve where he must have brought an arm up to shield his face – pero neither seem to be having an effect.

Kaliel has a gun. He levels it towards mi cabeza. My heart pounding, I duck behind the table. There's a whisperpop, and a hole explodes in the chair back, not far from my ear. Oye!

I stare at that hole, ice dancing down my spine, and by the time I look back up, Brill is taking the gun away from Kaliel using that same leverage motion Chestla had used to take the broom away from me. Brill drops the gun and kicks it over towards me. No y nunca. I'm not picking it up.

Brill chases Kaliel towards the kitchen. People are ducking under tables, screaming, moving back out of the way.

"Hey!" one prep cook shouts. "You can't come back here."

Kaliel pushes him over and grabs the guy's pizza cutter. Brill tries to take it from him, pero Kaliel slices Brill's hand deeply, splashing orange blood on both of them.

Mi vida cries out, holding his hand to his shirt, while Kaliel escapes out the back door. I hesitate. Brill's in pain.

Yet, if I stop to help him, I will lose Kaliel. Giving Brill an apologetic look, I chase the fugitive. "Stop, Kaliel! Por favor!"

Out in the alley, Kaliel hesitates, looks back with an expression I can't read.

Chestla comes up from behind him. "Where do you think you're going?"

Kaliel drops the pizza cutter, frozen by her alpha-predator vibe. Before he can recover, Chestla whips out a pair of handcuffs and secures his hands behind his back.

I rush over to Brill, who is standing still while the thin-fingered prep cook twists a long strip torn off a tablecloth around mi vida's forearm. The guy has rounded ears at the top of his cabeza, with shell pink interiors, and the fuzzy hair on the back of them blends into the sand-brown hair covering his head. His nose is small and flat, his black eyes oversized, whiteless and beady, his lips thin and pink, his arms improbably thin. The guy's grim frown deepens as he sticks a pasta fork into the knotted cloth and turns it tighter. Brill's jacket is crumpled on the floor.

"Mi vida, are you OK?"

Brill gestures towards Kaliel with his uninjured hand. "I thought this su was an Earthling." He's holding a balled-up napkin in his other fist, and orange blood is seeping through it. Mi vida's shirt's navy, pero even so, I can see the front of it is soaked and sticky. "I hit him twice. How is he still conscious?"

"He needs a doctor," the prep cook says. There's no question which guy he's talking about. Brill's lost a lot of blood already, and he's leaking more. Which is even worse for a Krom than for an Earthling.

Brill takes hold of the makeshift tourniquet, so the big-eyed guy can let go of the fork and tie it, pero the bleeding hasn't entirely stopped. "Wal. I'm not about to stand here and bleed out over a kalltet cut hand. I think Kaliel nicked a vein at the edge of my wrist."

Brill looks reproachfully over at Kaliel, pero Kaliel doesn't react.

Mi vida's trying to act casual, pero his eyes are a deep, worried gray. Krom cardiovascular systems are their weak point, and they don't rebound well from massive blood loss. My heart jolts. I could lose him, like he just said, over a cut hand.

"Come on, Killer," Chestla tells Kaliel. "We're going back to the *Fois Gras*." She turns to Brill, holding her hand out for the keys. "Hopefully I'll have some information for you by the time you get back from the doctor."

I pick up Brill's jacket. I think I can get the bloodstains out.

Brill pulls out his keys, pero, he hesitates about handing them over. "You're sure you're going to be there when I get done?"

Chestla rolls her eyes. "You're wearing a proximity band. Which may well have saved your life."

I look closer at the metal band, peeking out above the napkin edge. A deep scratch in the surface matches where the cut up his wrist abruptly ends.

"Sorry." Brill drops the keys into her hand. "I'm not used to working with people I can trust. I forget you gave Bo your claim on Jack's bounty." Brill closes his eyes, sways on his feet.

"You OK, mi vida?" I reach out to steady him.

"Wal, Babe. I'm just going to sit down for a second while you find out about that doctor." Brill looks up at me. His eyes are a dark, muddy gold. He holds up his injured hand. "Whatever happens, Babe, remember, this wasn't your fault."

Tears bite at the back of my eyes. "You're going to be fine."

"But if I'm not. I want you to know that you mean all the worlds to me. You're mi vida too. And mi corazón."

I wipe at my eyes. "So that's what you mean when you say Babe?"

"Pretty much." He cups my chin with his good hand, drawing me towards him and kissing me. For someone who says he's half-gone from me, he sure has a lot of strength left to do it with.

Six hours and one close call at the hospital later, we're back on the *Fois Gras*. I'm going to have to start carrying healing foam if I'm going to continue dating a Krom.

Brill doesn't seem to be thinking about how he nearly bled out in the cab, passing out in my arms.

He seems more concerned about the flexible coating on his cheek, where the doctors had sloughed away the frozen cells, then applied a pack over the raw flesh that's supposed to stay on for twelve hours to encourage generation of new cells.

They gave him a lot of pain drugs.

From the sofa where he's lying, he looks over at me, his eyes still unfocused. "Don't give up on me, Babe. We can make this work. Especially now that they're going to make me pretty again."

I keep thinking about how the nurse had explained it to him: "You can't regenerate frozen cells. No matter what the galaxy's cryostasis salesmen say, you can thaw a frozen humanoid cell, but they'll never figure out how to make it live again, even if it's not damaged."

I'd never thought about it before, but what had happened to him was pretty close to cryostasis.

Tawny's watching the news in the ship's holofields. "Guys? You hear this yet?"

Feddoink, the blob-monster, says, "Ambassador Grong, who was visiting Earth with a provisional tourist visa, has been declared dead, after being taken from the site of the Greene Memorial Snowboarding Extravaganza by ambulance and admitted to Martin Memorial Hospital."

I gasp. I know him. He was aboard *Layla's Pride*, for the conference. He was from Mardgar, the planet known for the best Kona coffee in the galaxy. They're on the hot-list for anything that comes out of a Krom First Contact. Claro está, they'd been interested in chocolate. Pero, he'd been one of the most likely delegates to change his mind about the invasion.

Feddoink continues, "Representatives from Earth are claiming the death was an accident, that Grong's injuries resulted from an improper understanding of Earth gravity. Many of our sources feel like this is one accident too many for a planet who exonerated a man who subsequently set off bombs on Zant."

I force myself to breathe. We finally have Kaliel. We were

starting to get things under control. Pero, the media's going to malcast Earth so bad, it might not matter.

"To get a feel for Earthling psychology, we're going to interview–"

Brill sits up suddenly. "Shtesh! A su passes out for a couple of hours, and look what happens!"

It's another hour after that when Kaliel wakes up. According to Chestla, he'd made it back to the ship, realized he wasn't going to escape, then passed out. Whatever he'd done to delay the effect of the darts couldn't last forever.

An hour after *that*, I'm still sitting across the table from Kaliel, trying to get answers. Tawny and Chestla gave up half an hour ago. I feel bad for the way Kaliel's hunched over, pero it was the only way to attach his wrists to the table.

"Por favor. Who really set those bombs?" I'm getting frustrated.

Kaliel's been uncooperative. Now, he just sneers.

From where he's lying on the sofa, Brill says, "You're making a lot of allowances for Dork Face's behavior, if you don't love him on some level."

Brill lost a lot of blood, and what's left has been laced with iron replacement drugs and painkillers. He sounds alchafuzzed. I should just let it go.

"Maybe you and I should run away together." It's the longest sentence Kaliel's said since we came aboard. He winks. It's smarmy, not sexy.

"Por favor." I can't hide my exasperation. "That's not helping."

"After all." Brill holds up his wounded hand. "He did this to me, shot at you… and still, you can't give up on him."

"A lot of people would have given up on you when you left me for dead," I snap. I take a deep breath. This isn't helping anything either, just bringing a color of pain to his irises. "Lo siento, mi vida. Mira, I believe you can care for someone as an amigo, even if you've been attracted to them. It's like your pendants. You can hold more than one heart in your hand."

"As long as that's all you're holding." Brill shakes his cabeza, careful not to disturb the gel covering half his face. "It so rarely stays that way. Unless Earth girls are *that* different from Krom girls."

There's a story there, pero it's not fair to ask him for it while he's in that condition. Maybe not a good idea to bring it up at all. I know he's had a couple of previous relationships, pero I never asked for details on the break-ups.

I turn back to Kaliel. "We know you bought massive amounts of salt and baking soda at that grocery store. Put that together with the fiber optics cable, the broken glass and the black whoosie-whatsits – and I got nada. What were you doing with all that stuff?"

Kaliel shrugs.

"I told you, Babe," Brill says, "we won't figure that out unless we find his ship."

I know what he said. I ask Kaliel, *again*, "So what did happen to your ship?"

He shrugs, again, the gesture so awkward in his hunched position. "Ditched it."

"At what point will you be ready to turn him over to Tyson?" Brill asks, like Kaliel's not sitting right there. "That was the deal, right? Tyson finds him a doctor and offers legal support? Then we can backtrack and look for the ship."

I bristle at this, even though it's what I originally agreed to. "The minute that happens, we get cut out of the loop."

Brill sighs. "Then what do you want to do?"

"No lo sé. I thought he would tell us something helpful, and then we would know what to do."

Chestla steps out of the galley, a sandwich in her hand. "Take him with us to Evevron. I have a friend who is a doctor. He's won Galactic awards for having developed new treatments for brain trauma. I can get him to do a work-up on Kaliel."

"That sounds promising," I agree.

Brill raises an eyebrow. "You told her I would fly us all to Evevron?"

Heat flushes my face. "Unless you want me to call Uber or something."

"Again, you could have asked." He pushes himself up off the sofa with his good hand and moves over to the command chair. "But I understand. You couldn't say no to a friend. I've been there." He's talking about the friend who had died in his arms, demanding one last promise – which gave it the same weight as the promise Brill had demanded of Gavin, on my behalf, when he thought he was going to die. "And I can never say no to you."

"De veras you're in any condition to fly this thing?"

"I've flown the *Fois Gras* with a concussion and a bullet in my leg before." Brill starts pushing buttons. He closes his eyes for a second, obviously woozy. "We should leave before news spreads about what happened in that pizza place. Until we announce intent to turn Kaliel over, anyone could still snatch him and claim the reward."

Which means I've put some of my closest amigos – and Tawny – in incredible danger.

"Of course," Brill continues, "your casual bounty hunter isn't going to be kalltet enough to follow us to Evevron."

CHAPTER TWENTY-SIX

It takes days to get to Evevron. We're getting close when Brill's phone rings. He looks at it, and then looks at me – almost out of sight in the galley, where I've been preparing breakfast – and his eyes go an embarrassed pale pink that contrasts with the maroon tee-shirt that he's wearing sans jacket, since he feels safe in his ship.

He turns his phone so that the video capture has the ship's controls as a background.

Who's he about to talk to that he wishes I don't know about?

His eyes shift towards a happy blue I know he doesn't feel. "Kam, Zaw." *Hi, Ma.*

Ma? Then why is he so embarrassed?

And then it clicks.

He's embarrassed of me. My cheeks flame. I've never seen Brill's family. After he'd confessed that they had no interest in meeting me, I hadn't brought it up again. A few days ago, when he thought he might die, I was worth more to him than anything. Pero now?

I can't help myself. Staying well out of the capture field, I move around to where I can see the front of the holo. Like all the Krom women I've met, Brill's mamá is beautiful, with flowing auburn hair, heavy on the red, a darker shade of Brill's strawberry blonde. She looks maybe my age, or even a little younger. Which is disconcerting, pero I should have realized it, because, hello, she's Krom. Right now, her irises are the color of steel, her mouth set in an equally forbidding line.

Brill's gaze flicks over to me, and I freeze, just as his mamá says, in Krom, "Please tell me you're not with that Earth girl right now."

Brill shrugs, cracks a smile. "OK, I'm not with that Earth girl right now."

I clamp down hard on the noise of protest that wants to come out of my throat.

"Your father has been watching the news, and he swears that he saw you in the background of a clip from that tragedy on Zant. And now there's been the death of another Galactic Citizen on Earth. I don't know what she's dragged you into, but things are about to get ugly for Earthlings stuck out in the galaxy. I don't want you to get caught in the crossfire, Tazoz." She just called him *baby boy*. There's a hint of pink creeping back into his eyes.

That's hardly fair. Brill's the one who got me involved in all of this. Surely he will tell her that.

"You're overreacting." Brill holds up a placating hand towards the camera.

Hs mamá gasps. "What happened to your wrist?"

Brill tucks his hand out of sight. "It's nothing, Zaw. Just a job that got a little messy."

Her eyes go an intense brick red, worried and angry and affectionate all at the same time – the exact color of maternal protection you'd see in a she-beast about to step between a predator and her cub. I hope never to be on the other side of that gaze.

"Where are you?"

Brill glances over at me. "It's better if I don't say. Look, Zaw, tell Sum I love him, and the girls I miss them. I gotta go."

She's still making another protest when he hangs up the phone.

Brill and I look at each other for a long time.

I cross my arms over my chest. "I'm not here?"

"Babe, I'm sorry. They'll come around eventually. Now's just not the right time."

He gives me a pleading look, pero I flee out into the hall. It feels like something is crushing in on my lungs, and somewhere during all of this, the IH has bubbled up again, leaving me shaking and spent.

I mean it when I say Brill's mi vida, my very life. Pero his life's so much bigger than just me. How am I supposed to deal with that?

I stop after about three steps when I see Tawny looking out her door at me, an I-told-you-so pity-smug look in her eyes.

She does not get to win that easily. Pero, Brill doesn't get to treat me like I'm not good enough for him, either. Not if he doesn't want his kalltet pendant back.

I walk back out there. His eyes are the color of remorse. "I promise not to do that again. I realize now that if I don't stand up for you, they'll never respect you."

Chestla nods with every phrase. I wonder what she said to him. And where those scratches came from on his arm.

The planet comes into view, and it reminds me of Chestla's nail polish, all purple and glittery. And swirling.

I look over at her. "Is that a jewel-toned dust storm, chica?"

"Unfortunately, yes. They're more common now, with the droughts. Which reminds me." Chestla goes to her cabin and comes out with a tri-folded garment bag. "You're a dignitary here. It would be a big favor to me if you could wear that."

I unzip the bag. A pour of lace escapes. I raise an eyebrow. "It's white, chica."

Chestla stares down at her hands. "I know, it's your least favorite color – those earrings you always wear excepted. But it implies status. How many people do you imagine can afford to keep white garments clean in a place like this?"

She's done me so many favors. I'm committed to help her get her future back. As I head to my cabin to change, I say back over my shoulder, "So where's yours?"

Chestla gives me a sad half-smile. She gestures down at her own top, which is white, too. The fabric is slightly flowy, with a square neck outlined by a strip of black decorated with a geometric pattern. "I'm auditioning to be a Guardian Companion, not a courtier."

Tawny comes out into the hall. She runs an appreciative finger across the lace. "Where's mine, you mean. That lace is gorgeous."

I manage a tight smile. There's probably a tiny camera lens somewhere on the fabric now, pero I can't spot it. "You coming with us, then?"

Tawny snorts a laugh. "I have to. The alternative is being stuck alone on a ship I can't fly in the middle of a sandstorm that might shut down the spaceport's visual communications. No thanks."

Which means she's been keeping up with everything, from inside her cabin. She's here by choice. She's had ample opportunities to book a shuttle back to Zant and taken none of them. She strolls over to where Brill is sitting, while I make my way into my cabin.

When I close the door behind me, I faintly hear Brill and Chestla talking. He doesn't sound happy. A couple of times, *shalshis*, the Krom word for danger echoes through at me. Chestla doesn't know much Krom. I guess they're trying to exclude Tawny from the conversation. As I'm pulling the white tunic over mi cabeza, I distinctly hear Chestla call Brill a kek.

The pants that go with the outfit are also white, though of thicker, more utilitarian cloth. I don't have any sturdy shoes to finish the outfit except for my black boots.

I go back to the bridge, take my seat on the modified sofa

between Chestla and Tawny and strap in, in case the storm's more than the stabilizers can handle. We're squashed together far from the command chair, pero the nav and closeup fields are showing plenty of jewel-toned chaos. I don't envy Brill right now.

Tawny leans forward, looking across me at Chestla. "You certain they're not going to arrest us all for harboring a fugitive the minute we touch down?"

"I've spoken to the Council of Elders. They and the Royal Family have agreed to offer Kaliel temporary sanctuary, until they're done evaluating him."

"And Tyson will have to honor that?" I ask.

"He can't charge us with harboring, but he can petition the Galactic Court to override the sanctuary. The council also won't fight it if Tyson snatches him and manages to get him out of atmo. They're only doing this at all as a favor to me."

Brill buckles the safety restraints on his command chair. He grabbed his jacket, so Krom-quick I didn't even notice. "I don't like trying to land in this weather. The winds are high enough to knock us into one of those skyscrapers."

I take a good look at the planet, and sure enough, now that we are coming in close, and the acceleration to bring us in through atmo has us committed, I see tall gray buildings poking up like spikes from the surface. It's mountainous and forbidding, like a lavender-tinted *Star Trek*y planet Vulcan. Maybe that kid back on Zant was right. You keep looking for fictional correlations long enough, you might find the real thing. That's ironic, since personality-wise, Chestla is the opposite of good old Spock.

Chestla says, "I'll serve as translator. Aside from diplomats and members of the council and the court, there's not going to be a lot of people who speak Universal. We don't get many visitors."

I look over at Kaliel. He's watching the instruments, and for a second, I can see a flicker of the old intelligence in his eyes, see him move his hands as though he would like to adjust the controls to bring us in safe. Something's different about his face, and I can see again the guy I kissed, the sensitive hero I'd been tempted to love. He catches me looking and blinks, before he stares back down at the table he's shackled to.

Nobody strapped him in for landing. I hope it's not going to be as rough as Brill said.

We burn through and the winds catch at the ship. Brill's superhumanly-fast hands race over the controls, making micro-corrections to the thrusters. My stomach feels loopy from all the juddering, pero we're going down on cue, heading for the spaceport's generous landing area. A sudden gust of wind hits us, and we're flung sideways, out over the sand, the distance magnified by the speed we were already traveling.

"That's going to make for a nice hike back," Chestla says.

Kaliel grunts, then lifts his face from the table, where the force banged his temple against the smooth metal surface. "Be sarcastic, but it really is a beautiful piece of land. Reminds me of the old days. And the longer the hike, the longer we get to keep breathing." It's the most vocal he's been since we captured him. Which I take as a good sign, even though he isn't making much sense. He's the only one facing muerte here, right?

I cock an eyebrow at him. "What old days?"

Kaliel's from Sweden. He has family in Brazil, and took his pilot training in Mexico – presumably at the megaplex in Guadalajara. Which is hardly a desert. At twenty-six, how many more old days could he have?

He blinks, looks confused, then shrugs. "Pilot training, at a tiny base in the middle of the Chihuahua Desert. Guadalajara was full that year, so we pulled the overflow facility."

It's plausible, pero he still sounds uncertain.

Brill's angling the external cameras to check on the outside of his ship. We've landed upright, without a scratch – if you ignore the graffiti and the dents from Tyson towing us.

"Do you want to try to move to the spaceport?" I ask.

Brill grimaces. "Ga. Not in this kind of storm. All it would take is one gust to tip us over, and then we'd have real problems."

Chestla's already unfastening Kaliel from the table, cuffing both his hands behind his back again. She's been in charge of moving him as necessary over the past few days, and he hasn't tried to fight her. She leans in close to his face. "I wouldn't suggest trying to run, not on this planet. That ravine leading into the river is going to look inviting, but trust me, you've got a better shot at surviving a Zantite jury."

I shudder, imagining all those Zantite teeth ripping Kaliel apart, pero he just shrugs. "Doesn't matter much in the scheme of things, does it, how I die?"

His voice is gruff and hoarse. I suspect it really does matter to him.

I remember the version of this guy who could have escaped prison in the middle of a riot, pero chose to stay to face an unjust death rather than to be seen as guilty – or a coward. I still keep wondering if the Kaliel I'm looking at now is some kind of doppelganger – pero, I felt like I'd glimpsed the real Kaliel a minute ago.

It has to be something going on inside Kaliel's mind.

So many things don't add up – unless there really is a virus. Fizzax never had explained how he knew Kaliel was going to make it back to the trial at the last minute. And Dghax had talked about a sickness aboard that crashed ship, busy becoming a reef in the Zantite ocean. Could it have been dormant on Zant for all those years? Maybe Kaliel had stumbled across something infected with germs while he'd been lost.

I hold my breath, waiting for him to say something else. He doesn't. Chestla pushes him towards the door. He rolls his shoulders, as best he can, given the confinement of his arms.

Chestla bounces the key in her hand, then tosses it to me. "You're still in charge of this guy."

Kaliel watches the key disappear into my pocket.

Chestla pokes him. "Unless you decide to turn him over to the police here, which should still count as beating Tyson."

I shake mi cabeza. "No y no. They'll just turn him over to the Zantites. The whole reason to challenge Tyson in the first place was to prevent that. We need answers."

Tawny pulls me aside. Her face is urgent, like she's got something very important to say. She pulls a tube out of her pocket. "You cannot go out there without sunscreen."

"En serio?" I try to turn away. We have important things to deal with here.

"Yes, seriously." Tawny opens the tube and starts applying cream to my cheek. "Your face is Earth's brand right now. You don't want our planet to look old and cracked, do you?

When the door opens, a blast of hot air hits my face. Brill drops the stairs, and the five of us walk out into the dust storm. Brill's got a couple of levbots carrying cases and cases of bottled agua. Tawny gives him an approving nod. Brill does something to the proximity band on his still-injured wrist, then he retracts the stairs and locks the door. The sand is already scratching at the bottom edges of the ship, piling up against the fins, further damaging the paint job.

It's going to be a long, hot walk.

We haven't gotten far when a vehicle trundling fast across the sand appears at the horizon, heading straight for us. Tawny flitdashes back towards the *Fois Gras*. The vehicle stops and a dozen Evevrons dressed in tight-fitting body armor pile out, surrounding us. There's an equal mix of guys and girls, a wide range of skin-tones and hair colors, pero they're all armed with identical staffs.

Brill's gun is in his hand, and he's standing in front of me before I've even registered that he's moved.

"No!" Chestla rushes over, pulling Brill's arm down. "Don't kill any of them. It's a test."

"A what?" Brill asks, pero he holsters the weapon, just as the delegation rushes us.

CHAPTER TWENTY-SEVEN

Chestla leaps at one girl, wrenches the staff away from her and tosses it to Brill. He manages to catch it, and then not be where his attackers expected him to be. He *did* learn something from sparring with Chestla. I wish I could say the same.

Kaliel is standing cuffed, unable to defend himself as one of the warriors swings at him. I jump on her back, dragging her to the ground. The staff's blow comes in low, at the back of Kaliel's legs, driving him to his knees. I scramble for the staff and as soon as she's unarmed, the Evevron backs away.

"So that's the test," Kaliel mutters. "Take the staff before they kill you with it."

"Doesn't that mean they're not going to hurt us?" My voice squeaks hopefully, pero Kaliel laughs.

"Don't count on it." He gestures with his chin at Chestla, who is locked in battle with a girl with yellow eyes.

Chestla has a staff too, now, which she raises to block a blow. The girl's staff slides over Chestla's, knocking mi amiga hard in the head. Chestla falls backwards and the girl stabs down at her with the staff. Chestla rolls out of the way, barely avoiding the blow.

So nope, they're not pulling their punches. Nunca.

And now I've got a staff and absolutely no idea what to do with it. I'm between Kaliel and half a dozen people who are trying to kill us, so I brace myself and try to steady my pounding heart. Most of the warriors are focusing their attention on Chestla.

From behind me, Kaliel says, "Let me free, and I can protect you."

I turn mi cabeza to look at him. His eyes are soft and gentle now, more the Kaliel I remember. I still haven't figured out what's wrong with him, pero my heart wants to trust him again. My hand twitches towards the key in my pocket. One attacker takes advantage of my distraction, and there's a staff arcing straight towards my nose. But before the blow lands, Brill flashes in front of me, shoving the guy wielding the staff away.

"She doesn't need your protection," Brill growls at Kaliel, who just shrugs.

"Suit yourself, man."

Brill grits his teeth. "Babe, get him back on his feet and away from the fight. But don't uncuff him." He points to a hole that he and Chestla have made in the formation, leading to the protection of a rock outcropping. About half of the combatants have been disarmed and are standing in a row, observing.

I brace myself with the staff as I help Kaliel stumble to his feet. He leans against me, and he's warm, the soap smell of his skin still clean and inviting despite the hike and the fight.

"Taga!" a female voice shouts, close behind me.

I whirl, and another warrior is there. I'm not sure what she said, pero she must have thought it cowardly to hit me in the back. The prey instinct rolls into me. The residual IH overrides it. I swing out wildly with my staff. The blow doesn't even land.

But it does earn me a smile from the Evevron, which crinkles up from her fanged teeth to her slit-pupiled green eyes. I swing again, and she backs away. My staff hits her foot, which is clad in a protective boot. It'd be easy now for her to knock me on the back of the cabeza.

The warrior laughs, and holds out her arm. In English, she says, "Oops," and drops the staff. I scramble for it, confused. The girl reaches into a pocket hidden in her body armor. She flashes me a picture. Of me. En serio? She's a fan?

I hold up her staff, and she gives me a salute, displaying a thick rubber bracelet on her wrist, printed with the Roman letters MIAG. And I get it. It's Tawny's tag line – *Mercy Is a Gift* – and it's caught on like wildfire. This girl's telling me she's offering mercy. We share eye contact, and a moment of mutual understanding. Then she withdraws towards the line of observers.

Kaliel stares after her. "Why would she do that?" He sounds like a little kid, genuinely confused and full of wonder. "She could have killed you, easily."

I shake mi cabeza. "I'll explain later."

We make it to the rocks. He leans back against the largest one, shifting to try to comfort his shoulders.

I look down. My white clothes are smeared with purple grit. "Fantastica. Chestla said the clothes are important."

Kaliel cracks a smile. "Don't worry. The Evevrons respect when dignitaries aren't afraid to get dirty. All those stains are actually a badge of honor."

I raise an eyebrow at him. "How do you know that?"

He shrugs. "Not sure. Just heard it somewhere, I guess."

He sounds confused again. I look at him, trying to block the noises of the melee behind us out of my brain. "So now that nobody else is listening, you want to tell me what went wrong back on Zant?"

Kaliel shrugs again. "Doesn't matter. I'll die for it, one way or another. Unless you let me go. All I need is a key, not so different from the one I gave you, that night in the rainforest. I helped you escape, no questions asked. Remember?"

My heart squeezes. "I can't do that."

"Of course you can." He licks at his lips, and I fall deeper into my memory of that night, when he saved me. When I kissed him. We both know that Frank would have shot me dead if Kaliel hadn't helped me get into that Jeep.

Heat's building at the back of my eyes and in my nose. "Por favor. Don't you understand? I'm trying to keep you alive, when all the bounty hunters and pirates out there would rather bring you in muerto."

Kaliel laughs. "This is so much bigger than you and me. And there's nothing either one of us can do to fight it. But it is so sweet that you care enough to try."

I put a hand on his shoulder. "Kaliel, the Zantites are going to execute you."

He looks me straight in the eyes. "And what complaints am I supposed to make?"

I was asked if I had any complaints, too, when a Zantite officer planned to execute me as a stowaway. I hadn't had any defense either. It's as close as Kaliel has come to an admission of guilt.

"If you explain, maybe we can think of a complaint."

He leans forward and kisses me on the forehead. "If you wanted me to live, you should have just let me run."

Chestla screams, and I turn. She's holding four staffs over her cabeza, and several broken ones have been driven into the ground at her feet. The row of warriors bows. The four of us managed to defeat three times our number. And the chances of them all being fans aren't that high.

Are Chestla and Brill really that good? What am I even doing here with them?

Somehow, Brill's standing between Kaliel and me. "Is everything OK over here?"

"Fine," Kaliel says.

Brill gives him a sharp look. "So now you want to talk?"

"Nope."

Brill gives *me* a look.

I shrug. "He didn't tell me anything useful either."

Kaliel pushes away from the rock. "We still have a long walk ahead of us."

"No." Chestla, still breathing hard, turns to join us. "We're getting a ride into town. Just as soon as we circle back and pick up Tawny."

"But I thought..." Real pain comes into Kaliel's eyes as he looks from me, out into the open landscape. It's like when we went up to watch the meteor shower back at HGB in Brazil. He'd had the same look then, trying to drink in all of life before his trial – and probable execution. He'd escaped that once, but now he's convinced again that he's about to die. He really wanted that hike, that last taste of nature and beauty and freedom.

He nods and follows us to the vehicle. Managing to wipe his eyes against his shirt before he gets in, he winds up sitting squashed between the girl who dropped her staff at my feet, and the guy who had tried to bash me on the head.

The girl says something to Chestla, who looks at me.

"She asked if there's any danger in cuffing his hands in the front, since it will be painful for him to ride like this."

I glance around. Kaliel's unarmed and there are fourteen highly skilled warrior-types between him and the door. I fish in the pocket of my pants and hand the girl the key. She keeps a hand on Kaliel's arm as she uncuffs him.

Suddenly, she gasps.

She flips Kaliel's forearm over and points at a discolored yellow spot, like a fading fist-sized bruise on his dark skin, with a single red bump at the center. She grabs his face in both hands, moving in close and staring into his eyes while speaking rapidly in Evevron.

Kaliel looks up at the ceiling, like maybe she'd instructed

him to. I didn't realize he spoke the local language. She sucks in a breath and says, "Feyese."

The other Evevrons in the vehicle flinch away from Kaliel, like he's contagious, Chestla included.

I look at Chestla, who stretches her hands before she answers. "The word means infected." She turns to the girl, and they exchange rapid Evevron. She looks back at me and Brill. "She believes he has a parasite. There was a rash of cases here a few years ago."

I have to keep myself from pumping a fist into the air and saying, *I knew it.* I'd guessed a virus, not a parasite, pero, I wasn't far wrong, no?

"What kind of parasite?" Kaliel asks. He sounds nervous, keeps looking at the spot on his arm like he's never noticed it before.

"Ekrin called it a mindworm." Chestla looks embarrassed just pronouncing the word. "She claims it can influence a person's thoughts. I don't know. I wasn't here when all of this happened. And apparently, it wasn't important enough for anyone to tell me about it."

"Like it wasn't important enough to tell us that we were going to be attacked as a test?" Brill asks. His eyes are a sullen apricot. I hadn't even realized he was upset over anything other than Kaliel.

Chestla's cheeks tint pink. "I did train you on how to pass it, didn't I? I was impressed by your rapid improvement."

Brill doesn't look flattered. I don't want to hear whatever he's planning to say next.

"It's over now, right?" I force a smile, looking from one to the other. "We can relax."

Chestla stares at me. "That was only the first test. I still must prove I can keep you alive on this planet for the next couple of days. I did tell you that coming here would be dangerous."

"Which means what, exactly?" Brill asks.

Chestla says, "Well, there's the hunt, for one thing."

I gasp. Chestla had once told me her true love had died on one of their hunts. Chestla's people may be the alpha predators on this planet, pero that doesn't mean there aren't other species here that come close second.

"Can we focus on me, for a minute?" Kaliel asks softly. "Wouldn't I know if I had a brain parasite?"

Chestla and Ekrin have another rapid conversation, and a few other Evevrons, who have been watching the rest of our exchange with interest, chime in, a couple of them tapping their foreheads, and one making the universal finger-twirling symbol for crazy.

Chestla shakes her cabeza. "The parasite's interaction with the victim's brain is subtle, introducing thoughts in such a way that the host usually thinks they are his own. But given your erratic behavior, and the slight bleeding at the edges of your irises–"

"What erratic behavior?" Kaliel asks.

"Tell us why you attacked a bunch of Zantites," I say.

Kaliel tenses and Ekrin catches his wrists. She cuffs him again. There's a long silence, before Kaliel says, "It just felt like something I had to do."

Chestla shrugs. "I'd say he's infected. That's definitely out of character for the Kaliel I know."

How does she even know him well enough to say that? She must have gotten his number from Kayla. She was going a bit stir-crazy in that rainforest.

"Is there a cure?" Brill asks. I can't read his face, or the brown tone to his eyes. He still looks almost like he's hoping it's fatal, pero there's a note of concern, too.

Chestla asks Ekrin, and both Ekrin and the guy on the other side have to hold Kaliel down as midway through the exchange, he starts trying to fight his way out of the vehicle. Either he – or the supposed parasite – understands Evevron.

After they subdue him, Chestla starts to say something, pero Kaliel interrupts.

"Jeez Louise, we're both sitting right here. It's cruel just calmly explaining how you're going to kill one of us."

By which he means the parasite. There must be a cure after all.

Ekrin says something, and Chestla translates for her. "You're part of a hive mind. What you are won't be lost."

Kaliel doesn't reply to that, pero he looks like he's about to throw up.

The vehicle stops and the doors open. The driver says over the intercom, in passable Universal, "She's hiding behind the ship."

Which isn't easy, given the design of the *Fois Gras*, which is all arcs and points. I'm surprised Tawny hadn't found a way to sneak back inside.

Everyone's looking at me.

"Que?"

Chestla says, "Someone's got to go out there and talk her into getting in this transport."

And I'm the only one they think she won't run from. I sigh.

"Cierto." I get off the transport and walk toward the ship. I shout, "Tawny? You OK back there?"

There's no response except the howling of the wind, then the crunching of my own boots across the ground. "Tawny?" Still no response. My stomach flops. She's out here alone. What if one of those lethalriffic creatures snuck up on her? The arched fins, the only points of the *Fois Gras* that touch the ground, are narrow, and I can see her sitting behind the far one, toppled forward over her own knees. "Tawny!"

I race around the ship. She's sitting at such an awkward angle, pero there's not a drop of blood on her. I move in close to check if she's got a pulse. When I touch her, she jumps and lets out a little scream.

"Bo, you scared me half to death!"

I put a hand over my racing heart. "You and me both."

She was shielding a holo from the sandstorm, a close-up of the Evevron girl showing off the rubber bracelet. Tawny pulls the headphones off her ears. "I told Gagnon that his releasing the MIAG plans for free for 3D printing was a stroke of genius. I couldn't have come up with a better fan club captain for you if I'd chosen him myself."

I look at her, stupidly unable to process this information. "I have a fan club?"

"Of course." Tawny looks at me like I really am estúpido. "Didn't you see them standing behind the protesters when we left the spaceport?"

She means when we'd left Earth in the first place to go to Zant.

"I'd assumed they were all protesters. It was hard to look past the signs with slogans and holos calling for my death. And then that one lady had tried to throw poo at me, remember?"

"Of course I remember." Tawny smiles. "She took one look at your entourage and dropped it on her shoes."

She means one look at Frank, who had been sitting in the driver's seat. I don't want to think about how I'm going to explain to him what just happened. He's not going to be happy I was in the middle of a fight. It breaks my brain how he seems to want to protect and kill me, at the same time.

"Vamonos. We've got a ride into town, if you're willing to take it."

Tawny looks relieved. "I lost all the gritfeeds the minute you guys got into that signalblocked transport. Did I miss anything important?"

I laugh, and then I can't stop laughing. All her cameras, and Tawny managed to miss the big reveal. "Did you miss anything?" I suck in a breath of dusty air. "Only that Kaliel's got a mind-altering brain parasite."

Her mouth drops open. She snaps it shut and straightens her back with resolve. "I can work with that. Can you get me an image of the parasite for the cameras?

CHAPTER TWENTY-EIGHT

Tawny is freaking out. "What do you mean I can't tell people about his brain parasite?"

We both look at Kaliel, who is leaning against the guy in the transport, snoring softly. The knock-out stuff they gave him was instantly effective. What was in it that was different from our darts?

Ekrin, who's standing next to Tawny now, having grabbed half of Tawny's electronics, says something else.

Chestla says, "It could jeopardize a plan already in place for eliminating the threat. That's all she's willing to tell us. You can ask the Council of Elders for your electronics back, but she's not letting you off this transport until you hand the rest of it over."

Tawny grabs Ekrin's wrist, apparently immune to the predator effect. She points at the MIAG bracelet Ekrin's wearing, then at Kaliel. "Nyash. Important. His life's important."

Ekrin nods. "OK. Good friend." Still, she gently removes Tawny's hand from hers and holds out her palm for the rest of the hardware. Tawny sighs and hands it over.

She hits Ekrin with a barrage of questions. "Where did this parasite come from? Is it native to this planet? How come nobody's heard of it before?"

Chestla translates Ekrin's answers as, "Nobody knows. Probably outer space. Space is big, and this parasite is subtle."

And the answers to Tawny's follow-up questions as, "Nobody knows. Nobody knows. Nobody knows."

I can say it now, *Uven coz. Nobody knows.*

It's plausible. After all, this parasite likely spread to Zant aboard that ship that's now becoming a reef off the shore of Letekka. The timing adds up right for that.

If those infected only betray subtle symptoms, it's not surprising that it's been almost a decade and nobody on Zant has noticed yet they've been infiltrated.

I imagine this hive mind spreading from planet to planet, blending in with the local population like sleeper agents back in Earth's Cold War era. Wherever it started, whenever this parasite found a way to go interstellar from its native planet, it's probable we will never find all the places it now calls home.

So why show itself so dramatically by bombing Minda's show? It makes no sense. Unless it assumed that would be considered normal behavior for Kaliel.

When the transport door opens, we're on a street out front of a blocky purple-gray building. Five young girls of varying heights wearing deep blue dresses are leaning against the wall, looking bored – right up until they spot Chestla. They race over to us, already chattering at her before she's even made it out of the vehicle. Two of the girls have yellow eyes instead of green.

The smallest girl wraps her arms around Chestla's legs, almost tripping her. Chestla ruffles the girl's hair. "Bo, these are my sisters. It is their duty to welcome me home."

I climb off the vehicle. "Tell them I am honored to meet them."

The tallest girl says in Universal, "It is we who are honored to have such a hero among us, as our sister's cesuda ma. Please regale us with your tales of adventure, after you have recovered from your arduous first test." She holds out a cup, pero Chestla puts a hand over mine.

"That's saltwater and herbs, meant to refresh and restore an Evevron warrior after vigorous exercise. It'd probably make you sick." Chestla takes the cup herself and drains it. She smiles at me. "It's good to be home."

Brill joins me on the sidewalk. He asks Chestla, "Five sisters, su? That's one more than me."

I think about my own two sisters, back on Earth by now. I'm not there to comfort them in the face of the tragedy they witnessed, to make sure that they're not having nightmares about Verex Kowlk's broken and bleeding body.

A wave of homesickness hits me so hard it's like a physical blow. I haven't felt like this since right after I moved to Larksis, fleeing a home where I no longer felt welcome.

When all of this is over, when we save Kaliel or lose him for good, am I going to want to be there with my sisters, watching them grow up? Eventually, is Brill going to want to go back to his own family? *Tell the girls I miss them.* That's what he'd said to his mamá. Even Krom, who have so much time, can feel the conflict between the call to adventure and the call back home. How do they reconcile it? How can Brill and I find a balance where we won't be torn apart?

Oblivious to what I'm thinking, Brill puts his hand in mine and squeezes. "That littlest one reminds me of your niece."

And my heart melts. Maybe there's hope for us after all.

It's only hotter and more humid inside the building. Gran windows have been propped open to allow for a light breeze, which makes a dusting of sand skitter against the raw stone floor. No wonder Chestla left for Larksis, if these people don't even have air conditioning.

The other warriors stayed in the transport, pero Ekrin follows us in, gestures us towards an empty waiting area with about twenty primitive-looking wooden chairs.

"Wait," I protest. "What about Kaliel?"

Ekrin shakes her cabeza, gestures for us to sit.

I try to bury my frustration. After risking our lives to get Kaliel back, and finding out I was right about his innocence, they're just going to take him?

I put a hand on Brill's arm, thinking how we're not sure how many more brain parasites there might be still on Zant. "We need to let Stephen know what he might be running into if he goes looking for Kayla. She could be infected too."

That would explain her buying a ticket and leaving her cell phone at the spaceport. We'd never even considered her setting up her own disappearance. Because she'd had no motive. But her parasite might.

"I'll call him." Brill moves off to one side.

I sit in one of the uncomfortable chairs. Tawny sits opposite me and sighs loudly. No lo sé if she's expressing annoyance at the loss of Kaliel – or of her electronics.

Chestla sits next to me, squeezes my hand. I'm hoping she's about to say something reassuring about Kaliel. Instead she says, "Thank you for this. Don't lose your nerve, and it will be OK."

I glance over at Brill, who is hanging up his phone. He leans against the wall, all casual cool in his brown leather jacket, with his arms crossed over his chest – though he's holding the injured hand awkwardly. I am hoping for reassurance, pero he just shrugs.

Well, fantastica.

A small door at the back of the room opens, and a guy dressed in a more masculine version of my white-pants-and-tunic ensemble comes through it. His eyes are hazel, which I've not seen in any of the others, and his brown skin shares the same warm tones as mine. He speaks Universal. "They are ready for you downstairs."

My heart jolts. That sounds ominous. What could be down there? A dungeon? A prison? A basement full of paperwork that needs sorting? Still, what else is there to do but follow him into the back room, and down the stairs?

He turns and flashes me a smile that, despite the implied good intention, makes me take a nervous step back. He says, "I'm sorry for the crudeness of your reception. There is an air-conditioning repairman strike on, and none of us could abide that stuffy room."

I hear agua running somewhere at the bottom of the stairs, and laughter. We come out into a short hallway with rubberized matting covering the raw rock, then take a right turn into an enormous roughhewn cave, much of it pure white stone, with veins of amethyst-tinted minerals threaded through it. At one side, a waterfall cascades into the space from somewhere unseen, into a pool that takes up most of the area. A couple dozen children in bathing attire modest enough to have sleeves play in the pool, and maybe thirty adults lounge in white chairs at the pool's far edge, wearing either tunic ensembles or similar swimwear. One of the adults jumps in, and the kids splash her, screaming in delight. Pero then they notice us, and everything falls silent, save the *chsssh* of the waterfall.

Our guide leads us around the pool, to a raised platform, and all the adults – save the one in the pool monitoring the kids – turn their chairs around to face it.

Our guide sweeps a hand in their direction. "Miss Benitez, may I present our Council of Elders."

Some faces out there don't look particularly old. Some do. The pairs of slitted eyes stare hard at me over high-boned cheeks. There's enough sheer predator pheromone here to override the IH, and I find myself unable to speak. I give a nod and do my best to smile. And not pee.

One of the most wrinkled faces belongs to a dark-haired woman, who stands and says, "Chestla. So good to see you again, my dear. I trust that your cesuda ma is coming into this pashed open, honest and free from any collusion of answers prepared in advance."

Chestla bows her cabeza. "Of course, Grammy. I have told her nothing of the tests to be faced, except that there will be a hunt."

"Good." Chestla's Grammy – no lo sé if that's gene-tied, or just a title – smiles. "Bodacious Babe, we need your honest accounting of the facts. And to secure that, we need your permission to administer a truth drug."

I try to talk, pero all that comes out is a squeak. Given the lethalriffic nature of Chestla's people, I probably wouldn't have even managed that without the artificial courage from the residual IH.

Chestla squeezes my hand. "May she have a moment to compose herself?"

I take a few deep breaths, feel my thudding heart slow a little as I try to force my mind to let go of the flight response. Once I'm able to speak I say, "It's not addictive, no? 'Cause I've already got one of those." I'm trying for a joke, pero it falls flat in the cool room.

Our hazel-eyed guide takes a bottle from a cooler leaning against the wall. It looks like a sports drink. "There are no lingering effects."

I look at Chestla. "Is this one going to make me sick?"

Chestla blinks. "I don't think so."

I take the bottle and uncap it. I'm expecting something salty, pero this tastes a bit like peaches and basil. I take a few sips. Everyone's still watching me expectantly. Chestla mimes upending the thing, so I drain the bottle. I don't feel any different.

After a few minutes, Chestla's Grammy starts talking to me about nothing in particular, waiting for the drug to take effect. I tell her about growing up in Chetumal, about mi mamá's show, and I assure her that I am very much a chocofan. She asks when the last time I had chocolate was, and I tell her I made chocoflan for everybody last night aboard Brill's ship, how

Kaliel, who dislikes chocolate, had refused to eat it.

This makes her look very happy. "Good, good." Grammy's golden eyes narrow. "Have you been alone with Kaliel at any point since the day he disappeared, back on Zant."

Brill makes a startled noise. "Now wait a minute–"

I can answer honestly. "No. We spoke privately for a few minutes today, pero that was in view of an entire complement of watching warriors."

"Has he hit you, kissed you, or offered you injectable drugs?"

I blink. "Que?"

"Babe, they're trying to figure out if you might be infected with whatever Kaliel's got." Brill uncrosses his arms, lets his hands hang loose at his sides. It's a passive move, pero it puts him ready for action. "Wal, he kissed her. But that doesn't prove anything."

"Of course not," Grammy says. "We are looking for the parasite's intent, not its effectiveness. We can test that physically."

Guide Guy takes my face in his soft hands. "Look up at the ceiling."

It's a beautiful ceiling, with skylights hewn into the rock. I study it for a good thirty seconds. He releases my face and shakes his cabeza.

"Good." Grammy's smiling again. "What did you eat the day he kissed you?"

I blink, trying to fight an overwhelming urge to rub at my face. All I can think about is what Kaliel had said that night. *He really wanted to do that.* Was *he* the parasite? Or Kaliel? Does it matter? "I thought this was supposed to be about Chestla."

"So did I," Chestla says softly.

"Of course." Grammy nods. "Tell me how you met Chestla."

I talk for a long time, about how I met Chestla, and how I met Brill, and how what Brill really wanted from me was to get close to chocolate as a commodity, right up until we fell in love.

I'm honest about how hurt I was, and how morally conflicted I still am over what a gray trader is and does, about how I'm afraid to ask sometimes about Krom or Brill's family or where he stands on certain things. And yet, I know that both he and Chestla will always keep me safe.

When I'm done, I look over at Brill. His irises are a deep sorrowful apricot, and I have no idea why. I have a hard time recalling what I've just said.

Grammy nods again. "That's very... interesting. You trusted Chestla with your life then... but do you now? Are you prepared to join her tomorrow on the hunt?"

"Prepared? No y no y no. Pero, am I willing to trust her? Of course. She is one of my best friends."

Chestla puts a hand on my arm. "Thank you, Bo. That means a great deal to me."

Something happens in the pool behind us. It starts with lots of splashing and ends with two kids crying. Everyone turns to see whose kids they are and to make sure nothing horrible has happened. These are people with families, with a basic level of decency.

I look several of them in the eye, then focus on Grammy. "What happens to Kaliel?"

"We will deworm him after the hunt tomorrow," Grammy says.

Brill snickers and looks significantly at me, and I know he's resisting making an Earth-pet joke. Chestla realizes it too and stares daggers at him.

Grammy looks confused, but continues, "In the meantime, we wish to study him, and to interrogate the parasite. We were unaware that this scourge had jumped to Earthlings."

That makes sense, even if it leaves Kaliel connected to a condemned part of a larger consciousness. It reminds me of when Kaliel had been wearing that lethal-if-cut tracking anklet, awaiting trial. Maybe he can comfort the mindworm.

Maybe – ironically – this experience will help him heal.

If we can just keep him alive after that. I'm sure Zantite law doesn't have a mind-worms-made-me-do-it clause. And the Zantite jury would never believe him anyway, especially if the Evevrons won't let us record evidence.

"When you say interrogate," Brill asks, "you're not intending to hurt the su are you?"

I glance over at him. The concerned deep green-gray of his eyes looks genuine. I wouldn't have thought he cared what happened to Kaliel. Maybe there's a lot more going on inside mi vida than I give him credit for.

Grammy shakes her head. "It wouldn't be fair of us to return your friend to his own mind harmed by us in any way."

"I want to be there," Tawny says. "I'm not going on your insane hunt, so I can at least observe."

The council members start looking at each other, and there's a brief murmur of conversation, and then Grammy nods. "Agreed." Then she gestures Brill over to her and touches his face, gently prodding the new skin, which is still a bit shiny and uneven. "I have a facialist named Cassandra that specializes in battle scars. Two hours with her, and that will hardly be noticeable." She grins. "Unless your people consider scars a badge of honor."

"Absolutely not. The badge of honor thing, I mean." Brill looks over at me. "I'd love to have the face back that she fell in love with."

Chestla insists that I stay with her, while the council offers lodging for Tawny and Brill at a nearby hotel. My friends are invited for dinner, though. Chestla's papá is a chef, so it's kind of a big deal. Tawny bows out, saying she's ill from being out in the sun. So an hour before dinner, it's just me and Brill sitting on a black leather sofa in Chestla's family's living room, waiting.

Chestla's family's "house" is the entire forty-second floor of one of the skyscrapers. It's spacious enough for all the kids, and feels like a comfortable place to hang out, pero the smells coming out of the kitchen are disturbing.

"Don't worry," Brill whispers. "I put enough provisions on the levbots with our water to last the three of us a couple of days. I gave Tawny something for dinner, and I can sneak you some food in here later."

"It would be rude not to eat *something*," I whisper back.

Brill's eyes go violet, showing amusement without having to laugh out loud. "I stopped worrying about who I might be offending after I got food poisoning on Cherdon. It's amazing how different our base biology can seem with races that still manage to cross." He wrinkles his nose towards the kitchen. "I mean, how do you mix their taste buds with mine?"

I raise an eyebrow. "There have been Krom–Evevron tewakelle?" That's the Krom word for an interplanetary gene-cross.

Brill does laugh out loud. "You've never heard anybody talk about a Duracell?"

"Like a battery?"

"Something about energy that just won't stop? It's Earth slang, uan I'm not sure of the exact reference. They're exceedingly rare. Like if tewakelle in general are rare, a Krom and an Evevron hitting it off long enough to reproduce is almost a myth. But most of those crosses wind up with book lungs *and* claws. The Evevrons recruit them young as special cops. The status and the preferential treatment tends to give them an attitude." He makes an exaggerated face like he's bitten into an unripe t'tel.

"You sound like you know this from experience."

Brill shrugs. "Tyson's partner when I first met him was a Duracell. In every sense of the word."

"What happened?"

The violet fades from Brill's eyes. "Guy thought he was invincible. From what I hear, he ignored Tyson's request that he wait for backup and charged into a den full of art thieves. Can't say it didn't make me happy, knowing he never walked back out."

Brill's never been the vengeful type. What would it take to make him happy someone's dead?

"This has to do with Darcy, no?" I hold my breath as soon as the words are out. Darcy was Brill's best friend, who died as a result of an illegal trade deal gone bad, before I had even met Brill. Jeska had implied that Tyson was somehow involved in Darcy's death. I've never pushed Brill to talk about it, and from the look on his face, now was a bad time to start. Can I blame it as aftereffects of the truth cocktail? "I'm sorry. I shouldn't–"

"No." Brill says it so loudly that the three little girls across the room look up from their craft project.

Brill touches my face, guides me to look at him. "I don't want you feeling like you have to tiptoe around me. If we're going to make this work, it's not fair for you to feel like I'm still hiding things. If you want to know about Darcy, you shouldn't be afraid to ask."

"OK." I swallow, hard. "What happened between him and this Galactacop?"

"Jeska told you how Darcy and I found those cases of expired Lotvrek in his aunt's basement?"

I nod. Darcy's brother had told me more about Brill's past than Brill himself. The illegal neural enhancers had brainmelted Darcy's uncle so badly he'd wound up in a mental institution. Which is why I'm still uncomfortable with the fact that Brill was trying to help Darcy sell them.

"Darcy told that to Inspector Know-It-All, but the su didn't believe him. Wanted him to name his source, promised to go easy if he could get a bigger arrest up the ladder. That's the flaw with letting the Inspectors qualify to collect bounties.

He beat Darcy to near unconsciousness. Finally, Darcy made something up.

"It was total nonsense, but the word got around that he had snitched. He fled the detention center while he was still on Krom because he suspected he would be killed, as soon as he got to prison." Brill closes his eyes, like this story has been waiting to come pouring out of him. "You know what the Codex says. A Krom is responsible for his own actions. If he breaks the law and is caught, he accepts the punishment rather than cause Galactic conflict. Darcy had been prepared for that, even joked around at the trial that he was finally going to have time to write that novel. But we don't turn our people over to die for crimes that shouldn't merit it. We appeal to the Galactic Court instead, when local laws are insane. He was within his conscience bounds to try to escape, rather than let himself be killed."

"I know." Well, maybe not the specifics, pero I've learned how important honor is to mi vida.

"I still have this vivid recurring nightmare about the day it happened." He hesitates, and I can see how painful this is to share. My heart hurts for him. "I'm outside my family's house, detailing their runabout, when Darcy crashes into it, uan he can't even control the wheel of the car he stole from the parking lot of the detention center. And when I pull him out, there's a hole the size of my fist in his chest. We manage to talk for a couple of minutes, while I cradle his head. I have his blood all over me, hear the rasp of his final breath... and then the nightmare switches to this surreal black and white, and I'm in a field, chasing someone wearing a black beanie, someone whose face I can never see, and when I wake up, I can't decide if that's supposed to be death, or justice or what that I'm running after."

"That part is just a dream." I hold him closer, comforting him.

"Darcy was shot by another Krom, at a detention center on our home planet, and the guard only thought he was dangerous because of Tyson's partner's lies."

"And Tyson didn't do anything about it?" I hear the note of disbelief in my own voice.

Brill opens his eyes. They're the color of clay. "How could he have missed what was happening on his own ship? There are rumors that Tyson killed at least one innocent Krom, early in–"

"You guys! I cannot believe this little guy is still alive!" Chestla's standing in the doorway, holding a brass and plastic cage. She looks from Brill's muddy eyes to my tense face. "Maybe I should come back later."

"Ga." Brill forces a smile as he forces his eyes to a greyish blue. "We're done talking old times. What little guy?"

Chestla puts the cage on the floor and removes the top. A fist-sized bug flies out of it and lands on her hand. It's like somebody crossed a ladybug with a wasp, only the yellow striped wings are an iridescent blue and the head's about three times too big. "This is my old hunting beetle, Tazma. They're only supposed to live to about ten, but he's at least twelve. I gave him to my sister for her first hunt, not long before I left. She wants me to borrow him back for tomorrow."

"It's a what, now?" Brill asks.

"A hunting beetle. They're just about the only thing fast enough to chase the things we're going after, and they send back echolocation signals we can trace. A couple of centuries ago, they were the miracle of modern genetic engineering. But now, everybody has at least one."

I point. "So that stinger on the back…"

"It injects a paralyzing agent to slow down the animal we're trying to catch. It doesn't always work, though."

Chestla's holding a potentially lethal pet on her bare fist – one that's not necessarily a match for whatever we're hunting. Agreeing to this was probably a mistake.

Chestla's dad calls to us from the kitchen. Chestla smiles and coaxes the beetle back into the cage. "Dinner's ready."

"About that," I say hesitantly. "I'm not hungry."

My stomach grumbles, giving lie to my words.

Chestla moves towards the door. "One bite of hefshig never killed anybody. That's my dad's rule – it's OK if you don't like something, but you have to at least try it. He even made it vegetarian, on account there's a Krom."

I look at Brill. He shrugs. Well, at least we'll have the story to tell of the time we tried hefshig.

The next morning, I'm sitting in bed, trying to decipher the newsfeed on the Evevron-language householo. I didn't sleep well last night, and I ate even less. Since Chestla insisted on guarding my door in case of other surprise attacks, Brill wasn't able to sneak me provisions, so now I'm grumpy and ravenous and willing to trade everything I have for a cup of coffee and a jelly doughnut. I've got the shakes something fierce, and I can't find my toothbrush, which I left last night in a bathroom shared by six girls.

Chestla knocks on the door, then comes in carrying another outfit. Gracias a dios, this one is a purple camo print tunic and pants – just like what she's already wearing. En serio.

Why can't I just once wind up somewhere where I get to wear a formal gown? So many other elements of my life feel like a telenovela, so why not that one?

"I hope you're ready to face your public this morning, cesuda ma. They're giving Tawny her camera drones to fly at the hunt breakfast."

I groan, but at this point it's mostly habit. "Bueno. I didn't really want to watch her snap."

I haul the curtain closed and look longingly at the bed. Pero this hunt breakfast had sounded imminent. So I don the camo-chic, and I'm lacing my boots when Chestla comes back with a steaming mug.

When I take it, Chestla studies my shaking hands.

I take a sip. "Withdrawal symptoms from the Invincible Heart. They're never going away."

It's hard to say that out loud.

"We all adapt." Chestla looks down at her own hands, stretches her fingers. "After I fell in the canyon, it took a long time to get over the pain. And longer to get off the pain drugs. I learned the hard way, you can rely on your friends, when you can't go on alone. If you don't shut them out." Like she had done, sending them away from her hospital room, and then leaving the planet. We aren't that different, not really.

CHAPTER TWENTY-NINE

A car arrives outside Chestla's place to take us to the hunt breakfast. When her parents and sisters hug her goodbye, it's desperate and lingering, like they're afraid they might be seeing her for the last time. The little one doesn't want to let go of her legs, even as we head for the door.

Chestla peers down into the hunting beetle's cage for the whole ride down the elevator, uncharacteristically silent. When she catches me watching her, she says, "We're taking the lead nefch." *Position? Vehicle?* "Which is always the most dangerous. And they just got me back, so it's natural they're worried." She nods down at the beetle. "Most of the time, though, everyone comes back fine. Like I said, this guy's been around for twelve years."

The car picked Brill up before coming to get us. He's sitting in the back in his usual leather jacket and tee combo. Chestla gets into the front, next to the driver, pero she turns around to frown at mi vida. "Did you not get the hunting habit we sent?"

Brill's irises go apricot. "I'm not wearing that."

I stifle a laugh, looking down at my own ridiculous clothes as I slide in next to Brill. "Sí... purple's not exactly Brill's color, chica."

Chestla sighs. "We're going into a heavily forested area, where many of the plants have picked up pigmentation from the minerals in the soil. It's not about fashion. It's about safety."

Brill shrugs. "Think of the leather as low-level body armor."

Chestla rolls her eyes. "Stubborn kek."

Brill grins. "Guilty."

"How about I see if I can get you guys some real body armor? A lot of people wear it under their hunting habits."

Brill's eyes go bright green, in intense excitement. "Really? Avell, su." His expression has hardly shifted, but it's the chromatic equivalent of jumping up and down like a kid getting candy.

"No promises." Chestla lapses into silence.

"What's up with the weather around here?" Brill asks. "I moved the *Fois Gras* to the spaceport this morning – after I dug it out from the dust storm. But that whole area is close to a lush forest."

Chestla says, "This region only has one major irrigation source, so we all fight to control the river. The city upriver built dams, and then we rerouted it to build our own; the changes in the flow pattern and the way people used the land turned swathes of this continent into a dust bowl."

Brill asks, "Are these conflicts ongoing?"

Chestla looks down at her hands. "It's more of a cold hostility. You won't be affected as long as you stay on this side of the banks."

So Chestla's people fought a war with Zant, while at the same time in the middle of a civil war on their own planet. Never underestimate the Evevrons.

My stomach grumbles. Brill passes me a packaged cake, which I eat as discreetly as I can. It's no jelly doughnut, pero at least the flavors are familiar.

Chestla's quiet the whole way to the breakfast, and when we get there, she's slow to get out of the car. I wonder if Brill's question hit some painful memory for her. She forces a smile that looks more like a grimace. "This is in our honor. Let's do our best to enjoy it."

The party is set up outside. There must be a hundred people here, in line for the buffet, seated at picnic tables, standing in clusters talking. I recognize Ekrin and several of her companions, Grammy, the hazel-eyed guy, a few of the kids. Ekrin is wearing her body armor. No lo sé whether that means she's joining us for the hunt. Guide Guy is wearing a hunting habit, based on black and gray, with only hints of purple. So he's going.

A camera drone shifts, catching the hazel-eyed guy's smile as Chestla approaches, then capturing our semi-dramatic entrance. Grammy sees us and waves. She picks up a pair of bowls that have been resting on the buffet table's edge. She carries them over and hands one each to me and Chestla. "The best portions for our champions."

It doesn't smell half bad. We chat with Grammy for a second. When she walks off, I ask Chestla, "What is it?"

"Nebra." She hesitates. "In Universal you call it Amethyst Rice. It picks up the color from the soil."

"Pero what are the black discs?"

"Meat."

The way she says it, I don't dare ask her to elaborate.

People are watching, so the only culturally acceptable thing to do is eat. The meat is alright, if a touch on the sweet side. The rice though – it's so salty that I can barely choke it down.

"Water? Por favor?"

Chestla looks towards the buffet table uncertainly. "That's rationed."

"Reshdo, Babe." Brill comes up to me, hands me a bottle from Tawny's stash. I crack the seal and gulp it.

Brill taps his fist against his chest, and there's a hollow clank. "This stuff is so thin, you can't even tell under the jacket."

He looks so happy, I can't help but smile. "Perfecto, no?"

"Ekrin got some for you and Chestla too." He points at Ekrin, enjoying yellowish custard with her amigos. She sees us looking and waves me over.

I follow Ekrin to a building where I layer the armor under my hunting habit. It's a long, flexible vest with Velcro for attaching the jointed sleeves.

My handheld rings. It's Tyson. I take it as a voice call.

"Where te bloodfire white rapids cold heart are you?"

I swallow, and that salt aftertaste is suddenly strong in my mouth. "In a changing room?"

I thought that might embarrass him. No y no. "Everyone is saying you have Kaliel. You're supposed to turn him over. That was the deal. Do you want me to have to arrest you too?"

I don't tell him we're supposed to have sanctuary, because that would mean telling him where we are. "I'll call you when the doctors are done with him." When the parasite is dead, and we know what we have to work with.

I hang up on Tyson while he's still trying to reason with me and head back to the party.

A train of open-sided vehicles trundles driverlessly up the street, halting where the car had dropped us off. The hazel-eyed guy punches a fist in the air, and at that signal, the Evevrons in hunting gear peel away from the picnic and race for these vehicles, with their huge tires and platforms attached to the back ends.

"Come on, you guys!" Chestla's already in motion, calling back to us. "We have the lead nefch."

Brill catches up to her with zero effort. I rush to join them.

Guide Guy's already in the lead vehicle – the same one we're heading for. He turns to Chestla, "Already leaving your cesuda ma behind, Stala?"

As he says it, his hazel eyes glimmer lavender, just long enough I know I didn't imagine it. Which means the guy's a Duracell.

I look at mi vida's face. Brill saw that glint of chromashift, and he's not happy about it. Pero, will he let that prejudice him?

"Shut up, Ball." Chestla shoves the Duracell's shoulder as she gets in next to him, leaving Brill and me to climb into the back seat.

The gun mounted to the back of the front seats is roughly the size of a rocket launcher.

"Are we expecting trouble, chica?" I ask.

"What?" Chestla looks back at me, puzzled.

I nod towards the gun.

She laughs. "That's just a hunting rifle."

"Buckle up," Ball says, even as he shifts the vehicle into gear, and we take off into the forest. Whoops echo up and down the line, from the other vehicles, as they start to break into a rangy formation.

"Ball's a Krom name," Brill says, leaning forward, so that he's close to the Duracell's ear. "With a similar meaning to mine. Instead of *Frost Flower*, it's something more like *Snowy Crag*."

"Wal." Ball doesn't turn around. "It happens to be my dad's name too. Reverae desha neb sawa shon?" Very loosely translated, *You got a problem with that?*

"Ga, su." Brill smiles, and this time it looks genuine. Relief floods through me. Brill gestures to his own eyes, while looking in the rearview mirror. "You didn't shift once yesterday, so I honestly had no idea."

Ball laughs. "My eyes only hit shades of lavender, and there wasn't anything funny going on."

"Really?" Chestla asks. "I never noticed that, even when we were little."

"That's because you saw them shift all the time." He makes eye contact with Brill in the rearview mirror. "I was the class clown. My dad still jokes they should have named me Parz."

The Krom word for laughter.

"You went to a regular school?" Brill sounds surprised.

"My dad insisted. Threatened to move us all to Krom if my

grandparents didn't stop pushing for me to be special. I've earned every accomplishment to my credit. I'd like to think I'm a better man for it."

I watch Brill's eyes, wait for the flash of color after the surprise fades. It's a soft blue. And there's no quick switch after. And that's what I love about mi vida. He doesn't let preconceptions about *what* a person is blind him to *who* they are. Given the culture he comes from, he's had to learn that skill the hard way.

"Don't listen to Ball," Chestla says. "He was horrible. He used to pull my hair."

Eh? Ball probably had a crush on Chestla when they were kids. Claro está, he has neither the chromashift or the ability to blush to give him away. And Chestla had had a crush on somebody else, so she might not have even noticed.

Chestla opens the lid of the cage on her lap. She puts her hand inside and comes out with the hunting beetle on her fist. She shields it from the air rushing past us with her other hand. "Are you ready?"

Ball nods, and Chestla holds her fist out the open side of the vehicle, and the bug is in the air. It's not the only thing out there. One of Tawny's camera drones has come along for the ride. The whooping passes through the formation again. We're all following Chestla's lead. She puts the empty cage on the floor between her feet and holds up the lid. She flips it over, and there's a holographic display of a dancing field of shifting colored light. What it represents, I can't tell.

Chestla can. "Twenty degrees to our right."

The nefch turns, slipping between two tall trees. There's a hint of movement ahead of us, the sound of something bulky crashing through the underbrush. I hope the hunting beetle managed to stun whatever it is.

Chestla keeps shouting course corrections, and the other vehicles are holding formation despite the breakneck speed and the uneven terrain. She gestures to the gun. "Brill, do you want to do the honors?"

He straightens the collar of his jacket. "I'm a vegetarian."

Well, not a strict one, but we all get his point. And I can see why a Krom/Evevron tewakelle is an exercise in contradiction.

For a second, I wonder why Brill came at all, pero then I realize – he's only here to protect me.

"Suit yourself." Chestla grabs the gun and pulls it over the seat as the vehicle skids to a halt. Apparently, we have surrounded the whatever-it-is. "Stay behind me, Bo."

I nod numbly, and force myself off the vehicle. Should I be insulted that Chestla didn't offer me the rifle? Honestly, I'm relieved. She bounds away, disappearing into the vegetation.

Brill moves Krom-fast, putting himself between me and whatever is going on beyond the next stand of trees. I hear a scuffle, and Chestla shouting. We race forward, pero before we can see what's happening, there's the crack of a gunshot and an animal scream. The injured beast – something like someone crossed the ugliest parts of a rat, an alligator gar and an elephant – turns and lashes out at Chestla with a whip-like tail. She flinches away, pero takes the blow across her shoulder.

Whoosh! Something sleek's flying through the air. Ball's oversized knife hits home in the creature's neck. The beast topples. Ball rushes to Chestla. "Are you OK?"

Given the look on his face, he didn't just have a crush on Chestla a long time ago. He still has a thing for her.

I look down at the dead rat thing, hoping Brill knows better than to make a joke about cats chasing mice. I'm a little nauseated, looking at that sinewy tail. Was that what we had for breakfast?

"I'm fine." Chestla's looking at her bleeding shoulder, not at the concern on his face.

Ball examines Chestla's injury, picking out a few shards of armor. "Thank the Codex."

Brill makes a small noise at this reference. His eyes are a soft brown, pero they tint towards green as he reevaluates this guy.

Ball looks over at me. "The tail barbs on kapursts are poisonous. But it doesn't look like that got through."

"I told you, I'm going to be fine." Chestla winces as one of the medics comes up behind her and applies foam to her shoulder.

"Then Stala, what were you thinking?" Ball grabs her arm roughly, turns her so that she has to look at him. "Why didn't you wait?"

Chestla looks from him, over at me. I feel my face going hot. She'd tried to protect me.

Ball scowls at me, pero he's talking to Chestla. "If you die trying to keep her from having to see danger, then what's the point of taking this test? Go throw your life away somewhere else." He hesitates. "Somewhere I don't have to see it."

Chestla's eyes go wide, pero other Evevrons are entering the clearing, half a dozen of them kneeling to efficiently butcher the alligator-rat-thing.

Brill gestures towards the vehicle, where the others are lashing freezer-bags of meat to the platform on the back of our vehicle. "We survived the hunt, so what's the big deal? We're done."

Ball clears his throat. "Does it look like that is going to feed an entire city for a week?"

As intimidating as the beast had been when alive, it doesn't look like much broken down. The hunt isn't over.

CHAPTER THIRTY

Back in the vehicle, Chestla's still in the front seat, pero the elevated excitement has drained out of her. I catch her glancing at Ball, like maybe she's never really looked at him before in her life. Could Ball's unrequited childhood crush be blossoming into something real as Brill and I watch?

The vehicle is moving more slowly now, almost like we're trawling for fish.

We are, kind of. The smell of fresh meat has to be attracting other predators for miles. I see a flash of movement in the underbrush off to our right, and then a minute later, I get the chicken-skin-raising impression that something is watching me.

My heart is thudding, and a sense of euphoria is building in my chest, the remnants of the Invincible Heart trying to gather into something useful.

A tree off to our left cracks as something heavy leaps from its branches, and a lumbering form reaches for the sky. Chestla releases her hunting beetle, and up and down the formation, others must be doing the same, because suddenly there's dozens of them thick in the air. The creature makes a noise like a high-pitched freight train as the bugs attack it. It turns around and bites one of them out of the sky – along with Tawny's camera drone. I can't tell which beetle it was, pero Chestla gasps. She looks down at her swirling hologram, just as all the colors fall flat.

"Tazma." She says it softly, pero she stares down at her hands, and it's the first time I've ever thought she might cry.

"Lo siento," I say. "Truly, I am so sorry,"

Chestla runs the back of her hand across her nose. "It's better than finding him dead in his cage. He was so old."

The vehicle is silent save for the engine noise as Ball revs it, giving chase. Chestla adjusts the holodisplay, and it comes back up, split into four quadrants. She's tapping nearby echolocation feeds from some of the other beetles. Her voice is even as she gives Ball directions, pero I catch her wiping her eyes.

The undergrowth is bceoming thicker and it's even more humid. We're getting close to the river.

We come out at the cliffs overlooking the bank. The snake-bug-hippopotamus thing's flying oddly, one insectoid wing flapping strongly, the other half-paralyzed. We're still close enough that we might be able to catch it before it clears the edge.

Chestla grabs the gun again, leaning out of the moving vehicle, ready to take a shot if Ball can get in range. Ball looks at her with renewed determination in his eyes and forces the vehicle even faster, out ahead of the pack of transports. We're running out of cliff and he's showing no sign of stopping. Chestla takes her shot, and the creature lets out another bellow, as it comes crashing to the ground, rolling head over tail, coming up glittering from the minerals in the lavender-tinted soil. It rolls over the edge of the cliff.

Ball slams on the brakes, and my seatbelt engages as we skid toward the edge. My heart's thudding, the echo loud in my ears as my hand clutches the seat, like that will save me if we crash. I hold back the screech trying to escape my lungs.

We have almost two feet of flat ground left when we stop. A wave of hunting beetles flies back up, heading for the other vehicles. Brill gives Chestla a long, mahogany look, pero she's already out, bounding over to the edge, looking down.

"Killing it's not going to make her feel better, Babe."

We follow more slowly.

There's a ledge partway down that the creature landed on. It's not dead. It is flailing around in pain. I can't help feeling sorry for it, pero Chestla's glaring at the iridescent wings with an intensity that should crumble them to dust. The beast looks up at us, makes eye contact with Chestla. It seems to feel the same way about her.

Brill looks troubled. "Are you sure that thing's not sentient?"

Chestla turns her glare on him. "We wouldn't eat them if they were."

"They're just dangerous pests, su," Ball says. "Sometimes they tunnel under buildings on the outskirts of the city, destroy property, kill people. But that's more of a swarming instinct than a conscious plan." Ball looks over at me. "In Earth terms, imagine the intelligence of a lion crossed with the bothersomeness of a mole."

Ball puts his hand on Brill's shoulder. His eyes flash lavender.

"What?" Brill asks.

Ball shrugs. "Didn't expect it to be real leather, su."

Brill shrugs back. "I don't like denim, su."

Ball smiles at the easy return of the casual address. "Naw, su," he emphasizes the Krom word this time. "I'm the last one to judge." He gestures down at the injured monster. "I value the Codex, but I'd still eat that thing."

The thing in question starts climbing back up towards us, leaving a trail of blood on the rocks. The monster's progress slows as the climb gets steeper.

Chestla pulls a coil of rope out of the back of the vehicle and fastens it to a stumpy tree not far from the edge. I hope the slender trunk will hold her weight. Brill moves over to help her, counterbalancing the weight as she climbs over the ledge.

Between watching her, and keeping an eye on the beast, I'm blindsided by the *screeking* noise as another flying snakapotamus – three times bigger than the one we were chasing – impacts the vehicle and slams it at us.

"It's another spuck!" Ball shouts, even as the car hits us, pushing me and Ball over the edge.

Brill can't rush to my aid without dropping Chestla.

Ball grabs onto me, trying to wrap himself around me to cushion my landing.

We're falling towards the ledge, and the injured snake beastie – the spuck – below us has its mouth open in anticipation. Ball kicks it in the nose as we plummet past, pero even so, it turns and catches his leg in its teeth, jerking us to a halt.

Ball pushes me away from him, towards the rock face, where I manage to grab on. Even as he's drawing both of his knives, he grits his sharp teeth and says, "Small cave... down there."

I start climbing, trying not to listen to the sounds above me as Ball and the spuck try to kill each other. There's still a long way to go. I glance back up. Ball slashes at the spuck's face, and it drops him. He hits the ground while I'm still climbing. The beast struggles to get turned around to climb downwards. I'm not going to make it down before the spuck, injured and lumbering as it is, catches up to me.

"Bo!" Chestla calls. She's balancing on the rope, trying to get off another shot, pero she's still so far away. The spuck and I are almost down to the ledge. The rifle blast doesn't even come close.

Moving as a blur, Brill comes vaulting over the cliff edge. I hold my breath. Krom can jump a lot farther than humans can, pero this distance is a stretch even for him. He lands in a crouch, then stands up, unhurt. His balance looks a little off, and I realize he's got a megarifle slung over his back. He swings it back around and fires. The snake-hippo lets out a sound like a whisper as it loses its grip on the cliff face and crashes to the ground at Brill's feet.

There's a deep bellow from overhead as the larger version sweeps back around. Brill rushes over to me, still moving superhumanly fast. "Jump, Babe," he calls. "I'll catch you."

I let go of the rock face, and once he's got me in his arms, Brill crushes me into an embrace so tight I can't even draw breath. "I was so afraid I'd lost you." He loosens up enough for me to reply.

"Impressive heroing, mi vida."

He grins, pero his eyes are still solid black, and it isn't me he's terrified for. We're racing around the spuck's still form, to where Ball is struggling to crawl towards the cave. Brill puts me down. "Hanstral, Babe, but I need you to help me carry him inside."

"What about Chestla?"

She's still up there, exposed, on the cliff face. And the dead monster's mate is in the distance, wheeling to make another pass.

Brill glances up at it. "We have to help Ball first. Chestla can take care of herself."

"No!" Ball protests. "I'm dead already. Help Chestla."

Ignoring him, Brill picks Ball up by the shoulders. I help as best I can.

It's a small cave, and Brill has to duck to get through the entrance. There's the dripping sound of agua from somewhere deeper inside.

"I got him from here." Brill shifts his grip and carries Ball into the cave. I turn back to check on Chestla, but the rope is empty and she's nowhere to be seen.

The larger spuck is diving towards the ledge. I duck back inside the cave, move farther into the safety the space provides.

Ball is lying on the ground near the water, and Brill's thrown off his jacket and taken off his shirt, his jeans incongruous with the body armor covering his chest as he presses the fabric against the worst part of Ball's wounded thigh. The gashes run the length of the Duracell's leg, from the lower calf, up onto the torso. Ball attempted to use his belt as a tourniquet, pero it's not stopping his life from leaking out all over the cave floor.

From the distant look on Brill's face, mi vida must be flashing back to Darcy's death. And somehow, it's like Ball's representing both Darcy and the Duracell who caused Brill's best friend to bleed out in his arms. I can't tell exactly what's going on inside mi vida, pero his eyes are shifting like a fireworks show.

The cave floor vibrates as the grande snake hippo lands outside and starts scratching at the entrance. Brill looks at the rifle, then at me. "Babe. He's a tewakelle, not a full Krom. Maybe he still has a chance if we can get him to the medics."

Ball gestures towards the mouth of the cave. "You'd have to get past that thing first. Spucks live in burrows, so you want to do something before it carves a way in here."

Brill presses even harder with the shirt, while staring at the cave entrance. Ball lets out a soft cry of pain.

"Hanstral, su," Brill apologizes. Then he gives me a pleading look.

I want to tell him that we can switch places. I could put my hands over his, and we wouldn't even lose pressure on the worst of Ball's wounds. Pero, mi vida needs to be there for this injured man in a way that's deeper than my fear.

I swallow hard. "You know I'm a horrible shot."

Still, I pick up the rifle.

Ball's face still has color, and he looks in good spirits for a guy who's in the process of bleeding out. He may not think we can help him, pero that doesn't mean we don't have to try.

I make my way back to the cave entrance. The snake-hippo is still scratching at the rock, and a big piece of it gives way. The spuck fills the field of view outside the cave. There's no way I can miss.

I fire the rifle, and the kickback knocks me off my feet, sending waves of pain through my shoulder with the old gunshot wound. I'm going to think of Tyson every time that spot hurts.

The beast bellows, and there's spurting blood, pero I don't think I hit anything vital. It thrashes and the cave mouth bursts apart. A flexible front foot comes inches away from me, almost like a giant hand with eighteen-inch long claws – blunted for digging, pero still strong enough to impale me. It makes a grab for me, and I jump backwards. The claws rake my purple camo shirt, echoing through my body, like nails on a chalk board. Pero, the body armor holds. I get the rifle up again, and as the snakelike cabeza comes at me, I fire.

There's a hole in the jaw, and in slow motion, it topples to the side.

And Chestla's standing outside, with a sword in both her hands raised high up over her head, like she was about to strike. She stares from me, to the rifle, to the prone monster.

She blinks. "Alrighty then."

Now that it's on its side, I can see that she was shooting the spuck too, putting several holes in its wings, busting up its back leg. Pero, that's not what killed it.

"You sure it wasn't sentient?" I take a deep breath. I've boiled lobsters alive, and steamed ghexxkt before, pero nothing I've cooked has looked me in the eye with malice like this thing did. Plus, the head shape's not that different from Tyson's.

"Absolutely." She puts a comforting arm around my shoulders. I wince because of the bruising to my old injury. "They're smart enough to set a basic trap, but they don't have a language or a culture, they don't pass wisdom on to their offspring. They can't pass empathy or self-awareness tests. And they kill indiscriminately."

"I guess that makes me feel better." It doesn't. Pero I don't have time to dwell on the strange numbness inside me right now.

Chestla stares at the claws on the spuck's limp forefoot. "I wish we could find a way to exterminate these things. We have little enough water as it is, and they tend to divert parts of the river into underground pools for their spawning grounds. You know the waterfall cave complex under the city building? That was originally the spucks' work." She looks past me, and I can see she's babbling because she's hesitating. "Where's Ball? Is he..." She can't finish the sentence.

I look deeper into the cave. "We have to figure out a way to get him out of here, chica. If..."

I can't finish my sentence either. *If it's not already too late.*

Chestla nods and her arm drops away from me. "How could I have been so blind, cesuda ma? How could I have missed seeing how he feels about me? Even after I've been away for all this time?" She hesitates. "It's like how I started to feel about Eugene. We were together every day for two months, and he never saw it. I suck at this love stuff." She turns, moving into the cave.

I follow her. Ball's starting to look pale. My stomach sinks, like I've swallowed a lump of Zantite fest bread. Brill shakes his cabeza, just a little.

Ay, no! No. Ball can't die. Not just because he's a nice guy, pero because of what it will do to both Brill and Chestla.

Chestla moves to Ball's side, takes his hand in hers. "We're going to get you back up this cliff. It'll be OK."

Ball squeezes her hand. "Don't bother. I'm not going to make it back up to the top. I already feel cold."

She stares at him. "Are you going to give up? Are you expecting *me* to give up?"

He grins. "Stala, you never gave up on anything in your life. That's what I love about you."

"So why didn't you ever say anything?" Her words come out almost venomously.

"Because you never even noticed me. Not really." His breathing is getting slower. And there's not a damn thing any of us can do about it. "Today, I thought maybe."

"Maybe what?" Her voice is husky and broken.

My own throat feels so thick that I can hardly swallow.

"I thought maybe you really saw me, for the first time. But I was foolish to think it would matter. There's no room now for might have beens."

"It might have been something wonderful," Chestla says. "I thought that, right after you yelled at me."

Ball closes his eyes for so long I think he's gone. Then he says, "I am jealous of Sleekadai. At least he died firm in the belief that you loved him."

Chestla sucks in air. "He knew?"

"Of course he knew." Ball's eyes flash lavender, even as his hand slips out of Chestla's. "What do you think he did when you sent him away from your hospital bed? He spent days in the waiting room, pestering the nurses for news."

"I never thought..." Chestla's voice breaks. She takes Ball's hand in both of hers.

"I'm glad that I could tell you. That I could in some measure heal your pain. That I..." He lapses into silence.

"That you what?" Chestla asks. He doesn't respond. She scoops him up in her arms and heads out of the cave. "No! I refuse to let it end this way."

There's an odd sound from somewhere deep inside the

cave, and then a breeze, which seems to be blowing in the wrong direction – from the rock face behind us. Chestla turns and bounds past us, deeper into the cave, disappearing into a crack in the wall that I hadn't even noticed.

"Chestla! Por favor!" I don't even know what I'm asking. For her to come back? For an explanation of what just happened?

I start to go after her, pero I look back at Brill. He's moved to the underground pool, where he washes off his hands and chest, the blood an indeterminate shade here in the shadows as it mingles with the agua. Then he puts his jacket on and, without his usual layering tee, zips it closed.

CHAPTER THIRTY-ONE

We find the opening at the back of the cave, follow a trail of dark smears through a maze of tunnels to where Chestla has busted open a door. It's a finished, air-conditioned room, incongruous with the rest of the space.

One wall is taken up with computers, and a large holofield. Near the opposite wall there's a tall counter inlaid with Bunsen burners and scattered with test tubes – some of them filled with dark substances. There's even a microscope set up with a slide in it. It feels like we've stumbled into the lab in a cheesetastic mad scientist flick.

Chestla's laid Ball on the floor. We walk in just as she wrenches open a metal box that's attached to the wall, next to an emergency eye-washing station.

"What is this place, chica?"

"Don't know. Looks like some kind of research facility. Maybe somebody trying to escape regulation. They could be cooking drugs."

She pulls out a gun filled with healing foam and a roll of gauze. I move to try to help her, pero she's reconstructing a person with foam and papier mâché. I don't have the skill to assist.

Brill digs through the first aid box. He hands me a pouch filled with clear liquid, and a syringe of something deep amber. Mi vida taps the syringe. "Don't give him that unless his heart stops beating." Then he turns away to explore the room, which is filled with old computers and lab equipment. "They have to be hiding something, to have set up shop somewhere this dangerous. And isolated."

I kneel next to Ball, on the opposite side from Chestla. He's stopped breathing. I still can't get over the certainty in mi corazón that seeing a still chest means he's dead – even if mi cabeza knows he's got book lungs. I feel Ball's wrist. There is a pulse, slow and faint. I release the short tube tucked up against the clear pouch, and try to figure out how to insert the needle.

Chestla's muttering in Evevron as she works, and she's got healing foam smeared across her face.

I rip Ball's sleeve, revealing a granite-muscled forearm with visible veins. That – and the pictures printed on the pouch's side – make it easier than I anticipated. The fluid looks thick. Considering Evevron biology, it's probably super-saturated saline.

The medics should be down here soon, to help us.

"Babe," Brill says from across the room, his voice high and nervous. I look over. He's sitting in a chair at a computer station. There's a floor-to-ceiling holofield next to him, and he's staring at the image in it.

It takes me a long time to figure out what I'm looking at. It's a giant 3D floating brain, made of an intricate grid of colored light.

My handheld rings. It's Tawny. I'm a bit surprised she hasn't checked in sooner. It's been a while since the snake-hippo ate her camera drone. If I don't answer, she'll just keep calling. And then, if I still don't answer, she'll assume the worst, and I don't want to be responsible for giving her a heart attack.

Before I can even say hola, Tawny says, "Can you take a couple of steps back? I can't tell what that thing is. And stop crossing your arms. You keep ruining my shots."

How did she manage to get a camera on the outfit Chestla

gave me this morning? I haven't even seen her since yesterday.

"Only if you trade me whatever gritfeed you got today of Kaliel." Which she wasn't supposed to have taken. Pero, I know she did.

She hesitates, her face set in mild disgust. "I'll send it to you if you want. But I warn you, it's disturbing."

"I can handle it." My voice sounds confident, though inside I'm cringing. Did they hurt him, after all?

Tawny nods. "After what I saw you do today, maybe you can." She points at me. "You surprise me sometimes, Bo. When I first met you back on Larksis – well, I doubt that girl could have taken down a dragon."

"It wasn't a dragon," I splutter. "It was a spuck. It's half bug. They don't breathe fire, or hoard gold, aren't super-intelligent–"

"Yeah, well, Bodacious Babe the Spuckslayer doesn't have quite the same ring to it, does it?"

I groan. She's already written the headlines. What's Mario going to think, reading about his hermana the dragonslayer? Ay-ay-ay. I change the subject. "Mija, what you're looking at is a giant brain."

From where he's sitting at the bank of computers, Brill adds, "I think these researchers are trying to make people immune to the brain parasites. It must have been quite an epidemic. Why didn't the Evevrons broadcast it, asking for help and warning others?"

He looks over at Chestla. She's intent on her work, doesn't seem to notice what we're saying. Pero, it feels extraño talking in front of her like this, about what her people ought to have done.

"They must have been trying to contain the outbreak." Tawny sounds like she's really thinking about something else.

"That's loco. This isn't ground zero." I fight the urge to cross my arms again. Then I almost do it, just to annoy Tawny. But I don't. Not with Ball dying on the floor twenty feet away.

"Ekrin explained at length about how nobody knows what planet these mindworms came from, or what they want. That's why the Evevrons wanted to study Kaliel."

Tawny laughs. "They know *something* they're not telling. I could get that just from the way they were questioning your pilot friend. They were trying to get something very specific. But they never did, and they were unhappy about it when they gave him the dewormer."

"They already did it?" Brill looks startled – and his rose eyes say he's upset. "Shtesh!"

Chestla looks up. "What's wrong?"

I figure out why Brill's unhappy before Tawny even asks, "Is it a problem?"

"They killed Kaliel's mindworm." Brill shrugs. "There were just some questions I wanted to ask."

"Because," I say, "if it was part of a hive mind, there was a good chance it knew what happened to Kayla."

Brill nods. "Among other things."

"Maybe Kaliel still knows," Tawny says. "They are treating him to a massage and facial down in the float spa."

"What's a float spa?" Brill asks.

"It's down in the complex under the city buildings. Back past the freshwater pool we saw yesterday, there's a saltwater hot spring."

The bottom drops out of my stomach. I blurt out, "I have a bad feeling about this."

I study Tawny, trying to see the real person beneath the fake smile and namedropping façade. I have no reason to think the Evevrons would hurt Kaliel, pero, I can't shake the horrortastic weight in the pit of my stomach. If I ask Tawny for a favor, I'm going to wind up owing her forever.

Doesn't matter.

"Por favor. Will you go check on Kaliel?"

She smiles, and for once it looks genuine. "I'm sure he's

fine. But if it will make you feel better, I'll go have a facial."
She reaches into her pocket and throws something into the
air. The holo shimmers, and now we're looking down at her.
She points up at the drone that's filming her. "Make sure you
keep monitoring this feed, so if there is trouble, you can call me
some backup." She slips her phone into her pocket.

I search for the bug Tawny'd been using to listen in and find
it on my shirt, a circle the size of a flea. I smash it.

A few minutes later, Ball gasps in a single breath.

Chestla leans over him, her words fierce as she examines
him for more gashes to caulk with healing foam. "That's right,
you damn Duracell. Breathe. You don't get to confess your love
and then die."

He takes in another breath, then his chest starts to rise and
fall more naturally.

I turn to Brill and whisper, "She's got him breathing again by
sheer force of will."

"You did that once for me," Brill says. Pero, he's still studying
the computer display. His eyes have taken on that troubled
color of sand again. "Look at this."

He does something to the screen in front of him, and the
brainpic in the holofield dissolves, replaced by an equally large,
equally complicated representation of a molecule, with each
element neatly labeled in indecipherable Evevron. Brill points
at it. "That's Pure275. They're not calling it that, but Babe, they
developed it here."

Pure275 keeps coming back up.

Someone was trying to poison everyone with it aboard that
SeniorLeisure tour vessel that Kaliel was set up to destroy.

A woman known only as Jane Doe was looking for a
warehouse full of Pure275-laced chocolate on the day mi papá
died. I'd followed that trail and found out that Pure275 had
been weaponized to kill people, back during the First Contact
war – and without it, HGB probably wouldn't have come out on

top. Earth might well now be run by a coalition of independent chocolate producers, instead of a power-hungry mega-corp.

Eugene just told us someone came into the rainforest in Rio and took all the Pure275-tainted chocolate we had found there.

Pure275 keeps coming back to HGB. And now Brill's saying it wasn't developed on Earth, pero here on Evevron.

My brain balks. "Which means what?"

His eyes shade to deep purple. "I'm not sure. But when HGB came out with it, wasn't Pure275 a jump ahead of everything else, selective in what plants it killed and relatively harmless? Genetically engineered to contain cacao from breaking out of the plantations... and geneflipping is a tech Evevron specializes in. Just look at those hunting beetles."

I can see where he's going with this. Forty years ago, in the middle of the First Contact War, Earth came close to ripping itself apart. Pero, there had never been aliens involved in it.

Or had there?

"So you're saying HGB got whizbangs from someone here to win the war?"

CHAPTER THIRTY-TWO

"When we were by that pool, and he knew he was dying, Ball said there was something going on on this planet that didn't add up. He didn't get the chance to elaborate about–" Brill's words cut short. He's looking behind me, at Chestla, who's standing now, staring at the hologram.

"What are you two looking at?" The small part of white visible around her cat-like pupils has gone solid red from crying, pero her face looks half-angry and hard.

Does she understand what she's seeing? If it really is Pure275, this implicates her people in a number of illegal activities that could cause sanction from the Galactic Court. Not the least of which is aiding in war crimes on another planet. People have been killed to keep smaller secrets.

Like Papá had, over two vials of liquid. I guess every planet does have its own Serum Green.

And Chestla – if she's in on the secrets here – just realized that we've found out about hers. Which makes her dangerous.

Unless, of course, I'm reading her body language wrong, and she's just as confused as we are.

"Is Ball…?" Brill just said dying. Why can't he say dead?

"He's got a pulse. For now." Chestla's covered in foam and blood, but she's still heavily armed. She sniffs and rubs her arm across her nose, and when her hand falls to her side, it's not far from the sword strapped at her hip.

A shiver goes through me as an echo of the prey response. My body has been afraid of Chestla before, pero this is the first time I've felt it in my heart. We're isolated here, and if Chestla is involved in the secrets Brill has been uncovering on the computer, she could keep us from leaving this room. Ever.

She's always seemed like such a solid amiga. I want to give her the benefit of the doubt.

Still. She hadn't wanted to come into this lab, not until she realized there was no other option. And she's been watching me like a hawk since we got to Evevron.

Pero, she's the one who asked us to come here, on this hunt.

"Ball didn't get a chance to elaborate about what?" she asks.

Brill swallows hard, and his hands move to the bottom edge of his jacket, shifting it, so that if he has to, he can draw his gun. "I was going to say about who we can and cannot trust."

No y no y no. Chestla's one of my best friends. And yet, her eyes are intense as she studies Brill's hands. Is it possible she knows her people's secrets – and is willing to do violence to keep us from uncovering them? Or that she's infected by the mindworms?

Chestla tilts her cabeza. "And now you're not sure if you can trust me? Just because I'm Evevron?"

Brill shrugs. "Family and homeworld's a strong indication of where most people's loyalties lie."

Chestla looks at me. "Have I ever once given you reason to doubt my loyalty to you, cesuda ma?"

"How did you know about this lab?" Brill asks Chestla. "How'd you know there would be medical supplies in here?"

Chestla blushes. "I didn't. When the air conditioning kicked on, I smelled henikix coming from inside the tunnel. Which means there was probably a first aid box. It's an analgesic with a particular odor."

"I don't smell anything," Brill says.

"You wouldn't. You're not Evevron."

Brill looks at me, his eyes questioning and shifting colors.

I turn to Chestla. "No, mi amiga. You've never given me a reason not to trust your word." I look from her to Brill. "You two have been good sparring partners, shared drinks, risked your lives for each other – and for me. Let's step this down un poco, muchachos."

"I'd be happy if nobody died today." Chestla unstraps the scabbard from her hip and lets it fall to the floor, the sword hilt clattering not far from Ball's shoulder. He doesn't so much as flinch. Pero, he is still breathing.

"Me too." Brill pulls his jacket back down and turns again to the computer. It's almost like it never happened. Almost.

For the first time, I truly understand how the First Contact Riots – people attacking former friends and neighbors with the belief that at least one hidden alien had been left behind after the Krom First Contact – had gotten so out of control, and I can see why the Evevrons decided to try to stop this mindplague without telling anyone about it. Because the last thing anyone needs is this kind of standoff on a galactic scale.

Chestla studies the molecule. "Why are you looking at Pure275?"

Brill explains his theory about Evevron's probable role in Earth's First Contact War.

Chestla's mouth falls open, displaying her sharp lower incisors. "And you thought I might be involved in the cover-up?"

"I already told you I'm not used to working with people I can trust." Brill's eyes are deep purple, still brainstorming. "But maybe you can give us some context. Did your planet have any unexpected gains forty years ago? Is there any partnership now with HGB?"

"Not that I know of. This is dangerous information. The Galactic Court sanctions executions for those convicted of war crimes. If entire villages of civilians were destroyed – if whoever built this place finds out we know what they did, they'd probably kill us to keep us quiet." She retrieves her sword from the floor and moves over to me, takes my arm. "Come on, Bo, we have to get you out of here, right now. You too, Brill. Before someone else comes to tell us it's time to go. I can't believe I busted the lock on that door."

She's digging for something in her pocket. She gets it out and crushes it between her nails, and suddenly the room smells like someone broke open about a dozen gallons of pine-scented cleaner.

Brill puts a hand over his nose and mouth. He sounds muffled. "Shtesh, you could warn a su." Pero, he shuts down the hologram and wipes his fingerprints off the screen with the sleeve of his jacket.

Over near the test tubes, Chestla sucks in a breath.

"Que?"

She gestures at the microscope slide. "I recognize that handwriting. Nobody else writes their hets with an extra swirl the way Leron does. He's one of the medics who came on the hunt today. The guy who glued my shoulder back together."

Dios mio! That means he's one of the people coming down to help Ball.

Chestla picks up Ball. "There's no hiding what I did getting in here, but if you use that bleach on the floor in here and we cover the blood spots in the dirt outside, no one will be able to prove for sure it was us."

I help Brill clean the floor. Well, I help a little. He's moving at Krom speed, and the rags are in the lab's biohazard incinerator before I've done much more than wipe my own hands.

"I'll cover the blood spots," he volunteers.

I catch up with Chestla, who's still carrying Ball close to her chest.

"The medics should be here any minute." Chestla rushes us toward the cave proper. We've barely made it out of the tunnel when an Evevron steps over the rubble at the cave entrance, calling, "Chestla? Where's Ball? Did I make it down in time?" before his eyes adjust enough to the dimness for him to see us at the back of the space.

He's wearing the bright green neck pouch that marks him as a medic, over his hunting habit. It's Leron, and he's alone.

Chestla freezes as the guy looks from us to the tunnel behind us. She takes a shuddery breath. "Yeah, Leron. He needs you. I've done everything I can."

The medic looks from us to the tunnel and back again. There's an odd look on his face. Has he figured out we've seen the lab? "What were you guys doing back there? You should have tried to get back up the cliff, to the medics with the ground vehicles. A child would know that."

He drags a lev-cot over and takes Ball from Chestla, laying the guy on it. Ball groans again. This time it's a little louder. That's a good sign, no?

Brill grabs my hand, and his heartbeat feels super-fast, even for him. I think he's still afraid Chestla's going to sell us out.

Pero, Chestla runs both hands over her face. "I was hiding in the dark. My cesuda ma came in to tell me not to feel bad about failing my test. Again. This time, I got somebody else hurt." Chestla's pupils are almost round in this dim light, and glittering with all the charm of Puss in Boots in the tooncasts. "You're not going to tell anybody I just couldn't face it, are you?"

Leron's eyes look sympathetic. "Of course not, Stala." Still, he takes one more long look at that corridor, and my heart starts thudding harder. He squints. "Did you set off a scent mask in here?"

She nods, shows him the crushed capsule still resting on her palm. "I didn't want to have to smell the blood."

That makes enough sense to Leron that he turns and escorts us to a small flying transport. Once we're in the sunlight, he stares down at Ball, examining Chestla's handiwork. "Where'd you get all the first aid supplies?"

My chest goes frío. How are we going to explain that?

"You know, su," Brill says. "Ball had a basic kit in the vehicle. I brought it down with me."

"Where is it now?" The medic looks skeptical.

Brill gestures at Ball's leg. "You're looking at it. We tore up the bag to make more bandages."

An alarm goes off on the cot.

Chestla turns toward Ball. Her voice comes out as a whisper. "No."

Leron shifts his attention. "He's crashing."

"Give Leron the syringe," Brill prompts.

The one Brill had said not to use unless Ball's heart stopped? My chest feels light and sparkly as I take it from my pocket and hand it over. There's not going to be any hiding where this came from, and we already lied and said we were never in the lab. But the only alternative is letting Ball die right in front of us.

Leron raises an eyebrow. "Now that doesn't belong in a basic first aid kit." Pero he's already turned away, moving to administer the drug.

After a few seconds that feel more like hours, Ball gasps in another single breath and Chestla hugs Leron. The alarm fades.

Leron pushes her away. "We need to get this guy to the hospital, now. But we're going to have to have a little chat later."

Chestla grew up with this guy. Surely that has to count for something when she has to tell him she never touched his computers, because she was too busy saving one of his friends.

Once we're all buckled in, Leron lifts off. He turns back to Chestla. "Have they officially told you you failed?"

Chestla cradles Ball's hand on her lap. "Why would they have to? Not only did someone else have to save my cesuda ma, she wound up in danger a second time and had to save herself.

And I nearly lost–" Her voice breaks, pero she forces herself to start again. "And I nearly lost a member of the hunting party."

"But she's still alive." He jerks a thumb at me, then down at the cot. "And so is he. That's going to count for something. Especially *because* she saved herself."

Chestla nods like she's considering his words, like that's still the important thing.

It's a quick journey back, and Leron lands the transport outside the hospital. We get to a relatively private waiting area where I check in on Tawny. The small gritfeed on my phone shows her moving way past the freshwater pool, towards a door that leads deeper into the complex. She walks down the hall with purpose, opening doors and not apologizing when they're not the ones she's looking for.

Kaliel's not in any of the massage rooms. Tawny keeps going. There's a sign that says something in Evevron above a stylized image of a person floating on a giant drop of agua. The float spa.

Tawny slides the door open, and there's Kaliel, alone in a shallow pool in a dimly lit space, his eyes closed, something like headphones over his ears. He's wearing one of the ridiculous swim outfits, and I want to laugh, pero then the camera shifts. He's not alone after all. A figure steps into the agua, holding a folded-up shower curtain high enough that it obscures his – or her – face.

The drone catches Tawny's tiny gasp, shifts to her as she looks around to improvise a weapon. She grabs a thick glass pitcher from the table.

The drone spins around. The figure in the pool is silently spreading out the shower curtain, as Tawny creeps closer to the edge. The figure swoops forward, enveloping Kaliel in the plastic and pushing him under. My stomach clenches, and my heart's thudding.

"No!" I shout loud enough that both Brill and Chestla turn around to stare at me.

"Hey!" Holo-Tawny shouts.

The figure looks up, pero where the drone's positioned, you still can't see the person's face. Tawny pegs the intruder between the shoulder blades with the glass pitcher. It's confettiglass, which breaks into three pieces, the confetti-shards sparkling down the would-be killer's back.

The person scrambles away. Kaliel's thrashing in the water. The heavy salt content is buoying him up, pero he's trapped inside the plastic, and there's probably enough agua in the curtain to drown him. Tawny shouts again at the person making their way out of the opposite end of the pool, pero she has to let them go if she's going to save Kaliel.

She jumps into the pool, shouting at Kaliel to stop fighting it, pero with those headphones on, there's no way he can hear her. She's fighting the plastic, and he's fighting her, and she's soaking wet with her short hair hanging limply against her scalp by the time she's holding the balled-up shower curtain, and Kaliel is standing up in the pool. He pulls off the headphones and looks at her uncertainly.

"Did you just save me, or are you about to finish the job?"

Tawny closes her eyes and brings a hand to her forehead. "Can't you see how much more of a headache it is for me if you're dead?"

CHAPTER THIRTY-THREE

Once Ball's settled, Leron takes us to the city building. He escorts us inside, through the stuffy waiting room, and back downstairs to where the council members are supposed to be waiting for us. Maybe he's afraid of what we're going to say. Maybe he wants to talk to someone here about what to do about us.

But we didn't disappear halfway here, so I'm feeling a bit more optimistic about this guy.

Before we're down the staircase, I hear Tawny's shrill voice.

"You can't be serious! Someone from this planet tried to *kill* him."

And Grammy, deeper and more calm. "You don't know that. You said yourself you didn't get a good look at the attacker. I understand there is a steep bounty on Kaliel. It is equally possible that he was attacked by a bounty hunter." Grammy sees us coming down the stairs and gives me a relieved smile. If she's hoping I can control Tawny, she is sadly mistaken.

Chestla walks straight up to the platform, moves to the center of it and falls to her knees, palms flat on the floor in front of her. Tawny moves out of her way, exiting the platform. Kaliel is already sitting in one of the lounge chairs. He gives me a devastating smile, which I force myself not to return.

Yep. Kaliel's back to his normal self. And I'm blushing. And from the way Brill's posture just stiffened, he noticed.

Grammy gives Chestla a sympathetic smile. "Stand up, Stala. You're not getting banished."

Chestla looks up, but doesn't move. "I should be."

Grammy says, "Nobody gets banished over a hunting accident."

Though it would be a convenient way to get her out of town. Which means the council probably doesn't have anything to do with that hidden lab.

"But it was my fault," Chestla protests. "If I hadn't been so angry that the spuck ate my hunting beetle, then we wouldn't have wound up that far out front of the rest of the group."

"You weren't driving, though, were you?" Grammy must have interviewed the hunting party before we got here. "And you weren't the one who stopped that close to the cliff."

Chestla straightens up, resting her hands on her thighs instead of the floor. "I haven't failed?"

Grammy looks at her for a long time. "The vote is still split. I advise you to move on to your interview with your potential companion while we deliberate. And please, please – take these two with you." She points to Tawny and Kaliel.

"Of course." Chestla taps her palms on the floor again, then stands up.

"Wait! I'm not done talking." Tawny tries to make it back to the platform, pero Kaliel intercepts her and walks her over to us.

Once the four of us are standing outside, I pull Chestla aside and ask, "Are you really still considering becoming this girl's companion? What about Leron? Won't it be dangerous to stay here?"

Chestla nods. "I'll be careful. But I can't say no now. The best place for me to unravel the secrets here is from inside the Royal Court."

"So you're not coming with us to help clear Kaliel?" My voice sounds smaller than I meant it to.

Chestla sighs. "Of course I'm coming with you. I'm not about to let you get eaten on Zant. But after that, if they let me, I have to be here."

"Is this 'interview' code for fighting flesh-eating water snakes or something?" Brill asks. "I need to know if I should keep the body armor on."

"It's an art walk," Chestla says. "But it's near a contested border."

An hour later, we meet up with a half dozen teenage girls and their entourage at the edge of a sculpture garden. And yeah, Brill's still wearing the body armor. So am I. Chestla insisted.

The girls are in the garden, sketching. We won't get to talk to them until they are done.

While Chestla is exchanging introductions with the girl's staff, Brill asks Kaliel, "Now that they zapped that thing in your head, do you still remember what happened to Kayla?"

Kaliel takes a deep breath. "You guys never found her? Not since that night at the club?"

I ask, "Don't you remember pawning her make-up bag?"

He blinks. "I was mad she dumped me."

If Kayla's infected, is it possible that they'd both been a part of the same hive mind and him not realized it? The Evevrons had said he probably didn't even know the parasite was present in his mind. That points to a stronger single consciousness, orchestrating its agents, whereas the distress of the single parasite inside Kaliel implies a number of individuals connecting to a central point. Which is correct? Can it somehow be both? Is it in flux?

Brill asks, "Can you remember anything specific that might help us find Kayla? Or help us stop these mindworms?"

Kaliel hesitates. He looks at Tawny.

She sighs. "I'll stop recording. Though I don't see how it hurts."

"Thanks." Kaliel runs his hands across his cabeza. "I can remember everything that happened – everything I did. And some of it, I'd honestly rather forget. I've never killed anyone up close like that. I'm not sure if I'll ever be able to sleep again. That's why they wanted me to try to relax in the float spa. I had a panic attack after the drugs wore off."

"It'll get better, su." Brill holds out his hand – the injured one.

Kaliel blushes. Looking down at the foamglued-together palm he says, "Man, I'm really sorry about that."

Brill shrugs. "Wasn't really you, was it?"

There's still an uneasiness between them that has nothing to do with brain parasites.

Oblivious to it, Tawny says, "But the million-dollar question is, why attack Minda's show? What do these mindworms gain by starting a war between Earth and Zant?"

Kaliel rubs at the back of his neck. "The big question's not who just tried to drown me in three feet of saltwater?"

Tawny glances over at the Evevron bodyguards, still talking while watching the girls sketch. "Absolutely not. Figure out what the mindworms are doing, and you'll find out who considers you a loose end. It won't work the other way around."

"I'm supposed to ignore the fact someone's trying to kill me?"

"Kaliel, sweetie," Tawny says. "The Zantites want to execute you. There's about a hundred bounty hunters who want to give them the opportunity. Your own planet has publicly stated they don't oppose that happening. You've got bigger problems."

"HGB disavowed me?" His voice sounds small. When Tawny nods, he asks her, "Then why are you still here?"

Tawny smooths the collar of Kaliel's shirt. "Because my bosses are being shortsighted. You're our best hope right now for avoiding a war we can't win."

"But that's the thing." Kaliel frowns. "I don't think these

parasites care what happens with Earth or Zant. It's hard for me to tell where my thoughts ended and its began, but I'm pretty sure it was angry at Minda because her show featured chocolate. They're scared of chocolate."

"That doesn't make any sense," Brill says.

Kaliel sighs. "Can't we just tell the Zantites about the parasites? That has to be enough to sway a jury."

Tawny and I share an uneasy glance.

I say, "The Evevrons made us promise not to tell anyone. They said it would disrupt a plan they have in place to destroy the mindworms."

"But that was before we found out they're lying to us," Tawny protests.

This time I share a glance with Brill. He shakes his head, subtly. Meaning he doesn't think Tawny realizes we found out the Evevrons had a role in the First Contact War. And he doesn't think we should tell her.

He's probably right. HGB's been keeping everything they did during the war secret. She might just make a recommendation to have both of us eliminated.

Brill says, "I'm surprised you haven't already broadcast the feed you have of the Evevrons killing the parasite. You said it's disturbing. It's bound to get attention."

Tawny presses her hands together, calling attention to the glowing trapezoidal jraghite ring she always wears. "I almost did, but I wasn't sure if it was the right play. I've got everything edited and ready to go if that's what we decide."

"You prepare for everything don't you, mija? I bet you even prepped my eulogy in case I didn't make it back from that hunt."

I mean it as a joke, but Tawny just blinks. "I've had your eulogy prepared since you volunteered to come to Zant. It's a very different version than the one I worked up when you got that cacao pod off Earth. You'd like this one."

A chill dances down my spine.

"We should wait until we know more about what's going on." Brill's eyes are deep purple again. "Diplomacy can be a fragile thing. You don't want to accidentally make it look like Earth is trying to shift the blame for a problem you created. And you don't want to start the war back up between the Zantites and the Evevrons. You'll wind up getting crushed between them."

"So what do we do?" Kaliel asks.

"We smile and make nice, and we get off this planet as soon as possible." Brill smiles and waves at Chestla, who's looking over at us with wide, worried eyes. "And then we find somewhere dark and deep to hide you."

"No," Kaliel says. "I'm not running. You can take me back to Earth, or you can take me straight to Zant, but I'm not going to let anybody start a war over me."

"That's noble, su." Brill sounds sincere. "In the meantime, we can piece together all the information. Maybe find you an out. I came ita, ita close to being executed by those Zantite sus myself. It's a horrible way to die."

I agree. Brill and I have both been in a Zantite's jaws, one heartbeat away from being cut in half. Kaliel doesn't deserve that.

Kaliel's cheeks go ashen. "All I know is I was building a machine."

"What kind of machine?" Brill asks. "What for?"

Kaliel looks like he's concentrating hard. Finally he huffs out a breath. "I don't know."

"Where is this machine?" Brill asks.

"It was on my ship. But after I got captured, somebody came for my ship, to finish what I had been doing. I don't know how I know that. And no, I don't know where they were going."

Brill asks, "Do you remember getting infected?"

Kaliel nods. "Jimena did it. She had an underwater

propulsion device that let her pop up next to me. She attacked me and in the struggle she hit me with an injector gun. I didn't know what it was then, just expected to pass out, or start hallucinating or die. But she towed me around the point and left me there, bobbing in about ten feet of water. Once I got to shore, it seemed urgent to do all these crazy things – starting with throwing my lifejacket back in the water – and silly to tell anyone I'd been attacked by a girl. I never realized I was being manipulated. Which is what has me freaked out the most."

Brill looks down at his phone, which is buzzing in his hand. His eyes shift through a few colors, landing on gray. "We have to go. Right now."

I try to see what's on his screen. "I doubt Chestla's going to go for that just now, mi vida."

Brill shows me his screen. "Gavin says Tyson's on his way. ETA a couple of hours."

My heart jolts.

Kaliel says, "I know. I called him."

We all gape at him. Tawny asks, "Why?"

Kaliel cracks an ironic smile. "Because Bo won the bet. I told you, I remember everything that happened while I was under the influence, and you guys were talking about it enough. Tyson agreed to try to help me. Of course, that was back when I thought I could tell him about the mindworms."

"Su," Brill says, pero then he can't seem to think of any way to finish the sentence.

"It's OK." Kaliel balls his hand into a fist. "If it comes down to it, I'd rather face a Zantite execution squad than get shaved on Earth, because at least that way I'll get to apologize to Minda. Maybe I can even warn her that she's still in danger. Maybe get some people interested in looking for Kayla."

I tell him, "Frank knows there could be another attack on Minda, and Stephen is retracing Kayla's steps." I try to think of a way to say it that doesn't sound morbid. "So if the worst does happen, people are already doing their best to honor your wishes."

"Thanks, Bo. That does help." The beginnings of tears glitter in his eyes, but there's no defeat there, not like when he was slated for the shave.

"But you know, muchacho, Kayla prefers you breathing, and she's mi mejor amiga, so we'd better work on figuring out how to honor *her* wishes."

Kaliel smiles. "You think we're going to get our happily ever after?"

I see where his will to fight this time has come from: his love for my friend. Por favor, let Kayla still be alive out there somewhere. For his sake.

Chestla walks over to us. "The council has decided. They need us back right away."

I look from her, over at Kaliel, and back. Brill said we would have at least a couple of hours. "Then we should head to the city building now."

"Babe," Brill protests.

"We'll make it as quick as we can, mi vida, I promise. Take Kaliel and prep the *Fois Gras* for takeoff."

"I told you, I'm not running," Kaliel insists.

Brill says, "It never hurts to have a plan B."

The transport pulls up to the city building, and as the door pops open, there's a loud screech from outside. I move to the windows, scanning for something horrortastic.

Chestla gets up and calmly walks to the open doorway, stepping down onto the sidewalk.

I follow her. "Is everything OK here, chica?"

She points down the street. "They must have caught one."

"One what?"

"When there's a hunting death, the animal that struck the killing blow is brought back alive, so everyone can see it, and respect the danger it represents – and remember to show more care next time. Then the animal is killed and the meat served once the mourning is done. When it's an injury, the surviving hunter is supposed to kill it, to prove himself still fit. We will leave the animal caged for as long as it takes the person to heal, to show we haven't given up on him. When that animal escapes – or is already dead – Ekrin's group is in charge of trying to find one like it."

Ekrin. The girl Chestla had had me fighting with a stick. I have no right to be alive.

Chestla misreads my hesitation. "Do you want to go see it?"

"No y no. I've already seen enough today."

"Me too." Chestla marches up to the front door, then she just stands there, unable to make herself open it.

I open it for her. "Whatever they say in there, you're the bravest person I know, and no one can convince me different."

"I'm more scared right now than I was facing off with that kapurst." And yet, she crosses the floor and leads the way down the stairs.

CHAPTER THIRTY-FOUR

When we're standing together on the platform down by the pool, Chestla doesn't look nervous any more. There's a fierce confidence in her as she makes eye contact with the people about to judge her.

Grammy stands. "Thank you, Miss Benitez, for sharing your time and energy with us over the past few days. Ekrin, especially, enjoyed the chance to get your autograph, and has requested that I pass along her offer to join your protection force." She turns to Chestla. "We have deemed the results of your test inconclusive. However, in one week, we will be running the standard admission exam, including the obstacle course at Nargo Canyon. If you can pass the test there that you originally failed, the position is yours."

"Thank you for the opportunity," Chestla says, pero she doesn't sound fizzbounced. Without saying anything else, Chestla leaves the platform.

I follow her. "Hey! Wait!"

She stops, but she doesn't turn around. "You know as well as I do that there's no way to get from here to Zant and back in one week."

"Then stay here and dig for information, and then rock the obstacle course."

She looks me in the eyes, and the prey instinct echoes through me again. "I promised I would help you save Kaliel."

As we're walking out through the building's upper floor, Ekrin comes rushing in, carrying a black metal briefcase. She holds it out to me, speaking rapidly.

Chestla translates. "There are a hundred doses of dewormer in here. You will need them if the situation on Zant is as dire as Kaliel's parasite claimed while bragging. Please be safe."

Then she turns and rushes away.

"She wasn't supposed to give us these, right?"

"Nope." Chestla keeps walking towards the door.

I make a mental note to have Tawny send Ekrin one of everything in the fan club goodie box. Once we're outside blinking in the sun, I turn to Chestla. "We're on our own now to find transportation back to the spaceport?"

She opens her mouth to say something. Pero, then her eyes go wide, and the slit pupils round out, like she's suddenly stepped into the dark.

She pulls a tiny dart out of her neck. She holds it out towards me, then collapses onto the pavement. I scramble to help her. She's breathing, pero she's out, and I'm not strong enough to pick her up and run away.

"Don't worry," someone says from behind me. "We'll give you a ride."

I look up into a mottled face, humanoid, pero with some of the qualities of a piece of granite. Grundt. Captain of the *Onyx Shadow*. From Chestla's surveillance holo.

A small black air transport lands in the middle of the street, and several of his companions pile out. Grundt grabs my arm and pulls me to my feet, while the others pick up Chestla and carry her into their transport. One of them picks up the briefcase of dewormer and pops it open, examining the injector vials before bringing it on board.

"We've never met before, Miss Benitez," Grundt says. "But you've given us a lot of trouble. Do you know who I am?"

I nod, then gesture towards where Chestla has just

disappeared. "Given your reputation, I'm shocked she's still breathing."

His grip on my arm tightens. "She shouldn't be the one you're worried about. She's asleep because it doesn't tend to go well when someone you're trying to recruit sees what happens to her previous crew."

Ice dances down my spine. Chestla got their attention, all right, with her snooping. "Then why am I still breathing, mijo?"

"Let's call it curiosity, mija." He says the Spanish word ironically, emphasized but unaccented.

I call Brill on my sublingual, pero he doesn't answer.

I try to fight Grundt's grip on me all the way to the transport. He doesn't push me inside exactly, pero he doesn't give me any choice but to walk up the steps.

I try Brill again. This time something's interfering with the castsignal. The whole vehicle's probably signalblocked.

Grundt turns me towards a minibar at the back. "You're supposed to be such a great chef, why don't you mix us a couple of drinks. But make one move towards the ice pick, and I will drop you."

I nod towards the front of the bus. "Us as in you and your friends, or us as in me and you?"

"Just me and you. They're kind of busy right now."

I walk over to the minibar and pull out a couple of glasses. The selection is impressive. In one glass, I mix together a cocktail that perfectly blends the four major flavor profiles. In the other, I put two cubes of ice, and a couple of inches of expensive Betarogian whiskey.

I drop some cheese I saw in the minifridge on a plate and go back over to where Grundt is sitting. He examines the two glasses and takes the whiskey. I sit down opposite him.

He takes a deep drink. "So why bring Johansson here, instead of claiming the bounty the minute you found him?"

I take a sip from my own glass, determined to keep this civil for as long as possible. "Kaliel's my friend. I helped get him exonerated after you guys framed him."

Grundt laughs. "And here I thought you did that just to get back at HGB."

I blink. "HGB?"

Grundt takes a shorter sip of his drink, studying me. "You have no idea that it was HGB that hired us, do you? There was a troublesome couple – the Benders or Basics or something – that were working with a remnant of the Nitarri to lay groundwork for a cacao plantation in space. We were given great latitude on how to handle the situation but not much time. The collateral damage was unavoidable."

All this time we've spent trying to figure out who set Kaliel up and why – and he's just telling me? Practically monologuing about it?

My stomach feels like I've swallowed all the ice in that little freezer. There's no way he would be this forthcoming if he was planning to let me walk out of here alive. My trembling hand sets the ice in my glass tinkling. I cover it by taking a drink. "Was it Baker?"

He snaps his fingers. "That's it. The Bakers. The ones who rescued those Nitarri kids that time."

I nod, like I even know what a Nitarri is. "Must have been them."

Maybe he'll read the shock slackening my jaw as just more fear. Kayla's grandparents weren't the collateral damage in the SeniorLeisure debacle after all. Kaliel was. And the fallout from it is following him even now.

We were never going to figure it out, because we'd been looking at it backwards. That kind old lady in Kayla's Anastasia video really was looking for hope. And HGB had killed her to quash it.

They'd actually framed one of their own pilots, and taken a huge publicity hit, knowing it could tip Earth into global war

– because it was less dangerous to them than letting someone break the monopoly on chocolate.

I wish I could at least let Chestla know she'd been right to keep looking, that HGB was too corrupt to keep a secret this big, even with all the possible repercussions.

There's no way she's going to join these guys. They're going to wind up killing her too.

I glance out the window. We're headed for the spaceport. "What happens when we land?"

Grundt ignores the question. "What did Johansson need here? And what are the vials in the briefcase? And what in the spredjenkiix was he doing at a health spa?"

"Wait. That was your crew that tried to drown the poor guy?"

Grundt smiles. "Not our finest operation."

"Just wait until I tell Tawny she went up against one of the galaxy's deadliest mercs. She's going to faint."

Grundt clears his throat and shakes his cabeza.

"Oh. Right." Because I'm dying soon – probably when this transport lands – and am never going to get the chance to tell Tawny anything. I drain my glass.

Grundt says, "Why don't you try answering my questions?"

He's not giving me any incentive to cooperate. It's not like he can kill me any more dead, no? Pero, I want to see his reaction, whether he already knows more about what's going on here than I do.

"Kaliel was infected with a parasite. We brought him here to be cured." Not quite accurate, but close enough. I gesture at the briefcase. "If you want to make points with Chestla, offer to help her stop it."

Grundt's already craggy face gets even harder as his lips narrow. "My curiosity's getting dimmer."

"Then test it yourself. I need another drink." I stand up, head towards the minibar. If he decides to shoot me in the back, so be it. This time I go for the expensive whiskey. I'm halfway back when the guy piloting the transport says something to us. It sounds like he's gargling Tic-Tacs.

Grundt gestures for me to sit, so I take the nearest chair. The pilot brings us down so light, the whiskey doesn't even slosh in my glass. Pero the shakes are back, so when I lift the glass from where I rested it on my leg, it looks like we've hit turbulence. I take a sip of amber liquid, smooth yet bracing.

Grundt's heading my way, and now there's a gun in his hand. "Hands behind your back and stand up."

My hands are sweating despite the ice as I set the glass down and put my hands behind me. He cuffs me.

My heart squeezes as the last of my hope dies.

He marches me off the flying bus, back out into the heat. We've come down a few feet away from the *Fois Gras*. I stop in shock, and Grundt grabs my arm again. He pulls me around to the front of the ship, where Brill is bound to have a good look at me, then he drags me around to where three of his companions are trying to break down mi vida's door.

The thrusters fire, then sputter out. Which means that while we were in the council chamber, these guys were quietly grounding Brill. And that the real reason I'm alive is to be Grundt's human shield.

CHAPTER THIRTY-FIVE

They pop the door, and Grundt pushes me through in front of him. The fish-smell residue hits me.

Grundt whispers, close to my ear, "It stinks like something already died in here."

Already. Seems like an innocent word, no?

The bridge is empty. When I look towards the galley, the unbolted dining table is on its side, wedged up against the entrance. Two of the mercs duck down low and flitdash across the open space. They pull the table out of the way. Grundt marches me forward. The galley's empty. Only… there's a tiny bit of plastic sticking through the seal of the refrigerator door, quite possibly Brill's assurance that he can get back out again. The racks from inside are stacked on top. I try not to look at them, pero Grundt still grins and focuses his men in behind him, all training weapons on the fridge.

Grundt opens the door… onto an empty space, save for a bottle of mustard and three bottles of white wine. There's a noise behind us and a blur as Brill streaks for the door. Pero there's an energy field across it, which he hits full speed. He bounces backwards and crumples to the floor.

I gasp.

"Relax," Grundt says, pero he tightens his grip on my arm. "He's not dead." He gestures two of his guys forward. "Yet."

The mercs haul Brill up and dump him onto one of the

chairs, still bolted into their tracks where the table used to be. He seems stunned, pero he's not unconscious, and his irises are black with terror as they bind him to the chair. After a minute or so, he comes out of it. "What do you want?"

"Where's Johansson?" Grundt asks.

"Ga, su, I don't know." Brill's eyes are still solid back, so it's impossible to gauge if it's a lie.

"Flip, burn him."

One thug pulls a brulee-style torch out of his jacket and lights it.

I look up at Grundt. "Por favor, don't do this. I can–"

My sublingual rings. It's Tawny. *Don't offer him money.*

Flip doesn't even get the torch close to mi vida's face before Brill says, "He's in the smuggler's hold past the head. The hatch is right in line with the door."

Flip hesitates. "Boss?"

Grundt shrugs. "Go check it out."

Brill says, "I'm really not a fan of torture."

Que? I ask Tawny.

I know your mom's loaded. You're going to want to offer him the equivalent of Kaliel's bounty to let him go.

I've gotten used to her cameras being all over me, pero how has she gotten inside my mind? *So?*

So. That makes you valuable. They kill Kaliel and collect the bounty, then ransom you and double their money. And they'll make sure Brill's in no condition to rescue you.

I swallow against a mouth gone suddenly dry. I don't bother telling Tawny that Grundt made it clear we're not walking out of here anyway.

Brill's looking at me. "Lo siento, Babe."

Grundt looks from me to Brill and back again. "Heartbreaking. But what did you expect when your security expert cracked through to our financial files? No one steals from us."

"Wait!" Brill splutters. "We're not thieves."

"He's talking about Chestla, mi vida." I look up at Grundt. "I know how this looks, and sí, Chestla can get a little overzealous. If she was in your financials, she was just trying to prove who hired you to set up Kaliel."

Grundt looks like he's just bitten into a lemon. "You expect me to believe that?"

"Boss," Flip says. "The hold's empty."

Brill's eyes go a brilliant green with surprise. "He was in there a minute ago."

"Kill the Krom," Grundt says. He looks at me. "I hate liars."

"No!" I jerk away from Grundt so hard I slip out of his grip. My hands are still cuffed behind me, pero I manage to get myself between Flip and Brill. "Por favor. Please."

Flip shoulders me out of the way.

"He's not lying." Kaliel opens the door to the baño. "I slipped out of the hold and was hiding in the shower."

He's got a dart gun in his hand – the same one Brill used on him. While everybody's still startled, he fires three times. A volley of gunfire comes back at Kaliel, who hits the floor, hands shielding his head.

Ten seconds later, Grundt's three darted mercs fall.

Grundt draws a weapon, and Kaliel holds up his hands as he gets slowly back to his feet. "I've already promised a Galactacop that I'm turning myself in. You hand me over, that puts you in line for the reward. Let these two go, and I'll walk out of here with you, right now."

"You'll be easier to handle dead." Grundt fires at Kaliel, who ducks back behind the doorway. I leap behind the metal table.

Grundt turns to Brill, growling in frustration. No! My heart freezes. Esto no puede estar pasando. *This cannot be happening.* There's a single kathud, followed by a metallic ping. Brill goes limp. I scream, before I realize what that second sound was. Brill's still wearing the body armor. Pero, he's playing dead.

And since he's stopped breathing, it's convincing.

The bullet must have bounced up towards the ceiling, because there's a crack and then a hissing noise, and a half-bubble, painted white to match the ceiling, pops open. A tornado of confetti flies out, and a banner unspools. The lead weight that's been attached to pull the banner open drops right toward Grundt's cabeza. He looks up, tries to bat it away, and while he's distracted, Kaliel barrels into him. There's the crackpop of the gun hitting the floor. Kaliel and Grundt are fighting, and it doesn't look like either of them are injured enough to give up.

"Mi vida, are you OK?" I race over to Brill, getting him untied from the chair using my still bound hands.

"Better than I have any right to be, Babe." He turns to the fight, looking for a way to help, pero it's almost over and when the confetti clears, Kaliel's sitting on the merc, the guy's arms pinned behind his back.

Brill starts picking the lock on the cuffs I'm wearing until they come free.

He twirls the cuffs with his good hand, then moves over and applies them to Grundt. "That should make a nice peace offering for Tyson. Kaliel wrapped up these guys with a bow."

"Which just leaves the three watching Chestla." I turn towards the door.

Oh, I wouldn't worry about that, Tawny bubblechatters. I forgot I'd left the channel open. Startled, I reflexively hang up.

"What does this mean?" Kaliel asks. He's holding up the banner. "It says, *How about now?*"

Brill laughs. "Mertex must have done that. He was trying to goad me into a practical joke war. And I just never triggered whatever was supposed to set it off. Remind me to thank him for saving our lives – if this stuff doesn't clog our air system." Even as he's speaking, though, the confetti starts to melt away.

There's a feral scream from outside, and whatever mechanism has been netting the door breaks apart, and there's Chestla, ready to charge inside. When she sees the bad guys already on the floor and the three of us blinking at her, she drops her sword arm, automatically doing the cleaning-the-blade swish before she puts the weapon away. "Ah, man."

Brill's looking at Kaliel, his eyes an embarrassed pink. "Look, su, I'm sorry I gave you up so easy. And then you turned around and risked yourself for me and–"

"Don't worry about it." Kaliel hands his captive – who is busy rolling his eyes at this bro-moment – over to Chestla. "You make Bo happy. And believe it or not, that's all I want for her."

Brill blinks a couple of times, and his eye color's different each time he opens them. "I misjudged you, su."

There's a heavy banging sound from somewhere overhead. "Can somebody let me out now?"

Brill moves the upended table back into place and jumps up on it. He helps Tawny down out of a hidden hold up inside the ceiling. I thought I knew my way around Brill's ship, pero even I've never seen that one before. While Brill's busy sliding the panel back in place, Tawny sidles over to me. "Are you sure you can't switch your affections over to Kaliel? It would really help sell the selfless, remorseful guy feedclip I just sent out. I'm having a hard time here, not being able to tell anyone *why* they should think he's innocent." She pinches my cheek. "Besides, like you said, Kaliel's hot when he's playing the hero."

"I didn't say that. Well, maybe I thought it, just for a minute–" With my sublingual channel open. Who knows what I could have been telling her. "You weren't recording that, were you?"

Tawny grins. "I wish. That commentary track would have been perfect for the FeedCast."

I roll my eyes. "Don't you think Kayla y Kaliel plays better, as an example of forgiveness?"

"I don't think we want to emphasize that Kaliel blew something else up in the past, or that Kayla is missing, do you? Team KayKay is played out."

"You have to call them that? It's going to break my brain. Kayla used to sign all her e-mails KayKay."

"I know." Tawny looks steadily back. "Where do you think I got the idea? But I for one am bored with KayKay and BeeBee. I'm still shipping hard for double KayBee."

"I heard that," Brill says, climbing off the table after fastening the panel in place. I hope he didn't hear all of it.

While Brill's ship might be grounded, the *Fois Gras*'s shower still works. I'm clean and dressed in fresh clothes, and I finally have a moment to myself, before I meet the others in the spaceport's restaurant. But I can't stop thinking about what Kaliel said about Jimena.

If she was infected, whatever she'd done or said to Frank hadn't been her fault.

Pero, when I call Frank I can't confront him about it. If he knew about the mindworms, he would have fought harder to keep Mamá from visiting Zant.

It takes him a long time to answer, and when he finally does, Frank looks like I woke him up. He's rubbing at a layer of salt-and-pepper stubble on his chin, the hair on his cabeza spiked wildly. Oh, right. It's the middle of the night on Zant. He's standing in an unfamiliar kitchen, pulling out a package of coffee grounds. "Make it good, Bo."

I do my best to explain without giving him details. "We found Kaliel, and he has confirmed the attack was on Minda."

The vestiges of sleepiness fall away from Frank. "Did he bother to say why?"

Is Frank even going to believe that Kaliel had a space parasite? "That's... complicated. Pero, por favor, talk to him before you put in a report about this."

Frank pours coffee into a machine on the counter. "You believe everybody deserves mercy, don't you?"

I nod.

Frank pushes the button. "Except me."

I blink at him. "What do you mean, viejo?"

He sighs as the machine makes a similar noise, heating agua. "You have no idea how much your mother values your opinion, how hard it is for her right now, knowing that you don't approve of me and her being together. She keeps telling me you're going to come around, but if you don't – she hasn't said it, but I'm going to lose her. And there's nothing I can do about it." He turns and takes a mug off the dish drain. "I'm a man of action, Bo. You're killing me here."

What would it mean, for me to show him mercy? To give him something he doesn't deserve but really needs? "Are you asking me to forgive you for mi papá's death?"

He looks gobsmacked. I probably have the same expression on my own face. He swallows visibly. "I guess I am. Though I've no right–"

"I don't know how to do that." I study his eyes, which are steady, accepting. "Lo siento. I wish I did."

He breaks the eye contact, watching the coffee brew. "That's fair. I gave up a lot when I took this responsibility for HGB. I can't expect you to understand how much."

"There is one thing I've been curious about, viejo." I hesitate. "How did you wind up with custody of Minerva?"

Mamá already told me Minerva's other grandparents are in an assisted living place and aren't in a position to provide for the kid long term. Pero, that's not what I mean.

"You mean what happened to my daughter and son-in law?" Now he looks like he really needs that coffee. "I lost both of them in a pirate attack. I encouraged my girl to improve the galaxy in a more positive way than what I've had to do. Minerva was only two when Sam and Noni left to provide aid to the colonists at Sertai. We lost contact with them after four days. The cowards that spaced all the volunteers had the gall to sell the aid ship at auction six months later."

My heart breaks for Minerva. I'd grown up without a father. I can't imagine what it had done to her to lose both parents in a spacejacking. "Did you ever forgive them, viejo?"

He looks at me for a long time, considering. "They never asked."

After I hang up, I walk out into the common area and find myself looking over at Brill, still wearing the jacket he stole from Jack. I understand a lot more about how Frank feels about mi vida, and anyone else who associates with space pirates. As everyone keeps saying, it's a thin line between a gray trader and a bad guy. The thing Frank doesn't realize, though, is that mi vida hasn't crossed it.

CHAPTER THIRTY-SIX

A few hours later, Ekrin and a couple of translators are giving Tawny an interview about what it's like to be a fan of a show you have to watch with subtitles.

That should keep Tawny busy for a while.

Which means it's just me, Brill, Kaliel and Chestla, sitting in Grundt's transport, drinking his booze, trying to figure out what to do with the dewormer.

Kaliel still intends to turn himself in to Tyson. We still have no idea how extensive the mindworm infection is on Zant – or who we can trust to tell about it.

I pick up one of the cylinders, feel liquid moving inside it. "What is this stuff, anyway? Could they replicate it if we send them a formula?"

"I know one way to find out," Chestla says. "Grundt's crew trades in pharmaceuticals. This transport is practically a mobile chem lab."

As if I didn't already have enough reasons to dislike the guy, he's a drug runner.

We move into the divided area at the front of the transport. It reminds me of the hidden lab we'd found in the cave on Evevron – only smaller and more organized. Chestla breaks open a vial of dewormer. She gestures towards a drawer, labeled in a language I can't read. "Get one of those slides."

I pull out what she's asked for, and hold it while she puts a drop of liquid in the center and places a cover slip on it. The microscope feeds into the computer's holofield. It comes up with a complicated projection.

Chestla gasps. "Would you look at that?"

"I am, chica." Pero, that doesn't mean I know what it is.

Chestla takes her handheld and plugs it into the computer too. She scans through the phone's files and throws up two other images. Chestla taps at the keys, and the dewormer molecule turns, lining up with the other two holocules. I can see the similarities.

Chestla says, "The molecule on the left is theobromine. That's the compound in chocolate that makes it similar to caffeine. I pulled this sample out of a brick of HGB dark."

At the mention of HGB, I automatically turn around and check the door. Even though we chose this space to talk because Tawny can't pick up feed in here.

Which means that Tawny didn't hear Grundt telling me that HGB set up Kaliel. I plan to keep it that way. She may be helping us out because we're important to Earth's PR right now, pero I don't want to test what will make her decide we're a liability. She's already recommended Brill's execution once, no? I'm still worried what I might have said to her when I was too panicked to pay attention to my sublingual.

"The middle diagram is a sample of the dewormer Ekrin gave us. There's a whole cocktail of other compounds to blunt the effect on the host's nervous system after the initial hit, but the active ingredient here is definitely an amplified theobromine molecule. It's a known poison. It's possible – though exceedingly rare – for humans to die from an overdose of it, just as they can die from an injection of pure caffeine. But there are Earth species – most notably dogs – that are extremely prone to theobromine poisoning. It interacts badly with the nervous system."

Kaliel grimaces. "Then it makes sense why after they gave it to me, I threw up and then had a panic attack."

"Sounds about right." She hesitates. "But for it to work at a dose that wouldn't damage the host, the parasite would have to be extremely sensitive to the compound. Almost intentionally so."

Brill says, "So for the mindworms, it's literally death by chocolate?"

"Chocolate, and anything else that contains theobromine. The mindworms would also be susceptible to tea and acacia berries from Earth, and probably skenza from Wanrog 3 and bleck from Taqu. They are both similar xanthine alkaloids to theobromine. But this is so specific that things containing caffeine wouldn't be a problem, even though caffeine and theobromine molecules are so similar." Chestla wrinkles her nose at him. "Interesting that you put it that way, though. Here's the rest of what's in HGB Dark."

She's color-coding the highlighted compounds, so that even I can't miss it. I say, "They liquified cacao to fight these parasites, no?"

"That's just it. Those highlighted compounds aren't naturally occurring in cocoa beans. But they show up in Serum Green." She brings the third holocule to the center. "We originally isolated these three compounds, which cause addiction with remarkably few side effects. But you take those away, and you take away the theobromine compound itself, and Serum Green and the dewormer are identical."

I'm trying to put this together. "Which means that either HGB gave Evevron the dewormer formula when they got hit by the epidemic – or your people made it and asked HGB to put it in the chocolate."

"But that doesn't fit," Chestla insists. "These mindworms infected this planet roughly eight years ago. Serum Green's been in HGB's chocolate a lot longer than that. The date stamped on the vials Eugene and I found of Serum Green in that lab in Rio means the formula is – at a minimum – twelve years old. And I doubt it's the first batch."

Brill's eyes have gone purple with concentration. "I keep coming back to something Tawny said. About how it seems like they're trying to contain information on the parasite – uan maybe this *is* ground zero."

"The timing still doesn't add up," Chestla says. "Unless someone was planning ahead for a possible outbreak…" Her eyes go wide as she realizes what she's just said. "Awwww, geesh, they were. Do you know what this means?"

"That we just figured out what Evevron got out of giving HGB Pure275 so they could win the war. They needed a commodity with galactic appeal, one where they could control the supplier by funneling everything through a single company, making sure it all had a dose of Serum Green." I speak slowly, lining up the pieces in my own mind as I go. "They were engineering in a failsafe before they even started with their genetic experimentation. Kaliel, you said the mindworms fear and are angry about chocolate, no?" Kaliel nods, so I continue, "Maybe these researchers were planning to create a creature that couldn't infect anyone that had consumed theobromine."

"That's plausible, Babe. At the time of the First Contact War, chocolate was a food-fad, spreading fast across the galaxy. But I think it's worse than that. These researchers would have wanted chocolate to spread faster, and they probably didn't expect HGB to actually hold onto the monopoly. They probably assumed that by now, people would be growing chocolate across half the galaxy. But by making chocolate addictive, they increased demand, even if the chocolate grown remotely wouldn't have that same addictive aspect. With the precarious position Earth was already in, Earth held onto chocolate even more strongly. Now that addictive need for chocolate has driven everyone to the brink of war." Brill's eyes are intense purple. "That addictive factor has to be why the coalition won't just wait for the Krom cacao plantation to mature, even though they know my people will share. Otherwise, why go through that much expense and loss of life?"

Chestla grimaces. "That's a lot of probablies."

And every one of them could get people she cares about killed. If this gets out, it could well restart the war between the Evevrons and the Zantites – and who knows how many other species, who will be mad at being forced into addiction? Not to mention the potential sanctions and/or executions by the Galactic Court.

Certain types of genetic experimentation are forbidden by that court. And that could get Chestla's people in serious trouble. Because there's one implication to all of this that none of us seem ready to put into words. If Serum Green was added to HGB chocolate because the Evevrons intended to engage in genetic experimentation, and the mindworms are afraid of it, logically, the Evevrons intentionally created the mindworms.

They didn't tell anyone that the infection had escaped their planet, because they're afraid of the punishment that could be brought down on them.

"But why would they have created these things in the first place?" I ask out loud.

"Maybe they were trying to come up with something like a sublingual," Kaliel volunteers. "Though I don't know why they wouldn't just use an actual sublingual. We know that tech can't go rogue."

"Supersoldiers," Chestla says. "Maybe. We're in the middle of a civil conflict with the cities that share the river. The ability to make coordinated attacks in the woods would come in handy."

"We could be dealing with someone trying to bring about the end of the galaxy," Brill says. "A mad scientist trying to take away individuality and free will to bring peace and end all war."

We all just stare at him.

Kaliel busts out laughing.

"You really have been watching too much bad science fiction holo, mi vida."

"It doesn't matter what it was. It wasn't supposed to get out." Brill looks at Chestla. "There's no plan in place for stopping this plague, is there?"

"Probably not." She closes her eyes for a long moment. "But I don't think many people know that. Ekrin's been my best friend since we were little kids. I don't think she'd intentionally lie to me." Chestla looks over at me. I can see the hesitation and conflict there, and I know what she wants to ask.

Before she has to break her pride or her word, I say, "Amiga, I know how much you want to come with us to Zant. Pero, you have to stay here and finish connecting the dots for us."

"Tell them you decided you can't leave while Ball's so badly hurt," Brill says, his voice thick. He's still connecting Ball to Darcy, on a raw emotional level. "That's something your great-grandmother will understand." He puts a hand on Chestla's arm. "I wish we could all stay until he's out of danger."

"Are the doctors going to take him off the critical list soon?" I ask.

Chestla stretches her fingers. Her nail polish is chipped, one of her claw-nails torn. "He was making jokes this morning about one-legged hunt captains – even though the doctors are saying they might be able to save his leg. But he's still so weak. And they haven't downgraded his condition. I... What am I supposed to do if I lose him?"

"You're not going to lose him," Kaliel says. "It wouldn't be fair."

Chestla stares at him, like she's willing herself to believe that because it's fair, that's what will happen. Pero, she says, "We don't have cemeteries here. We burn the bodies and mix the ashes with clean salt, which goes into the Cave of Memories, where water trickling through forms it into blocks of minerals together with the person's ancestors."

"That's not the same cave where we hid from the spuck, is it?" Brill asks. Is he afraid he contaminated the agua with Ball's blood?

"No," Chestla says, and Brill looks relieved.

"Are the families cool with those people being kept in cryostasis?" Kaliel asks.

Chestla tilts her cabeza. "What cryostasis?"

Kaliel says, "When I was going down to change for the float spa, I got lost and opened the door to a room where there were five people in cryopods. I didn't think anything of it, since the door wasn't locked. But unless you guys have unraveled the secret to bring popsicles back from the dead, it feels like those people are missing out on some important rites, or something."

Chestla looks shocked.

Brill puts his hand on her arm again. "Are you sure you want to investigate all of this? You could find out unpleasant things about people you grew up with, people you care about. It's a lot for us to ask."

Chestla looks up at him, her face fierce. "Then they shouldn't have lied to me."

The transport door opens. Tyson's standing there, his snakelike head cocked in curiosity. We knew he was coming.

Still, I shudder, and for once it's not instinctual fear. It's because of how much his cabeza looks like that of the spuck I had killed.

I know it was just an animal. I know they're planning to eat it.

Pero unlike everyone else here, I've never done anything like that before. And looking at Tyson, his animated face, so similar to the one I had put a hole in, is making it clear that

I have not processed the emotions that come with that. I'm having trouble breathing evenly.

Tyson tilts his head. "Who lied to you?"

Chestla snaps, "Does it matter?" Then her face changes, and she looks like she's about to apologize.

Before she can, Tyson shrugs. "One of you guys lied to me. Tere are no prisoners in the hold aboard te Krom ship."

"Shtesh!" Brill's a blur, exiting the transport.

I follow, looking back over my shoulder to say, "There were three Evevron guards watching them fifteen minutes ago."

All of which are gone now. Along with pretty much everything in the main part of the *Fois Gras* that's not screwed down. Ay, no. I step into the galley. They even took the silverware. And they broke Brill's fridge and stove. Grundt's crew didn't seem the type to go in for petty theft. They must be muy muy furioso.

Brill pokes a finger through the hole in his jacket. "Babe, we have to get off this rock. Now."

Brill's ship is grounded and busted. At this point, his insurance is going to consider it totaled. Pero, the *Fois Gras* is Brill's home. It would take a lot for him to be willing to leave it.

Tyson puts a hand on Brill's shoulder. "You still owe me a passenger. Plus, I already have one on board tat wants to talk to Bo."

Brill and I glance at each other. *Who on Larksis could that be?*

CHAPTER THIRTY-SEVEN

As the ramp comes down on Tyson's saucer, my heart starts thudding fast. The last time I'd stepped off this ship, it had been as a criminal, going back to Earth to face a judgement that nearly got me shaved. The time before that it had been as a fugitive, running from Tyson just before he bit me. The mere thought of getting back aboard *The Open Grenade Party Sunshine* has me nearing hyperventilation.

Pero, staying out in the open's no good either.

I climb the ramp, and my eyes zero in on the cell that takes up the far half-circle of the ship's main level. The cell is occupied by a guy in a black sweater and tight black leather pants. He has a long, pale face with a green cast to it, like someone cosplaying that painting *The Scream*. He smiles when he sees me, leaping up and moving to the bars. He clings to them, pressing his face as far forward as he can. In Universal, he says, "As I live and breathe, it's Bodacious Babe Benitez herself."

I blink. "And you are?"

"Oh, we've met." His grin gets even bigger. "A number of times. The first time, I was Hector Valencia, in Earth's rainforest, but causality for me gets all mixed up, so maybe he wasn't the first."

My chest goes frío. This hombre has to be being influenced by a mindworm, right? It's the first time I've talked to someone I know is infected. It's odd how the victim's personality still seems to color how the mindworm talks.

Pero, if that same parasite had infected Hector, also known as CyberFighter321, that means the mindworms are infecting Earth. Somehow, when it had just been Evevron and Zant, it hadn't hit home the same way.

Scream guy continues, "You stopped the Evevron girl from killing Hector Valencia, even though he had hurt people you care about. So why spare his life?"

I move closer to the bars, pero not so close he could reach out and grab me. "Because I value life, mijo. It shouldn't be taken away lightly."

Brill makes a startled noise, and I realize I've just quoted him. From a long time ago.

"But why? What makes one person's life so special? As a Sympathetic Mindhugger, I have hugged many people, and their thoughts are not so different from Hector Valencia's, brutish and mean. Well, except maybe Kaliel Liam Johannsson. All he wanted was approval and love."

I blink. Why value an individual like Hector? "Because Hector was once a child, filled with hope, and life hurt him, and he was angry. But he still had the potential to change, to be more and better than what he was."

"No." The guy's smile falls away. "He doesn't."

This muchacho really does have a problem with causality. Hector Valencia was executed by HGB months ago, and Scream's still using the present tense.

"I believe otherwise." I lift my chin, look the guy full in the face. "And even if he didn't, life is still a gift that shouldn't be squandered. My life, his life—" I point at Brill. I know Fizzax was infected with the parasite when he'd tried to execute Brill, down at the channel on Zant. Then I point at the guy I'm talking to. "This guy's life."

"What is up with this guy, anyway?" Brill asks. "When Kaliel was infected, he was still more or less in control of himself."

Scream puts his thin hands on his face. "Dashtin Kure has taken too many flawed neural enhancers. He rarely pays attention to or filters what he says. My suggestions come right out of his mouth, without me having to push very hard. I could override all of my mindhugs – had to do that to Kaliel Liam Johannsson in order to save his life when the Zantite guards attacked – but overriding on a regular basis would be unkind."

"How many people have you infected?" I ask.

"Six hundred and twenty-three." Dashtin looks at his shoes. "I have tried not to be greedy. Though expanding more would help keep me safe."

My stomach fills with ice. Over six hundred people. There's no way we can find them all.

Brill says, "Mr Kure deserves enough dignity to keep what's left of his brain for himself. The kind thing would have been to leave him be."

Dashtin frowns at Brill. "So even in this form, with a brain this guy is barely even using, you approve of killing parts of me?"

"I do," Kaliel says from behind us. He and Tawny walk in the door. Tyson raises the ramp behind them. Kaliel looks down at the briefcase full of dewormer that's in his hand.

Dashtin frowns, his eyes weakening, absolutely betrayed. "You don't mean that. I sat so gently in your mind. I protected you, gave you the skills you needed to survive."

"You forced me to do things that will give me nightmares for the rest of my life. An individual's life only matters because it's the sum of that individual's choices. And theirs alone."

"I guess this means we've settled the question of whether or not to tell Tyson about the mindworms," Tawny says, slipping on her headphones before anyone has a chance to respond. She heads for an empty spot on the wall near the door and sits down on the floor to start sorting feed, ignoring us, because she can't use any of this.

Tyson's still standing in the middle of the room, mouth open, reptilian tongue moving slightly in the gap between his fangs. Finally, he recovers. "Tat's te defense you were telling me about? Te mindworms made me do it?"

I'm afraid the shock's going to send Tyson's bureaucratic little heart into overdrive. I hesitate before I add, "Pero, when Kaliel told you he had a defense, he didn't know that the Evevrons don't want us telling anyone about these mindworms."

Tyson groans. "And I'm supposed to save his life? On Zant?"

Brill gestures towards Tyson's command station, with the central sphere that looks like an oversized trackball. "Sweet setup, su. Can we see it in action?"

Tyson pats the control panel. "You did say you were in a hurry to get off tis rock."

"You should be," Dashtin says. "You barely have enough time as it is."

I'm tired and frustangerated and a little freaked out, so I rise to the bait. "Time for what, mijo?"

Tyson lights up the controls.

"Wait," Brill says. He does something to the proximity bracelet. It looks exactly the same to me, pero Brill's pained face shows how much it hurts him to leave the *Fois Gras* – even graffitied and disabled – behind on this planet. He probably doesn't expect to see it ever again.

"You intrigue me, Bodacious Benitez," Dashtin says. "I've seen you be brave and seen you be kind, but I want to know if you are smart enough for those qualities to matter. You have exactly six days, three hours and twelve minutes to stop me from hurting people you love in the most ironic way possible. If I succeed, we will see how you feel about the value of my life then. And to show a gesture of goodwill, I will release my hug on this wreck of a mind."

"Wait!" I shout, not sure if it will do any good. "Por favor.

My friend Kayla. Did you hug her? Where is she? Is she still alive?"

"The Nitarri girl? She's alive. But she's not who we're playing for. And you're not getting any more clues. I really must be going."

"Wait!" Brill says.

"What?" Dashtin sounds annoyed.

Brill shrugs. "Who named you Sympathetic Mindhuggers?"

"The ones who engineered me did."

"Pero why did they make you?" I ask.

Something subtle changes about Dashtin's face. It's slacker, less focused. I get no answer.

Why would the Evevrons have intentionally created something as monstrous as this Mindhugger? Something that sees people as nothing more than interesting variables to run experiments on? Were they really trying to create a fleet of supersoldiers, able to coordinate an attack?

Poor Kaliel, at the mercy of such a cold, amoral force.

And poor Chestla, if whoever made it figures out that she knows. I fear for her, back on their planet.

"So where are we headed?" Tyson asks.

Six days. "If it's somebody I left behind on Larksis, they can forget it. We're weeks away. So it's got to be either Zant or Earth. And either one will be cutting it close." I feel paralyzed. I've never realized how equally centered Evevron is between Earth and Zant. It's about five days, either way we go.

"Zant it is," Tyson says.

"How'd you decide that?" I'm still flustered.

"Kaliel promised to show for trial on Zant, anyone following us is less likely to land on Zant, and you said Zant first, which means tat subconsciously you tink tat's te more likely spot." We're already in motion. "If you tink of a compelling reason to go to Eart instead, you have twelve hours for us to turn around."

Kaliel's still standing there, watching the brainmelted guy as he moves back to the bunk, pulls a table close to him and starts putting together about a million-piece puzzle involving different shades of blue. That's the thing about bad neural enhancers – on some level they can still turn a person into a genius, pero at the expense of everything else. Brill's also watching those thin pale-green hands moving puzzle pieces, and I wonder if mi vida's thinking about the drugs he and Darcy were trying to sell – which were of just this sort. I wonder if he still believes that putting all commodities out there – with a few war-mongering or suicide-inducing exceptions – is still the best way to prevent conflict. He said I could ask him anything. Pero what if I'm not sure I want to know the answer?

Kaliel looks down at the case of dewormer in his hand. "I wish that thing had stuck around a little longer. Then I'd have really given it a piece of my mind. Slowly and painfully."

"If you actually mean that, su, then I did misjudge you." Brill nods towards the guy in the cell. "And so did he."

Kaliel is silent for a few beats. "I guess I don't. It's just – I can't explain how much of a violation it is to be manipulated from inside your own mind. And I'm about to have to die for the things it made me do. I know it must look like I keep volunteering to play the martyr, but I like breathing. A lot. And there's a girl out there who loves me, and I just found out that she's alive somewhere, lost or hurt, and I won't be able to go to her. It's not fair."

"No, it's not fair." Brill crosses his arms, and his jacket shifts, showing his injured wrist. "But you can't be angry at the Mindhugger. It's like a child – a stupidly powerful child – trying to learn what it means to be a person. You heard what it told Bo. It doesn't understand what an individual is, so it doesn't understand why it should value a life, not even yours, though it spent time inside your mind. Getting mad at it is like getting mad at a shark for attacking a surfer that looks like a seal from under the water." He's taking my side of the argument he'd witnessed between me and my brother the night we'd all watched *Jaws XXII*.

"Then who should I get mad at?" Kaliel snaps. He pushes the case of dewormer into Brill's hands.

"It told us it was engineered. You should be mad at whoever created it." Brill's face doesn't look somber often, but when it does, he seems older than he really is, the weight of all that Krom history settling into the corners of his eyes and the edges of his mouth. "There are some things people have no right to do. Just ask Tyson for the letter of the law."

Tyson swivels around in his command chair. He's already got his sun lamps on, so he looks both spotlighted and thrown into shadow. "Mindhacking has been illegal since te foundation of te Galactic Court. It's one of te few times Galactic Law trumps local law – like with cases of attempted colonization of a civilization's home planet." Dios mio, he sounds so much like a lawyer. He'd have become one too, if life was fair. "Anyone making – or ordering the creation of – a mind-controlling parasite could face execution. And te organism itself would have to be destroyed. Do you have any idea who created it?"

Kaliel's face has lost color. Maybe, like me, he's thinking of all the council members we met on Evevron watching their children play in the pool. Because it's pretty obvious that they created the mindworms. We just don't know why.

"I'd rather not say without proof." Now that's the Kaliel I know. He puts his hands in his pockets. "So what do you guys know about the Nitarri?"

CHAPTER THIRTY-EIGHT

Brill shrugs. "There's not many Nitarri left. An ecological disaster destroyed the core of their planet a couple decades ago. The royal family was completely wiped out, and nobody could decide who had the right to lead, so they wound up scattered on planets in the nearby star systems."

"So why would that thing have called Kayla one? I've met her parents and–" Kaliel's eyes go to the floor and he swallows. "And we all know about her grandparents. They're all as human as Bo and me."

But then it all drops into place. Grundt had said Kayla's grandparents had saved a couple of Nitarri kids. I had assumed the merc had been talking about *other* niños, with their own grandchildren safe at home. Pero Scream had called Kayla the Nitarri girl.

And with what Brill just said about the power vacuum with the loss of the Nitarri royal family… "Estás jugando conmigo!" *You've got to be kidding me!*

Everyone in the room looks up at me – including Tawny, despite the headphones. Heat creeps into my face under the sudden scrutiny.

Pero, it's just about the only novela trope we've been missing: the secret princess and the hidden child.

"What?" Kaliel asks.

"Did Kayla ever tell you her middle name?"

"No." Kaliel rubs at the back of his neck again, not noticing this time. "What does that matter?"

"It's Anastasia."

Tyson and Brill are both blinking at me in confusion. Mi vida's not of Earth, so his knowledge of our history before First Contact is patchy.

Pero, Kaliel's blinking at me in a different way. "That sounds like something out of a bad knock-off of *Star Wars*."

"And your whole personality switch looks like something out of a telenovela," I point out. "Doesn't make it any less true."

"Will one of you tell me what you're talking about?" Brill asks.

"Sí, mi vida. As soon as I've talked to Stephen." Pero, how do I even start that conversation? Hola, Steve, are you secretly an alien prince? He's going to hang up on me. Unless it's true.

I open my sublingual channel.

Stephen answers immediately. *You have news.*

I do, actually. Kayla's alive.

The noise that echoes through my mind is practically a sob. *I told you she was. Where is she?*

I hesitate. Was it cruel to give him hope when I have so little information? No. He deserves to know. *We don't know where, pero we believe we know who has her. I have to solve a loco puzzle before I get any more information.*

OK. Where are you stuck?

I sigh. *I haven't even started working out the puzzle yet. Pero, it might help if we at least know who the players are.*

I don't follow.

I have to say it eventually. *Is there any chance that you're... not of Earth?*

There's silence in mi cabeza for a long time. Pero, I don't think he's hung up. Finally, he says, *You've been talking to Claire.*

It's my turn to be confused. Why would I be talking to Stephen's ex-wife? *Que? Stephen, this isn't a joke, nunca. The mindworm called Kayla that Nitarri girl. If Kayla's an Earthling, then that means he was talking about the wrong person. And she may not be alive after all.*

His voice is almost a whisper inside my brain. *You know there aren't any aliens living on Earth. It's hard enough for them even to get a travel visa.*

Sí, I know that's supposed to be true.

Pero, I can sense a hesitation. Finally, Stephen bubblechatters, *Did I ever tell you I enrolled in the pilot training program on Earth, before I shipped out for the mining corps?*

I'm trying to follow the whiplash turn in the conversation. *Okaaaaay.*

My dad got me out of having to take the physical. I assumed it had to do with scarring on my lungs from when I kept getting sick as a kid, but now I'm not sure that would have let me out of the program. I've never seen a doctor other than my dad. Which isn't weird, in and of itself, but there's this thing that happened between me and my sister when we were kids and I almost died from a lung infection. He hesitates, but obviously he's been wanting to tell somebody this for a long time. *I was only eight years old, and I convinced myself later that it had to have been a hallucination, but I swear Kayla put her hand on my forehead and pulled out the fever. She was singing that weird song she picked up somewhere, and the song took away the pain, but at the same time she was telling me inside my mind that I didn't get to chicken out and die on her.*

I temp-mute my side of the sublingual signal. "Sí, muchachos. Definitely aliens."

"Exiled prince?" Kaliel asks.

"Ni idea."

Ever since then, I've wondered if I could be an alien. I told Claire my theory once, after she accused me of not understanding her emotional needs. I think that's what got the divorce papers sent my way.

I snort out a laugh. If Claire divorced Stephen because she decided he was crazy, maybe she'll want him back if he can prove he was right. I've always thought there was still something between those too, anyway. *Stephen, what's your middle name?*

Kent. Why?

"Like Clark Kent?" I'm so startled, I say it out loud. Brill looks at me quizzically as I dissolve into uncontrollable giggles.

What is so funny? Stephen sighs in my head. *My grandpa used to laugh every time he said it, too. I don't get it.*

Tell you later. I hang up. "Stephen's middle name is Kent. And he's an alien being secretly raised by human beings on Earth."

"Ven, from your viewpoint, I'm actually the second alien you've dated." Brill's eyes are lavender with mirth.

I manage a straight face. "Sí. Who knew I got dumped by Superman?"

Brill pulls a pout. "I thought I was Superman. *Faster than a speeding bullet* and all that."

"I'll give you that, mi vida." Yet I can't help touching his jacket where the bullet went through it. If it hadn't been for the body armor... let's just say Grundt had a good bead on mi vida's heart. "But you're not indestructible."

"Stephen's indestructible?"

"That's not what I meant."

Brill's eyes are still lavender, so no lo sé if he even meant the question seriously.

"And to think, I'm dating a princess in hiding," Kaliel says.

"Maybe," I remind him.

His shoulders slump. "You're right. She might not want me with this much blood on my hands."

Oye! "No, loco boy, we don't know for sure she's a princesa." The Kayla I know is still going to want Kaliel, if we can find a way to keep him alive. And if we can find her. "Stephen's fizzbounced at the possibility he's not an Earthling, pero Kayla's never liked uncertainty or surprises."

Kaliel sighs. "And I've brought her nothing but that."

"Oh, no, muchacho," I tell him. "You don't get to go being depressed again."

Brill laughs. "I can see why Stephen'd be excited, though. Every kid dreams of being something different, no matter what they start out as. It's the whole unique-means-special thing. There was a brief time when I wanted to be a cybernetic cop, uan the kids in one of the shows I watched. I had a fantasy that I'd get kidnapped and taken to the lab."

"You?" Tyson scoffs. "A cop?"

"Wal. Me." Brill's jaw juts out. "You and me could have been partners. I'd inevitably mess up, and you'd look the other way. It'd be perfect, since that's what you're so good at."

Tyson moves over to Brill, and suddenly he's about nine feet tall, towering over mi vida, studying him with those whiteless eyes. "I tink you'd better explain tat remark."

Brill shrugs. "Like when your partner beats a guy you've taken into custody unconscious, just to get information."

Tyson blinks his translucent eyelids. "When did tat happen?"

Brill stands and faces him. "I saw all the bruises on Darcy Hayat, su. He wouldn't have lied to me about where they came from."

Tyson sucks his mouth inside out again, his spine coiling down some of the extra height. "Are you talking about his first escape attempt? He made sure I was knocked out before he re-wired te lock on his cell, but Yernell didn't drink te drugged coffee. I woke up in te airlock because Hayat had been in te process of spacing me. Your friend apparently put up quite a fight before Yernell put him unconscious."

Brill's bitter laugh breaks my heart. "Darcy didn't try to escape. And I'm sorry to be the one to tell you, but *apparently* your own partner drugged you. Darcy told me you were in the loft the whole time. It might have made him feel better if he'd realized you were knocked out, and not the world's biggest hypocrite."

Tyson stands there frozen for a long moment. Then he says, "Yernell always was an ass."

Brill turns away, paces over to the cell bars. I follow him over, take his arm.

"Does it make *you* feel better, mi vida?"

"A little," he admits.

Dashtin stands up from the bunk and asks, "Do any of you have any gum?"

CHAPTER THIRTY-NINE

I call Mamá. "What are you going to be doing in six days?"

She's sitting in the Green Room with Minda. They're watching one of Mamá's flashback-casts from last year's ChocoFest. "The same thing we are doing every day, mija, making a new show."

"We've been alternating," Minda says, "so six days from now, we will be showing Lavonda's work. This one, probably."

I glance at the FeedCast playing behind her. It's covering nine different ways to enjoy hot chocolate, as prepared by top chefs throughout Brazil and Bolivia. There's nothing in it that feels like a particular opportunity for irony.

Pero, the divas still seem the most likely targets for the mindworm's test.

"Can you cancel that show? Maybe at the last minute say one of you is sick."

"Absolutely not," Minda says. "If there's a possibility of danger, we will amp up security, limit the audience to people we know. But I will not give in to fear."

I sigh. If fighting Mamá on something is impossible... just try fighting Mamá and Minda put together. "Where are you FeedCasting from?"

"They repaired the old set," Minda says. "Frank says it is more secure to keep using the same space." She makes a *ppfft* noise. "Have you ever tried fighting him when he's determined about something?"

Ignoring the irony, I tell Mamá, "We will be there as soon as we can."

"You do not have to do that, Bee." Mamá gestures at Minda. "Estará bien." *We will be fine.*

Heat burns the back of my eyes. I've spent too much time avoiding Mamá, each of us trying to prove that we don't need the other. "This time, I'm going to be there for you, Mamá."

Her eyes glitter with sudden moisture. "Maybe we can cue up one of your flashback shows. Get you sympathy. You need it with so many people lobbying for you to be recalled to stand trial."

I was pardoned, in exchange for doing the tour on Zant. I've left the planet and haven't exactly lived up to the original bargain. That could put me back in line for the shave, if the judge really pushed. "You're going to help by showing everyone what I was like as an awkward teenager?" I cringe, thinking about my first cheesetastic role.

"Exactly, mija. I want them to see why I love you."

Mi mamá and I can patch up what went wrong between us. I can tell she wants to.

As long as we get there on time to keep her safe.

Pero, what if I'm wrong and the threat is to Earth? More people I care about are there than on Zant. I call Mario, tell him, "I need you to take all the girls and get out of town."

He's shocked, pero he listens.

After I hang up with Mario, I pretend to be enthralled with looking up something on my phone, while I call Tyson using my sublingual.

Tyson looks at his phone, then up at me. He slides out of his control chair, then taps Brill on the shoulder. "You mind watching te controls for a minute. I gotta take tis."

Brill moves over to the trackball. "How do I fly this thing?"

"Just let me know if anyting on the panel turns red." He

flashes up the ladder and answers the phone. *Why all the secrecy?*

Because I don't want Tawny to hear this, and there is at least a chance she hasn't managed to slap a camera on you.

Tyson asks, *What's on your mind?*

Are you planning to tell the Zantites about the mind parasites?

Tat's te responsible ting to do, Bo. He sighs. *But Kaliel asked me not to.* I'm not sure when that conversation could have happened. Maybe they've been texting? *He believes te mindworms are holding his girlfriend hostage. He wants me to rescue her before te parasites get attacked.*

And you're going to go for that? I'm surprised.

Kaliel called it a last request. Tyson sighs even more heavily. *Brill once said I didn't understand te difference between te spirit of te law and te letter of te law. I tink te spirit of the mindhacking laws – which favor saving te victims whenever possible – means I must try.*

What about Kaliel? He's a victim, too.

Tyson is silent for a long time. *I'm doing my best to help him.*

Then don't take him back to Zant.

Whether he was controlling his own hands or not, tose hands are covered in blood. Tat's a letter I can't ignore.

After that, it's a long and awkward ride to Zant, with no privacy. We're all sharing the bathroom in Tyson's loft, because the only other facilities are inside the cell with Dashtin. And we're sleeping wrapped in blankets on the floor.

There's nothing here for me to do. Tyson has no galley. He just eats those pre-packaged rations. Brill brings down several boxes of those, along with flat after flat of agua. We won't go hungry. Pero, there's no coffee to ease my shakes. And no chocolate.

Keeping the holo small enough to fit in my hand, since I'm a bit embarrassed how much I still care about what the people back home think, I selfiesearch FeedCast Wannabees. Forty-seven percent of responders think I should get shaved. That horrorstat is actually down from sixty-two percent, at the time

I left for Zant. That is surprising, and in some ways encouraging.

There are a couple of new sub-polls connected to my already extensive entry.

Brill Cray Real Deal or Wannabee? herocasts Brill leaping off that cliff and shooting the spuck to save me. A whopping eighty-six percent say real deal.

Team Kaliel or Team Brill? herocasts Kaliel trying to surrender himself to a group of anonymous space pirates to save me. There's a roughly sixty/forty split, in Brill's favor.

There's no mention of Kayla. It's like the minute she shadowpopped from that club, she ceased to exist.

Should Bo and Kaliel Get Shaved Together? starts with a close-up of me and Kaliel dancing. Thirty-seven percent say yes.

Brill wanders over. "What are you looking at?"

"Nothing." I start to close the malcast. Pero, if I want Brill to trust our relationship, I have to be as open with him as he was with me about Darcy. "I've been selfiesearching the public opinion polls."

He starts watching the holo. "You need a better source for news."

Heat creeps into my face. I should have known he'd criticize me for looking at fluffcasts.

Then he points. "In that sub-poll, these sus spelled my name Brill Clay."

I laugh and watch his eyes turn violet. "You're not mad that they keep shipping me with Kaliel?"

He sits down next to me. "Your fans expect a love triangle. That's what Tawny's spinning them."

CHAPTER FORTY

The engine is making noises, just like the first time I was aboard the *Sunshine*. At which point, Tyson had had to stop then for repairs. My heart sinks.

We wind up stuck at a tradepost, and there goes our day of leeway. Tyson won't even let us get out, in case we might be spotted on the security feeds.

Chestla calls me on my handheld, and I sneak up to Tyson's loft to talk. I'm fairly certain Tawny hasn't bugged me again.

"I've been doing a little research. Leron bought that I didn't know anything, and I took the opportunity to lift his password." Chestla pops up stat-sheets onto my phone of three Evevrons, two guys and a girl, somber-eyed and stuck-up looking. I can still hear her talking, even though I can't see her any more. "These are the three researchers who created what they called the Sympathetic Mindhuggers."

"Sí, chica. We've met your planet's take on supersoldiers in the flesh."

"Supersoldiers?" Chestla blinks, confused. "No. I was wrong about that."

I am confused también. "Isn't that what this mind plague was supposed to be?"

"No. The Evevrons were trying to find a way to halt prison overcrowding. They wanted to create a biological system for positive reinforcement. They thought they could end the need for prisons altogether by having the Mindhuggers more or less program people to be kind to each other."

That's chilling. What gave these scientists the right to take away a person's free will – even a criminal's?

This is why mindhacking's illegal.

Even if you think you're doing the galaxy a favor.

"If it was supposed to be a force for good, chica, then why did it influence Kaliel to kill people?"

"Something went terribly wrong. Like with most monsters, what they created isn't what they intended. They didn't expect it to become sentient. And they certainly didn't expect it to cause a telepathic hive mind. Check this out." The stillholo dissolves to a gritcast, where these same people are sitting in chairs, and there's a group of five other Evevrons sitting opposite them. The difference is that the group of five – they're each cuffed wrist and ankle to their seats.

The most stuck-up looking of the trio reads off a tablet. Chestla's provided auto-generated subtitles for my benefit. "Do you now regret your attempts to blow up the dam?"

"I regret getting caught." The guy closest to the camera rattles his cuffs. His face is narrow, his cheeks sunken in. The others make noises of agreement, and all start rattling. The caption cites him as Chevros.

"Yeah," agrees the prisoner the captions label Des Sah.

"I can't say I'm sad to hear you say that, because if you had shown any signs of remorse or rehabilitation, you would not have been considered acceptable candidates for our pilot program." He points towards the camera. "This is a historic day, recorded for posterity. This is the day that we eliminate the need for prisons on this planet."

The five – three guys and two girls – look nervously at the camera. The lady on the researcher's side opens a case and removes a silver injection gun.

"What's that?" one prisoner squeaks. The caption labels her

Awn. She has a round face and a pert nose and cascades of curly black hair, though she's as thin as the rest of the prisoners.

"This," the muchacha says, "is the future. Each of these cartridges contains the dormant form of one Sympathetic Mindhugger. It will attach to the appropriate parts of your brain, where it will reinforce positive, socially acceptable thoughts, and discourage anti-social behavior. After your observation and testing period has ended, you will be able to leave this prison to become productive members of society."

"I didn't volunteer for no pilot program! Neither did my wife," Chevros protests, even as the lady approaches him and presses the silver gun against his neck. He whips his head around and bites her.

"Agh!" She pulls her hand away, bleeding, and checks to make sure all her fingers still work. "You see? This is exactly what got you here."

The bumpclip ends, and Chestla's face reappears. "Those cryostasis pods Kaliel saw? That's those five."

"They froze patient zero?"

Chestla nods. "Someone did. The original three researchers didn't survive when their research escaped. They underestimated what they'd done. When the parasites became telepathic, it allowed their hosts to anticipate each other's movements. And then a separate consciousness started to emerge that helped them coordinate their efforts to spread across the region. But the core of that consciousness was imprinted by what it learned from five criminals."

"So how come the whole planet's not infected?"

"These creatures weren't engineered to be able to reproduce. If you want another one, you clone it. It's not a quick process, and the clones have to be kept in a super-cooled solution that keeps them dormant until they can be introduced into the bloodstream of the would-be host. That tends to make the hive mind selective about who it infects." She hesitates.

"But if they ever found a place where they could set up reproduction laboratories, the population could start increasing exponentially."

Chestla looks worried.

"What are you not telling me, chica?"

"It's just – Leron's involved somehow. How could my friends have done this? The five you call Patient Zero were desperate people, on the opposite side from mine in the river dispute. They hurt my city, but they only did it because they were dying from lack of water. You can see the malnutrition, just looking at them. Two of those five were married to each other, and had a son. You saw Awn and Chevros. He really cared about her. It was a truly tragic love story. I– I'm too close to all of this. Had it happened on the other side of the river, that could have been me and Ekrin and Ball being kept on ice."

Five days in, Brill's sitting against the wall watching the guy in the cell work his puzzle, and I'm leaning on him, checking the news.

When I move away from his shoulder, he pats my hand. Then he asks Tyson, "What did this su even do?"

"Transporting stolen goods. By te time I found him, he'd turned te stuff over to anoter pilot and was counting his cash. We know the cargo originated on Eart, but we haven't verified what it is, or where it was headed."

"Zant," Dashtin says, dropping another piece into his puzzle.

"What did you say?" Brill asks.

"I was supposed to take it all the way to Zant. But I stopped, and someone who wanted to buy a box of it came on board. My passenger didn't like that." He lapses back into silence.

"Who hires a mentally defective pilot?" Kaliel asks.

"Somebody who doesn't want anyone curious about what they're flying," Brill replies. "He's probably good with spatial things. If it's a gretis run, you're not likely to need sharp reasoning skills."

The whole thing's still odd. If a whole transport worth of something's stolen, someone's missing it. So why doesn't Tyson know what it is? Unless... Eugene had said the people who broke into his lab had taken the boxes of poisoned chocolate that had been laced with Pure275. That wouldn't have been reported to the cops.

We'd assumed it had been HGB moving around their own stuff, pero what if it wasn't them?

It's a huge logic leap. Still, I approach Dashtin and ask, "A box of what?"

He shrugs.

I pull up HGB's main site and show him their logo. "Did it look like this?"

He nods. "But marked out."

"Oi! No." I turn back to Tyson. "There's a whole transport out there full of Pure Chocolate. And it's headed for Zant. That can't be a coincidence."

Tyson tilts his blade-like head. "If it's pure, ten what's te problem?"

The problem is that I'm not supposed to know about it.

Pero, this is one secret I have to share.

"Pure275 is the herbicide HGB uses to keep cacao contained inside the plantations. There was an entire storehouse worth of chocolate that had been contaminated with it."

Tawny's staring at me from her spot on the floor. She already thought I knew too much. I can practically feel her filling out a requisition form for Frank's assassination services on my behalf.

Pero, mi mamá is in danger, and no matter what happens to me, I have to save her. I continue, "Hector Valencia was in that room. If he was already infected, the mindworms knew the poisoned chocolate was there."

"It'd fit what Dashtin said about irony," Brill says. "Everyone is trying to kill off these mindworms using chocolate, so they kill off some of us using the same method. Plus, it makes half the galaxy afraid to eat anything with the HGB logo on it."

Tawny makes a tiny noise. I glance at her. She looks about to pop. There has to be a way I can talk her into leaving Brill out of her report. He wouldn't say anything, nunca.

I shake my head. "Pure275 is considered safe on Earth because you have to eat a ton of it, or breathe the weaponized version to wind up muerto."

Tawny lets out a louder noise. She didn't realize we knew about the weaponized Pure, either. Oh well, they can only execute you once.

"Maybe they added something to it?" Brill suggests. "There's nothing else that makes sense."

"We have to warn them that a couple tons of choco-poison are headed their way." I step far enough away from Tawny to avoid crosstalk with her sublingual – though not her glare – and open the channel. I call Frank's phone, pero I get a polite, clipped message. *We are sorry, but this user does not exist.*

Ice crashes inside my stomach. I try Mamá, who has a different service. *Lo siento mucho! Este usuario ya no está disponible.* Translation: *So sorry! This user is no longer available.*

I try Minda's set. There's a blanket out of service message for that entire section of Zant. I fumble for my handheld. It isn't hard to find the news.

A Zantite reporter, reading off a tablet he isn't holding all of the way out of the capture field, is speaking mid-feed when I pick it up live. "...and Minda's show will go on as scheduled, despite the numerous sabotages in the area. They're planning to string some old school communications tech together to force the signal out, so stay tuned for an early morning broadcast. We expect restored phone service by the end of day tomorrow."

I appeal straight to Tawny. "If they're using the same

foodieholo Mamá showed me, it's going to be a choco-stravaganza."

Brill looks at Tyson's charts. "We're going to be cutting it close, but we should still make it."

A little later, Tawny's coming back from using the bathroom in Tyson's loft, and I'm on my way up. We cross paths at the top of the ladder. She's been quiet, ever since she found out we knew about the Pure Chocolate. She gives me one of those plastic smiles.

I can't take it any more. "Can we be honest for a minute, muchacha?"

She lets the smile fall away. "Are you sure you want that? Most people think they're ready for brutal honesty, but once they have it, they want the candy-coated ignorance back."

I finish climbing the ladder. "You know me. I've never been one to leave the veneers alone."

"I know that, Bo. And that's the pity. You have to know the truth about everything, even the secrets that are keeping everyone safe. You feel so deeply, want so much – and that's exactly what's going to get Brill killed."

My heart clenches. "Brill? I thought the threat was against me."

Tawny pulls out her tube of lotion, smoothing on the soothing fragrance. "It's too late for threats. It's bad enough that you hold so many secrets in that pretty little head of yours, but to have someone so mercenary as a Krom privy to our weaknesses – how are we supposed to trust where his loyalties lie?"

"He's loyal to me," I say fiercely.

"For now," she shrugs. "But his loyalties haven't always been consistent in the past." She tries to put the plastic smile back on, pero it doesn't quite fit.

It's hard to tell if she's supposing what might happen, or if she's telling me Brill's execution's been signed off on.

Whichever way, it's clear she holds me responsible. My heart's pounding in panic. There has to be a way to change her mind.

"You should have just been happy Kaliel escaped the shave. He was. We put a tracking anklet on him, and practically slid his neck under the blade. And even he knew better than to push to know why."

So Tawny knew that HGB had baited Kaliel into blowing up that vessel. She'd known he'd been tricked into believing he was under attack by space pirates, and could still smile at him back in Rio, when he was under the same roof at the HGB processing plant, awaiting trial – and execution. She'd been going to just let him die.

How could she *do* that, when she knew he was innocent? And if she could do that, then there's no way to convince her to spare Brill now.

I force myself to look her in the eye. "Are you still going to help us save Kaliel?"

For a second, I imagine there's a glimmer of shift, just around the edges of her irises. Pero, eso es imposible. She's HGB. She *is* Earth. Only, now that I've found out Kayla's not, I'm seeing aliens everywhere.

"Kaliel's still important to preserving peace. I'm going to do what I can to save him, but I won't deny my own loyalties to do it. HGB has asked we honor the Evevrons' wishes not to disclose information about the parasite."

In other words, she's not going to show the feed of the mindworms because if someone digs deep enough, they're bound to find out Earth helped the Evevrons with the cover-up. And everything will come out about Serum Green. Which I hope she still doesn't know I know about.

I move past her, trying to ignore the way she's watching my hands quiver from the IH shakes. "Maybe you should try being loyal to the truth, mija."

"Not all secrets are bad, Bo." The ice blue of Tawny's eyes is intense. "Look at your friend Kayla. Her secret's kept her alive these past twenty-odd years. She's never going to know how much her family sacrificed for her and her twin, even though she's not theirs by blood. And she doesn't need to."

I stop. "What do you know about it?"

She fiddles with the headphones draped around her neck. "Me? I'm not old enough for all that ancient history. But if you ask Frank about ecological disasters involving a planet's core, he might tell you. Or it might push him far enough to finally shoot you. You're not going to be happy anyway until it comes to that."

I blink in confusion. "Frank caused an ecological disaster?"

"No! Why do you assume we're the bad guys in everything?"

"Because you usually are?"

"You can't afford to still be that naïve." Tawny takes my hand in hers. "I know you. You're going to want to shout out the truth about these parasites to any Zantite who will listen. But if you don't – if you show a modicum of restraint for once – then just maybe no one has to find out how many of Earth's secrets Brill knows."

CHAPTER FORTY-ONE

When we land, there's a party of about two dozen Zantites waiting for us. We're watching enhanced gritcast from inside the ship, and the group includes both Mertex and Fizzax.

Is that the jury? Are they going to execute Kaliel right there on the pavement?

"Kaliel." I move over to him, take his hand in mine.

Brill stares at me, not even trying to hide the jealousy in his irises. And yet, he walks over to us and puts a hand on Kaliel's other shoulder. "It's not too late, su. We can turn this bread loaf around. I have friends that can hide you so long the Zantites get tired of looking."

"I did not hear tat," Tyson says.

Brill looks at him. "Don't tell me you aren't thinking the same thing. This isn't justice, and you know it."

Tyson puts his hands on the big trackball, like he's actually considering leaving. Then he shakes his cabeza. "Te law is all tat holds society together. And I cannot break te trust put in me to uphold it."

Brill looks at Kaliel. "I liked it better when I thought he was a hypocrite."

"It's OK. I agree with him." Kaliel takes a deep breath, and I can't help but wonder how many of those he has left. "It sucks. But I agree." Then he looks at me. "Don't give up hope."

I squeeze his hand. "Lo siento."

He grips mine back. "I said, don't give up."

I stare at him. I thought he'd been taking this all too calmly. "You have a plan."

"It's a long shot." Kaliel stares at the door. He has to be holding onto every moment, trying to freeze time before he steps out there. "You guys know the truth. That may have to be enough. Since I probably won't be able to, tell Kayla…" His voice breaks. "Tell her I wanted to give her my grandmother's ring."

"Suavet ita hanstral," Brill says. *I am so very sorry.* "But we're running out of time to get to Minda's set before the Mindhugger executes its plan. We have to open the door."

"Right." Kaliel straightens his posture, moves closer to the door.

Brill gives him a closed-fisted salute. "Safe journey and true heart, Kaliel."

Kaliel hesitates. His journey is going to be anything but safe. He can't know how much that means, for Brill to bid farewell to him not only as an equal, but as a close friend. Kaliel smiles. "Thanks."

Tyson lets down the ramp, and the group outside bring weapons to bear. It's not quite dawn, so they're indistinct outlines against the light coming out of the saucer. The air is cool, the first bit of color smearing the sky. A night insect clicks, rhythmic and alone, somewhere nearby. It promises to be a heartshatteringly beautiful day.

Brill adjusts the body armor under the collar of his tee. He made me put mine on too. Who knows what the Mindhugger has waiting for us? "You do realize if Tyson puts us down as the ones who turned Kaliel in, we're getting half the reward. It's about five times what we got for Jack."

I still haven't figured out when a Galactacop can or can't claim a reward. I remember Tyson once saying he wasn't about to turn bounty hunter.

"I don't want blood money," I shudder.

Brill shrugs. "Let's make sure we use it for something he would have approved of."

Kaliel holds up his hands as Tyson walks with him down to meet them. Brill and I follow. Tawny's right on our heels, ready to tackle me if I say anything she doesn't like.

I told Brill what she said. He'd gotten her alone and flat out asked her if she'd sent another recommendation he be assassinated, and she said she hadn't. Yet.

Kaliel gets to the bottom of the ramp, and the Zantites form a circle around him.

Police Chief Dghax steps forward. "Mr Johansson, you killed nine people on this planet. For that you are to be executed. Have you any complaints?"

He's going to say no. And then he'll die.

Kaliel says, "I do. I dispute the charges, and ask for a civilian trial under the Cadmar Treaty. I am a citizen of a planet protected by the Galactic Court, and therefore eligible. I also request a complete medical and psychological examination, as other medical treatment has uncovered a growth in my brain that may have impaired my judgement."

Tyson is nodding along. He's obviously coached Kaliel. Fizzax and Mertex are also nodding along. What's going on here?

Dghax's mouth falls open. He looks at Tyson. "Are you going to represent him?"

Tyson shakes his head and points at Tawny. "She is."

Tawny looks just as shocked as I am.

"This will take some hours to arrange. That type of trial requires the presence of those who have been wronged by the crime in question." Dghax looks troubled. "Will you waive the right to complain of mental anguish due to the delayed judgement and to being detained under threat of execution?"

"I willingly waive such rights."

They all nod at each other, and Kaliel walks away with them. He looks back, once, staring at Tyson, and it's light enough out now to catch the intensity of his gaze. Tyson coils down his spine, back to his resting height. Somehow, he seems even shorter, like the weight of Kaliel's final request is pressing down on him. I understand how he feels. We have no leads. So how are we supposed to find Kayla?

"Wait up!" Tawny hurries after them. "Apparently I need to talk to my client!"

I look over at Tyson. "So how come I never heard of this treaty, mijo?"

He plays with the angles of his mouth. "Because most of te time, it's just delaying te inevitable. You have to be able to claim an interplanetary misunderstanding. And it doesn't apply to cases involving military law, or directly involving te king, so if I had invoked it for you aboard the *Layla's Pride*, tey'd have just laughed." He can't have forgotten that call from Garfex, asking him personally to find Kaliel. Tyson's just not mentioning it to the potential executioners, since Garfex didn't bother to show up for this. Tyson gets the kind of trial he wants, without actually lying to anyone. He so should have been a lawyer.

Brill asks Tyson, "Do you think it will help this time?"

Tyson shrugs. "If not, at least it keeps Tawny from itching our scales, which is hot springs fizzy wine delicious."

Brill's scanning the spaceport. "There isn't easy public transport here."

We don't have time to call a cab.

"Mertex!" I call.

Murry stops, waits for me to catch up to him.

"Por favor, can we get a ride to Minda's set? It's urgent."

Mertex's eyes go wide. "What's wrong?"

"We can explain on te way," Tyson says, as we head towards Mertex's vehicle.

Tyson takes the seat next to Murry, while Brill and I slide into the back. We give him an abbreviated version of what's been going on – one that doesn't mention that the people in the process of sabotaging Minda's show are infected by brain parasites.

I feel guilty. Who knows how far the infection has spread? People really should be warned.

But if I speak the truth, Brill and I probably both wind up on HGB's hit list.

Mertex looks alarmed enough, as he sucks in air through an open mouth, showing off all six billion pointy teeth. "Why didn't you call and tell me this?"

"We tried," I protest. "The phones are down."

"All of them?" Murry pulls his own phone out of his pocket. "Then how did Dghax know for us to meet your saucer?"

"I spoke to him shortly after we left Evevron." Tyson's tilting his mouth in again, pero Mertex doesn't seem to notice how troubled he is. "I wanted to emphasize tat Kaliel was coming in peacefully. I didn't want any misunderstandings on te tarmac." Tyson hesitates. "But I told you tat when I called you, remember?"

Mertex laughs. "Oh, right." He looks at his phone. I catch a glimpse of the castsignal gauge. It's topped. Pero, he says, "That's weird. But it makes me feel better. Because, you see, Minda and I went on a date yesterday – just coffee, nothing serious – and I was starting to freak out that she hadn't called me back yet."

You know how when people are lying, they tend to talk real fast and add unnecessary details? Murry's doing that. We don't have to see the bruise on his skin to know he's infected, pero there it is, on the back of his wrist.

The sun's up now.

We're going fast down a highway.

Tyson unbuckles his seatbelt.

Brill glances down to make sure my seatbelt's on. I brace myself, not sure what's about to happen. Tyson's armed, pero if he's concerned about not hurting the victim here, he'll be careful with Murry, right?

Mertex puts on his blinker. He's heading away from the set. He puts one hand down on the seat beside him, and it comes up holding a weapon.

Tyson lunges at him.

The tires squeal, the wheel jerks, and my stomach lurches as we angle off the road, bumping our way through a field of haraggaha plants, the purple pulp splattering our windshield as we mow it down. Ay!

Mertex and Tyson are fighting in the front seat, grunting and cursing, as we careen out of control. Mertex flails an arm, and the front driver-side door flies open. Mertex flips Tyson up, like he's trying to bite the Galactacop in half, pero Tyson turns the momentum into a forward roll that pulls him out of the door. He takes Mertex with him.

I'm frozen, for a shocked second. That's all it takes for Brill to get his seatbelt and squeeze between the two front seats. Pero, before he can manage to punch the brake in a configuration sized for a Zantite, we burst through the last row of sugar plants and hit a ditch, which jolts us to a stop. My seatbelt engages so hard it takes my breath away. Brill's cabeza comes close to the windshield, pero doesn't go through it.

He looks miraculously unhurt when he slides back through the seats. "Babe, you OK?"

"Sí." I try to unbuckle the seatbelt. The buckle's jammed.

Brill takes out his pocketknife. He's still cutting through the strap when Tyson drags Mertex up to us.

The Galactacop blinks, and one of his translucent eyelids looks discolored.

Brill nods downwards, at the busted axle. "This thing's not going anywhere."

Tyson hefts Mertex back into the vehicle. "Yeah, well neiter is he."

I can't tell if Murry's breathing.

Tyson pulls out a couple of zipties and starts fastening Mertex's wrists and ankles, threading the tie-ends through either side's door frame. Tension melts out of my shoulders. At least the guy's alive.

The car's trunk got thrown open in the crash, and there's a dent where something heavy hit it on the way out. Not far away, in the middle of the sugar plant pulp, there's a familiar metal lock box.

Eh? It's the one those Zantites had salvaged from the wrecked Evevronian ship. Why would Mertex have that? Unless… maybe it means something to the mindworms.

The lock broke open on impact. The guys are busy with Mertex, so I take a quick look inside. Amazingly, this box had remained watertight for almost a decade. There's a locket, engraved in Evevron. I can't read the inscription, pero inside, there's a paper picture of Awn on one side – and of an infant Evevron on the other. There's also a packet wrapped in red paper that looks suspiciously like explosives. And a holo-keychain showing the image of Chevros. And stacks of papers I can't read. And a gun.

I close the box. This belonged to one of the minds that had made up the first tier of the mindworms. Pero, Awn had never made it onto that ship. What does that mean?

Is Awn part of the mindworm? Or was it in love with her?

"Shouldn't we just deworm him?" Brill asks.

Tyson pats his jacket pocket. "We need to ask his parasite a few questions. I've got a stimulant shot tat should pull him back to consciousness."

"We're already running out of time," I insist. "You talk to him. We're going to look for another ride." I hesitate. "Remember, that's not the parasite's body, right, mijo?"

Tyson looks at me with distaste. "You know me better tan tat, Bo." Then he looks at Brill. Brill's eyes go a confusing tannish-green-gray color. Tyson looks away, embarrassed.

"Come on, Babe." Brill starts walking, in the opposite direction of the road. "There has to be a farmhouse somewhere back here."

We're even farther away now from Mamá and Minda. Frustration burns through me.

And still, mi vida is hurting. I take his hand, doing my best to keep pace with him. "Are you going to be OK?"

"You know what? I think I am." Brill looks down at me, smiling sadly. "I told Kaliel not to be mad at the parasite. I'm the hypocrite, if I can't let this go. Darcy's dead, but so is the su who got him killed. Ven let the dead blame the dead."

"Te amo, mi vida." It's taken a lot to get him to this point. I hope he really can find peace.

"Love you too, Babe." He squeezes my hand.

Soon, we find a complex that is more full-on sugar-processing plant than farmhouse. There's a row of tanker trucks off to one side. I guess they process some of this stuff as syrup. Looking at them, Brill's eyes turn green.

"Are you planning to borrow one of those?"

"Not without permission." Brill makes a face. "Can you imagine the punishment for auto theft on this planet?"

I shudder. "Probably about the same as for everything else."

"Wait here and look lost. Like you might cry or something. You used to be an actress."

I know he meant it as a compliment, pero pain spikes through me that is almost physical. I was supposed to have been a star, but my short career had crashbanged so hard I'm still trying to climb out of the emotional crater.

Brill starts talking to a couple of guys standing near the complex's door. He mimes something crashing into a divot – our truck hitting that ditch. He points over at me. They talk for a couple more minutes, then something changes hands and Brill walks back to me, holding a set of keys.

"They let you borrow the truck, mi vida?"

"Only after I bought the cargo." Brill pulls the tanker's steering wheel down as low as it will go and adjusts the seat all the way forward. He still looks like a ten year-old trying to drive his dad's truck, barely able to see over the dash, and stretching his legs out from a position perched on the edge of the seat. "They charged me about twice what it's worth."

By the time we take the long road around to where we went off course, Tyson is standing at the edge of the field, waiting for us. He's holding the case of dewormer.

"Where's Mertex?" Brill asks.

"I left him attached to te car."

Mi vida nods at the dewormer case. "You didn't do it yet?"

Tyson hands him the case. "You had more questions for te last one. He will be waiting for you when we come back."

"We should take him with us now." Brill strides into the field. "And I want his phone."

"I agree." I follow mi vida.

Pero, when we get to where we left the vehicle, it's been rocked over on its side, and the passenger door – now the upper door – has been ripped off its hinges and cracked apart where the tie had been threaded through it. Brill's looking at the door, so I step up onto the side of the car and look inside. There's no sign of blood, pero there is something silvery and clear shining at the edge where the driver's side floor joins the door. My chest fills with ice. "Oye! Por favor no."

I swallow fear around a lump in my throat, remembering Murry picking up the syringe of the Invincible Heart that I'd dropped in frustbarrisment. I climb into the car, pick up the syringe, and longing cramps my gut as I examine the small amount of inky residue swirled through with gold, like a secret galaxy that leads to power and euphoria and freedom from the shakes.

"Babe! Don't!" Brill's leaning into the car, looking down at me, and I realize I've brought the needle of the syringe right up to my arm. I drop it. Heat burns through me, starting with my eyes and nose, then flooding into my chest and arms. Poor doomed Mertex. I can't help but picture him staring at the yellow bandage they'd put on my arm after I'd been injected with this stuff. *You'll tell me if it's amazing, right?* His stupid smiling, excited face.

A few tears escape. After a minute, I get it under control, and Brill helps me back out of the vehicle.

I run my sleeve across my nose. "He never would have done it."

"Done what?" Tyson leans against the wrecked vehicle and uses the hard surface to scratch his back. I realize he doesn't really know Mertex.

"Murry thought he was a coward. He once told me that the ultimate act of bravery was for a Zantite soldier to take a dose of the Invincible Heart." Because, in the Zantite biological system, it is guaranteed death, after the euphoria and rage that fuel a mission have run their course. "He was fascinated with the stuff, pero he valued his life."

"Which is not cowardice, by the way," Brill puts in.

I nod. I'm already talking about Mertex in the past tense. Which is fitting, since he is a dead man walking – err, raging. "He never would have dosed himself."

Brill's eyes are pure mahogany sorrow. "The Mindhuggers still don't understand what it means to be an individual. Think about how calmly it suicided one of its own parts inside Dashtin on board the *Sunshine*. And remember what Ekrin told it? Nothing you are will be lost. How is it supposed to understand what it means to lose everything that a single person is?"

Tyson looks somber. "What is it about Mertex Makanoc tat will be lost?

It's an oddly philosophical question, coming from him. I guess finding out that someone got tortured on his watch – even if it was years ago – has really gotten to him.

I manage to keep the tears inside, at least for now. "He was such a geek. I never knew anybody as into movies y mas as he was. He even thought it was chido that time I kicked his butt. I was trying to kill him, and he was picturing it as an action scene fit for a cheesecast."

"We can mourn him later," Brill says. Though he pauses to offer the car a close-fisted salute. "Right now, we need to make sure the mindworms don't use his teeth to leave us mourning anybody else."

The box with Awn's things is gone. Mertex must have taken it with him. There's at least one individual these mindworms seem to care about. But why? Awn's been dead a long time.

We trudge out of the field. The tanker only has one row of seats, and Tyson's the best suited to drive it, so I find myself squashed up against Brill in the almost double-sized passenger seat. Mi vida's body is warm against mine, even through the leather jacket and the body armor, and his arm around my shoulders is about all that is keeping me from dissolving. It feels like his heartbeat, hummingbird fast against my cheek, is somehow steadying my own, like the pendant in the bag at my feet's supposed to do for a Krom.

We should all have some sort of visible sign like that, to show the world when our heart is breaking with grief.

I sniff. "You know how most lies have a kernel of truth?"

"Yeah, Babe?"

"Well, I hope Murry wasn't lying about having that date with Minda."

CHAPTER FORTY-TWO

We have to get to Minda's set before they start melting chocolate.

"What is your plan when we get tere?" Tyson scratches at his shoulder, keeping his other hand firmly on the wheel. I wish he would keep both hands on the wheel. We are going pretty fast.

"I'm going to ask you not to tell anyone the chocolate's poisoned, por favor."

"Bo, tat's—"

"Just hear me out. These brain parasites want people to stop eating chocolate. Which everyone will do if they know a batch got poisoned. Which gives time for the number of infected people to multiply exponentially by the time we rescue Kayla." I know the mindworms would still need a lab. Pero, I'm appealing to Tyson's emotions. "Which you promised Kaliel you would do."

Tyson shows me his fangs. It's body language without human equivalent, and I'm not sure what it means. He looks back at the road before he closes his mouth.

"What's the Earth saying, in for a penny, in for a pound, eh Tyson?" Brill grins.

"Do you even know what tat refers to?" Tyson asks.

"It's about one of the card games they play for money. The psychology that makes it easier to stay in once some of your money is committed." Brill doesn't sound sure, though. After all, Krom don't gamble.

"Actually, it has to do with obsolete Eart law. Once you got behind and owed a single penny, you might as well borrow a whole pound, because te penalty for nonpayment was te same." Tyson turns towards the set. "If someone gets hurt here, tere will be consequences. For all of us."

I point out the windshield. "We have to destroy the chocolate – and make it look like an accident."

"What are you pointing at?" Tyson squints into the distance.

"That's Minda's set. The storeroom is on the left. If we were to crash into it, and if this tanker full of sugar syrup were to spring a leak, it would all be ruined." Tyson looks hesitant, so I add, "Brill already bought the syrup, and I'll pay for the truck and the damages."

"How do we know tere's not anybody in tere?"

"There probably won't be. Ni idea how to make sure. Too bad we don't have a Zantite here to use his x-ray vision." It's a joke. The Zantite augmented heat-based vision isn't strong enough to see through metal – or I wouldn't be here. I hid from them twice aboard one of their own warships. Claro está, I didn't realize that they even had heat vision then.

"But these might be." Brill pulls out the goggles Fizzax gave him. "Some of the other settings are stronger." He puts the goggles on and adjusts them. "I can see a ton of heat signatures off to the right. There's one on the left. But it's moving back out of the way."

"I want to see," I say.

"Later, Babe." Brill takes off the goggles and slips them into my bag.

"All right ten." Tyson opens his mouth and shows his fangs to the road. We're pushing his moral boundaries to the edge here. I hope it doesn't break him.

"Brace yourself, Babe. This thing doesn't have airbags."

Tyson floors it. We cross the last stretch of road. The engine roars. The storeroom wall is getting closer.

We crash into it, through it, the impact pulling tight on the seatbelt Brill and I are sharing, metal crushing in around us.

Two tons worth of chocolate spills out of broken boxes with the HGB logo crossed out on them, some of the bricks bursting out of their wrappers, a few others flying through the windshield.

Glass shatters.

I duck as a block of HGB Dark comes flying at mi cabeza.

I look over at Brill, afraid he might be bleeding again, pero the body armor seems to have done its job protecting his arm and shoulder. We pile out, not having to fake looking shocked as people rush towards us.

We don't even have to rip open the truck's tank. A strong piece of rebar did that for us, raking a hole down the side. Phosphorescent sugar syrup is leaking all over the boxes, coating the chocopoison. If this mess is going down the drain – if that drain is even anything other than decorative – it's moving slowly.

Tyson looks down distastefully as chocolaty sugar syrup coats his boots and the cuffs of his pants. He heads to the ledge at the pool's edge, to walk around the mess, rather than through it.

Frank is one of the first people to make it over to us. He looks worried when he sees me tottering through the mess. Pero the look he gives me when he sees Brill standing next to me – a mix of disappointment, frustration and frío determination – sinks me to my core.

Without him having to say it, I can tell his orders have changed. He's a reluctant assassin, evaluating his target's troublesome girlfriend.

I'm guessing Frank was hoping Brill had dropped off his radar, and he wouldn't try real hard to find him, because if he can't find him, he can't end him, nunca. And here we are, making a scene too public to ignore.

No y no. Tawny said if we kept our mouths shut, HGB would forget about mi vida. She said the megacorp wouldn't even have to know how much Brill knows.

I don't think she lied.

I think she underestimated the ruthlessness of her own company. There must have been something in the feedcasts Tawny's been sending of our exploits that gave HGB a red flag, or maybe they just want to sever my connection with Krom, now that the rest of their media-spin isn't going well.

And now they want Frank to kill Brill so that he's no threat to their secrets – and so that they can keep me in line.

A small noise escapes my throat. Frank starts to say something, pero Tyson and Brill push past him, onto the set. Tyson scratches his back again, against a corner of the fake wall, before heading farther in to look for Mertex. The doomed Zantite has to be here, somewhere.

Mamá is standing there, staring, holding a box of HGB dark. I gesture her towards me, urgently. She brings the box, gracias a Dios.

I tell her, "Pretend to trip and drop it in the goo."

She raises both eyebrows at me. "Oh no! This is too slippery, mija!" She throws the box. It lands with a plop in the rising sugar syrup. Frank and Mamá and I, we're all covered with phosphorescence. It's beautiful.

I hold my hands up, and Mamá holds up hers, and it's like I'm a niña again, and we're making holopaintings in the park. She's always loved a piece of art called Starry Night, loved to mimic little pieces of it, and right now it looks like we've fallen into it. I make eye contact with Frank, and his expression is soft, looking at the glow with a child's wonder. For a moment, it feels like he could fit, a star in my constellation.

"The chocolate was all poisoned," I say. "But don't tell anybody."

Frank scoops up a handful of glowing syrup. He empties the syrup, holds out a glowing hand. "Come home, Bo." I don't think he means it literally. "HGB will welcome you as a hero. We need people as resourceful as you to keep Earth safe, and it would be so much easier if we weren't working at cross purposes."

It's a beautiful image, healing the crack between me and my planet, bringing in a generation of peace.

Pero, then I remember the look he gave me about Brill. HGB is bloodthirsty, and even from the inside, I wouldn't be able to change that. Frank has more blood on his hands than phosphorescence, and I don't want any of his guilt on mine. "HGB is poison too, viejo."

Frank looks at the residue on his hand. "You are oversimplifying things again."

I turn away from him. "Mamá, por favor. Is there any more of this chocolate out there?"

"The show does not start for another half an hour. We have barely started prepping." She looks rattled, though whether from finding out she's standing in a lake of poisoned chocolate, or because of what Frank and I just said to each other, I can't tell.

"Oh, gracias a Dios!" I hug mi mamá close. She returns the embrace, weakly. "If you see anyone eating chocolate in here, take it away from them, OK?"

I look past her at Minda, still working to set up, while casting worried glances over this way. Dozens of audience members in the waiting area are looking our way too, pero the security guys won't let them down past the stands.

Brill and Tyson are crossing the room, peering into corners, and the security guys are looking nervously at them, until Fizzax says something that seems to calm them.

There's a flash of movement back behind the staging area. I motion to Frank, then bring a finger to my lips, careful not to touch my mouth with the tainted goo. He follows me, and I sense more than see someone moving from the back out into the hall, towards the exit door. Someone big enough to be Mertex. Frank pulls me to a stop, moves to check it out.

Frank on a regular day versus a Zantite hopped up on IH. I don't want to see either of them get hurt, and I'm honestly not sure which one I should be more afraid for.

The exit door bangs open, and Frank's moving fast. I follow.

When we hit the alley, Mertex hasn't gone far. He's crouched with his head in his hands, groaning. At first I think the IH has already run its course. Then I realize the miscalculation the Mindhuggers made. Well before the IH kills Mertex, it's poisoning his parasite. And unlike whatever quick fix the Evevrons gave Kaliel, this is unpleasant for both Murry and the thing in his cabeza.

"Atento," I tell Frank. *Careful.* "He's had a dose of the Invincible Heart."

"Poor kek." Frank draws his weapon, a grim frown on his face.

"Stop," I grab for his gun arm. I never would have dared to do that before. Frank draws back before I can make contact.

I'm half-afraid he's going to turn that gun on me, pero he looks at me quizzically, somehow still keeping an eye on Mertex. "He's dangerous, he's dying, and he's obviously in pain. Putting him down would be a kindness."

"He's not a dog, Frank." I've seen him show more actual kindness to that stupid corgi. "And none of this is his fault. Besides, I need to talk to him."

I step closer to Mertex. Stooped down as he is, he's almost my same height. He looks at me. "You were right, Bodacious Benitez. There's a lot here that should have been saved."

I suck air. How does he even know I said that? Was there some kind of transmitter in the car? Or could the Mindhugger have had someone in that field, listening?

It sounds like I'm talking directly to the Mindhugger again, no? I shouldn't be. The IH wasn't supposed to fry Mertex's brain. "What do you mean, mijo?"

Mertex blinks those hunormous whale eyes. "Didn't you say that to me? I thought... but I can't remember when."

So Murry, then. Pero the mindworm's still there. "Mijo, I need to know where Kayla is."

He bares his teeth and grumbles deep in his throat, and I have to stop myself from flitdashing. I still feel an urgent need to pee. The irritability brought on by the drug growls in his voice when he says, "Why would I know that?"

I swallow hard. "Because I can tell you're going to be really good at guessing today. If you were going to hide Kayla somewhere, where would it be?"

He groans and clutches his cabeza again. Pero when he opens his eyes again, he says, "It would have to be across the teeth, on the far island. Somewhere deep."

"Deep?" I ask. "What does that mean?"

He grits his teeth, looking irritated again. "I don't know. Just deep."

And that's all I'm going to get. Frank clears his throat. I almost forgot he was there.

"You are going to explain all of this to me later." It's not a question.

"Sí, viejo." I'll gladly tell Frank anything he wants to know, keep him talking long enough for Brill to flitdash. I hope mi vida understood Frank's expression. I hope he's already gone. "Murry, mijo, por favor. Is the game over, now that we destroyed the Pure Chocolate?"

"It would have been the perfect form of irony, wouldn't it? He thought of it a long time ago, back when the troublesome couple took off ready to spread their theobromine poison across the galaxy. Only, it took too much tainted chocolate to kill an Earthling. So he added a catalyst to the dairy they were supposed to use today to magnify the effect. It would have been almost instant, almost painless."

Troublesome couple? It takes me a couple of seconds to put that together with the missing boxes of Pure Chocolate that had somehow found their way aboard the CaptureVista, the SeniorLeisure vessel Kaliel had been tricked into scuttlepunching.

It had been an unnecessary double-whammy, so if HGB sent the black ship, they wouldn't have been behind it. Chestla had never found leads on who was.

"The mindworms tried to poison the Bakers?" Kayla's poor grandparents never had a chance. "Pero, it didn't work, because somebody else blew them up first."

"It had started working." Mertex looks at his shoes. "There were several cases of illness among the staff, and one death. Plus a visiting Zantite dignitary, who died almost instantly. Zantites are surprisingly susceptible to Pure275."

Which is interesting, because the Zantites and the Evevrons – who created Pure275 – have a history of war.

"Pero, now. This game. Is it over? Did I pass the test?"

"You won major points. But there's one more piece of irony left. The people you care about are the ones saying the show must go on, even after Kaliel disrupted it. Even after you destroyed the chocolate."

That means Mamá and Minda. I look back at the closed exit door. My heart sinks.

"Murry, what did you do?"

"I–" He collapses, writhing on the pavement. Then he goes still and lets out a long sigh, like some excruciating pain has been released. Pero, then his eyes fill with horror, and he looks up at me. "What have I done?"

He's on his feet, pushing past us back into the building.

Frank looks alarmed. "You really don't think I should shoot him?"

I follow Mertex, calling back over my shoulder. "He's back on our side." It takes me a second to realize what I just said. As long as Frank's supposed to hurt Brill, we'll never be on the same side. Pero we both want to protect Mamá, and in this moment, that's enough.

CHAPTER FORTY-THREE

Mertex races down the hall, and I see what he's looking up at: the mechanism built to push a giant sculpture of Minda out over the stage, where wires are supposed to float it down for the opening scene. Just like the beginning of *Hearts Wanted*, where Minda played a young actress in the chorus of a theater company production where everyone twines ribbons around a sculpture of the theater's first diva – only, in honor of Mamá's chocofootage, this one's made of chocolate. It's at least three times as big as the chocolate sculpture Brill had nearly been frozen inside.

The fluorescent pink wires are flopping loose against the sculpture's shoulders. Minda's staring inside one of the ovens, so focused she doesn't even notice that the contraption is moving overhead. There's a bang, and the oven door goes dark with splattered cake batter. Minda flinches. Her mic is already on. She says a guttural word in Zantite, then mumbles, "I thought I had this down."

Mamá, who was on the other side of the kitchen, moves closer to help her.

My heart freezes. "No!"

"Minda!" Mertex shouts, dashing towards her, as the choco-statue starts to wobble.

Brill could easily get there in time to snatch both of them out of the way. If he's still here.

As I run towards the two divas, I quickly scan the set, hoping he's here to help, hoping he's not, so Frank can't find him.

Mi vida's here all right, pero someone has darted him again, and he's standing inside a ring of cops, looking woozy. I glance over at Frank as we both race towards mi mamá. Is he really planning to destroy my love, my heart, my life?

Mamá backpedals from the rage-powerful Zantite barreling towards her. Mertex grabs Minda, shoves her out of the way as the sculpture falls, dropping him squarely under it. Minda's high-pitched wail as he disappears shatters the entire row of glasses on the table, pops half the lights. The sculpture cracks in half. Even after nearby Zantites drag the chocolate pieces off him, Mertex doesn't even try to get up. From the way he's lying, something's broken, low in his back.

Minda looks up at where the sculpture was perched, and moisture glitters in her eyes. "Why did you do that?"

He shrugs, his shoulders moving the choco-rubble that covers the floor. "Because that's what you do when you love someone."

"You what now?" she says, and it's only half a joke.

"I love you. And I'm glad I'm getting the chance to say it, even if it's too late to do anything else."

She looks at me, alarmed. I shake my head, just the same way Brill had when I'd walked into that cave asking about Ball. Only, unlike Ball, there's no chance of Murry improbably surviving this. Mertex may look full of vitality, pero there's no filtering the IH out of his blood.

It's even harder to be on this side of the head-shake.

Minda bursts into tears. I've never seen a Zantite cry before. It's not pretty.

Tyson moves over to us, watching with sympathy in his eyes. Has he lost someone he loved, too? Or is he sympathizing with Mertex, who is receiving punishment for something he didn't do?

"I've been given the Invincible Heart." Mertex holds up a hand, cups Minda's face. "I just want to know, though, before I sleep – why me?"

"What?" Minda sniffs.

"When we were on the warship, why pick me, when all the other guys were bigger, stronger – funnier?"

She runs a finger along his jawline. "None of them were as beautiful on the inside."

OK. I can't take it. I pull out the goggles Brill stuck in my bag, and flip them back to the setting that will let me see as Minda sees. I gasp. There's a fine filigree of red heat lines glowing on both of them, outlining veins and touch points and the swirl where they're both blushing. And Mertex really is beautiful.

"Let me see tat." Tyson elbows me, and the instinctive fear hits me again when I look at his reptile's face through the goggles. He's more or less one temperature, though there's collected heat somewhere deep in his cabeza. I'm guessing that's the core of his brain.

I hand over the goggles, and when he looks through them, he draws a breath, like a little niño. I wonder what it must be like to see through Zantite eyes – as filtered through a Myska's vision. He scratches the back of one hand with the other, idly, like he doesn't even realize he's doing it.

Minda's tears fall on Mertex's shirt. "You never did remember, when we were little kids. When I first moved here."

Mertex looks confused. "I thought you came here after I left."

She takes both his hands in hers. "That's when I came back. We only lived here for a couple of years. When I returned they said you had enlisted."

"I don't..." Suddenly, he smiles, displaying all those shark teeth with the same geeky eagerness he's always shown. "Were you the girl with the doll? And the flower-print replacement leg?"

Minda blushes even more solidly green. "That leg was part of why we moved the first time. When my dad got in trouble, some of the girls injured me when they tried to drive me out of my learning pod. And when I came here – the social order had already been set. I didn't think anyone was going to accept me until you..." Minda looks up at the rest of us. "It's not common for people from this region of Zant to move far from their families, unless there's no suitable pod for their children. My mom and I were alone. I was getting bullied until one day Mertex stopped it, and the girls apologized."

I've seen Minda in a dress – see her now, on her knees by Murry – and now that she's outgrown the flowers there's no way you could tell she has a prosthetic. That kids would be so cruel as to snap off her leg when she was already hurting over whatever happened to her papá – when Minda told me that people get over buzzbashing and unpopularity, she'd been speaking from experience.

Mertex looks at the rest of us too, like he's just realizing his impending death has an audience.

I move closer to him, bending down on the opposite side from Minda. Murry's the only one in this room who can come close to understanding my addiction. The need, the power, at the same time the raw fear that it's going to end you. "So the feel of the Invincible Heart. You'll tell me if it's amazing, right?"

He manages a laugh. "You know as well as I do how bad it sucks. Especially now when it's telling me to leap and run, take on the worlds – only I can't move my legs." He takes a deep breath. "Promise me you won't die like this."

He knows about the betting pools on how long it's going to take me to give in. He can feel the drug's power, its seduction – and he's channeling all that rage into looking back at me, challenging me to say I'm stronger than this. And yet, it's un prometo I can't quite make.

"I promise you I will do my best, mijo, with all my might."

"Then your success is assured." He holds out a hand, touches mine, completing the formal exchange. Pero, it isn't just a formality. He means it. "The crash after IH comes on fast. I've got a little while, but I don't want everyone watching."

Just like in a Zandywood holoshow, where the camera turns away before death arrives.

"Then I'll say goodbye now." I take Minda's oversized hand in mine. "Mertex told me once that if he had to die, he wanted it to be in your arms. That he wanted you to sing him the lullaby from *Wandering Wild*."

Mertex's face turns solid green, all the way across the bridge of his nose. "But that was when I never thought it would be possible."

"I wish we had more time," Minda tells him.

Tears fill his oversized eyes, pero they don't fall. "I've always been a coward. I'm so scared right now."

"A coward?" Minda protests. "A coward wouldn't have done that to save me."

"That's right." Fizzax steps from behind me, kneels by Mertex. "I'd be scared right now too. Did I ever tell you my uncle took the Invincible Heart? I was a kid at the time, and I thought it was fascinating and cool and oh so brave. But I'd never do it."

They don't need me here. I turn away, as Tyson moves to help them transport Mertex somewhere a little more private.

I look for Brill, where I'd seen him ringed by the cops, pero he's not there.

Ice tickles down my spine. I'd thought he'd be safe in their custody, at least until this was over.

Pero, no y no. Nunca. Frank's already leading Brill towards the gaping hole we crashed the tanker through. I race over, reaching the storeroom door just as they make it around the lake of syrup. Brill is still darted, still looking nauseated. His eyes are solid black, and he frowns at me like he was hoping I wouldn't get caught in the middle of this. Pero he stops moving, and Frank looks back to see what's causing the hesitation.

I dash across the receding pool of syrup, the sticky mess sucking at my shoes. "That's a little cowardly, don't you think, Viejo?"

Frank sighs. "It would have been easier for everyone if we'd gotten out of here without you noticing."

"At least take the dart out, and let him say goodbye."

"And have him run? I'm getting too old to chase a Krom."

"Babe, it'll be OK." It won't. And Brill knows it. He looks like he wants to reach out to me, pero his hands are cuffed behind his back to keep him from pulling out the dart. "At least I know the su."

That's loco. Where's the comfort in getting a bullet from someone you know, instead of from a stranger?

I try one more time to appeal to Frank. "There's a Galactic Inspector here, and dozens of witnesses who saw you take him."

Frank nods. "The cops handed him over to me, for questioning. And I didn't lie to them. We are going to have a little chat first."

First. My heart feels like ice. "You know he doesn't deserve this."

"Come on." Frank puts a hand on Brill's shoulder, starts walking him across the parking lot. "Get in the van."

"Jimena didn't deserve it either." My voice comes out softer than I'd meant for it to, more raw with emotion. "Ask Brill why when you have your little chat."

A blush breaks across Frank's cheeks and nose, pero he's still acting like he hasn't heard me.

Brill manages the step up onto the back seat of the van despite the dart and his handicapped balance.

"No!" I race over to the van, pushing Frank out of the way. I manage to get the dart out of Brill's neck, prying the embedded device out with it, and get turned back around to–

Bang! Pain blooms through my chest.

I'm wearing the body armor, pero the force of it still takes my breath away. I sit down, hard, on the floor and glance at the neat hole Frank just put in my shirt. From the front seat, Botas whines. Frank has him strapped in, pero he's pulling at the restraints, trying to come to me.

Brill makes eye contact with me, and when I nod that I'm OK, mi vida looks reproachfully at Frank. "You promised not to do that."

"Kek." I'm not going to ask what kind of deal he made, not when every breath hurts. "You know this is my fault for digging into HGB. I don't want you to sacrifice yourself for me."

"I love you, Babe." He shrugs. "Besides, they'd already cuffed me. So it wasn't much of a concession."

"Get out of the van, Bo." Frank doesn't look like he's about to apologize for shooting me. And he's not about to pretend he knew I was wearing body armor.

"Babe. Everything I told you before still stands. Even the part about Gavin." Brill's main concern is taking care of me. He still looks ill. It will take a while for the dart's effect to wear off – if he even lives long enough for that to happen. "You'll wear that pendant for a good long time, won't you? And then if you want Kaliel or somebody else – well, I'm OK with that."

"Mi vida, I–" I reach up and kiss Brill, hard and deep, for a good long time. Frank's going to have to shoot me again if he wants to stop it. This really is our last beso. And I don't know how to say goodbye. When we finally break apart, I look at Brill. No pet names, no laughing hope of reprieve. "Brill Cray, eres el amor de mi vida. Verdaderamente. Siempre pensaré en ti." I'm glad he's learned enough Spanish that I can say it that way, in the language of my heart. *You truly are the love of my life. I will think of you always.*

"Babe." He looks like he wants to reach out for me again.

"Bo." Frank says it softer this time. "Out now."

I step off the van and Frank closes the door.

Minda's still got her mic, and she's turned the speakers up loud. Behind me, I can hear her start singing.

The van drives away.

I sink to my knees, my chest sparkling with shock and aching from the bullet. Frank might as well have shot me for real. Because that's one loss too many. All I want is to blunt this pain.

Rex isn't still here on shore leave, pero he gave me his number when he left – and I hadn't been able to make myself throw it away. No matter what I just told Mertex, I'm about to call the unethical doc's assistant, because he has to know someone here who can get me a dose of the Invincible Heart.

I need courage to confront Frank and make him look me in the eye one more time as I tell him I'm going to do everything in my power to break everything that belongs to HGB. And if I'm still high on IH, who knows what might happen?

Rex has just answered the phone when Fizzax walks up to me, still on my knees in the parking lot. He kneels across from me and arches one of those almost non-existent Zantite eyebrows at Rex. He puts a hand on my face, makes me look at him. "This is trying your best? Mertex's heat lines haven't even faded yet."

I hang up on Rex. Fizzax is part of the group of cops that just handed Brill over without a second thought. I look at him steadily. "How am I supposed to be strong without him?"

He tilts his cabeza. "Without Mertex?"

"Without Brill."

"Brill's gone?" Fizzax had been in with Mertex and Minda. He'd missed the entire thing. I don't have the strength to explain it right now. Let him assume for the moment that Brill just left. Fizzax purses his rubbery lips. "I haven't known you that long, but from what I've seen, your strength has never come from someone else. Come back inside, and let's talk. Minda's got a bar in there, and I make a mean bexarkk. Best thing for a broken heart."

CHAPTER FORTY-FOUR

Minda turned the choco-fiasco into a memorial concert for Mertex and for Verex Kowlk. They've been going for hours.

I am hiding out in the Green Room, waiting for Mamá to bring me clean clothes. Fizzax got called away after one drink to question everyone about what happened to Mertex, and I slipped away while he was getting his orders. If he finds me in here, I'm going to claim accident – Mertex accidentally stabbed himself with the syringe when the car went into the ditch, Tyson's foot slipped off the brake when we followed him here, those wires just never got attached right to that statue. In my version, Murry's a hero. As long as Tyson doesn't contradict me.

I'm still shaking with shock and heartbreak and need, so when I text Stephen what Mertex said about where Kayla is, it takes me a couple of tries to get it right. I'm not up to talking, so I'm relieved when he texts back. *Heading over to the other island as soon as I find my shoes.*

I'm too broken right now to even be curious what Stephen's doing that he lost them.

There's another text I didn't even notice come in. It's from Rex. *Are you OK? You didn't say what you wanted.*

I want Brill back. I have trouble breathing every time I think about what is happening to mi vida right now. If he's still talking to Frank, he must be so scared. When his heart stops

369

beating – if it hasn't already – will I somehow know?

I took off the dented body armor when I examined the bruising on my chest. Now, I take the paladzian pendant out of my bag. The crystal glitters, beautiful, perfect.

The door opens while I'm putting the pendant on, tucking it under my shirt, close to my shattered heart. Brill may not even be dead yet, but it doesn't matter. Unlike Minda, I won't be there to hold him when it happens. Unlike Chestla, there's no way for me to demand mi vida not die on me.

Frank probably won't even give us his body back, so there can be a proper funeral.

Minda sees what I'm doing and gasps. She wraps me in a hug. "Oh, sweetie."

It feels good, like the compression is holding my world together. When she lets me go, I feel lost. I'm still covered in dried glow syrup, and it feels like I'm a string of stars, let loose in the galaxy to float away. I'm losing my friends, one by one. And Kaliel is next. The time they set for his trial is less than an hour away.

Mamá comes up behind Minda, carrying a dress for me. "What's wrong, mija?"

I glare at her. "If you wind up with Frank, I will never speak to you again. Nunca."

Mi mamá looks like I slapped her.

I turn to Minda. "At least you got to say goodbye."

Minda hugs me again. She doesn't ask what happened to mi vida. "Tell Kaliel goodbye as soon as we get there. Plus anything else important you have to say. This kind of trial – with the victim's families there – it's not likely to go well. And you know our justice is swift."

I take the dress from Mamá, who is looking more and more puzzled.

I tell Minda, "Kayla's the one who needs to tell him goodbye. Can't they delay this until we find her?"

"I wish it was that easy." Minda rubs at her leg. I wonder whether it's the real one or the join for the prosthetic. "I've arranged for a transport to bring as many of us as possible to support Kaliel. It leaves in nineteen time segment partitions."

I still can't wrap my head around the way Zantites tell time.

Mamá looks confident for the first time since she walked into the room. "She means roughly fifteen minutes, mija."

I gesture down at my syrup-covered, gently-glowing clothes. "Then I'd better hurry."

I clean up the best I can, and am just sliding on a fresh coat of lipstick when Minda knocks on the door. "You ready?"

I follow her out to the transport, where Mamá, Valeria and most of the crew are piling in. I wind up sitting next to Tyson. I still don't feel like talking. I try to make that clear by staring out the window. He lets me, for a good long while.

They're holding the trial in an open-air coliseum. Which means that at least Kaliel will get one last look at the sky. Ay, no! No, I've got to stop thinking like that. Tyson may be planning a miracle.

I look over at him. He's got the sleeve of his jacket pulled up, examining a damaged scale. The skin underneath is a soft pinkish gray. "Are dragons on Evevron like dragons on Earth? Or are tey more like me? Tis body is sturdy. Are tey harder than me to kill?"

This trial must have him thinking about his own mortality, the way the pendant heavy on my neck has me thinking about mine. I manage a sad little laugh. "Dragons on Earth aren't real."

"Which is a shame, right? Some of te tings tey've done with tem in te holos is impressive." I'd never have pegged Tyson as a guy who watches Earth movies. Pero, this is the first time I've ever sat and just talked to him. He shakes his cabeza. "But I mean te extinct ones."

"Dinosaurs?" I think about it for a few minutes. "They're

more like dinosaurs. Spucks are smart, as animals go, pero, they're not people. And they certainly don't have your sense of justice."

Tyson's tongue flicks out between his lips. "Your compliment makes me bounce sparkle premier night champagne."

I glance out the window again. We're getting close now. People are lining the streets. Yet when I look closer, I blink in surprise. Many are holding up MIAG signs. Less than half of these people are Zantite. There are visitors here from dozens of different worlds, wearing shirts that say things like, *Team BeeBee AND KayKay*, and, *Save the hero, save the girl!* There are some holding up pictures of me – heavy on the theme of dragonslaying – and even a group of a dozen Scarzilan girls wearing hoodies with stylized images of Brill's face emblazoned across the back. The whole thing's done in black and white – except for the eyes, which are a different color on each hoodie.

When I see the one where Brill's eyes are lavender – mischievous and laughing – I look down at my hands, which are trying to dig holes in the top of my thighs. I have to force myself to keep breathing.

I still can't accept he's gone. When a Krom's unconscious, the eyes go clear, like a marble with a network of orange veins behind it. I can't dwell on what his eyes must look like now, not if I'm going to be in any condition to speak for Kaliel.

I try to focus on the scene outside the window. What Tawny's artist has done for Kaliel is nothing short of amazing. It's taking six people to hold up his most elaborate piece, a moving mural of various versions of Kaliel fighting space pirates. People around it are holding up signs that say, *Live to fight another day!* in about a dozen different languages.

That hurts too. Right now, my love is either dead or dying.

And yet. It's the opposite of the signs at the spaceport when I was leaving Earth. I wonder, after watching Tawny's spinwash of my exploits, if those people who were there that day all still feel the same way – if they'd rather be watching me die today instead of Kaliel. If they still think I sold out my planet's future. If that lady's still angry enough to want to throw poo at me.

And if any of that even matters, when there are also this many people – some of them Earthlings – who came all this way to show their support.

When we get off the transport, Minda takes my hand and pulls me through the crowd, to where Kaliel and Tawny are standing flanked by Zantite guards.

"Here." Tawny hands me a *Mercy is a Gift* tee with an olive branch – with one of the tree-dwelling booger-picker creatures perched on it – underneath. It's a hideous green color that matches my nails.

It's the last thing I'd have expected for her to approve for my wardrobe. I pull it on over my dress.

"Bo."

I turn back to her. "Que?"

She takes both my hands in hers, but it feels different than the fake-friend gesture she's made before. "Just so you know, I wasn't the one that gritcast feed back to HGB headquarters of those particular pirates walking into Brill's ship. I meant to keep my promise to you."

Is that a manipulation? Is she angling to keep my cooperation, now that her leverage is gone? Or was it an apology?

Pulling my hands out of hers, trying to keep tears from running down my face, I turn to Kaliel, and he throws his arms around me, wrapping me in a crushing hug. His face close to my ear, he says, "Thank you so much for coming. I didn't want to die alone."

Kayla's not here, his family didn't come, and no lo sé how many actual amigos he has left, since they mostly abandoned him during his first trial. Which just leaves me. I hug him back as hard as I can, and there's comfort there, between two people who've lost everything. And I can kind of understand what

Brill said about there being a measure of comfort in him going with Frank instead of a stranger.

I can't lose Kaliel too, so I try to hold onto him forever. Pero, he releases me.

I tell him, "I thought you had a plan."

"Well, yeah, but then Verex Kowlk's entire fan club showed up and went and sat in the victim's section, and I don't think Tyson was expecting that." He casts a distressed look out into the coliseum, at a crowded section of seats marked out from the rest in black marble. Someone is trying to lead Minda over to sit in it. She refuses, points to a place farther down in the regular seats where Mamá's sitting. With Frank.

Which means it's done. "Oye!"

My love is dead. I shatter inside.

"Hey, where's Brill?" Kaliel asks.

That's what I want to know. I make eye contact with Frank, and he looks steadily back. Anger starts to break through the numb wall of grief. What did you do with mi vida's body, you kek? Where do I need to go to grieve? I had thought Brill was dead once before, and it nearly broke me. I need to see him, cold and ruined, to find closure.

Tawny'd as much as said Brill's execution had been green-lighted because they suspected Brill knew the megacorp had hired the crew of the *Onyx Shadow* to frame one of its own pilots.

Pero, is that what they told Frank?

I don't care if he is a weapon. If Frank approved of the "collateral damage" murder of a whole transport full of abuelitas, and chose to eliminate the guy who'd found out about it, he is even colder and crueler than I'd believed.

Tawny has to know Brill's already dead. She has to know it's tearing me apart inside. She says, "They're starting. You need to find somewhere to sit, so I can call you to speak later."

"Can I sit with Kaliel, por favor?"

Tawny nods and for a second there's actual sympathy in her eyes.

I move around her, and follow Kaliel out to his rows of seats.

I recognize some of Verex Kowlk's fan club members, filling the victim's section. Half of them are in Minda's club too. Many smile when Kaliel steps into view, and my stomach turns at the sight of all those white teeth, ready to tear mi amigo to nothing. He doesn't matter to them, not really. They're just angry the object of their obsession got taken away.

I do feel a pang of sympathy for a female Zantite, sitting apart from the other victims, weeping into an oversized handkerchief. Pero, she doesn't even look at Kaliel. I doubt whether Kaliel keeps breathing matters to her either.

Tawny's perched on the end of the long bench seat, then Kaliel, then me. Tyson comes to sit beside us. He scratches his ankle with the toe of the other boot.

"Brill's really not coming?" Kaliel asks.

"He wanted to be here." I glare over at Frank again, pero I can't hold onto the anger in the face of the heartshattered heat biting at the back of my eyes. "I can promise you that."

After the long introductions and formal language about complaints, Police Chief Dghax, one of the four Zantites sitting in judgement of this case, asks Tawny to state her objections to the summary guilty verdict, which is to stand unless proven otherwise.

Tawny moves into the center of the colosseum, and asks Doc Sonda to join her. Turns out Sonda's a pediatric brain surgeon, and thus an expert. Sonda does so, turning the space around her into a giant holo of a brain. It's so like what we saw on Evevron I get a strong wave of déjà vu. Sonda was one of Mertex's friends, and her giant jaw keeps quivering as she explains the abnormalities in what we're looking at. So much loss, in this one space. So much pain.

I don't know whether anyone told her what's really going on, pero she refers to the mindworm's remains as an "inoperable growth" woven into parts of Kaliel's brain, with a larger mass down towards the base of his skull. The mindworm looks huge and dark in the hologram.

Kaliel makes a tiny unhappy noise. When I look over at him, he whispers, "All of that is still in my head?"

"Relax," Tyson whispers over me. "It will dissolve away, given time."

Dghax asks, "Is this going to prove fatal?"

Sonda points at her diagram. "Whatever treatment he received on Evevron stopped the growth rate flat, and has relieved the pressure on the brain. The scan shows pockets in the tissue where something that was pressing into this lobe seems to have liquified. Kaliel claims the treatment he received was proprietary, so he cannot reveal the few details he knows."

Dghax says, "So if he were to be spared, he would be able to live a normal life?"

That raises angry murmurs from the crowd, pero Sonda nods.

After that, the psychologist comes out and says that Kaliel is contrite, and that he now seems rational, calm and unlikely to repeat his actions. The psychologist looks at Kaliel and shakes his head in wonder. "He doesn't deny that he did it. But the way he described what happened, it was like his perceptions had been re-wired, and the overwhelming feeling was that he was afraid of Minda and convinced that destroying her was the only way he could survive."

The psychologist reads specific details from Kaliel's account.

It sounds like Kaliel was describing what the mindworm was feeling, as filtered through his own brain. Brill was right. Psychologically, it is a child. And where we've seen it as aggressive, it's scared. Several times, Kaliel's report mentions homesickness, abandonment.

The psychologist continues, "Impaired perception is an

untraditional defense, but we are talking about alien physiology, and this entire trial is being held because of a treaty that found we had unjustly executed twelve physicians whose only crime was not understanding *our* physiology."

The unhappy grumbling turns into a chatterclash, pero at the same time, the judges look like they are actually listening. I look over at Tyson, who looks a little smug.

Then Tawny calls me to testify about Kaliel's character.

I'm not sure how long I can stand out here before I break down. I try to keep it as succinct as possible, speaking around the lump of emotion that keeps trying to stopper my throat. "Kaliel has saved my life more than once, and I've seen him put the welfare of others before his own. He could have run from this trial. It's a big galaxy. You probably never would have found him. But he was more worried about the damage he'd done between your people and mine. He showed up here willing to die to heal the breach. I beg you to let him live, pero if you don't, you should at least save his heart. Because that took courage."

That sends shock waves through the audience, and I'm afraid it was the wrong thing to say. My chest feels frío, my fingers like ice. Zantites take their customs seriously, and if they think I want them to honor a coward, even in death, it could sway them the wrong way.

Pero, look at him.

Kaliel's barely older than me, his body still in perfect condition, his eyes clear and unafraid. He's a lot more heroic than me. And he's about to be ruined. My hand goes to the mourning pendant around my neck, under the tee-shirt. "He's a good friend, and I seem to be running a shortage of those these days."

I turn to go back to my seat.

"Wait," Dghax says. When I stop, he asks, "What's that you keep playing with around your neck?"

Heat flames into my face. To these Zantites, it's a forest fire of emotion. I pull the pendant out. Dghax's eyes go wide, along with one of the other judges. The other two probably have no more idea what a paladzian pendant is than I did when Brill gave it to me. My throat thick with emotion, I manage, "Like I said, they're in short supply."

Before Dghax can ask what happened, I slip back into my seat and tuck the pendant back under my shirt.

"Very persuasive," Tyson says softly.

"I meant every word." It comes out forcefully, although Tyson hadn't implied otherwise.

Kaliel points at the pendant, starts to ask what it is, pero Tawny tells him it's time for him to go up there to speak for himself.

"But your grief has you even more impassioned. You miss Mertex." Tyson flicks his tongue. "So if Kaliel lives, you won't be so alone."

I bring a hand to the bridge of my nose. He said Mertex because he doesn't think I'm ready to talk about Brill, pero I am. "That's what this Mindhugger can't seem to understand. That you can't just replace one friend with another. I'm going to miss Mertex, because he was cómico and had a good heart, pero not like I'm going to miss Brill. Dios mio, I wasn't kidding when I called Brill my life."

Tyson scratches at the back of his blade-like cabeza. "Wat happened to Brill?"

Could he really not know?

Tyson's a Galactacop. There's a delicate balance here between my need for justicia, and my need for discretion, and no lo sé what powderkegs get blown open if he confronts Frank. "There was an accident. I'll explain later."

I turn my attention back to Kaliel. Dghax just asked him what he has to say in his own defense.

"Thank you for the chance to apologize thoroughly for the

pain I've caused." Kaliel turns, finds Minda in the audience. "Especially to you. You have showed kindness to my friends, and promoted understanding between our planets." Minda's work has actually been in an effort to keep her planet from invading ours, but there's no way Kaliel's going to say the i-word. "I have no way to repair the damage I've done to all your good work." He turns to the victims' section. "I don't know any of you the way I know Minda, but I regret what I've taken from you." Kaliel holds up his hands. "There's blood here and I know it. Even though I didn't mean it, that changes nothing. I don't deserve my life. But I beg you. My girlfriend is missing, and she's never hurt anybody. Delay this sentence and let me live long enough to find her. I want my last act to be something that brings good."

Beside me, Tyson hisses. He didn't coach Kaliel to say that. Tawny's just standing out there, looking bewildered. The judges ask her if she has anyone else who wishes to speak.

When she concedes the colosseum floor, the victims' representative moves to help the weeping girl descend from the stands.

And as much as they seemed to be considering the logic of Kaliel's arguments, looking at the judges' sympathetic eyes now, Kaliel's doomed.

I can already feel the fuzzy detachment where time stretches out, like I'm about to be in a car wreck. I want to flitdash down the street, past my new fans, and hide somewhere while Kaliel dies. But he asked me to be here. And I couldn't be there for Brill.

I've got the shakes. It's not so much the IH as having my emotions wrung out over and over. I'm not sure I can handle this. Pero, I won't abandon Kaliel.

The girl blinks her whale eyes. "I'm Willa. I am – was – married to Yex, one of the cameramen killed in the bombing."

"Does your heart long for justice?" one of the judges asks.

Sí. They're going to eat Kaliel in about three minutes. My guts are churning with nausea.

Willa grabs a fresh handkerchief from her pocket. "Yex was a curious man. He always wanted to understand the story behind the story, so I've been trying to understand why he died. I've been following Bo's exploits, and after seeing what she's gone through to save her friend, I really do believe mercy is a gift she deserves. I want to give Kaliel back to her. As long as he then stays far away from here."

Just about everyone in the audience turns to stare at me. And I realize I'm crying, heavy feo tears that have to be looking horrible on camera. I stand up. The only words I can manage to get out are a breathy, almost inaudible, "Thank you."

"Wait a minute." The president of Verex Kowlk's fan club is on his feet. "You don't get to decide that."

Someone else shouts, "Mercy is a gift!"

And then I can't make out anything distinct, because they're all shouting. The people on the streets outside hear it, and they take up the chant. *Mercy is a gift.* Kaliel's staring at Willa, wide-eyed, like maybe he hallucinated what he thought she'd said.

I can't believe they've latched onto Tawny's saying either. Media spin and emotional manipulation can do wonders. For once, just maybe, it's something good.

CHAPTER FORTY-FIVE

By the time the judges get everyone quiet again, there's still a division among the victims. The main ones still clamoring for justicia are Verex's fans – though even some of them fall silent when Tawny taps into the holofield and plays that montage of people willing to support mercy as a concept – including me – and Verex himself.

Nobody has invited her, pero Minda steps into the center just as the spin-holo ends. She looks at the fan club. "It was my set, and my show, and Verex was there at my request. And I can forgive. If you let him live, I will vow to take responsibility for Kaliel's actions until Kayla Baker is found."

The fan club president stares at her, his mouth hanging open. "But why?"

Minda blinks, and I realize she's trying to hide tears. "Because I'm a sucker for a good romance and a happy ending."

Just the same way Mertex was. Minda didn't get her happily ever after. I can see why she'd want someone else to.

I can see the fan club swaying, one sympathetic face at a time. Most are Minda fans too – and they're more concerned with seeing her happy than Kaliel dead.

When the judges finally look over at them, Dghax asks, "Are you even bringing a complaint against the Earthling any more?"

"I don't think so?" The fan club president clasps his hands

together like he's not sure what else to do with them. "We allow his mind-problem defense?"

The judges call Minda and Kaliel over to them, so they can be heard over the crowd, which is starting to disperse.

Dghax tells Minda, "You are aware that you will be held accountable for this Earthling's actions until he leaves the planet, and that he is forbidden from ever setting foot on Zant again once his business with you is concluded?"

Fizzax walks over to them.

"I so vow," Minda says.

"No," Fizzax says. "I vow. Mertex would have wanted to protect you. I misjudged him when he was alive, drove him to leave town over something he might not even have done. Let me at least make a gesture to his memory."

Tawny mumbles something about an interview, leaving me and Tyson sitting on the bench alone.

The Galactacop looks at me. "Speaking of Kayla, I've been thinking about wat Mertex Makanoc said about her being somewhere deep."

I raise an eyebrow. I didn't tell him that. He must have gotten it from Frank. "Eh?"

"I have a map of te island in question, and tere are tree spots I tink tat could refer to. I want you to come look."

"Sí, but give me a minute. I still need to give Frank a piece of my mind." I'm still so mad and crushed and lost over what Frank did to Brill. I march over there.

Frank eyes me steadily. He's standing alone, since Mamá has gone to join Minda. I slap him. He rubs his jaw, but otherwise doesn't react.

"I want to see him." It is supposed to be a demand. Pero, it comes out a whiney plea.

"Trust me, Bo, you really don't." Sympathy shines in his eyes. I didn't expect that. "Just wear your little necklace and hold onto your memories."

"I thought I *could* trust you."

He sighs. "I told you a number of times what I am and why. Duty before emotion. Always. You can't really be surprised." A strange look crosses his face, and he looks over at Mamá and Minda and Tawny. "Though it's painful when things don't turn out the way you want them to."

Because he knows I'm going to tell Mamá that he made Brill disappear. I study Mamá, beautiful and over-the-top and all corazón. Then I look back at Frank, and the angerzentment overtakes the grief. "Mamá and I have just started putting our relationship back together. Pero viejo, if she lets you back into her life, then I will never speak to her again. And that will be your fault, too." I look at Mamá again. "If she doesn't believe me, I'll show her the bruise on my chest. And if anything happens to her because of that, I'm done. No show. No tour. You might as well have executed me with mi vida."

"If it makes you feel any better, I knew you were wearing body armor. The outlines were obvious. But you ought to get it replaced, since the structural integrity's shot." Frank half-smiles. "No pun intended. There's still a lot here that you can't possibly know."

I do have a few theories. Like about the real reason Brill is dead. HGB thinks that without him, and with Chestla on another planet, they can woo me back or break me to their needs. I had worked it so that I was indispensable to their diplomacy – and then I'd left the planet with Brill. In a way, it's my fault. Right?

I have to ask, "If I had said yes to joining HGB, would that have changed anything?"

Frank considers me gravely. "Probably not. It just would have put him on the opposite side from you with all those secrets still in his head."

Those secrets are gone now, along with all the humor and charm that was in there, too. And the bravery.

Tawny sidles over to Frank. "Sawyer. We need to talk."

She takes his arm, pulls him away.

I look over at mi mamá. I need to talk to her, seriously and soon, pero right now I don't think I can bear to put the words Brill and muerto in the same sentence. Just thinking them is like stabbing myself in the chest.

"Don't be stupid." Frank's voice floats over from the other side of the wall.

I race up the aisle and peer over the wall's edge behind the top row of seats. They're below me, in an alcove created by a stand of trees and a water feature. Tawny says something else, and Frank's entire face goes pink. They exchange a few more quick words.

Frank raises his voice. "I'm not showing you the body. That's disrespectful to a guy who let himself get caught saving my life – a lot of lives."

My breath catches. Won't come back out. *The body.* Brill's body. That casual way Frank said it makes it real.

Tawny tries one more time.

Frank replies, "Haven't you played on her grief enough already? If you show that, don't you think there will be questions as to who put that bullet in his heart?"

A hand drops on my shoulder, and I squeak as the hand pulls me back away from the wall.

"Did you hear something?" Finally, Tawny's loud enough for me to hear. Now that she's not going to say anything else useful.

"Are you ready to go?" Tyson asks.

Kaliel is still talking to the judges. Apparently, what happens for him now is more complicated than it sounded. "Let me send Kaliel a quick text where we're going, so he and Minda can meet us there."

I send the text. Almost immediately Kaliel sends back a single, *K* and about ninety holo-smilies that float up and pop into digital confetti. He's fizzbounced that he gets to live. I know how he feels. I've been there.

I want to be excited for him.

Maybe I'll get there, in a little while, pero right now, I just feel raw and numb.

My handheld rings. The number's coming in as Zail Cray. Brill's mamá. He must have given her this as a contact number before he got a new phone. My stomach sinks, though I didn't know it had anywhere else to go. She must have been watching the news.

When I answer, she's standing with her arms crossed over her chest, the camera propped on something near her eye level. "Tell me I misunderstood."

"I'm so sorry–"

She takes a step closer to the camera. "Tell me my son's not dead. That you aren't the type of person who would let me find out that way."

I can't look at her. "Lo siento. He had his cell phone on him when Fr... when he was taken. I didn't know how to contact you."

Her arms drop down to her sides. "So you haven't seen his body? You don't know for sure he's dead? My son's resourceful, Miss Benitez."

I want to hope with her. If I hadn't heard Frank say that to Tawny... I swallow against a dry throat. "The people that took him – I asked to see the body. They told me it was better if I didn't."

Zail's eyes go the color of pain. Still she looks at me sharply. "I told him you were going to get him killed."

And that breaks me.

She can see it, too. Her face takes on a hint of sympathy, pero then it goes hard again, and she hangs up.

CHAPTER FORTY-SIX

I'm back inside the *Sunshine*, looking at the maps using Tyson's ship-mounted householo. Looking for Kayla's about all I have to hold onto right now. That, and finding a way to destroy HGB that won't leave Earth in smoking ruins. ·

The ship's cell is empty. "What happened to your prisoner?"

Tyson shrugs. "I turned him over to te local autorities."

"That's nice." I'm still trying not to break down crying again.

"Bo, I'm sorry."

"For what?" He's just about the only one who hasn't tried to hurt me, this time around.

"For tis." He grabs me around the waist and lifts me off the floor. He holds me against him with one arm, and I can feel his strong, even breathing as he uses the other hand to open the door to the cell. The cuff of his jacket shifts, and I can see he's wearing the locket Awn had left in her lockbox like a bracelet around his wrist.

I suck in air as frío dread tickles across my skin.

"Por favor! I can't go back in there!"

Pero, there's nothing I can do as the heavy door clanks shut, closing me in. "Oye!"

This is getting ridiculous. Between me and Kayla and Brill, people have been kidnapped more times on Zant than the heroine in the telenovela I was on as a niña was in season two.

"I didn't hurt you, did I?" Tyson sounds concerned he might

not have realized his own strength.

"No, loco boy. Pero, why am I in here?" Though looking at that locket, I already think I know why.

Tyson scratches idly at the back of his hand again. "I didn't tink you would understand what te Mindhuggers are trying to do here. Tey want to trust you. Tey have shown you mercy, and tey want you to show tem mercy in return."

My chest goes cold. I should have known all this *Mercy is a Gift* garbage would backfire. Mindhugger-Tyson lights up the controls and the ship lifts off. I have no idea where he's taking us.

"What do you mean they've shown me mercy?"

Tyson turns, an amused smile stretching his lips. "Can you guess when I got infected?"

Eh? Tyson already knew the Mindhugger existed, so it didn't even try to hide itself, the way it had with Mertex and Kaliel. It is amazingly adaptable. I think back, try to push the pieces into place. When would Tyson have encountered it? "After Mertex took the Invincible Heart to escape from the car?"

If it had happened during the original fight, Tyson would just have let Mertex go the moment Brill and I headed across that field.

"Exactly. He had a tiny injector hidden in his hand that slipped between two of my scales. And as my hug was unfolding and attaching into my consciousness, the first ting we heard was you saying that Murry should have been saved. So he did tat. For you."

"No, it – he didn't. Mertex is dead."

"Physically, yes. But te Mindhugger looked in Mertex's consciousness to find out what made him so important to you. It liked what it found tere – wanted a friend – knew Mertex had qualities tat you admired – so it took tat consciousness and absorbed it. Each piece of him is a biological computer. He filed and replicated all Mertex's memories. He tinks of himself as

Murry now." Tyson taps the side of his cabeza. "He's what he was before, but at te same time, he's a shy, nerdy Zantite who keeps me tinking about feedholos I've never seen."

That sounds like Mertex, all right. "And what does he want?"

"He wants to be safe. To not be hunted everywhere he goes, attacked at every turn. He left his planet because tey were trying to exterminate him."

I can sympathize with that. I can't see a way to fix it – the thing's a parasite – pero I can sympathize. "Why is he interested in me?"

"You surprised him, when he was Fizzax Clunssas. He intended for Fizzax to eat Brill Cray, because we thought Brill might have witnessed Jimena Duarte infecting Kaliel Johannsson. But when you volunteered to die, it caught his curiosity. He had intended another mission for Kaliel, who had already left te planet, and wasn't sure he would make it back in time. He was afraid tat Brill would die, and he wouldn't get to see why you were so attached to each oter."

The timing of Kaliel's return hadn't been an accident. The Murry worm had been afraid of losing his little experiment. That means us being outside when the bombs went off on Minda's set hadn't been an accident either. Only – it was more than an experiment. He'd been captivated by the idea of selfless love. I think about that box, hidden all that time beneath the ocean, of the locket dangling from Tyson's wrist. "The couple that froze in the cryopods. That was one of Murry's first experiences, no? Pero, he didn't understand what it meant to be an individual, so how could he understand amor – except as something he needs but doesn't know how to get."

"But he wants to. He's starting to understand love, and he hurts for you. You and Brill belonged together, like two pieces in Dashtin's puzzle. And you alone – it's not right. I heard you talking to the HGB agent, eavesdropped on you eavesdropping. Murry tinks I should track down Frank when we're done here."

"No!" I take a deep breath. "Por favor, no. Hurting him won't change anything. I want Frank to look me in the eye and apologize, that's all. And then I never want to see him again."

After I've said it, I realize that's true. It's like Mamá said. If I hold onto this angerzentment at him, it will destroy me. It won't bring Brill back. It won't heal the rift between me and HGB, or between me and Mamá, or between Earth and the galaxy. That moment of weakness when I'd wanted to take IH and confront Frank, and see where the rage took me – that dissolves in my heart into a puddle of shame.

"Brill was both heroic and flawed, and I loved him fiercely, both when he deserved it and when he didn't. And because I love him, even though he's gone, I won't do anything in his memory that he wouldn't have approved of."

I don't have the time or the emotional endurance right now to explain to the mindworm how much this loss is going to hurt. I need to find a way out of this mess, out of this cell, around the lump in my throat that keeps threatening to choke me. When I have control of myself, I ask, "So what happened with Fizzax? Did Murry release the hug on him after he wasn't useful?"

Tyson bows his head. "Tat was heartbreak snowfall cancelled series. After he consumed te t'eobromine in tose cookies, te part of Murry tat was him died. It was like what happened when Jimena splattered tat chocolate on her arm and mouth, only she didn't absorb enough to kill the hug – just to make both of them sick."

"Oye! Poor Jimena."

Tyson blinks. "You feel sorry for her? Even tough she was planning to kill you at te capital?"

"Que?"

"You and Kayla. It was supposed to look like a murder suicide. After all, she'd been paid to start a war."

Once I get over the shock enough to draw a full breath, I ask, "Who paid her?"

"Enemies of Zant, tat wanted te Zantites distracted. She didn't ever tink about who. Just about the money. Murry didn't tink tat was right. He wants you to be happy."

"What does Murry want from me now?"

"He needs you to get him Stephen Baker."

I was following this, right up until then. "As in Kayla's brother?"

CHAPTER FORTY-SEVEN

Tyson explains, "Murry needs both Nitarri twins, and he doesn't want to risk Stephen getting hurt in te capture."

I groan. I keep putting every guy in my life in danger. "What can he do with a couple of Nitarri that he can't do with anybody else?"

Tyson scrunches his mouth in, concentrating. Finally, he blows out air through his lips. "Yeah, I'm not really sure about tat."

That doesn't sound like the logical, methodical Tyson I know. It's extraño. He knows he's being manipulated inside his own mind, pero he thinks he's enjoying it. "You have no idea what the parasite in your cabeza is planning to do, and you have no problem with that?"

"I know tat it is not going to be darkness crying awards-show pain. He's not tat type of person."

"Even if he just had you snatch me? It's been almost a week since I managed to eat chocolate. The theobromine has to be out of my system by now. Why not just infect me to get me on your side?" I hold up my hands quickly. "Not that that's an invitation, nada, nunca."

"You've made it clear tat's not what you want. And what Murry wants more tan anyting is a friend." Tyson gestures towards a box under the bunk. "Take a look."

"Friends don't ransomsnatch friends, amigo." I pull out

391

the box. He's given me a change of clothes and some food pouches and agua. A thought hits me. "Pero what about that beso? When Kaliel kissed me."

"Murry wasn't trying to infect you. Tat was Kaliel's impulse, magnified by te mindworm's curiosity about what a kiss felt like, and why Kaliel thought he shouldn't have it. It was Murry's first kiss. You made quite an impression." He scratches at his ankle with the opposite boot again. "Change now, and I'll be back in a minute to destroy te old clothes. Tere's bug blockers in here, but tat won't work once we get outside. Can't have Tawny tracking us now, can we?"

I take off the MIAG tee. I never thought I'd feel so naked without one of Tawny's cameras. Tyson's given me a thin black sweater and jeans. Which gives me no clue as to what we're about to do.

When he comes back for the bundle of clothes, I ask, "So where are we going?"

"To find Stephen. Eat and rest. We will be tere soon." He holds out his hands to take what I've pushed through the bars. His hands are shaking.

Mine are, too, pero I have an excuse. I gesture at his solid boxer's knuckles with my chin. "You OK?"

"Bluebird Zandywood jumpfest. Sweet nap dreams."

Annnd… that's what you get when you have Tyson channeling Mertex. I'm going to miss this guy when I get regular surly Tyson back. I have several injectable vials of dewormer in my bag, and I have to find a way to use one of them. Because, as adorable as this version of Tyson is, it's not right that he's not in control of his own mind.

There's something else in the bottom of the box, a thick yellow envelope about the size and shape of a pencil case. I open it. Inside, there's a syringe full of swirling gold and hero stuff and death. "Tyson, what is this?"

I know full well what it is. What I really mean is *why is it here*.

"It's what you want, more tan anyting. Murry wants you to have it since he knows it won't kill you like it killed Mertex."

Tyson moves over to his command chair, fires up his heat lamps, checks the controls one last time, and falls asleep. Well, that's familiar at least. He sleeps like a rock. I wonder if the parasite sleeps too, or if it's awake in there, processing whatever's still coming in through his senses.

The shirt he gave me has a convenient pocket on the sleeve. I slip a vial of dewormer into it. And then I sit on the bunk, trapped in the cell with my overwhelming need and the liquid that would scratch the itch in my blood and no one to stop me from taking it. Except me.

I slide the syringe back into the envelope, put it back in the box and put the box back under the bunk. No one would blame me. Everybody caves eventually. And the IH might give me the strength I need to escape when Tyson opens this cell.

Without realizing it, I've pulled the box out from under the bunk. I pick up the yellow envelope.

I've resisted this longer than anyone else. Maybe it really is time to blunt the pain of losing mi vida.

Pero, if I take it now, it will be that much easier to give in next time, and soon I'll be dead.

I'm not going to sit here and torture myself, because I know that in a matter of minutes, I will open the envelope and uncap the syringe. Before I can change my mind, I put the envelope on the floor and stomp hard on it. There's the satisfying crackcrunch of breaking glass, the liquid soaking through the envelope paper.

Tyson stirs. It's been less than fifteen minutes. He does something else to the controls, and we're boomeranging back planetside to Zant. It's possible we never even left atmo.

Once we're down, Tyson moves over to the cell. He gestures towards the diagram of the island where Kayla's supposed to be, zooms the image in to a single stretch of coastline. Chances are we're very close to her now. And her brother is here somewhere. Because I told him to come.

"Call Stephen and tell him to meet us here." He points to a restaurant at the water's edge.

"No." I cross my arms over my chest. I can feel the vial of dewormer there, the outline distinct against my fingers.

"Why not?" Tyson looks puzzled.

"You cannot ransomsnatch a person, take over someone they trust, not tell them what's going on, and still expect them to help you."

"I thought we were friends now." Tyson's whining. It's not a good "look" for him.

"We are. Pero, Stephen is my friend, too. I'm not going to put one amigo through something feartastic to help another."

"But we're not going to hurt Stephen." Tyson's mouth drops open, revealing his fangs. "Tis is because Murry tested you, isn't it? He's sorry about tat. He didn't understand what it means when a person dies – not until he stayed inside Mertex until the very end, felt what it's like to have your consciousness – your very you-ness – slipping away. He regrets Mertex's death very much, regrets attempting to have Fizzax eat Brill, and Kaliel try to cut him open. He's very sorry tat Brill is gone and you are alone. Like he's alone. He wants you to forgive him – like they forgave Kaliel."

It's like my chest is caving in. "Oh, mijo. They forgave Kaliel because they could see he wasn't going to hurt anyone any more. Murry has to hurt people to live. Or has he found a way around that too?"

"I refuse to be a dog!" Tyson shouts.

I flinch back away from the bars. The mindworm had said it could push through any host. I just hope it's not hurting Tyson's mental functions to do it. "Who said anything about a dog?"

"I tried being tat corgi Frank Sawyer always has with him. It... wasn't satisfying. No hands, limited sensory input, brain that works like mush. And worst of all, dogs can't talk. I broke tat hug after two days." Tyson dips his cabeza, that dangerous snake-flex movement sending chills across my arms. He shows me his fangs again. "I need to be a people. And nobody's going to volunteer for tat."

This isn't working. I need Tyson to let me out of this cell. "Sí, OK. I get it now. If I call Stephen, you promise not to hurt him?"

"Cross my heart and hope for pie."

I'm not sure if it's Tyson, Mertex, or the mindworm that originally heard that cliché wrong, pero I manage not to laugh. "I'll call him if you let me out of the cell."

"Call him, and when he gets here, I'll let you out. Use your handheld, so I can hear. I've blocked te signal for your sublingual."

"Holding me prisoner isn't going to make me trust you."

Tyson tilts his cabeza. "But it's te most logical, expedient way to get what I want."

"Logical and expedient doesn't get you friends, mijo," I sigh. There's an exit door on the other side of those bars, and there's a vial of dewormer in my pocket. And neither of them are doing me any good while I'm trapped in here. "Haza. I'll call him."

When Stephen answers, he says, "You are not going to believe the conversation I had with my dad. He said Grandma pulled me and Kayla out of a burning building in the middle of an ecological collapse when we were like two. That's where that scar on my shoulder came from – the flameproof sheeting came unwrapped a bit. I can't wait to tell Kayla. You have news, right?"

I'd forgotten about that scar, the one that wasn't a birthmark and he never could figure out how he got. It's been a long time since that brief period when we'd been a couple.

"Kayla's not hurt, is she?"

"No." I clear my throat. "No, nothing like that. Mira, Tyson wants to go over some maps with you. Can you meet us at that little Peruvian place on the corner of the island?"

He blinks. "There's no Earth-based restaurants here."

"Oh, my *mistake*." I emphasize the word *mistake*. "It's Pakksceran."

Come on Stephen. Put it together. That one time – the only time – we went together to the drive-in holotheater, it had been for a cheesetastic mystery set in Peru. And the scene in the restaurant had been a setup.

Stephen smiles. "I can see why the slip. They have a savory chocolate dish there a little like mole. I had some last night." Is he really that dense? Or is he that good of an actor? I'm going with dense, unless he proves otherwise. And, if we both survive, I'm going to give him a crash course on the difference between Mexican and Peruvian cuisine. He says, "I've been checking out basements in public buildings all over this island, so I'm close. I can meet you in about twenty minutes."

"Perfect." I hesitate. "Stephen, you know I love you, right?"

Now if that doesn't clue him that something's wrong, nothing will.

He looks at me strangely. "You know I've still got a thing for Claire, right?"

Some people just do not get subtle. At least when he gets captured, he may have enough theobromine in his system to keep Murry from infecting him.

After I've hung up, Tyson says, "The Nitarri are te strongest naturally telepathic species in the galaxy. Some of tem can kill you with teir minds." He sounds fizzbounced when he says the last part. Just like Mertex would have been. "Stephen should be able to find his sister. But she's still refusing to call out to him."

Mi amiga must be so scared, trapped with Murry. My heart aches for her. "Did you tell Kayla she's Nitarri?"

"Why would we have to tell her what she is? How could she

be twenty-five years old and not know she can broadcast her toughts and metabolize heat?"

My handheld rings. It's Chestla. I almost don't answer it, since Tyson's still in the same room – though he seems preoccupied reading something.

Pero, when I do answer, it's Leron looking back at me. Chestla had said the Evevron medic was involved in the Mindhugger cover-up. Now he has her phone and a threatening look on his face.

Leron raises an eyebrow at me. His golden eyes are almost the same shade as Tyson's. "Are you alone?"

I look over at Tyson, who is watching with interest. "Not exactly. I'm hanging out with one of your old friends. A very Sympathetic one."

Leron looks confused for a moment. Then his feral cat's eyes go wide as he realizes I mean the Mindhuggers. "Is that so? And you're sure you're still yourself?"

He's asking if I'm infected.

"So far at least. You can check my eyes if you want." I bring the phone in close to my face and look up at the ceiling. I'm trying to hide my anxiety, pero I'm sure the flush to my face and the subtle camera shake is giving me away.

"Good. Good. We don't know what would happen if one of those hugs wrapped around your sublingual."

I shudder. Could I wind up an idiot or a vegetable if Murry changes his mind and infects me?

"How about Chestla?" I ask. "Can you put her on the phone, so that I can see she's still herself too?"

As in, still breathing.

"Can't do that," Leron says. He turns the camera so that I can see Chestla slumped on the floor. My chest and gut fill with ice. He's killed her. No y no y no!

Pero, then she takes a deep breath, and I can see her chest rise and fall. Relief floods my limbs.

Leron turns the camera back at himself. "I don't want to have to hurt her. We all liked Chestla back when we were kids together, and Ball's one of my best friends. For his sake alone, you know?"

Leron knows how close he came to losing that friend. I can't help but picture Brill cradling Ball, doing everything he could to keep the Duracell from bleeding out. Mi vida fought so hard to keep other people safe. To keep me safe. And now Brill's gone. I swallow back the thickness in my throat. "What do you want, then?"

"I want to know what you plan to do with those holofiles she sent you. Everything she's been doing is right here on this phone. And if it goes public, do you know how many of us are likely to die? The Galactic Court doesn't show mercy when you've created a plague."

Tyson's face is impassive. I don't think he's listening.

I swallow. "I thought the people involved in the experiments on those criminals were dead."

"Then you haven't seen the e-mail Chestla sent you. We realized right away that they shouldn't have been experimenting with sociopaths. The proof that we covered it up, conducted further experiments trying to correct our error – that's enough to warrant executions for the entire team I'm assigned to. I'm too young to die, Bo."

"You have more to worry about Chestla saying something than you do me." I've always been dedicated to exposing the truth. And yet, I'm willing to hold on to this secret.

Sí, it has something to do with Grammy and Leron and the others, Chestla's friends who have gotten caught up in something they can't control. Pero, it has to do with Murry too.

I'm fascinated with him. And there's something that's been nagging at my brain that's finally making sense. "Can I ask you something?"

"I guess." Leron shrugs.

"The original researchers. Were they infected when they died?" I had assumed mindworm-hugged people had killed them. But what if they were part of Murry, killed by normal Evevrons out of fear?

Leron grimaces, showing me his incisors. He looks like he isn't going to answer. Pero, finally, he nods. "I think so. I'm pretty sure. The rumor is they were trying to spread the plague offplanet."

This threat to the two divas with the poisoned chocolate – Murry had been testing me to see what I would do, so that he could learn. That makes perfect sense if his second formative tier was made up of researchers. He'd seen what they'd been doing to the first tier of him through their eyes, with all their justifications. He couldn't know that those justifications had been wrong. And when someone died as a result of Murry's experiment, he realized on his own that what he had done was unethical.

Murry is developing a conscience.

I realize that I want to help the Mindhugger.

Pero how? Nobody's going to willingly share their brain with a parasite.

I think about Evevron's giant vermin, how the spucks' faces look like they *could* be from Tyson's species, and that sparks a half-formed idea. I wish I had the old Tyson to run it by. He'd know the lines between biogramming a new sentient species to share your planet and unlawful mindhacking. "Can I ask you a weird question?"

Leron looks at me warily, pero he nods.

"Those spucks. You're sure they're not sentient?"

He looks offended. "Surely Chestla has explained that our people do not eat any animal even suspected of being sentient–"

I miss part of what he says because an alarm starts chirping, and Tyson moves over to silence it. He pulls up a holo of what looks like the outside of his ship. There's a flash of movement. It could have just been a bird, pero Tyson's studying it.

"Sí, I know they're supposed to be just pests. Pero those front feet of theirs, do you think they qualify as hands?"

Hands that could dig new waterways, reshape the planet if the spucks ceased being destroyers and became a people.

"Maybe. But they don't use tools or anything–"

He thinks I'm still trying to prove them sentient. "But they could?"

He nods. "Theoretically. We've gotten away from the point of my call. I was threatening Chestla."

"Don't bother. I'm going to try to fix this for everyone. If I can. It's a long shot, and Murry here might not go for it." I look over at Tyson, remember that conversation he and Brill had about how every little kid wants to be something special and unique. The mindworms are already unique. Maybe, though, I could convince them to be something with an even higher cool factor – at least chido for someone as geeky as Mertex. If Mertex's personality really is in there, he just might be willing to limit himself to one non-sentient species that meets all his qualifications – decent brain, hands that can use tools. The only one missing is the ability to talk – pero, maybe he'd give that up for the chance to fly.

I'll need the Evevron's help – especially Leron – if I'm even going to have a chance of pulling this off. "Tell Chestla her cesuda ma begs her to help you, at least for now."

Leron's mouth drops open, his brilliantly white predator's teeth glinting in the synthetic light where he is. "Anything else?"

Tyson drops the ramp to the ship and steps out onto it.

"Sí, por favor." I drop my voice to a whisper. "One more hypothetical question. What could you do with two Nitarri and a giant machine built out of two black somethings, glass, copper and a roll of fiber optic cable?"

Leron blinks at me. "Overload someone's brain from a distance? Or supercool something, I guess."

My chest goes cold. Murry-Tyson had been talking about how the Nitarri can assassinate people with their minds. He's going to force Kayla to use her telepathic powers – which she doesn't yet know she has – to kill people.

"Hang up." Tyson opens the door to the cell. He's looking dark and dangerous again, even though he's using his boot to scratch his ankle again. My heart sinks.

"Geesh." Tyson strips off his jacket and scratches his back against the wall. He's wearing a short-sleeved tee that emphasizes solid muscles.

I sever the connection. "Leron guessed it, no? You're planning to find a safe place by getting rid of the people who are already there. From far enough away that no one will ever guess it was you."

The Mindhugger's plan is brutally simple: Amplify Kayla and Stephen's brainwaves to create enough feedback to kill every person on Evevron. And then repopulate with the hundreds of individuals Murry had already infected.

CHAPTER FORTY-EIGHT

"My plan is justified. Awn and Chevros's son was sick. He was going to die from the scanty water rations. Tey weren't criminals. And tey weren't sociopaths. Tey just got caught on the wrong side of a conflict." Tyson's filling the cell door, at his full height. He opens his mouth and hisses at me, and a drop of venom appears at the end of one of his fangs. Tyson's not in control in there any more.

The ramp is still open behind him, offering a single slice of freedom. Maybe I can slip around him.

"You think more deaths is the answer?"

"It is te only logical conclusion. Do you know what tey did with te child, after they killed us? One of te council members adopted him." Tyson coils down his spine, like he's going to strike. "I'm sorry, Bodacious Benitez. You mustn't warn them."

Which means he's going to kill me. I back towards the bunk.

I feint like I'm going to dodge right, then I lunge left, and still Tyson's right in front of me, moving like agua.

I cannot believe that five minutes ago I wanted to help this thing find its place in the worlds. Or that I thought it would be safe to have Evevron populated by a horde of gene-doctored telepathic dragons. In this case, mercy is not a gift – it is a mistake.

"You really are a plague," I tell the Mindhugger as the back of my knees hit the bunk. I pull the vial of dewormer out of my sleeve pocket and drive it towards Tyson's arm, right above the elbow, where there's a gap in the scales.

He catches my wrist, squeezes the bones together hard until I drop the vial. He sounds even more like a little kid when he says, "I trusted you. I wanted to – I mean – how could you?"

Through sheer instinct, I anticipate his strike. I grab the thick pillow off the bunk and bring it up in front of my face. His fangs go deep into the fabric, and a second later the pillow is soaking with venom. A few drops are still falling from his fangs when he wrenches the pillow away from me and throws it to the floor.

That takes the fight out of me. No chance here of a dry bite. I watch his fangs in frozen terror as he rears back. At least I won't have to wake up mañana with the fresh pain of remembering Brill's dead. Or deal with the IH shakes.

I hope the venom acts quickly. I know from experience it's not going to be painless.

Tyson strikes again. This time, he goes for my torso instead of my face, and when I duck back, rolling onto the bunk, he catches one of his fangs on the paladzian, and there's the ringing sound of a knife against a sharpener as the fang pulls free of the chain, which is miraculously still intact. Without that three-inch disk of metal, Tyson would have pierced my chest.

He's starting to get really mad now. Well, let him. I hope killing me ruins his fangs. And then I realize I don't want that, because the real Tyson will have to live with the dental problems. He grabs my hand, pulls it to his mouth like he is about to kiss it.

"Any last words?"

"Mercy is a gift?" It's a question.

Tyson's face scrunches in irritation. "Last lies then."

He centers my hand under his right fang, preparing to pierce it slowly to prevent any more mistakes, and a drop of venom falls onto my skin.

"Por favor, Tyson." What kind of last words are those? He's not listening anyway.

Time stretches out, giving me time to question every choice that got me here. They were all mistakes, every single one, ever since I'd listened to Frank about keeping my mouth shut over Serum Green.

"Stop!" I imagine it's Brill's voice.

Eso es imposible. My life must have started flashing before my eyes.

Pero, Tyson hears it too. He turns. He doesn't let go of my hand. "Put the gun down, Brill Cray, or I'll–"

Brill fires. I scream. My heart clenches. Brill – impossibly alive – just shot a cop in the face.

Tyson doesn't fall. He hisses, then turns to look at me. There's an oversized dewormer dart sticking out of the side of his face. "You know it will take a few minutes for him to die."

He means the mindworm. Even knowing the hug is about to be broken, Tyson is still unable to think for himself.

Tyson wrenches my hand up towards his mouth.

Tears dance in my eyes, pero I can't break the grip he has on me. If Brill's alive, do I really have to die here? I ask, "What happened to the guy whose scales were supposed to gleam with innocence?"

Tyson hesitates. I think I got through to the real him. I can see it isn't going to last. Still, it provides an opening.

Brill's a blur, flashing across to us. He jumps up on the inspector's back and grabs Tyson around the neck, pulling him off balance so that he can't strike. "She asked for mercy, you kek!"

Tyson's prying at mi vida's hands, which are laced together so tightly that the fingers are going white. If Brill lets go now, Tyson will be able to bite him.

Time has stretched out like taffy.

And in between the heartbeats, Brill's facing his nightmares. Brill once ran from Tyson, leaving me for dead, because he thought Tyson was corrupt and murderous. And this version of the Galactacop isn't going to hold back death.

Tyson staggers backwards. He bangs Brill against the cell bars. Mi vida grunts, pero he doesn't let go.

Even more improbably, Gavin walks in. "Want me to shoot him for real?"

"Ga." Brill's voice is half a groan as Tyson bangs him against the bars again. "We're friends now."

Suddenly, Tyson stops moving. His arms fall to his sides. He stares off into space for a few moments, and then his hands start shaking. He makes fists to stop it. "You can let go now, Cray."

Brill doesn't budge. "How do I know the parasite's not just telling you to say that?"

"Because if you don't, I'm going to arrest you for assaulting a police officer."

Brill looks over Tyson's shoulder at me, his face uncertain. "Babe? Do you think it's safe?"

Tyson was already infected, so checking his eyes wouldn't help. Not that they have any whites anyway. I ask, "Tyson, how are you feeling?"

"Dark cloud poison strikes achy. And like your boyfriend is about to dislocate my spine."

Not a geeky holo reference in the bunch. "I think it's OK, mi vida."

Brill climbs down off Tyson. He holds out his hand. "No hard feelings?"

Tyson takes his hand. "Nah. After all, you just had a good excuse to shoot me, if you were still holding a grudge over your friend."

Gavin moves over to us. The gun is still in his hand, pero pointed down. He uses the other hand to offer me a formal closed fisted salute. "Bodacious. It's good to see you again."

We both know that's an exaggeration. I arch an eyebrow at him. "What on Larksis are you doing here?"

"I came to pick up Brill." Gavin holsters his gun. "But the kek got it into his head that you were in danger and wouldn't leave." He turns towards Brill and raises his voice, "Despite the fact that he's supposed to be dead."

That's the side of the faked-your-own-death trope you never see on a telenovela. The person just disappears, and you're not supposed to wonder about how they got out of the erupting volcano – or off the same planet from the murderous HGB assassin who claims to have successfully killed them.

"I'm glad he didn't listen to you." I look down at the bead of venom running down my hand and quickly wipe it onto the bunk. The area's not stinging, so I hope it's not being absorbed through the skin.

Gavin looks at the venom-soaked pillow, and at my ripped sweater, which reveals the paladzian glittering against my bra. It's not even chipped. He looks at Brill, concern etching his features. "That close, su?"

I half-laugh. He means the pendant, and Brill's close call, not mine. "You don't know how close you came to having me as your trevhonell."

Gavin's eyes go lime green. He looks at Brill. "*That* close, su?" Then back at me. "I have to look out for you now?"

I blink. "He didn't die." Doesn't that make a death promise non-binding?

"So?" Gavin says.

I guess living doesn't dissolve having expressed your deepest death-crisis wishes.

"If it makes you feel better, Babe, Gavin wasn't asking me to abandon you. He wanted me to call Frank." Brill moves in close and unfastens the chain from around my neck. Removing the death pendant that just saved my life.

I kiss him – just a brief brushing of lips on lips. "I don't get it.

If you escaped from Frank, como he'd say he shot you? Or was the whole thing las imitación? This broke me, Brill."

That's the thing about telenovela tropes, especially *faked-your-own-death*. A lot of the time they don't make sense, don't serve any purpose except to jerk with the audience's emotions. And being inside it – instead of just watching – is wrenching.

"It wasn't a ruse. He had orders to kill me. He meant to do it, too, when we got in the van." Brill looks down at the pendant still in his hand. "He drove me out to a cove with a lot of thick plants and soft sand, and he had a shovel and everything. But we talked for over an hour, and after that he said you were right, I didn't deserve it. Then he took me to the spaceport and said if I disappeared – permanently – that solved HGB's problem and his just as well as if he'd revoked my breathing privileges." Brill's eyes go solid black, thinking about it.

"I can't believe Frank bucked a direct order, mi vida, after all his talk about being a weapon."

Brill looks thoughtful. "The tipping point was when I told him about that shadow ship showing up at my front door. I gave him proof that HGB framed one of its own, and that rattled him." His eyes shift towards green. "You ever think if you weren't on opposite sides, you could really get to like someone? We had the best conversation."

"He was going to kill you, mi vida!"

"But he didn't. And that's fascinating. I don't know what kind of power you have, Babe, but I think you and Tawny broke Frank. Mercy's not something I ever would have expected from that su."

I'd discounted the whole MIAG thing as just a trite saying Tawny came up with, even after seeing it in action at Kaliel's trial.

I was wrong. Mercy really is a gift.

And mercy really does beget mercy.

I can trace the chain of mercy all the way back to the day I got kidnapped by Fizzax. If I hadn't shown mercy when Fizzax's life was in my hands, there'd have been no basis for Tawny's campaign. And if she hadn't shown mercy to Kaliel by using her precious resources, and if the Zantites hadn't been willing to show mercy too, Kaliel would have died. If Frank hadn't seen us fighting for Kaliel, if I hadn't said I believed Earth had given me a gift by sparing my life, Frank wouldn't have been impressed by the far-reaching power of mercy, and wouldn't have started to question his role in HGB. He'd have obeyed orders and shot Brill in the parking lot in front of me, instead of talking to him in the van. He'd never have been swayed to spare mi vida. Which means Brill couldn't have been here to save me. And I'd be dead too.

The power of that takes my breath away.

Brill's fist closes tight around the pendant. "Frank also said that if he ever saw me again, he'd have to put a bullet in my head after all, before anybody on his side realizes I'm alive."

I don't want to let myself understand what that means. Pero, I have to face it.

"You're leaving, no?" My chest and arms go hot, while my stomach feels frío.

That's another side of the trope the telenovelas never show the audience. There is some comfort to knowing he's not dead, pero I'll still never get to see him again.

"Not with you still in danger." Brill cups my face in his hand. "But after this is over, I may have to. Lo siento, Babe. It's not what I want."

I kiss him. Not another last kiss. Just un beso.

When Brill finally breaks it, Gavin and Tyson are both standing there, looking awkwardly into space.

"We have to go." I quickly explain what Murry-Tyson made me do. "Stephen's going to be at that restaurant any minute now, and Murry's not going to pass up a chance to snatch him."

Tyson's still staring off into space.

"You OK, su?" Gavin asks, putting a hand on his arm.

Tyson starts. "Yeah. Just thinking."

Gavin's eyes are going purple. He's examining a clone of the data Chestla sent me, in the holofield of his handheld.

It's data I didn't share. Brill having access to my phone is one thing, pero this is ridiculous.

"Oye!" I say.

Gavin ignores me. "We could destroy the mindworms, using whatever device it has built to kill off the Evevrons. The way it attaches – and how it is weirdly liquid… it would probably explode if the Nitarri overloaded the hosts' brains."

My mouth drops open in horror. That's murder. And not just of the mindworms – the hosts too.

Even Brill looks shocked. "Su."

Gavin shrugs. "I'm open to a better solution. But there's no way to close the barn gate on this one. That would at least keep the parasite from spreading. You told me yourself that it has only limited itself because it feels relatively safe. We start fighting it, it could take over half the galaxy to keep us away from its center."

"What about your Codex?" I protest. "I thought you guys were all about not causing pain and not fighting back. Go to jail rather than cause offense, no? You won't even wear leather!"

"We're all about providing peace," Gavin retorts. "And the Codex provides for self-defense. Your culture's history contains nothing like our lost eras. You don't know what it is like when the worst happens."

"Su," Brill says, "self-defense is only allowable in cases of immediate personal danger – when there aren't going to be intragalactic repercussions."

"And that interpretation is up to an individual's conscience," Gavin retorts.

Tyson flicks out his reptilian tongue. "I'm not sure wether

destroying something like Murry is really justice. He's developed a personality, and is rapidly evolving a moral code. It could be argued tat he is no longer te scourge tey engineered."

Brill studies Tyson. "Are you saying that you're willing to not report this?"

"If tere is a way to bring peace here, who would make a formal complaint? However, I will not remain silent about te murder of six hundred infected individuals." He scratches his back against the cell bars. "I'm not getting fat or anyting, am I?"

"Que?" It takes me a second to remember the real Tyson doesn't know Spanish. "What?"

He shrugs. "I feel like I'm molting. Myska don't do that once we're adults unless we've changed size significantly. Flash-awkward horror castle. So itchy. I never thought I'd have to go through this again."

"You look the same to me, su," Brill says.

CHAPTER FORTY-NINE

Gavin has a little runabout in his ship, which we take down to the restaurant. I look over the information Chestla gave me on the way. I don't understand the raw data, pero she's given me lots of helpful notes.

We drive up, and there goes Stephen, swaying groggily away from the restaurant in between two Zantites.

I start to open the door, to chase after them, pero Brill takes my arm to stop me.

"Better to follow them, Babe. Find out where they're holding Kayla."

"Sí." I move my hand back onto my lap. "Shouldn't we call Kaliel?"

"Ga. He's too far away. Plus he'd have half the cops on this island trailing him, which would be dangerous for Kayla – and me. I'm still supposed to be dead, remember?"

He has a point. "Then shouldn't we at least call the Evevrons and warn them?"

"Warn them to do what?" Gavin asks from the driver's seat. "Put on tin foil hats and hope their brains don't explode?"

The Zantites pull Stephen into a car and turn out onto the road.

"Tere is one ting tey could do." Tyson looks back at me from the front passenger seat. I'm sitting behind Gavin, so I can see the hesitation on his face.

"What, mijo?"

"Murry's alone. But he wasn't te whole group the Evevrons originally hugged. Tere was anoter consciousness forming in the worm inside Awn. Part of his plan includes reviving her. If te Evevrons let him talk to her, ten maybe… I dunno."

"That's a rather romantic notion for you, Tyson," Brill says. "You sure you're feeling OK?"

"I'm a little soft right now. I lost someone once, and having tat guy in my head brought it back up again. She would have loved te idea of love transcending death, at least once." He grumbles, deep in his throat. "But I'm sure one of you idiots will do something stupid enough to have me back to my right self in no time."

It's a loco idea. If reviving a frozen Mindhugger is even possible, someone on Evevron would have to volunteer to be infected with it. And after the two parasites talked, that person wouldn't be able to be "cured," or Murry would just get set off again. And he'd be even more destructive, having lost the one individual his formative members had loved.

Actually, though, there had been two individuals proto-Murry-Chevros had loved. There'd been a second photograph in that locket.

Someone Murry might actually still be able to talk to.

I text Leron. *What happened to Awn's child?*

If one of the council members adopted him, that niño had to have been in the pool with the rest of the council's children. I probably saw him at the hunt breakfast. He's less than ten years old and already carrying a legacy of so much pain. Pero, he's Murry's brother or son, or however the Mindworm would think of him.

If we can remind him there's one person on Evevron he cares about, maybe he will spare all of them, for the sake of the one.

Leron texts back, *That kid was always sick. He died last summer. Why?*

Leaden cold sparkles through my chest. Obviously, Murry already knows that his son-brother-whatever is dead. That explains some of the anger when Murry-Tyson had talked about the child being taken. *Never mind.*

"They're slowing down," Gavin says. He pulls us off to the side of the road.

The Zantites turn in at a parking lot across the street. It's an aquarium.

"When Mertex said somewhere deep, did he mean underwater?" I look over at Tyson.

Pero, Tyson's shoulders have gone rigid, and his neck's arched back. He's staring straight up at the ceiling. Now that can't be bueno.

"Gavin," I start.

"Way ahead of you." Gavin puts a hand on Tyson's arm. The Galactacop doesn't stir. Gavin takes a key fob with a large jraghite at the center out of his pocket and places it on the back of Tyson's hand. The jraghite glows based on body temperature, and on Tyson, it starts to fade, then flares. Then it fades again. Which means Tyson's temperature regulation is all over the place. "But if I bring him to a hospital, they're bound to ask questions about the thing in his head. And there goes your big secret."

I pull out my cell phone. "I know a brain surgeon. She was a friend of Mertex's. I'll have her meet you there."

Gavin nods. "You two be careful in there." He points at me. "Especially you. I am not listening to Brill whine all the way to whatever backwoods star he winds up hiding out on because he's grieving."

As we head towards the aquarium, I ask Brill, "Did Gavin just express concern for me?"

"You'd better get used to it." Brill squeezes my hand. His eyes have gone a deep purple-gray. "Do you think a Myska molt could be brought on by a neurological imbalance? Like the parasite didn't agree with him even before we killed it?"

"Maybe."

My handheld rings. It's Chestla, standing with both Ekrin and Leron. Chestla looks groggy. "You're alive! Leron thought he saw a Myska at the edge of your holofield before you hung up. But then you texted, and he was convinced someone else had your phone."

"You guys are the ones in danger." I give her a short recap – leaving out Gavin's proposal to fry Murry's hosts – and on impulse, I throw in Tyson's theory about the other mindworm. "Pero, that's loco, right? Who would let themselves be infected just so two parasites could talk?"

"It is feasible, though." Leron pulls a handheld out of his pocket and starts inputting something. "The Mindhuggers can survive indefinitely when frozen. That's how they are kept in the dormant state before injection – they contract down to a single pearl."

"If it survived the death of the host long enough to reach cryostasis," Chestla says, "then you should be able to re-inject it."

Leron's cheeks go red, and he studies his device. "I've seen the reports. Those five went into the cryostasis pods alive. And conscious. Their brain tissue has been sampled for study, but only after the process was complete."

Chestla turns to stare at him, the horror in her eyes reflecting what's chilling my own heart. I can't imagine what it must have been like, to be put into a plastiglass coffin and have them pump cell stabilizers into you for hours, before being quick-frozen. The claustraziety. The knowledge that this punishment far outweighs the original crime. Last thoughts about a child being left behind.

How long had Murry stayed inside their minds?

The wave of sympathy for all he's been through almost caves me in.

"What?" Ekrin asks. She looks confused.

Brill rubs at his face, where the damaged flesh used to be. "At least I was unconscious when Mertex tried to freeze me."

"It was a mistake to fix a mistake," Leron says. "I don't want to add another one to the pile. Can you imagine what trying to hunt these parasites down one by one and eliminate them will be like? How many hosts will die in the process? And if they manage to find somewhere with a big enough lab to start to seriously multiply, the problem becomes impossible to stop."

Chestla translates to Ekrin, who replies, when translated back, "This is why the Earthlings lose in every version I have seen of *Invasion of the Body Snatchers*. It is an unwinnable proposition."

Then Chestla speaks for herself. "I'd like to talk to Murry, if he's willing. I want to apologize on behalf of my people. I have failed you several times. I only hope that, if I fail you again, Murry's vengeance brings my shame to a quick and painless end."

"You're not a failure!" I take a deep breath. "I will try to let him know."

Pero, how am I supposed to do that?

It's hard to hang up and leave her horror-heavy. Pero, I have no choice.

CHAPTER FIFTY

The aquarium is open to the public. It's anticlimactic, pero we just breeze through the front door.

We suspect Kayla is somewhere below us, but that doesn't narrow things down enough. The main building alone is five floors, and the map shows outside exhibits too.

"At least whatever they're planning, they need Stephen alert to do it," Brill says. "Ven, we have a little time."

"Sí." But this much time? It could take us half the day to search this place. "Pero, mi vida, Tyson seemed frustrated that Kayla wasn't using her telepathy. What if Murry gets *too* frustangerated with her?"

"Then we had better do this smart." Brill points to a specific spot on the map. "What do you think, Babe?"

It's a round exhibit that takes up the majority of the bottom floor. *Living Jewels of the Deep.*

The word deep *could* just be a coincidence.

"We better go check it out, no?"

We move into the quiet blue stillness that comes when you're surrounded by glass y agua. There are people here, Zantite and otherwise, pero it's not crowded.

Brill makes a startled noise.

I follow his gaze, expecting trouble. He's looking at the back of a girl wearing a hoodie with his face stenciled on it. The eyes in the image are slate gray, and Brill's real ones are chromashifting to match. I forgot he hadn't seen those. "You OK, mi vida?"

"It's going to be a bit harder than I realized to be dead right now. One picture on somebody's feed, and Frank and I both have problems." He takes my hand and squeezes it just a little harder than necessary. "I've never been famous before. What do we do now?"

I kiss him on the cheek. "Celebrities don't shimmerpop when they're not dressed up or trailing a cloud of fans. Act normal, and chances are nobody will notice, no? There's a ton of offplanet tourists here because of Kaliel's trial. It's a miracle, pero we blend."

I want to run to Kayla, now that I think I know where she is, pero that will call too much attention. As we wander down the hall, pretending to be captivated by the exhibits isn't hard. Earth's sea creatures are extraño enough. Some things in Zant's oceans are downright weird. I pause to watch a small tank where dozens of feathery water-caterpillars with long legs that end in pinchers are building a wall out of pebbles to divide their space in half.

A girl's voice says, "Bo? Bo Benitez?"

I turn. She's humanoid, pero her pinched-forward chipmunkish face isn't familiar.

"Sí," I admit.

"I'm a FeedCaster, and it would virafizz if I could get an interview about how you feel about Kaliel being pardoned." Brill's still facing away, and she looks at him curiously. "I do want to say how sorry I am about Brill." The feeds had to make some conclusion about what that pendant had meant, and somebody heard me say there'd been an accident, so Brill's death by mysterious accident had already virafizzed. "Who's this?"

Brill turns towards us, his eyes that steady blue he uses when he's trying to mask other emotions. They'd better not shift, given the lie I'm about to tell.

I wipe my hand across my eyes, like I'm about to start crying. "This is Bob. He went to pilot's school with Kaliel. I don't have time for more than a picture, pero do you want to interview him about his parents' sheep ranch in Oklahoma?"

She wrinkles her nose, then seems embarrassed she couldn't hide the gesture. "That's OK. Amazing how much he looks like Brill, though."

"I look like a spider to you?" Brill taps a fist to his chest – a very Krom gesture, actually – and manages to look insulted as he says, "One hundred percent human."

At least he remembered to say *human* instead of *Earthling*. And his eyes stay sky blue.

"So just the picture then?" the girl says hopefully.

"Sí!" I drape my arm around Brill.

The FeedCaster smiles weakly. "Just you, if you don't mind."

I pose with the caterpillar crabs. Afterwards, as we're making our way towards the escalator, Brill says, "You think she bought that?"

"Eso espero, mi vida." *I hope so.*

She's not following us, at least.

He lets his eyes go violet.

"Que?"

"Just thinking how upset you got with me for being a good liar. When you're capable of pulling off that kind of performance." He gestures behind us.

"There's a difference between lying and acting. And I'm not great at either, no? Or my holostar career would have taken off."

"Babe." Brill stops walking, grabs onto my hand. "You can't believe that. I've watched every show you were in and–"

"All two of them." I'm touched that he took the time, especially for the half-season of *Un Corazón Demasiado, One Heart Too Many*, where I was the daughter's best friend, who mysteriously shadowpopped never to be seen again.

"Wal. All two of them." Brill pulls me forward, and we start walking again. "You were better than the girl who played the daughter on that show where they stuck you as the sidekick. A lot of things came together to crash your career, but lack of talent's not it."

"Mire usted?" *Really?* His sincerity blows me away.

The lights dim progressively as we take two escalators to the bottom floor. It's supposed to represent a descent into deeper parts of the ocean. Some exhibits here are lit by black light.

We approach the rounded glass tank that takes up the middle of the room. The glass wraps around a metal cylinder, which is so wide that there's only about a two-foot gap between the metal and the glass. This minimizes the amount of water needed to show off the creatures clinging to the cylinder's surface. They look like brilliantly-colored gemstones. With stalk-eyes and rings of tiny glittery frond-hands. They've formed a mat that goes up to the top of the water level. The exhibit is breathtaking.

That cylinder's wide enough to have a whole room inside it. It has to be where they're keeping Kayla. Pero, how do we get inside?

The cylinder goes all the way to the twenty-foot ceiling. The exhibit glass is only two-thirds that tall. Up near the ceiling, there's a small door leading inside the cylinder, and a narrow platform with a ladder down the outside of the back of the tank. Brill puts his hands on the rungs and steps up on the ladder.

"Are we going to climb it?" I whisper.

"Bob from Oklahoma feels entitled to see what's inside that tube. Act like you have the right, and nobody will question it." He starts climbing. "The skills of a trader and the skills of a celebrity aren't so different."

Nobody questions us, though this one Zantite kid stares openmouthed as we make our way onto the platform. He points, says something to the guy he's with. The guy glances at us, nods curtly, and then pulls the kid over to look at an inky blob in the next tank. I guess it's common to see non-Zantites in service jobs. I move to the door and turn the wheel that opens it.

A matching ladder inside the cylinder descends two levels, into a wide well-lit lab, bigger than the footprint of the building above it. Two float tanks on the far side of the room below look like giant black Cup Noodle containers with holes cut in the side.

Stephen and Kayla are huddled up on a Zantite-sized sofa next to each other. They're both wearing silver circlets on their heads. One of Stephen's hands is cuffed to one of Kayla's, and one of each of their ankles is cuffed to the metal sofa leg between them, a third of a way along the couch's length. Brill isn't the most skilled Krom I know when it comes to picking locks, pero those he can probably manage.

There are four Zantites down there, too, absorbed in their work.

Stephen used to keep his phone on vibrate. Hoping he still does, I call him over my sublingual. He looks startled, pero the phone stays silent. Furtively, he answers it. *Bo, I've been captured. But I know where they're keeping us. I told Gavin—*

I do too. Look up.

When he does, feedback squeals in my head, and then my own words, in my own voice echo back over the hardware. *I do too. Look up.* It hurts. I stumble backwards.

Brill catches me before I fall into the agua.

Gavin's right. We could use Stephen to kill these things, if not for the cost to innocent bystanders. And if it didn't feel so wrong.

When I get righted again and peer back inside the door, Stephen snatches the circle off his cabeza. *Sorry about that. I'm not sure how all this works.*

I have a couple of guesses, based on Chestla's notes. This would be easier for Stephen if he'd had a sublingual to practice with, pero his and Kayla's parents had adamantly opposed either of them getting the tech. Dr. Baker was probably more afraid it would mess up something in their Nitarri heads than that the tech'd get hacktacked.

Can you distract them so we can come down to you?

Brill can pick the locks, and then we can sneak Kayla and Steven out of here. Which should stop the Mindhugger's plan to reclaim its home planet. It's still going to be a threat to the galaxy, pero let's solve one problem at a time.

Kayla stands up and announces, "I have to pee!"

The Zantites all look at her in unison as she starts rattling the ankle cuff against the sofa leg, like in that gritcast of the first day of the Mindhugger's life.

All four of him stand frozen, their heads at an identical tilt, staring at Kayla as Brill and I make our way down the stairs. It's creepy.

We're halfway down when the little door slams shut above us. The echo of the bang in the metal jolts through me.

One Zantite turns. He's tall, with a scar running down the middle of his forehead, bisecting his nose. "Come down here, Bo. Murry is glad you came. He wanted you to see this."

The others all nod, but it's not so uniform this time, which helps. It's the first time I've seen more than one infected person in the same place. They're all part-Murry – part-themselves. And my brain is having difficulty wrapping itself around that. I address the one that spoke to me.

"Mire usted? He's happy to see me, when he just tried to kill me."

The Zantite's whale eyes look sad. "Yeah. Sorry about that. We need to think more carefully before we take the life of an individual. We would have missed you."

I find myself smiling at that.

Plus, I just realized why we're here.

Tyson said the Mindhugger is rapidly developing a moral code. Minda said I'm a good teacher. I have to teach Murry that holding hugs on sentient beings is wrong. If he willingly gives up the hold on his hosts, maybe we can find somewhere for him to belong.

"What happens next time you get angry, mijo? These guys you've infected now tend to chompcrush people they're unhappy with."

The Zantite chews at his hunormous rubbery lip. "They won't do that. Come down from there. Unless you can melt metal, you have no way out of here. I have several dozen pieces of myself outside."

"Babe?" Brill taps the gun in his jacket.

"No, mi vida. What would that help?" He'd just be killing the victims and putting Murry beyond our reach forever. Where Murry would then multiply until he takes over the galaxy. The only way we're going to win this is through logic and kindness. The mindworms said they wanted mercy. I have to try to believe that mercy can be as powerful for Murry as it was for Frank. "I'll come down if you tell me what you're going to do next time someone makes you angry. Something that leaves them breathing."

The Zantite starts to say something, but then looks stumped. "What do you do?"

I wasn't expecting that. "I step away from the situation if I can, so I can calm down. And then I come back and tell them why I'm angry."

Zan-Murry nods. "Like with Jimena Duarte. She made all those mistakes, and when she was afraid you'd fire her, you came back and encouraged her." He looks up at Brill. "And how you didn't let your friend kill Gideon Tyson, even though Tyson believes he has deeply wronged you."

Brill looks at me, his eyes slowly turning burnt orange. "I get what you want us to do here, Babe." He jumps off the ladder and flashes over to the Zantite – who flinches away as though expecting violence – and takes both enormous hands in his. "I know you're angry about Awn, and about Dek." That must be Awn's son. How is this the first time I've heard his name? "But the people who hurt them are dead. Tyson may not have been there for my friend when Darcy needed him, but he wasn't the one who hurt him. Me blaming him – that was wrong. That was me trying to make sense of my own pain, trying to find logic in it."

"But it's not fair." The Zantite's lip is quivering. "None of it is fair."

Brill hugs the Zantite to him, like the guy's a little kid, even though Brill only comes halfway up the guy's chest. "I know–" Brill's voice breaks, and he has to start again. "I know these are difficult emotions to process, and nobody programmed or prepared you to have to deal with them. You've been hurt from the day you became aware, and rejected ever since. And that's not fair. But you can't hold onto it. Because if you do, it will make you a monster. And I don't think that's what you are."

The Zantite hugs Brill so hard and so long that it's a good thing mi vida doesn't have to breathe. Then Zan-Murry pushes Brill away. "You hurt people. You shot at Mertex, back aboard that warship. Tyson and Mertex both think you've killed people. How can you tell me not to do the same?"

Brill is silent. There is no easy answer to that question. How do you explain the difference between self-defense and vengeance to a being with the psychological maturity of a seven year-old?

What Murry needs is an out, a viable choice that will let him be something more than a parasite, so he can live long enough to understand. My half-baked idea about talking him into becoming a people of dragons – maybe it's not a mistake after all. I pull out my handheld and call Chestla. "You muchachos didn't eat the spuck Ekrin and her crew captured yet, no?"

My breath catches at my own bluntness. Because the only way they would have done that already is if Ball had died.

"No. Ball's not even out of the hospital yet. They're about to transfer him to the physical therapy ward, but it will be a while before he's strong enough to kill a beast that size."

My shoulders relax in relief. "If Leron really can salvage that parasite out of Awn, inject it into the spuck. And let it go."

"But cesuda ma–"

"Please. Trust me. I don't have time to explain."

Zan-Murry says, "What are you doing up there?"

"I want you to talk to some of the people you want to destroy." I come down the ladder and hand Zan-Murry my phone. "Remember what you said about mercy? They're about to beg you for some."

There are still tears in the Zantite's eyes. "All I want is to go home."

Come on, Chestla. Tell him you'll take him back. That your people made him and now you'll take responsibility for him.

Chestla starts apologizing for her entire species, pero the Zantite's lips move into a hard line. He points at Leron, who seems to be edging out of the frame, trying to keep his face turned away. "You! You froze us."

Leron holds up his hands. "I didn't have a choice. I was just a lab assistant."

We had assumed he'd only helped with the cover-up after. Hadn't he said he'd looked at the records, to know what had happened that day?

Chestla turns to glare at him. "You said it wasn't your mistake."

"It wasn't. They said if the consciousness was inside the original test subjects that we could stop the plague. Five lives in exchange for the galaxy. And they made it clear that if I'd said no, it would have been six."

My heart sinks. How could he not have told us?

"Oh, Ler," Ekrin says.

"This?" Zan-Murry protests. "This is your case for mercy?"

He throws my phone on the floor, then grabs both me and Brill – who doesn't even try to dodge – and bares his teeth. I struggle against his grip, pero it's like iron.

"You said you absorbed all of Mertex's memories," I say. "Don't you remember trying to freeze Brill? The guy who was just trying to comfort you? He forgave you for that, remember?"

Zan-Murry opens his mouth, wide, and moves my face right up to his lower lip. Then he takes a deep breath through all those open teeth and puts me back down. "You told me to take a minute before I do something I regret. And I would miss you. So don't talk to us while we finish setting this up."

The other Zantites cuff me to Brill, and we find ourselves attached to the end of the giant sofa opposite Stephen y Kayla.

Frustangerated heat builds in my eyes. We were so close!

CHAPTER FIFTY-ONE

At least Kayla looks reasonably healthy. I lean over Brill and look past Stephen to ask mi amiga, "How long have they had you down here?"

"Since that night at the club. I got in a cab headed for the spaceport, then the car filled up with sleeping gas, and I woke up here."

I look down at her ankle, cuffed to this sofa. For weeks. "Oh, chica!"

"Oh. No." Kayla points towards a door on the other side of the lab. "They built a suite of rooms over there, with a bathroom, and they've fed me and brought me clothes. The only freaky thing was they kept asking when Stephen was going to show up, and hadn't I called him yet. When they knew darn well I didn't have a phone."

"They expected you to realize you're telepathic," Stephen points out. "And just, you know, call me."

She pokes his arm. "I told you, that's crazy. We're not aliens."

"On this planet you are," Brill points out.

Kayla glares at him. They've never had the easiest relationship. "At least if you're here, it means Bo wasn't after Kaliel after all."

She'd missed everything that happened after that night at the club. It's too much to sum up. I just tell her, "Tawny's bumpclip of me and Kaliel was holonique."

"Then where is he? Why didn't he come for me instead of you?"

"He's been looking for you, but he'd got a whole group of cops watching him." Brill lays the end of the cuff that had been around his ankle on the floor. He may not be the best with locks, pero he gets there eventually. "We couldn't have told him where we were going and still have a chance of sneaking you out."

Brill starts on the cuff holding me to him.

"Stop acting like you're so innocent!" Stephen shouts in the direction of the Zantites.

I'm so startled, I jump.

"Shut up, su!" Brill grabs for Stephen's arm, pero it's too late. Brill slides his foot back, so it will look like he's still cuffed to the couch.

Zan-Murry turns around. "What did you say?"

Stephen pales at that intense stare. Pero, he swallows and straightens his posture. "You keep shouting your thoughts at me. You feel guilty, and it's ripping you up. Let's count it all up, and see who owes mercy to whom." Stephen jerks the arm that's still attached to his sister, trying to point. "Kay, the Mindhuggers snuck poisoned chocolate aboard our grandparents' ship. If it hadn't got blown up, everyone on board would have died anyway. It feels guilty about the one guy who did die. Or was it two?"

Kayla stares at Zan-Murry, open mouthed.

"They were researching ways to kill us. The Baker couple had already created slow-metabolizing theobromine to keep us from spreading. We couldn't let them mass produce that." This is news. Grundt had said Kayla's grandparents were working with the Nitarri, but they must have had some connection with the Evevrons too. Murry looks away. "We don't feel guilty. We feel justified."

Kayla lets out a horrified squeak. Zan-Murry turns and

walks away.

"Por favor, chica." I reach towards her with my free hand, pero there's too much sofa and too many people between us. "You forgave Kaliel, remember? Don't make Murry angry now. We have a chance to–"

"It's not even sorry," she protests.

I try again. "Stephen said something about a song you sang one time when you were kids, a song that took away pain. Can you sing it to Murry?"

"I thought I dreamed that." She looks skeptically at her brother. "I've been trying to figure out where I found that song for my whole life. I went to culinary school mainly for the linguistics sampler classes, trying to hear something like it." Kayla's expression is dreamlike. Then it hardens. "I don't care what you all keep saying. I'm not an alien, and I don't have any superpowers."

"Pero, Kayla, you do. And you need to use them to balance Stephen."

"No, Kay," Stephen insists. "You need to support me. Brill's friend Gavin sent me some data, and I've been studying it."

Claro está. Gavin wouldn't have trusted me to take care of this. I'd have thought he'd have had more faith in Brill, though.

"Gavin called you?" Brill sounds disappointed.

"He didn't tell me what decision to make. But he thought I deserved the facts." Stephen glances over at the Zantites. He drops his voice to a whisper. "When we go into that machine, we can take whatever they're trying to send to the Evevrons and send it back to the mindworms. We can kill every single one of these parasites, wherever they are in the galaxy."

Brill's eyes go black. "If you do that, you'll kill all the hosts."

Stephen blinks at him. "Have you never seen *Invasion of the Body Snatchers*? Or *The Thing*. Or *Alien*. Or... or *Bowfinger*?" He's pushing it on that last one, and he knows it. "It's the only chance we have to stop this plague. How are you people forgetting that this is a parasite?"

Brill drops the cuff from around his wrist. "Enough. I'm going to try talking to Murry again."

"Careful, mi vida." I squeeze his hand, then I turn and look hard at mi mejor amiga. "We can change the script. This isn't *Body Snatchers*. It's *ET*. And we can help him phone home.

"Chestla looked at the data too. Her notes said the parasites work like biological computers, which were designed based on *your* telepathic abilities." There really is some kind of connection between the Nitarri and the Evevrons. How did I not see that before? "It's like you have a natural sublingual, that also works like a switchboard. Whatever FeedCast they give you, throw it away. It's white noise to us non-telepaths anyway. So toss it and then connect the mindworm to the mind that's like it on Evevron."

"I can't do that, Bo. I can't help either of you. Because I am *not* adopted." Her voice gets louder and more hysterical with each word.

And it's out.

What she's really hurting over.

"It's true, Kayla," Stephen says somberly. "Dad says we're the last of the Nitarri Royal Family."

I try for a smile. "Isn't it fantastica that you're a princess? You always wanted to be famous."

Kayla's hands twist together, forcing Stephen's cuffed wrist to go with them. "But... I can't be adopted! How was Gran not my gran? We were so close. Why would she have lied to me?"

I look at mi amiga, in so much pain. "Probably *because* she wanted you two to be close."

"She did it because she wanted us to be safe," Stephen says. "We're in danger if anyone finds out what we are. Mom, too. All that moving around when we were kids – that was for us, not her."

Kayla stares at him. "That would explain why Mom was so

upset when HGB started broadcasting those bumpclips of me and Bo talking about chocolate. I thought it was because I was being exploited." Her face crumples, as she sniffles. She takes a deep breath, gets control over herself. "I don't want anyone in my head. When I was a kid – it couldn't have been real. I can't let the nightmares back in."

"Nightmares?" Stephen asks.

"Yes. Your nightmares." And then Kayla hits him with them. Chestla said Nitarri can only interact with non-telepaths via electronic receivers, like my sublingual, or as painful white noise, which I get a dose of. They can exchange communication, not read minds. Pero, Stephen covers his cabeza, like he's ducking away from something flying in at him and lets out a little squeak.

"I'm so sorry." Kayla stares at the floor. "I didn't mean–"

Zan-Murry's heading back over to us, holding Brill off the ground by the shoulders of his jacket. I'm running out of time.

I say, "Remember how you told me your abuelos chose your middle names? Your abuelita named you Anastasia for a reason, muchacha. Everyone loved that princess, right? Would someone who thought of you like that want you to kill anyone here today?"

"Kay, do you really think they're going to let us live when this is over? If they're doing it this way so no one will be able to trace it back to them, then the four of us are all loose ends."

"No, Kayla, it–"

Stephen interrupts me. "*It* is willing to commit xenocide. Bodacious, your bleeding heart is going to get a whole planet killed. You know your little ad campaign? I say mercy is a joke."

I'm looking at Stephen now. "*He* is learning what death even means. He's almost there!"

"I want my hat," Kayla sniffs, not responding to either of us. "Gran and I bought it together."

Kayla always wears that hat when there's something difficult she has to do. Until now, I never realized why. That hat means she's accepting this.

Zan-Murry drops Brill in front of the sofa. The three other Zantites stop a little behind.

"I saw it earlier." Brill leans down and pulls the hat from underneath the sofa. He passes it to Stephen, who passes it to Kayla. Kayla clutches the hat.

Zan-Murry says, "Now cuff yourself back and give me whatever you picked the lock with."

Brill does as he's been instructed. When he unzips his jacket to hand over the lockpicks, there's a glint of metal, and I catch Zan-Murry eyeing Brill's gun.

"Let's get this over with." Zan-Murry gestures for the other Zantites to uncuff Kayla and Stephen and move them into the tanks. "Before we lose our nerve."

I can't see what's going on, have no idea if I've gotten through to Kayla. All I can see is that Murry has no idea he might have been out-thought, that he is in fact in danger.

"Por favor, Murry." I turn to the scarred Zantite. "There's another way. Let me explain."

He's not listening to me. He's still eyeing the gun. He reaches to take it out of Brill's jacket. Brill lets him. The Zantite opens it, verifying that it's loaded. "If you believe what we are doing is wrong, why didn't you shoot us to stop us?"

"Because the people you are manipulating here are still alive. And if you release the hugs you have on them, these choices you've forced them to make – they aren't responsible for that. Killing them would be murder."

Zan-Murry stares down at the gun. "But the lives of a few to save a whole planet…"

He has no idea how close Brill came to making that choice when we first came in here. Pero, I'm not going to tell him, not when he's looking at the gun pero seeing the cryostasis pods where he first heard that idea being whispered to Leron.

Instead, I tell him what Brill told me. "I'm sorry that happened to you. You have a choice whether you let it destroy you."

Brill says, "Vengeance is going to leave you cold inside, su. These people are the closest thing you have to family. If you do this, you'll never be able to understand why they made you, or why they hurt you. I think they did it because they're scared, just like you are, and because they didn't know how else to take responsibility for what they'd done."

The Zantite is dripping tears again. "Why do you care? I'm a plague. A menace. A·monster."

"My people have been called all that, too, su. Plus a few more creative things." His eyes go violet for a second. Probably he's thinking of the more outrageous ones. *Conan? Zombie? Spider-Man? Ferengi? Kus'hepp?* Or maybe something I've not even heard. "They're just words. You can learn to ignore them if your purpose is powerful enough."

"Murry. If you raze your planet and go back there," I ask, "what will your purpose be then?"

Zan-Murry comes to stand by me. The other Zantites are talking to each other, calling out numbers, adjusting something. He looks down at me. "Do you think I have one?"

I shake mi cabeza. "Nothing justifies what you'd have to do to a planet worth of people to make them populate Evevron."

Zan-Murry blushes green. "My only other choice is to die."

"What if your purpose could be ridding Evevron of one of its worst pests, and re-engineering the rivers so that everyone can have enough water?" I've looked at the topomaps, and those spucks' powerful burrowing claws should just about be able to do it. "You get to be the good guy instead of the plague."

The scarred Zantite glances at the tanks. "It's too late."

"No, it's not," Brill protests. "You've done some wrong, wal, but we can still fix this."

"I mean, it's too late now. The machine's online, and there's no turning it off. We've already fed the distortion into the Nitarri's minds, and they have no choice but to pass it on. My family, as you called them, are all about to die, and there's no forgiveness after that." Zan-Murry looks down at the gun. "I've miscalculated here, haven't I? Most individuals value the life of every other individual." He looks over at Brill. "Even the few who would have had to die to save the rest of them. They'll never let me have peace, even in a space of my own. They'll hunt me forever." The Zantite turns the gun towards himself. "When I realized I was the monster, I should have found a way to just fade away."

"Ga!" Brill is off the sofa, as far as the cuffs will allow, lunging for the gun, which he can't reach. He's dragging me with him as he manages to inch the sofa closer.

"Who are you trying to save?" Zan-Murry asks, stuffing the gun in his own jacket. "Him or me?"

"Both." Brill swallows visibly. "All of you. That's a lot of hosts for you to take with you." Mi vida gestures over to a platform near the tanks, where one of the other Zantites has climbed up and picked up a lethal-looking drill, now dangling carelessly from his hand.

Murry is capable of releasing his hugs on most of his hosts – pero, not all of them. According to Chestla's data, he needs at least four to hold onto the knowledge he's gained, and even if he drove himself down to his barest state, he can't release the last one. Not from the inside.

Brill should be suggesting he let most of them go, minimizing the loss of life if the Nitarri do decide to execute Murry or if he does decide to suicide, pero mi vida's saying, "You're just a child. There's got to be a way to–"

The whole room lights up, like prism sparkles through a disco ball in the middle of an exploding sunrise, and the white-noise ambient feedback hitting my brain makes me clutch at mi cabeza and cry out in pain.

It doesn't matter what we wanted to do. We're out of time.

"Are you OK, Bo?" Zan-Murry puts a hand on my shoulder.

I can't think clearly enough to speak.

Murry's hand clenches suddenly.

Stephen screams.

I stare at the scarred Zantite, waiting for blood to come out of his eyes or something. Either he's going to die, or he'll be so spooked we'll all wind up infected.

Pero, a slow smile spreads over his face – Mertex's smile on a more muscular mouth.

"Que? What's happening, Murry?"

"I'm talking to her. She says she found a way to talk to their radio, and they want us to come home. That they'll share the planet with us." He's shedding tears again, huge wet drops that are falling on me. "They know what I was planning to do to them, and they don't care. She says they understand where my feelings were coming from, and they're sorry. But she doesn't even know what that means. Should I trust she's got it right?"

"Yes, mijo. Por favor."

"She's flying. We've never felt what it's like to fly."

"You'll tell me if that's amazing, too, no?"

"Bo, it is. It really is."

CHAPTER FIFTY-TWO

Stephen is sitting on the floor by his tank, soaking wet, holding his cabeza, groaning. Kayla's kneeling in front of him, repeating, "I'm sorry. I'm so sorry."

Kayla looks up at me. "I could feel you getting through to him. He really does want to reconcile with his makers." She looks over at the scarred Zantite. "I couldn't let Stephen reverse that signal back at you. I nearly killed my own brother to save you. Do you understand?"

Zan-Murry's mouth drops open. "You would have killed yourself too, trying to process that kind of overload while looking for all of us, spread out so far. Two Nitarri aren't actually a hive mind, you know. You can't sacrifice parts of yourself. And there's only a thirty-four percent chance it would have worked before you died."

"You considered that possibility?" Stephen asks weakly.

Zan-Murry shrugs. "We didn't think you'd be stupid enough to try it." He peers curiously at Kayla. "What *did* you do with the signal?"

Kayla's cheeks go red. "I didn't have much time."

"What did you do?" Stephen asks warily.

"I needed to shift it away from the Evevrons, but I didn't have much control, and yeah, everything was starting to overload. I think… maybe… I obviously can't read minds – not even primitive ones – but I may have exterminated a species of rats. Or possibly scorpions." I bet she means the kapursts, the muy grande monsters with the poisonous tail barbs, like the one that nearly killed Chestla. Kayla takes off her hat, studying the brim. "I hope it wasn't a lynchpin in the ecosystem."

Brill and I help Kayla get Stephen to the same hospital where Gavin took Tyson, while Zan-Murry takes a formal holocall with the Evevron council.

On the way, I watch Tawny's interview with Minda, still at the scene of the trial, with people milling around behind them, trying to mug for the holocorder. It's the first time I've seen Tawny step in front of the camera.

Holo-Tawny says, "Everyone knows King Garfex's law is absolute. Has what happened here today changed anything?"

Minda looks down at Tawny and smiles. "Garfie may act like he does everything on a whim, but he's extremely logical. And he cares what his people think. He's rescinded laws based on popular opinion before. An invasion requires money and resources, and if we can prove to him that this one would be unpopular, he just might withdraw."

"And what impact will *this* have?" Tawny pops up a holo, pure razzicast of a person unaware they're being recorded. It's Queen Layla, sitting at a table with a couple of Zantite courtiers, a MIAG bracelet visible on her massive yellow wrist as she hoists a glass of pineapple turpentine.

"She'll have a giant headache tomorrow," Minda grins and Tawny flinches back.

"Really, Miss Frou." Tawny sounds flustered.

"Kidding." Minda puts a hand on Tawny's shoulder. "Though have you ever had one of those? She's on her third one. Seriously, though, mercy isn't a common concept in our legal system. Layla's a trendsetter. Can you imagine what would happen if that caught on – not just as a fashion statement, but really caught on? It wouldn't just change the relationship between Zant and Earth. It could revolutionize my planet's entire legal system."

I close the holo. We've arrived at the hospital.

They put monitors on Stephen, pero the initial exams don't show measurable damage. He's going to have to wait his turn for the specialists, though, because they're still working on Tyson.

We tell Gavin what we know about Stephen's condition, and he gives us a dumbed down version of what Doc Sonda told him about Tyson. The Myska's brain stem is shaped differently than most other bipeds, and the mindworm tendrils wrapped oddly around it when the parasite unfolded. Now that the worm is dead, the part that liquified isn't pressing back, so the tendrils are pulling to one side. The structural interference is killing Tyson. They're trying to remove the foreign matter, pero it is delicate work. One mistake could leave him paralyzed – or muerto.

Gavin says, "I need coffee. That place across the street has an approved cleanliness rating. You sus want me to bring you back anything?"

He leaves, promising sandwiches and double-shots – or the closest acceptable thing to that he can find. He turns back, raises an eyebrow at Brill and looks significantly at me. "I'm leaving after we eat. If you're still coming, then, well."

Then Brill had better tell me goodbye.

Gavin doesn't want to eat anything made on Zant. The real reason he's going on a food run is so that we will be alone so Brill can share his heart. Gavin really has started looking out for me.

So now Brill and I are alone in the little waiting area deep in the hospital, between the ER where they're still operating on Tyson and the room where Stephen is recovering.

My throat keeps wanting to close up, pero if I start crying now, I won't be able to stop.

"Babe," Brill says, wrapping me in his arms. I can't believe this might be the last time I get to feel the leather of his jacket against my cheek, breathe in the smell of him. "You going to be OK?"

"You have to go." I already sound nasal and sniffly. That's not the way I want him to remember me.

"Just when you forgave me for running away from you last time." He hugs me tighter.

"This is different, mi vida." Then, he'd abandoned me, when I was in over my head and said cabeza had a price on it. "This time, I'm asking you to go. I want that heart of yours to keep beating, even if this is breaking mine."

He kisses me, hot and intense, and I wind up backed against the wall. I'm breathing hard, holding onto him like he literally is my life.

A nurse walks by and clears her throat. "Not allowed in here, you two."

We break apart. My lips are still tingling, my whole body flushed. Brill's eyes tell me he's embarrassed she said that, pero, he looks ready to ignore her and grab me again.

He clears his throat. His voice still comes out husky. "Maybe this won't be forever. HGB's power will eventually crumble. Maybe at some point, Frank's loyalties won't matter."

I'm still standing there, trying not to dissolve away, when Frank walks in. All that heat in my blood turns to ice. I try to whisper *no*, pero no sound comes out.

Fifteen minutes later and mi vida would have been gone.

Sí, Brill broke his promise to Frank about not seeing me again, pero he had a good reason. Frank should realize that.

Only Frank doesn't seem to be looking for us. The assassin is making a bee-line for the nurse's station. Brill grabs me and kisses me again, hiding his face behind my hair, pulling me against his warm, solid body. It's different this time, urgent and frightened.

Frank has stopped behind us. I break the beso, look into mi

vida's terrified eyes. My heart starts thudding even faster.

"Damn it, Brill." Frank pulls the gun from his holster. "Don't run. We can do this easy, then Bo and I can walk out of here safe." He looks over at me. "Mercy is a waste of time."

"He was just leaving," I blurt. "You don't have to do this."

"I can't take any more chances." He starts screwing a silencer onto his gun. "Turn around, Bo."

"No." I'm not going to make this easy for him.

Brill flitdashes, while I try to block Frank's path. Frank knocks me out of the way, and I land hard on my backside, feel pain in my ankle. Frank takes his gun in both hands, steadies himself and takes a couple of dead earnest shots at mi vida, who is a blur. My heart freezes. Brill keeps going. He really is fast enough to dodge a bullet. Frank takes off in pursuit.

I scramble to my feet, chase after them. The ankle hurts, pero it takes my weight as I try to catch Frank, who is fast for a fifty-something. Brill flashes away, turning down a hallway farther down.

For all his not wanting to make a scene, Frank shouts, "You make me track you down, and people you care about are going to get hurt. HGB knows where your family lives."

"You didn't expect him to stand there and let you shoot him," I protest, catching up to Frank. Mi vida may have come to terms with death, pero he wouldn't be the same person I fell in love with if he'd been willing to do that.

We're running side by side now.

"Jrekt!" Brill's shout is still echoing in my heart when there's a crash, the sound of something breaking, a heavy thud. Some guy who's not Brill leaps into the hallway, sees Frank's gun and runs away. The guy's wearing a maintenance-type uniform. Frank lets him go, which means he doesn't expect this to take long, that I can count mi vida's life in just so many fleeting breaths.

When we get to the corner, part of it is blocked by a floor waxing machine, and the whole hallway looks glossy. Brill

skidded on the slick surface down a good fifty feet of hallway
and ran into a solid oak desk. He's trying to get to his feet pero
can't seem to get purchase on the slick tile.

I don't dare try to tackle Frank, not after how easily he'd
chosen to shoot me last time I'd tried to save mi vida.

Frank's gun tracks Brill as mi vida finally manages to
stand up.

No lo sé why Frank hasn't shot him yet. I guess he wants to
give Brill a moment of dignity first, time to dust himself off and
face this. Frank's also giving my heart time to break.

This isn't right. A Krom's supposed to be able to outrun any
bullet he sees coming. Even if mi vida can still backtrack faster
than a human across that shimmer of wax, it won't be fast
enough to keep Frank from anticipating his course.

I step between that gun barrel and mi vida, find myself
skidding on the slick floor, grabbing onto Frank to keep from
falling. He jerks the gun off to the side, doesn't shoot me.

"Por favor, Frank. Don't kill him. He's my life."

Frank pushes me away, pero not hard enough to knock me
over. "Give me one sensible reason why not. I told him to stay
away from you, or he's going to get all of us killed."

He recenters his aim.

"How about that he just saved an entire planet, because you
let him keep breathing one extra day. Imagine what he can do
with a lifetime – a Krom lifetime." I slide my feet even closer
to that gun barrel. We both know I'm not wearing body armor
this time.

"You mean that, Babe?" Brill sounds surprised, and that gets
a smile out of Frank.

"I really do." I'm still looking at Frank.

He's not looking at me, though. He's looking over my head
at mi vida. "What's she talking about?"

Brill's eyes slide from black to an embarrassed pink-gray.
"I hugged the mindworm and taught it vengeance is empty.

It's a long story. I'd love to get to tell it to you. For a long time. In detail."

Brill's begging for his life.

Frank laughs. "I bet you would."

Frank doesn't want to do this, or he'd already have pulled the trigger. I know he's all about duty over emotion, that eventually he's going to recover that frío detachment that let him kill mi papá even after Papá's final plea had been for his family's safety.

I say, "It's my fault Brill knows about the *Onyx Shadow*. He doesn't care about HGB's secrets."

Frank winces. "I looked into it. Those morons weren't authorized for all those collateral targets."

I step closer, have to catch my balance while trying to keep eye contact. "So it was a mistake all around, no? I won't say anything about it as long as Brill lives. He's leverage. I cooperate for the rest of the tour, instead of flying to Krom to tell them what happened. You can sell that, right?"

Frank stares at me. "And even with him to back you up, you aren't going to go public? Even though you can prove you were right? The big bad company didn't look out for the best interests of the weak. All that?"

I shrug. "It's common knowledge in the galaxy, if not on Earth. Grundt thought I was una idiota for not already having figured it out. The truth doesn't need me as its champion this time." I look back at mi vida. "Pero, he does."

"We kept your secret about Serum Green," Brill points out. "I promise. I'll disappear."

Frank looks like he's wavering. I did break him. Or at least put a crack in his hard, impassive moral code. Then his eyes harden. "You both know you're not going to be able to stay away from each other. I already told my superiors he was dead. How am I supposed to explain away him turning up alive?"

"Miraculous recovery from a presumably fatal gunshot wound?" I point at mi vida. "He'll let you put a scar on him." I don't dare look at Brill. He'd been so worried about the damaged flesh on his face scarring. What I've proposed would have to look like it should have killed him. "We're in a hospital, viejo. It can't be that hard to find something here to mark him."

"So I look sloppy, but not downright rebellious?" Frank taps the gun barrel against his free hand. "I can almost live with that."

"So can I," Brill says. "Scars are sexy. Right, Babe?"

"Breathing is sexy, mi vida. Come on, Frank." I stay centered in front of him. "I know you say you're a weapon, pero don't you ever want to be more than that? You can convince them he doesn't need to die."

"I couldn't make any promises. He might still have to disappear again." He lowers the gun. "If I did this, you would have to make sure that nobody else sees him until the wound looks like something that's healing. Give me enough time to figure out what to do."

"I promise, Frank. I'll take him to Minda's. Where tonight, I'll make dinner for us and you and Mamá. I'll even make biscuits for Botas."

Frank smiles. "You'd do that?"

"Only if Brill's there." I make a face. "Because if he's not, I'm going to feed you laxatives the next time mi mamá's not looking."

"Fair enough." Frank considers this for a few moments. "It's impossible, though."

My heart lurches. Brill lets out a soft, disappointed noise. Frank's going to follow his orders after all, and I'm going to have to see Brill's muerte.

Frank raises the gun again, his finger tensing on the trigger. Something's warring in his face as I flinch away.

"But just because I won't be there doesn't mean you shouldn't be." Frank relaxes his posture and holsters the gun.

I blink in amazefusion and shocked relief. "Viejo."

Frank waves his hand at Brill. "Come on, Romeo. Let's go make you pretty."

"Sexy," Brill corrects, even as he gives me a confused look and tries to make his way towards us without falling again. "And not Romeo. Even I know Romeo dies."

Brill's walking away again with Frank. Pero, this time it's OK.

"Hey, viejo."

Frank turns around.

"Lo siento about slapping you, back at the trial."

"Don't be sorry. I almost deserved it." Frank doesn't seem to notice Brill's eyes turning gray, then black. "That slap gave me perspective on why I didn't follow through. Probably what changed my mind just now."

I think about that shovel, about how close mi vida came to lying in a shallow grave, and chicken skin puckers its way down my arms. "How's this supposed to work, Frank? We're stuck on opposite sides."

He taps the gun in his holster. "I think we're making progress."

"Why are you here, anyway?" Brill asks. "At this hospital, I mean."

Frank looks embarrassed. "There's a medical team in the process of pulling an unknown lifeform out of a galactic inspector. I'm supposed to find out if they know what it is."

And if they figure out it's been bioengineered, then he's supposed to kill them all for being too smart.

I cross my arms over my chest. "And you think HGB's giving you a rock-solid moral code?"

Frank rubs at his nose. "I never said that. I just said they're doing the best they can to give Earth a future in a galaxy full of creatures more physically powerful and technologically advanced. I wasn't there when they decided to incorporate what you call Serum Green into the formula. But I had faith they had a good reason. And now I know they did. It buys us time to exterminate these mindworms before they destroy the galaxy."

Brill and I look at each other and burst out laughing. Frank looks flustered. "What?"

"We took care of that." I manage to stop laughing long enough to say, "As long as HGB's secrets aren't the only ones you're willing to keep."

"Don't worry, Babe. I'll fill him in on everything he's missed." Surely he'll leave out the part about the Evevrons and the First Contact War. "I can convince him Doctor Rimga is on our side. Nobody has to die here today."

Now that we're all calmer, I notice Frank's eyes are red, like he's been crying. Which should be impossible, no? I doubt it has anything to do with his assignment, or with Brill.

"Are you OK, viejo." I gesture at his eyes.

"I will be. Your mother asked me what had you so upset at me, so I told her I shot him." He gestures with his thumb at Brill. "I had to sell it, even to Lavonda. That's why I can't be there for dinner. It'd be a little awkward since she broke up with me."

Brill's eyes go pale rose with wonder. "You sacrificed your happiness? For me?"

Frank shrugs. "It was never going to happen, anyway. Not after how I came into contact with this family."

I reach out, put a hand on Frank's arm. "I'll talk to her, viejo."

Frank's mouth drops open. "You'll what now?"

"You heard me." I take my hand away, drop it down by my side.

"I never managed the olive branch," Frank says softly. "I couldn't find Kayla."

"She's about two doors down," Brill says, pointing.

As they walk away, I consider what I've just done. I think I forgave Frank. And gave him a place in my life. I wonder if I'll regret that.

But this time mercy was the gift he needed me to give. And I needed to give it. I feel lighter now, more whole.

CHAPTER FIFTY-THREE

I find Kayla in Stephen's room. She's sitting in a plastic chair, that hat rolled up in her hands. Stephen is asleep.

"Hola, Princesa." I make a show of knocking on the open door. "You have to admit being the Anastasia that Lived is cooler than being Princesa of Chocolate."

Kayla makes a face. "Yeah. I'm the Princess of the People Who Can Kill You With Their Mind. That's going to make people feel real comfortable hanging out with me. At least they're still putting your face on chocolate bars."

I take a chair next to hers. "Tyson has fangs, pero he doesn't usually use them, Mertex had all those teeth, pero, the only person I ever saw him try to chompcrush was me. Unlike Murry, you aren't likely to accidentally hurt someone in a fit of anger. So I don't see the problem."

"But I could." Kayla flips over the hat. "My mom – my gran – someone should have told me how to control this."

"Seems like you did that just fine on your own." I take her hat and straighten it out. She controlled her telepathy so completely, she convinced herself she didn't have a gift at all. "They couldn't tell you how to be Nitarri. They're all human."

She's nodding along with me. She's coming to terms with being adopted.

We lapse into silence.

Kayla takes her hat back and puts it on. "I wouldn't mind so much except – OK, that's a lie, I'd still be totally upset – but it's not fair to Kaliel. He's a straightforward kind of guy. And now I've got all these secrets, and oh, let's not forget I could kill him with my mind. I won't blame him if he doesn't want to be with me any more."

"That depends." Kaliel's standing in the doorway, out of breath, like he ran all the way here. "You going to let me in on those secrets?" He takes one deep breath, then adds, "Sorry it took me so long to get here. Getting away from Tawny and those FeedCasters was impossible."

Kayla goes to him. "I don't even know what my secrets are yet. I might need help figuring them out."

"Then I'm your guy." Kaliel goes to kiss her, pero, she puts a couple of fingers to his lips to block him.

"They did tell you about the whole could kill someone with my mind thing?"

"Yeah. I'm never going to not feel safe again, with you here to protect me." He goes for the beso again, and this time she lets him.

They're standing in the doorway, so there's no easy way to leave.

"Babe," Brill says from out in the hallway. "We have a problem."

My heart lurches. Por favor, tell me he's not bleeding uncontrollably again.

Kayla and Kaliel move apart so I can get out. Brill's face is pinched with pain, and he's holding his jacket away from his chest, pero nothing seems to be bleeding through his shirt.

"You OK, mi vida."

"I will be. If I have to have a scar, this one looks pretty cool." He looks over at Frank, who is regarding us with impassive eyes. "Somebody took a picture of Kayla coming in the front door of this place, and it's virafizzed, so we're about to get mobbed. Frank has emphasized the importance of me getting out of here without being seen."

"But what about Tyson?"

"I'm sure he knows better than to tell anybody I'm still alive."

"Mi vida, we're waiting to see if he makes it through surgery."

"I know that." Brill takes a deep breath, breathing in and in and in. "But there's nothing we can do to help."

Just as I turn towards the operating theater, the door swings open, and Doc Sonda pulls gloves off her hands. She looks somber.

"Oh, no." The invincible Galactacop can't be gone too.

Sonda sees us, and smiles. "He made it."

Something releases in my chest. Tyson's alive. Truly, nobody's dying here today.

"Then why so glum?" Brill asks.

"Because we still won't know for another twelve hours or so whether there's paralysis or brain damage."

"We can't stick around for that," Frank says.

"I know." I look back at Kaliel and Kayla. "You two will let us know when there's news?"

"Of course," Kaliel says.

"So here's what you say, por favor. You and Stephen found Kayla trapped in a hole somewhere, and Stephen hit his cabeza climbing down to her. Can you do that?"

Kaliel sighs. "I suck at lying, and it's never gone well when I've talked to the media."

I remember his first interviews after the SeniorLeisure debacle. "No kidding, muchacho."

"I'll take care of it," Kayla says. She pats Kaliel's arm. "You just be the strong, silent type and look embarrassed for being a hero."

"Now that I can do."

Frank, Brill, and I rush for the door and the anonymity

of the van. Only, the parking lot is already crawling with FeedCasters and galactourists who want to see the follow-up of Kaliel getting set free. The love story. The happily-ever-after.

Frank looks unhappy, pero he's not doing anything drastic, so Brill and I may still get our happy ending too. If we can just figure this out.

"This is humiliating." Brill's voice sounds muffled.

"It's better than a bullet, mi vida." I have him by the hand – the puffy, black-felt hand.

"I can't see, and there's no way I could run. Do you have any idea what it's like for a Krom not to be able to run?"

I feel bad for him. Really I do. Pero, I giggle. I can't help it. It's cómico seeing Brill dressed up as a giant chocolate bar.

"It smells horrible in here," he complains.

"You can't wash those things." Kayla's wrapping the loose end back onto a spool of surgeon's thread. "Just be glad I could make it shorter."

"What was this thing even doing here?" Brill loses his grip on the basket he's sort of holding through his other giant puffy hand. It hits the floor, and a couple of chocolate bars fall out.

"It's from the play the volunteers do every week for the children's ward," Sonda says. "You'd better hurry. We're not going to be able to keep them all outside much longer."

I reach down to pick up the bars. They're HGB Kiddie Bars, pero someone has slipped an extra label over the top that says *Free Chocolate is the Best Chocolate*.

I arch an eyebrow at Sonda. "What exactly is this play about?"

Sonda giggles.

"This is ridiculous," Frank mutters.

"In for a penny, in for a pound," Brill says from inside the costume. "The minute you spared my life brought you to this."

"I've always hated that expression." Frank scowls. He looks

at me. "Tawny is never going to let me live this down. And I can't even tell her why I'm doing it."

No lo sé what's so embarrassing for him. He's not even wearing a costume.

"Smile for the cameras, Frank, and tell Tawny it's to impress mi mamá. Which is true." I hand him his own basket of candy, give Kayla one last hug, and then head for the door. I don't even look back to see if they're following me.

The minute I open the door, several FeedCasters slip through the line of hospital staff trying to hold them back. I'm still not comfortable with the press. I could still get blindsided by someone bringing up my less than stellar past, or my ethics regarding chocolate. Pero, I brace myself and go out acting confident.

One reporter, who looks human pero probably isn't, says, "Senorita Benitez, do you really believe your own ad campaign, or was it a ploy to get Kaliel's life spared – again?"

I look over at Frank, who is helping Brill waddle down the stairs, holding mi vida's hand since he can't possibly see. Some of the children in the crowd are already running over to them.

I smile over at the camera. "Mercy sometimes comes from unexpected places."

They've made it to level ground, and one kid grabs Frank around his legs. He pats the kid on the bald yellow cabeza, then pretends to pull a chocolate bar out of the divot that serves the small Zantite as an ear. It's easy to see him having been a papá, and now an abuelo.

Someone comes running towards me, and Frank's eyes go hard. He shakes the kid away and moves in my direction. It's the lady who tried to throw poo at me back on Earth. Frank seems to recognize her, and he slows his urgent pace, pero he's still heading over here. She reaches into her bag and I flinch away. En serio? She's going to try to do it again?

"Lo siento."

I open my eyes. She's holding out a choctastic Bundt cake floating in a bubble bag, and she looks embarrassed by my reaction.

"I..." She looks down. She's wearing a MIAG tee-Shirt. "I wanted to apologize. But maybe it was a mistake to think you'd eat something I made."

"Thank you." I take the cake. "It looks delicioso. Perhaps we could share it."

I hope Tawny's getting this. I've been keeping up with myself in the feeds. There are still people on Earth calling for my death, pero now there's one less. And if we can show this kindness to each other in front of the galaxy, then Earth might find itself one step farther from an invasion.

Brill nearly trips over his own giant feet as he waddles up behind me. He steadies himself using my shoulder. He whispers, "You're going to save me some of that, revwal?"

EPILOGUE
Six Weeks Later – Kaimoan City,
the planet Evevron

Chestla grabs my hand. "This is what I wanted, you know."

She sounds like she's trying to convince herself. "That's what you keep telling me. Is there something I'm missing, chica?"

Chestla lets my hand go. "Eugene acted like I wasn't even there when I was, and now that I'm not, he won't stop trying to talk to me. I told you. I'm done with him. But at the same time – I don't want to be making another mistake."

"So what are you going to do?" I look out at the amphitheater. Construction dust dots the ground near the far side, where they added the giant platforms.

"I'm going to go out there. This is what I've always wanted, and Eugene would never come to Evevron. Besides, I have Ball to take care of. He's going to need physical therapy, and I don't want him to have to go through it alone, not like I did after I was injured." She looks at me intently. "I'm needed here, cesuda ma."

I pull at the white lace covering my wrists. "I'm not going to be your cesuda ma much longer. You should stop calling me that."

"If you want. But I'm not going to stop helping you. Your people have a history with mine. We both need to know the truth."

"I know. I still haven't made my peace with HGB, pero I can't dig into it, yet. I have to go back to Zant and finish filming. I promised Minda. And it makes sure the Global Court doesn't have grounds to revoke my pardon. Minda's setting up drinks with her and Queen Layla and a number of Zantite courtiers. They all want to hear about how hard I fought to save Kaliel. The queen serves as the king's chief advisor, and Minda wants to present a petition her fan club has organized against the invasion. We're finally getting somewhere, chica."

I look over to where mi vida should be sitting, and I can't help but grasp the pendant I'm wearing, pulling it away from my heart. Every day, I take it off the minute I'm out of public view, pero, Brill says it still makes him feel distant from me. The way he says it makes it sound biological, not symbolic. I hope Frank comes through with a message that they've rescinded the assassination order for him soon. I've almost convinced myself – almost – that Frank's not going to swing back around and carry out his order if that covert stay of execution is denied.

Only a few people know Brill is alive. That does not include Brill's mamá. She asked me to send his things home. When I told her his ship had been lost – since he obviously still needs his things – it didn't go well.

He's temporarily switched ship IDs with Gavin, since it's easier for someone who is alive to file an insurance claim. I'd gone on board before the *Fois Gras* got hauled in for repairs. Brill had cut the power, and in the absolute darkness, amidst the hum of life support tapping the back-up generator, the bridge took on a pink and yellow glow, finger-painted with swirling constellations of flowers. Up on the ceiling, in giant yellow letters, it had said, *Mertex M Was Here. How about now?* It had been beautiful and dorky and perfect.

That in-the-know list does include Tyson, who said that as long as Brill isn't getting any monetary gain out of being dead, he isn't doing anything illegal. I still can't believe the

Galactacop agreed to keep Murry's secret, considering the deaths the mindworm scourge caused. Tyson is mid-molt – once the process gets started there is no stopping it, even if the neurological problem is reversed. He looks ridiculous, with patches of scales missing entirely. I can't help but laugh when he leans over and says something sincere to the Evevron sitting next to him.

Chestla's friends are all out there, sitting on the first rows. It must be nice to have it so clear-cut, what you want and where you are supposed to be. Then I notice someone missing, and fear tickles through my chest. "Where's Leron?"

I'm afraid he might be imprisoned or dead. Surely nobody decided his lies were that severe, not considering all the wrongs we're burying here already.

"He's not ready to face Murry." Chestla looks over at the platforms. "I can't say I blame him."

Everyone goes quiet as a humming of giant bug-wings fills the air. Six muy grande snake-hippos come into view, landing easily on the platforms reserved for them. Four of the dragons sploot flat instead of sitting – a gesture they must have picked up from their time being Frank's corgi. The other two – both the smaller female variety – look at their companions reproachfully. Those are the other consciousness, the not-Murry that still doesn't have a name. Though I think she'll wind up calling herself Awn.

Interesting the way she and Murry seem to be instinctively trying to differentiate themselves from each other. A hive mind made up of individuals. Two hive minds that are individuals. It's enough to break your brain.

The two smaller spucks make a noise. The four parts of Murry get the hint and sit up a bit more formally.

There's a bit of uneasiness in the air, I'm afraid one of the Evevrons is going to attack one of the spucks. But the moment passes. I have no idea how the council spinwashed this to convince everyone to stop eating the dragons. Pero, it seems to be working.

They asked me to keep in regular contact with Murry to continue helping with his socialization. And in exchange, the Evevrons are going to publicly denounce the invasion of Earth.

I would have done it anyway. Murry needs a friend or two. We all do.

Pero, I want to make sure that I have the right information before I interact with him again, and Chestla's been working with the team to help with the former parasite's transition into civilized society.

"How do you know Murry released the hugs he had on everyone else?"

"The ones who knew they were infected came here, went on the hunt with us, injected copies of the para – of the consciousness – into the new species themselves. The Royal Court compensated them handsomely for their trouble, so I doubt they would have brought accusations, even if they hadn't become complicit by that final act. And then…" Chestla points over to Kayla, who is sitting between two Evevrons, looking terrified. I can't blame her. The predator pheromones are thick here, and even I'm having trouble keeping my knees from shaking. "She went back in the machine – willingly – and checked for extensions of him. It only takes a few weeks for the solid parts of an expired Mindhugger to dissolve away, so hopefully, we won't have anyone extracting one while it's still in a condition to be identified."

A dragon makes eye contact, and surreptitiously holds up a hand, waving at me. I wave back, and it breaks into a hunormous, toothy smile. My sublingual rings.

Hi, Murry.

Hi.

For a moment, we just look at each other across the amphitheater.

You want to go flying later?

You know it, mijo.

It's an odd balance. Murry is trusting the Evevrons not to eat any more of him, imprison and experiment on him, or kick him off the planet. The Evevrons are trusting Murry and the other dragon-consciousness not to mindhack them or try to take over the galaxy. And both sides know that if Murry does try expanding again, or if the secrets between them get out, all it will take is a couple of Nitarri and a giant machine to stop the plague. I have no idea what balances out the Nitarri. I'm not sure I want to know.

Chestla goes out there. Grammy takes her hand and addresses the audience as much as her. "You know how proud we are of you. We had already approved you, so you didn't have to take the obstacle course again, but you insisted and not only passed, but showed unexpected innovation in solving some of the challenges. But the real test was whether you could keep your word and successfully protect your cesuda ma's friend, and Kaliel's life was indeed spared." A lot more was spared than that, but they're keeping it under wraps, even here. "Therefore, we would like to offer you a position on the council, rather than as a Guardian Companion."

Chestla scrunches up her nose. "I thank you for the opportunity, but you know I'm not cut out for that."

So they make her a Guardian Companion. Two others who also passed the obstacle course become palace guards. And then we all go to a massive party at the sculpture garden.

Chestla is laughing, holding out a bowl of mystery meat, telling us we don't know what we're missing, when her eyes go wide, and she swallows hard. "Eugene?"

Eugene is indeed walking towards us, in all his nerdy glory. "Hello, everyone."

"What are you doing here?" Chestla asks.

"I wanted to see your ceremony thing. But I guess I missed

it. I couldn't leave until the test results came in."

"What test results?" Chestla asks. She's blushing. He may be late, but she's obviously flattered that he came. She turns and looks back towards town, where Ball's still lying in a hospital bed, holding what Chestla said to him when he was bleeding in her arms close to his heart.

Well. That got complicated quick, no?

"I was analyzing a plant virus." He pulls off his backpack and takes out a jar. There's a cacao pod, floating in clearish liquid. It is crusted over with white scales. "I can't get anybody at HGB to believe me, but this will destroy all cacao plantations on Earth within the next five years."

I catch one of Murry looking at us. He looks away. I call him using the signal signature from when he called me.

Do you know anything about this?

I may have engineered a plant disease out of the Pure275. In case you went to Earth instead of Zant, there would have been a few… surprises. I undid everything else, but that – Murry waves a hand at the jar – *has no cure.*

My chest goes frío.

Oye! That got real complicated. Real fast.

Which seems about par for my life these days.

I'm not sure now if I'm heading back to Zant to keep my obligation – or if I'm going to Earth to help solve this new problem. Either way, we have to keep chocolate flowing through this hungry galaxy.

ACKNOWLEDGMENTS

I want to thank my readers. It just blows me away every time one of you mentions how much you love Bo or Chestla or Brill. (Yep, those are the main ones. Everyone seems to love Chestla best, TBH. You'd be surprised how many people have said they wished Mamá would just wise up and ditch Frank, and I told them to just be patient and watch where that arc's going. What do you guys think now?) Seriously, thank you for caring about these characters and their problems in my zany 'verse. We all have limited budgets of time and money, and the fact that you liked the first one to come back for book two – just, wow.

I also want to thank the Robots, especially Marc Gascoigne, fearless leader of the whole Robot crew. Your support of the Chocoverse has meant a great deal, and I wish you all the best. *Trut openheart bubblecloud want,* as Tyson would put it. I'm not crying, you guys, you're crying.

The other robots that will always be special to my heart, no matter what:

– My editor, Lottie Llewelyn-Wells, who helped me take a too-long manuscript and whittle it into something more emotionally resonant than I ever imagined it could be. I learned a lot about pacing this time around, and how to help readers retain information. Thanks soooooo much, Lottie!

– My publicity manager, Penny Reeve (and her cat Fizz!), who kept me on track and got the word out about the Chocoverse so the people reading this could find *Pure Chocolate* in the first place. Also, she's fun to Skype with. You are the best, Penny!

– The guy who handles everything else, Nick Tyler, who kept everything running smoothly, made me files, and handled silly debut novelist questions. You rock, Nick!

– My first Robot editor, Phil Jourdan, who pushed me to build up the Space Opera stakes in the Chocoverse. Dominos he helped me put in place in *Free Chocolate* have started falling in this one. Long time no chat, but you are still *awesome*, Phil! Thanks again for everything.

– Former Robot, Mike Underwood, who was the first Robot I met, and the one who took a chance on the Chocoverse in the first place. Safe journey and true heart, Mike.

Of course, I also want to thank my agent, Jennie Goloboy, who's done a lot of hand-holding and patiently explaining over the past year – but has also called me on it anytime I've tried to do something the lazy way and kept me focused. Which is why having an agent who gets what you are trying to do and sees what level you could be reaching for is so important. Thank you Jennie! For everything!

Thanks also to Eduardo, for proofing my Spanish this time around. I owe you so much actual chocolate! (Any remaining errors are my own.)

And to Rachel and James of X27 Films & Media who did the *Free Chocolate* book trailer (along with everyone else who helped out in it, especially Monica, Jasmine and Ethan). Everyone, you have to see it! Either on YouTube, or the AR site. So gorgeous.

I want to give a shout-out to my Novel 1-6 class over at UT Arlington. They've shared the past year with me, week by week, and have been AMAZING cheerleaders. A bit after *Free Chocolate* came out, the first time I used an example from my own work to illustrate a point, I realized that half the class had read it. I had to just stop for a second because having them nod along, remembering the details of something I wrote, was so overwhelmingly cool.

And obviously Cassie, Monica (yes, same Monica) and Tessa, for keeping me sane and listening to my writer-problems while at the same time helping me have a life outside of writing. Sorry about that one time I sat through that entire game of *Apples to Apples* with my headphones on, editing. It sounded like everyone was having a blast. Love you girls!

I can hardly believe how many wonderful, supportive people I have in my life right now. Even if you weren't specifically mentioned, thank you all!

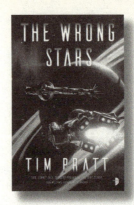

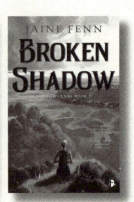